Graphic Classics:
JACK LONDON

Graphic Classics Volume Five
2003

©2003 MARK A. NELSON

EUREKA PRODUCTIONS
8778 Oak Grove Road, Mount Horeb, Wisconsin 53572

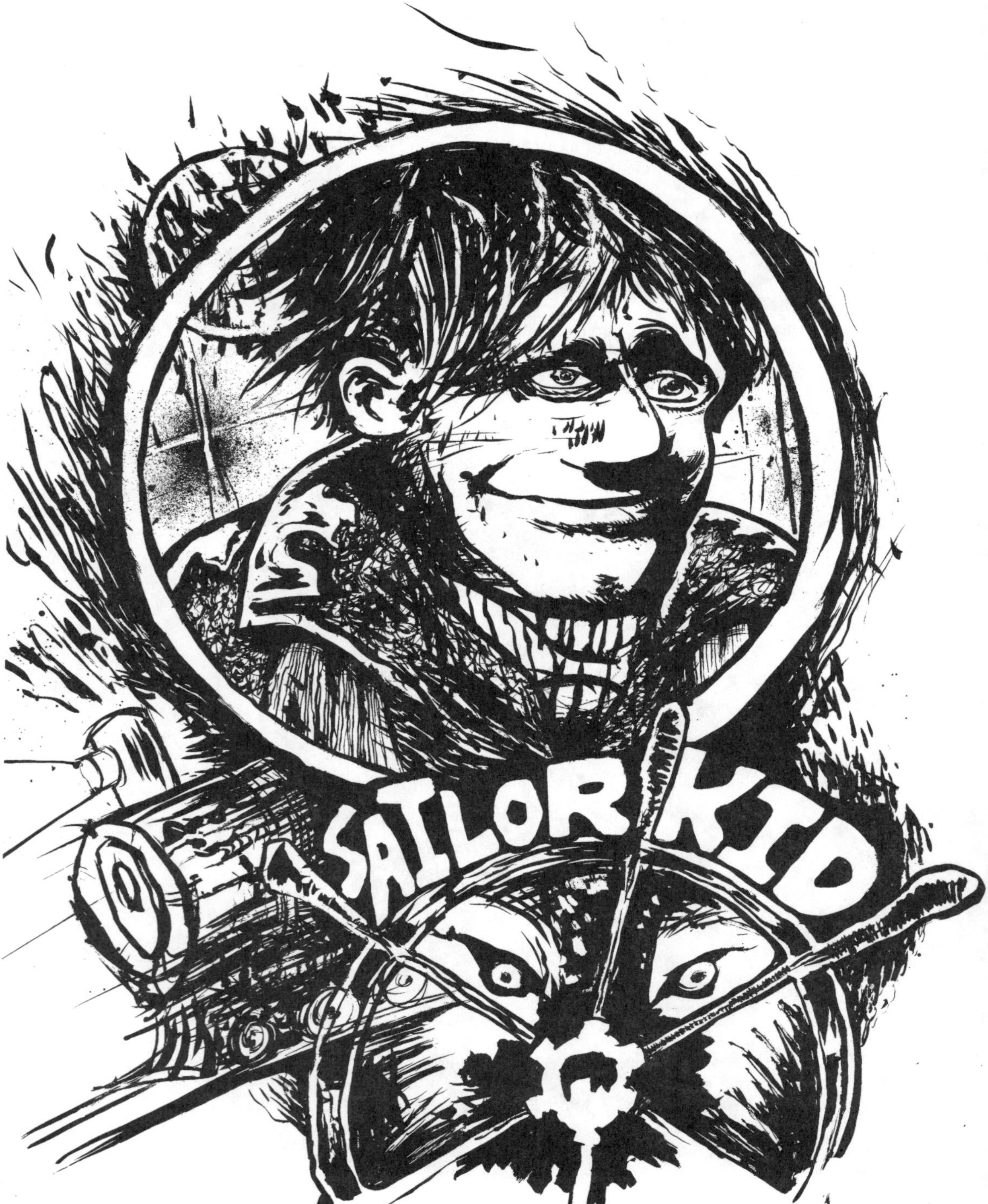
SAILOR KID

Jack London earned the nickname "Sailor Kid" in his early years as a sailor and vagabond.

CONTENTS

Graphic Classics:
JACK LONDON

Cover illustration by Arnold Arre / Back cover illustration by Michael Slack
Additional illustrations by Mark A. Nelson and Marc Arsenault

Graphic Classics: Jack London is published by Eureka Productions. ISBN #0-9712464-5-9. Price US $9.95, Canada $15.95. Available from Eureka Productions, 8778 Oak Grove Road, Mount Horeb, WI 53572. The Graphic Classics website is at http://www.graphicclassics.com. Tom Pomplun, designer and publisher, tom@graphicclassics.com. Eileen Fitzgerald, editorial assistant. This compilation and all original works ©2003 Eureka Productions. All rights revert to creators after publication. Graphic Classics is a trademark of Eureka Productions. Printed in Canada.

Illustrations and comics: Cover ©2003 Arnold Arre / page 1 ©2003 Mark A. Nelson / page 2 ©2003 Marc Arsenault / page 4 ©2003 Roger Langridge / pages 6-17 ©2003 Studio Jay-Bee / pages 18-26 ©2003 Sputnik Studios / pages 28-33 ©2003 Peter Kuper / pages 34-41 ©2003 Jeremy Smith / pages 42-48 ©2003 Kostas Aronis / pages 50-61 ©2003 John Pierard / page 62 ©2003 Gerry Alanguilan / pages 66-73 ©2003 Hunt Emerson / page 74 ©2002 Rafael Avila / pages 83-88 ©1989 Rick Geary / pages 89-97 ©2003 Anne Timmons & Trina Robbins / pages 98-104 ©2003 Lesley Reppeteaux / pages 105-115 ©2003 Matt Howarth / pages 116-130 ©2003 Milton Knight / page 132 ©2003 Spain Rodriguez / pages 134-139 ©2003 Roger Langridge & Mort Castle / back cover ©2003 Michael Slack.

The Leopard Man's Story by Rick Geary was originally published in different form in *The Bank Street Book of Creepy Tales* (Pocket Books, 1989) Reprinted by permission of the artist.

INTRODUCTION:
EIGHT FACTORS OF LITERARY SUCCESS

by JACK LONDON

©2003 ROGER LANGRIDGE

I WAS BORN IN SAN FRANCISCO IN 1876. Almost the first thing I realized were responsibilities. I have no recollection of being taught to read or write, though I could do both at the age of five. As a ranch boy, I worked hard from my eighth year.

The adventure-lust was strong within me, and I left home. I joined the oyster pirates in the bay; shipped as sailor on a schooner; took a turn at salmon fishing; shipped before the mast and sailed for the Japanese coast on a seal-hunting expedition. After sealing for seven months I came back to California, and took odd jobs at coal shoveling and long-shoring, and also in a jute factory.

Later, I tramped through the United States from California to Boston, and up and down, returning to the Pacific coast by way of Canada, where I served a term in jail for vagrancy. My tramping experience made me a Socialist. Previously, I had been impressed by the dignity of labor. Work was everything; it was sanctification and salvation. I had fought my way from the open West, where the job hunted the man, to the congested labor centers of the Eastern states, where men hunted the job for all they were worth. I saw the workers in the shambles of the Social Pit; and I found myself looking on life from a new and totally different angle.

In my ninteenth year I returned to Oakland and started at the High School. I remained a year, doing janitor work as a means of livelihood. After leaving the High School, in three months of "cramming" by myself I took the three years' work for that time and entered the University of California. I worked in a laundry, and with my pen to help me, kept on. The task was too much; when halfway through my Freshman year, I had to quit.

Three months later, having decided that I was a failure as a writer, I gave it up and left for the Klondike to prospect for gold. It was in the Klondike that I found myself. There nobody talks. Everybody thinks. You get your true perspective. I got mine.

In answer to your question as to the greatest factors of my literary success, I will state that I consider them to be:

Vast good luck. Good health; good brain; good mental and muscular correlation. Poverty. Reading Ouida's *Signa* when I was eight years of age. The influence of Herbert Spencer's *Philosophy of Style*. Because I got started twenty years before the fellows who are trying to start today.

Because, of all the foregoing, I have been real, and did not cheat reality any step of the way, even in so microscopically small, and cosmically ludicrous, a detail as the wearing of a starched collar when it would have hurt my neck had I worn it. My health was good — in spite of every liberty I took with it — because I was born with a strong body, and lived an open-air life, rough, hard, exercising.

I came of old American stock, of English and Welsh descent, but living in America for long before the French and Indian wars. Such accounts for my decent brain.

Poverty made me hustle. My vast good luck prevented poverty from destroying me. Nearly all my oyster-pirate comrades are long since hanged, shot, drowned, killed by disease, or are spending their declining years in prison. Any one of all these things might have happened to me before I was seventeen—save for my vast good luck.

Read Ouida's *Signa*. I read it at the age of eight. The story begins: "It was only a little lad." The little lad was an Italian mountain peasant. He became an artist, with all Italy at his feet. When I read it, I was a little peasant on a poor California ranch. Reading the story, my narrow hill-horizon was pushed back, and all the world was made possible if I would dare it. I dared.

Read *Philosophy of Style*. It taught me the subtle and manifold operations necessary to transmute thought, beauty, sensation and emotion into black symbols on white paper; which symbols, through the reader's eye, were taken into his brain, and corresponded with mine. Among other things, this taught me to know the brain of my reader, in order to select the symbols that would compel his brain to realize my thought, or vision, or emotion. Also, I learned that the right symbols were the ones that would require the expenditure of the minimum of my reader's brain energy, leaving the maximum of his brain energy to realize and enjoy the content of my mind, as conveyed to his mind.

A word as to the writer of today:

For one clever writer twenty years ago, there are, today, five hundred clever writers. Today, excellent writing is swamped in a sea of excellent writing. Or so it seems to me.

Editor's Note:
This Introduction is taken from a letter by Jack London published posthumously in **The Silhouette** *magazine, February 1917. Jack London, the most popular writer of his time, died on November 22, 1916 at the age of forty.*

A THOUSAND DEATHS

story by
JACK LONDON

adapted & illustrated by
J.B. BONIVERT

©2003 STUDIO JAY-BEE

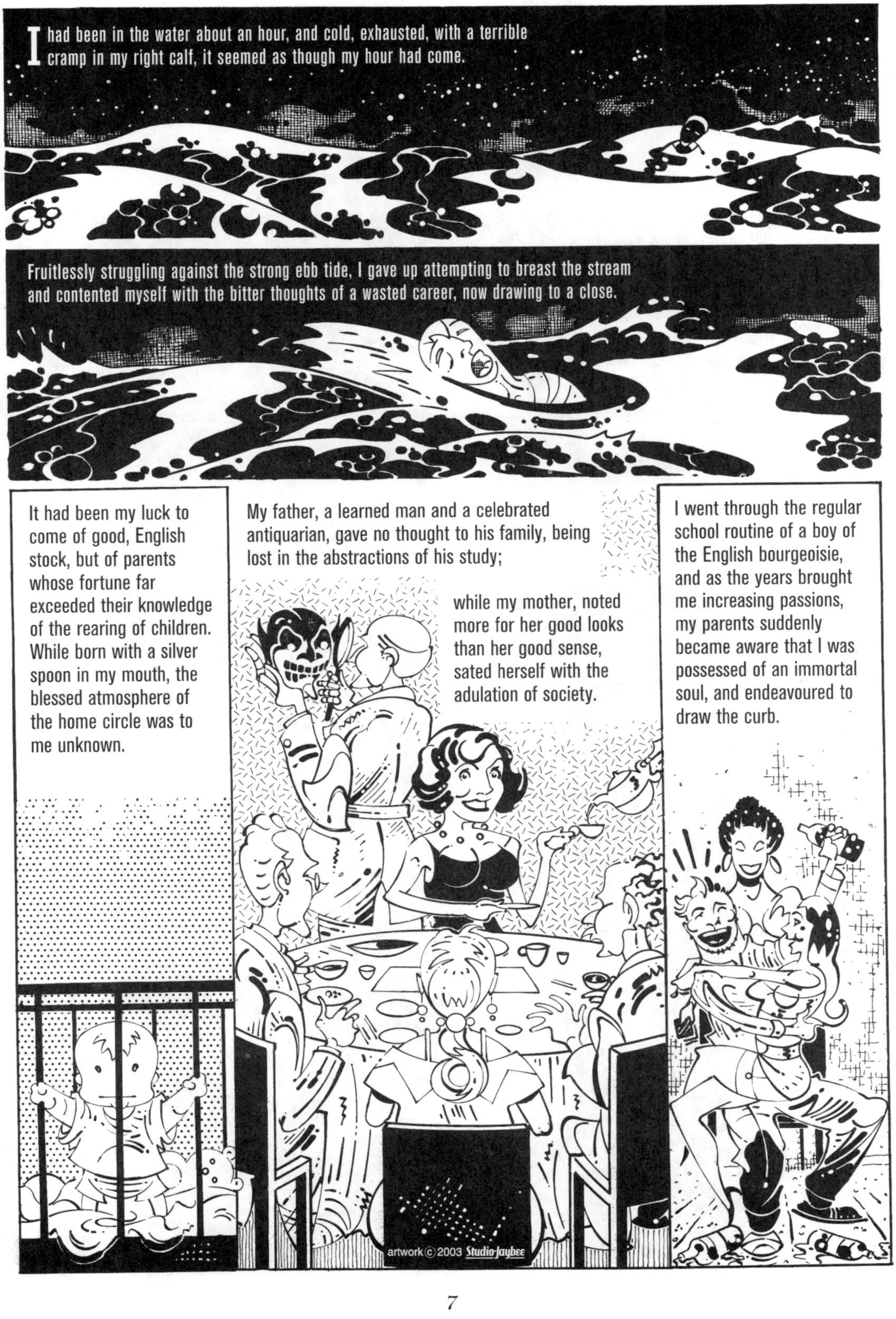
I had been in the water about an hour, and cold, exhausted, with a terrible cramp in my right calf, it seemed as though my hour had come.
Fruitlessly struggling against the strong ebb tide, I gave up attempting to breast the stream and contented myself with the bitter thoughts of a wasted career, now drawing to a close.
It had been my luck to come of good, English stock, but of parents whose fortune far exceeded their knowledge of the rearing of children. While born with a silver spoon in my mouth, the blessed atmosphere of the home circle was to me unknown.
My father, a learned man and a celebrated antiquarian, gave no thought to his family, being lost in the abstractions of his study;
while my mother, noted more for her good looks than her good sense, sated herself with the adulation of society.
I went through the regular school routine of a boy of the English bourgeoisie, and as the years brought me increasing passions, my parents suddenly became aware that I was possessed of an immortal soul, and endeavoured to draw the curb.
artwork © 2003 Studio-Jaybee

But it was too late; I perpetrated the most audacious folly, and was disowned by my people, ostracized by the society I had so long outraged, and with the thousand pounds my father gave me, with the declaration that he would neither see me again nor give me more, I took a passage to Australia.

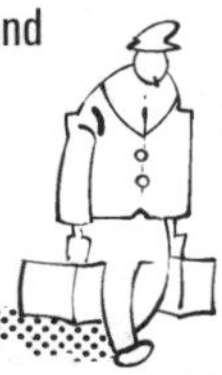

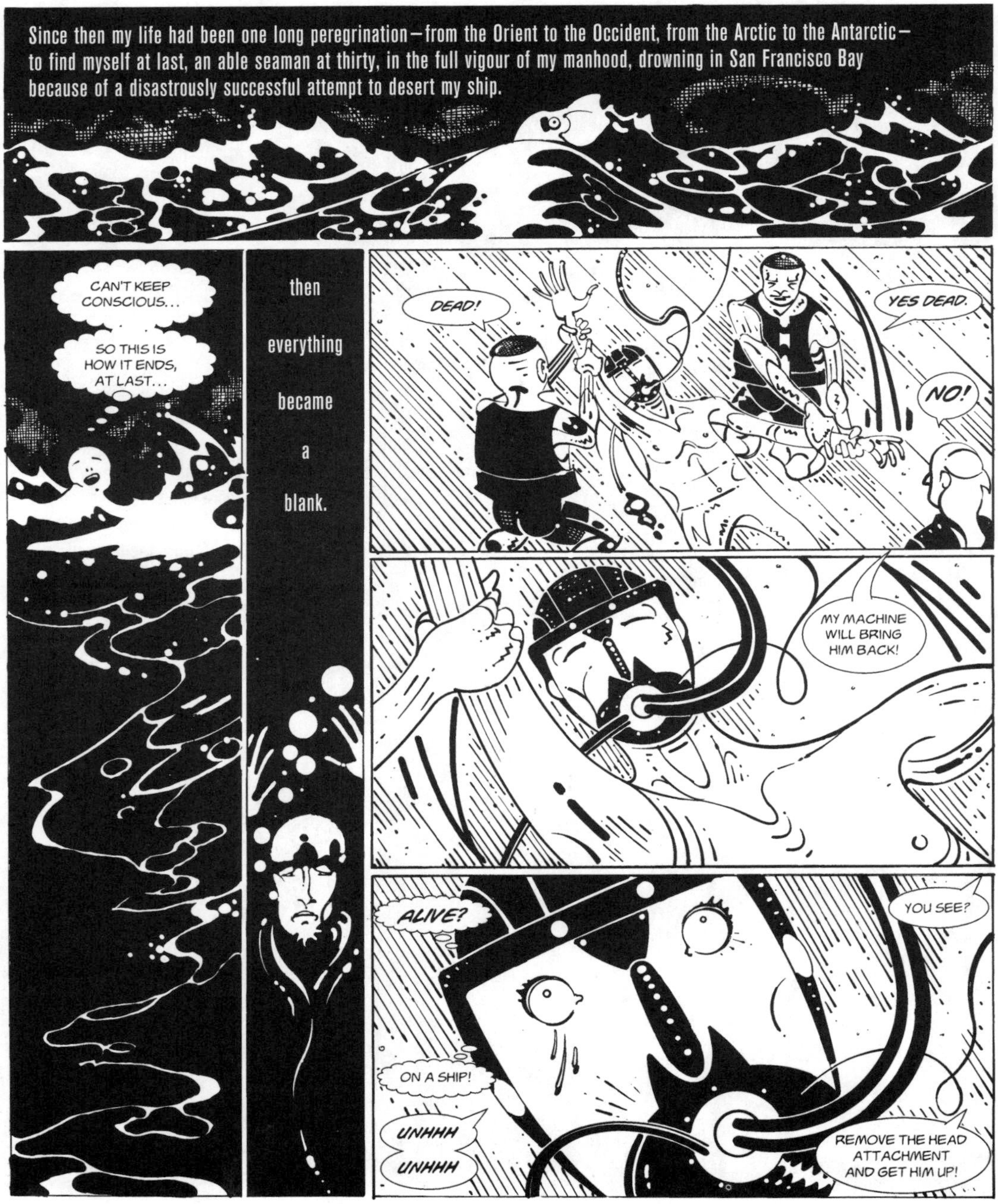
Since then my life had been one long peregrination—from the Orient to the Occident, from the Arctic to the Antarctic—to find myself at last, an able seaman at thirty, in the full vigour of my manhood, drowning in San Francisco Bay because of a disastrously successful attempt to desert my ship.
CAN'T KEEP CONSCIOUS...
SO THIS IS HOW IT ENDS, AT LAST...
then everything became a blank.
DEAD!
YES DEAD.
NO!
MY MACHINE WILL BRING HIM BACK!
ALIVE?
YOU SEE?
ON A SHIP!
UNHHH
UNHHH
REMOVE THE HEAD ATTACHMENT AND GET HIM UP!

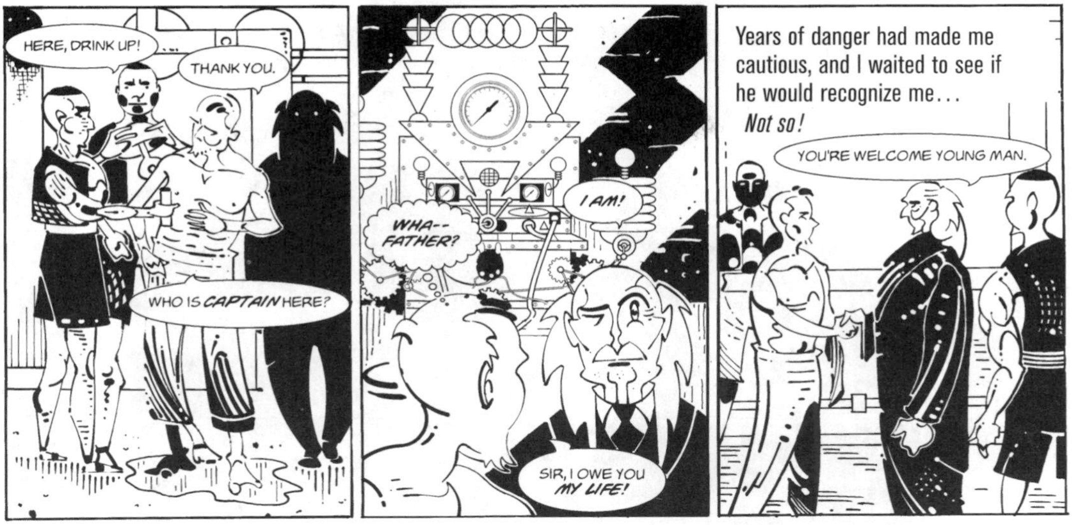
HERE, DRINK UP!
THANK YOU.
WHO IS CAPTAIN HERE?
WHA-- FATHER?
I AM!
SIR, I OWE YOU MY LIFE!
Years of danger had made me cautious, and I waited to see if he would recognize me...
Not so!
YOU'RE WELCOME YOUNG MAN.

Leaving me to the care of his men, he fell to revising the notes he had made on my resuscitation. As I ate the handsome fare served to me, the rattling of blocks and tackles began on deck, and I surmised that we were getting under way.

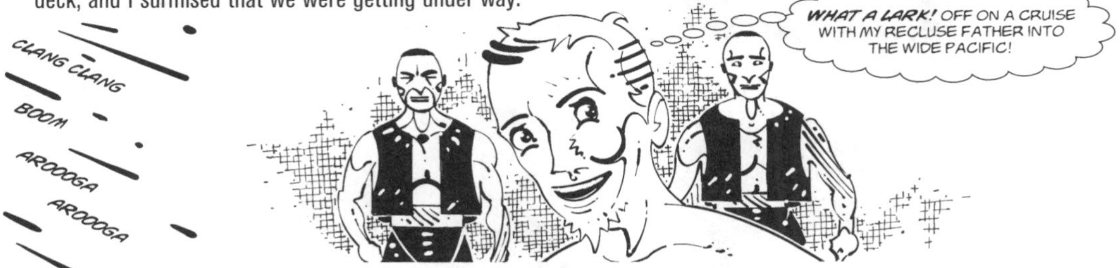
CLANG CLANG
BOOM
AROOOGA
AROOOGA
RATTTLE
WHAT A LARK! OFF ON A CRUISE WITH MY RECLUSE FATHER INTO THE WIDE PACIFIC!

Little did I realize, as I laughed to myself, which side the joke was to be on. Aye, had I known, I would have plunged overboard and welcomed the dark depths from which I had just escaped.

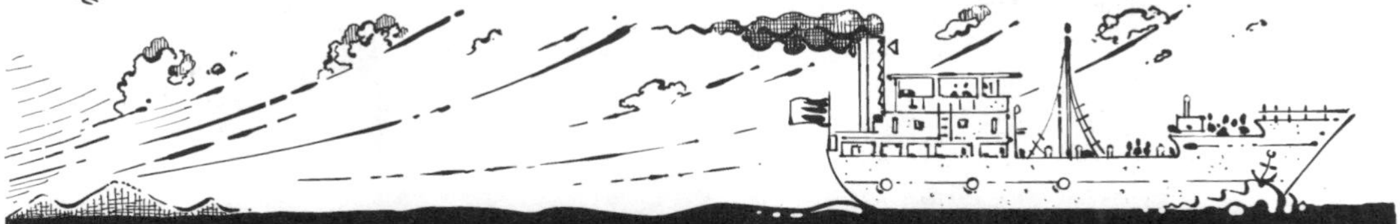

I was not allowed on deck till we were beyond the last pilot boat. I appreciated this forethought by my father and made it a point to thank him heartily. I could not suspect that he had his own ends in view, in thus keeping my presence secret. He assured me that the obligation was on his side, as he had constructed his apparatus for the vindication of a theory concerning certain biological phenomena, and had been waiting for an opportunity to use it.

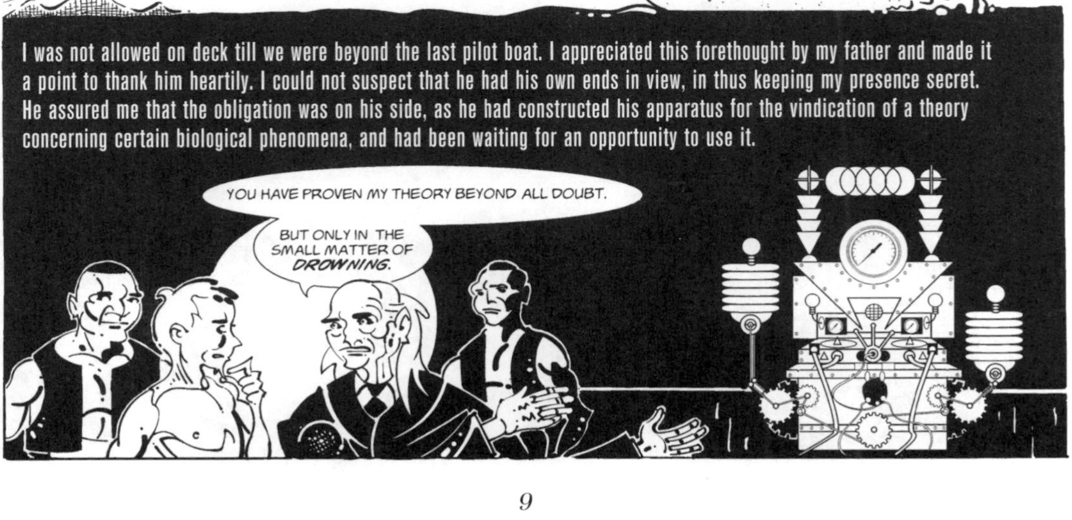
YOU HAVE PROVEN MY THEORY BEYOND ALL DOUBT.
BUT ONLY IN THE SMALL MATTER OF DROWNING.

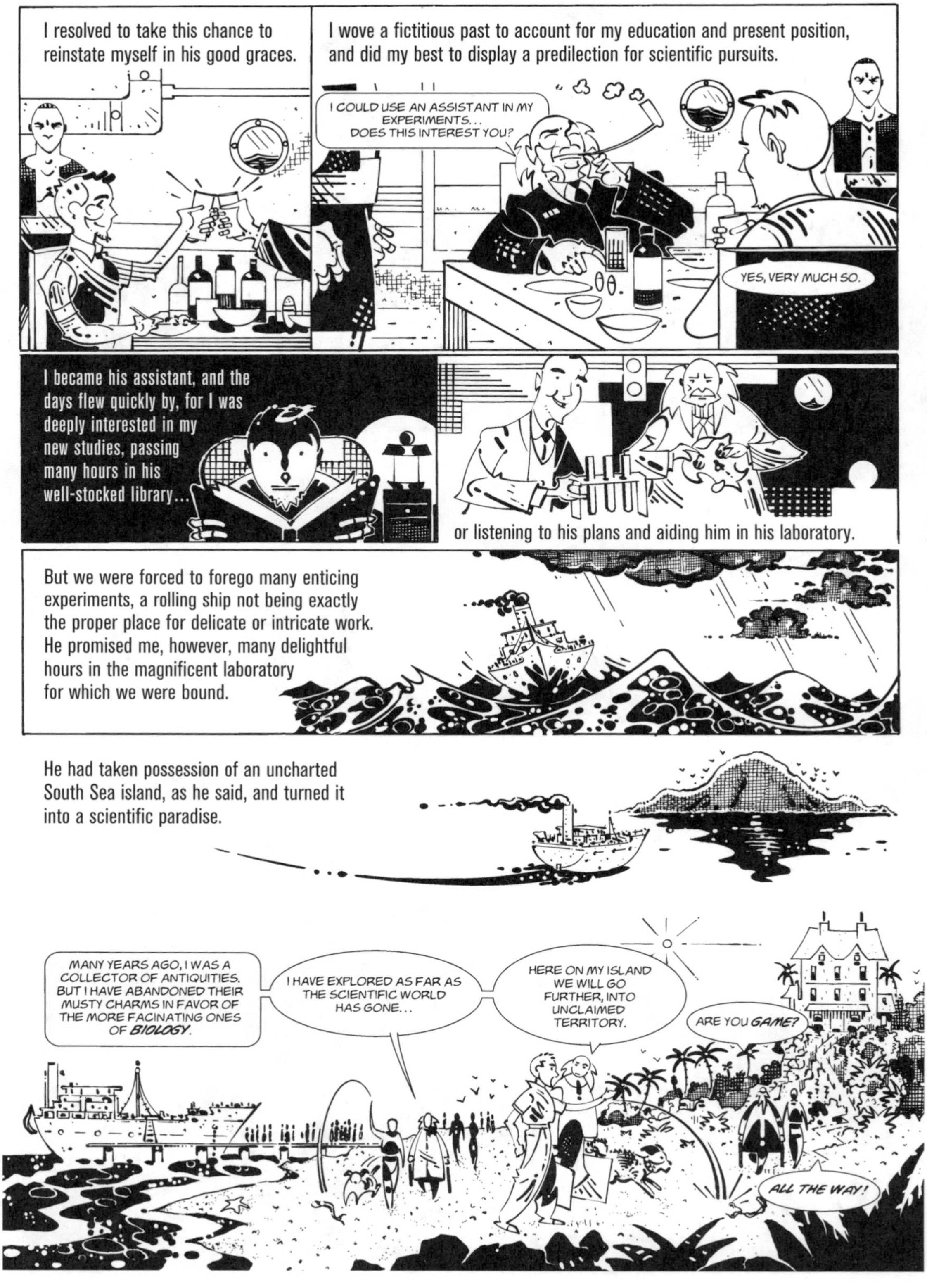
I resolved to take this chance to reinstate myself in his good graces.
I wove a fictitious past to account for my education and present position, and did my best to display a predilection for scientific pursuits.
I COULD USE AN ASSISTANT IN MY EXPERIMENTS... DOES THIS INTEREST YOU?
YES, VERY MUCH SO.
I became his assistant, and the days flew quickly by, for I was deeply interested in my new studies, passing many hours in his well-stocked library...
or listening to his plans and aiding him in his laboratory.
But we were forced to forego many enticing experiments, a rolling ship not being exactly the proper place for delicate or intricate work. He promised me, however, many delightful hours in the magnificent laboratory for which we were bound.
He had taken possession of an uncharted South Sea island, as he said, and turned it into a scientific paradise.
MANY YEARS AGO, I WAS A COLLECTOR OF ANTIQUITIES. BUT I HAVE ABANDONED THEIR MUSTY CHARMS IN FAVOR OF THE MORE FACINATING ONES OF BIOLOGY.
I HAVE EXPLORED AS FAR AS THE SCIENTIFIC WORLD HAS GONE...
HERE ON MY ISLAND WE WILL GO FURTHER, INTO UNCLAIMED TERRITORY.
ARE YOU GAME?
ALL THE WAY!

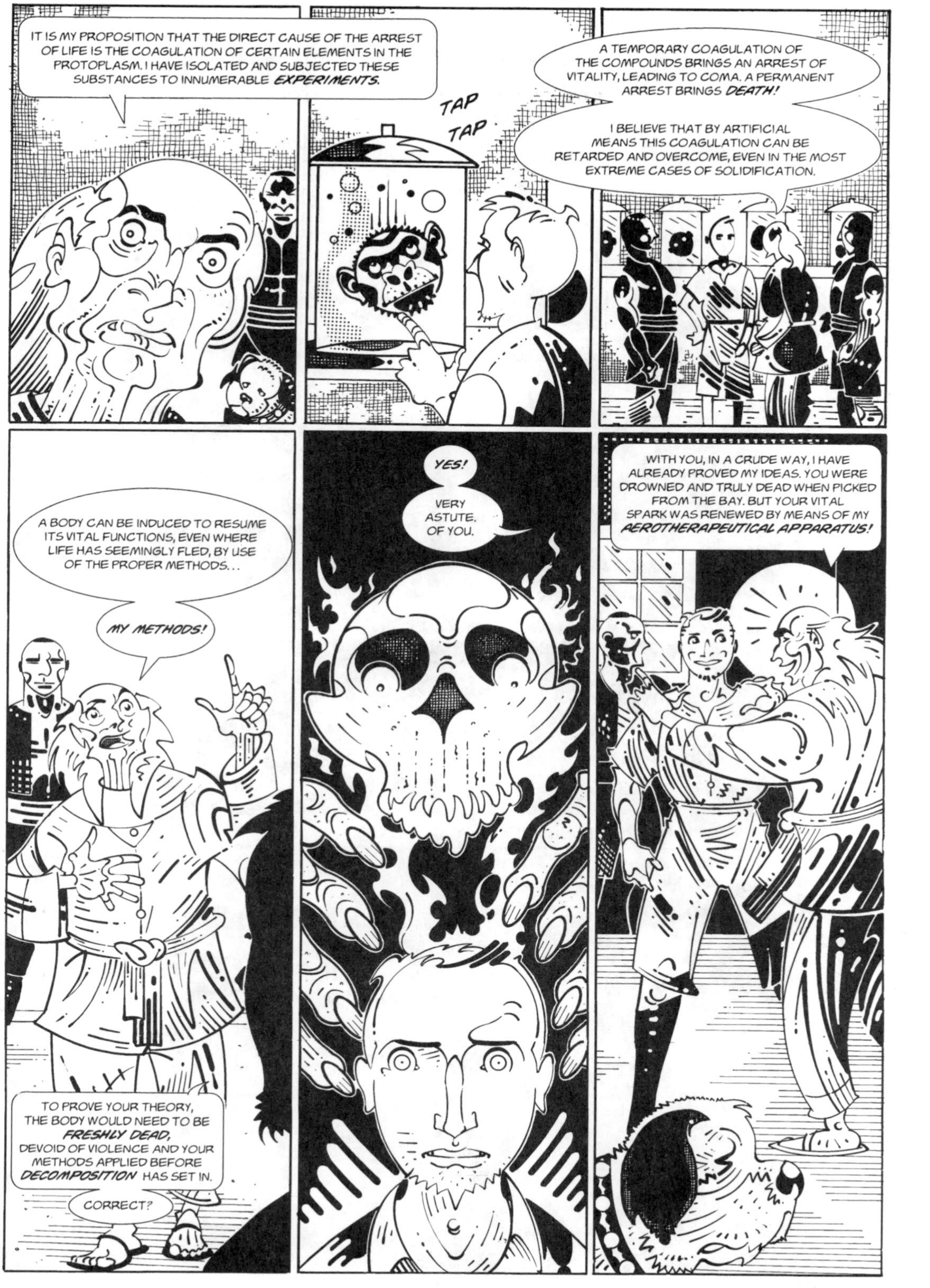
IT IS MY PROPOSITION THAT THE DIRECT CAUSE OF THE ARREST OF LIFE IS THE COAGULATION OF CERTAIN ELEMENTS IN THE PROTOPLASM. I HAVE ISOLATED AND SUBJECTED THESE SUBSTANCES TO INNUMERABLE EXPERIMENTS.
TAP TAP
A TEMPORARY COAGULATION OF THE COMPOUNDS BRINGS AN ARREST OF VITALITY, LEADING TO COMA. A PERMANENT ARREST BRINGS DEATH!
I BELIEVE THAT BY ARTIFICIAL MEANS THIS COAGULATION CAN BE RETARDED AND OVERCOME, EVEN IN THE MOST EXTREME CASES OF SOLIDIFICATION.
A BODY CAN BE INDUCED TO RESUME ITS VITAL FUNCTIONS, EVEN WHERE LIFE HAS SEEMINGLY FLED, BY USE OF THE PROPER METHODS...
MY METHODS!
TO PROVE YOUR THEORY, THE BODY WOULD NEED TO BE FRESHLY DEAD, DEVOID OF VIOLENCE AND YOUR METHODS APPLIED BEFORE DECOMPOSITION HAS SET IN.
CORRECT?
YES!
VERY ASTUTE. OF YOU.
WITH YOU, IN A CRUDE WAY, I HAVE ALREADY PROVED MY IDEAS. YOU WERE DROWNED AND TRULY DEAD WHEN PICKED FROM THE BAY. BUT YOUR VITAL SPARK WAS RENEWED BY MEANS OF MY AEROTHERAPEUTICAL APPARATUS!

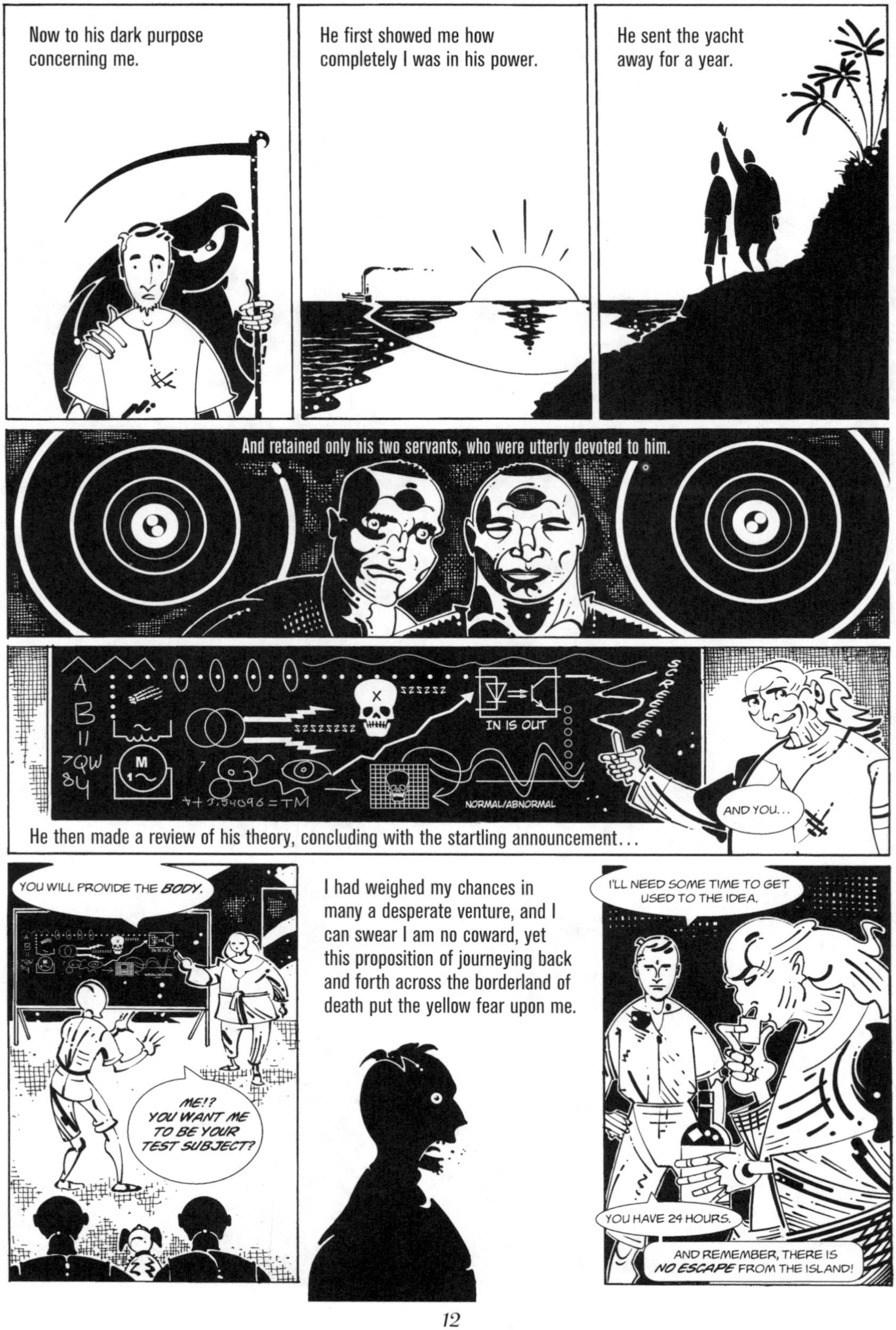
Now to his dark purpose concerning me.
He first showed me how completely I was in his power.
He sent the yacht away for a year.
And retained only his two servants, who were utterly devoted to him.
IN IS OUT
NORMAL/ABNORMAL
AND YOU...
He then made a review of his theory, concluding with the startling announcement...
YOU WILL PROVIDE THE *BODY*.
ME!? YOU WANT ME TO BE YOUR TEST SUBJECT?
I had weighed my chances in many a desperate venture, and I can swear I am no coward, yet this proposition of journeying back and forth across the borderland of death put the yellow fear upon me.
I'LL NEED SOME TIME TO GET USED TO THE IDEA.
YOU HAVE 24 HOURS.
AND REMEMBER, THERE IS *NO ESCAPE* FROM THE ISLAND!

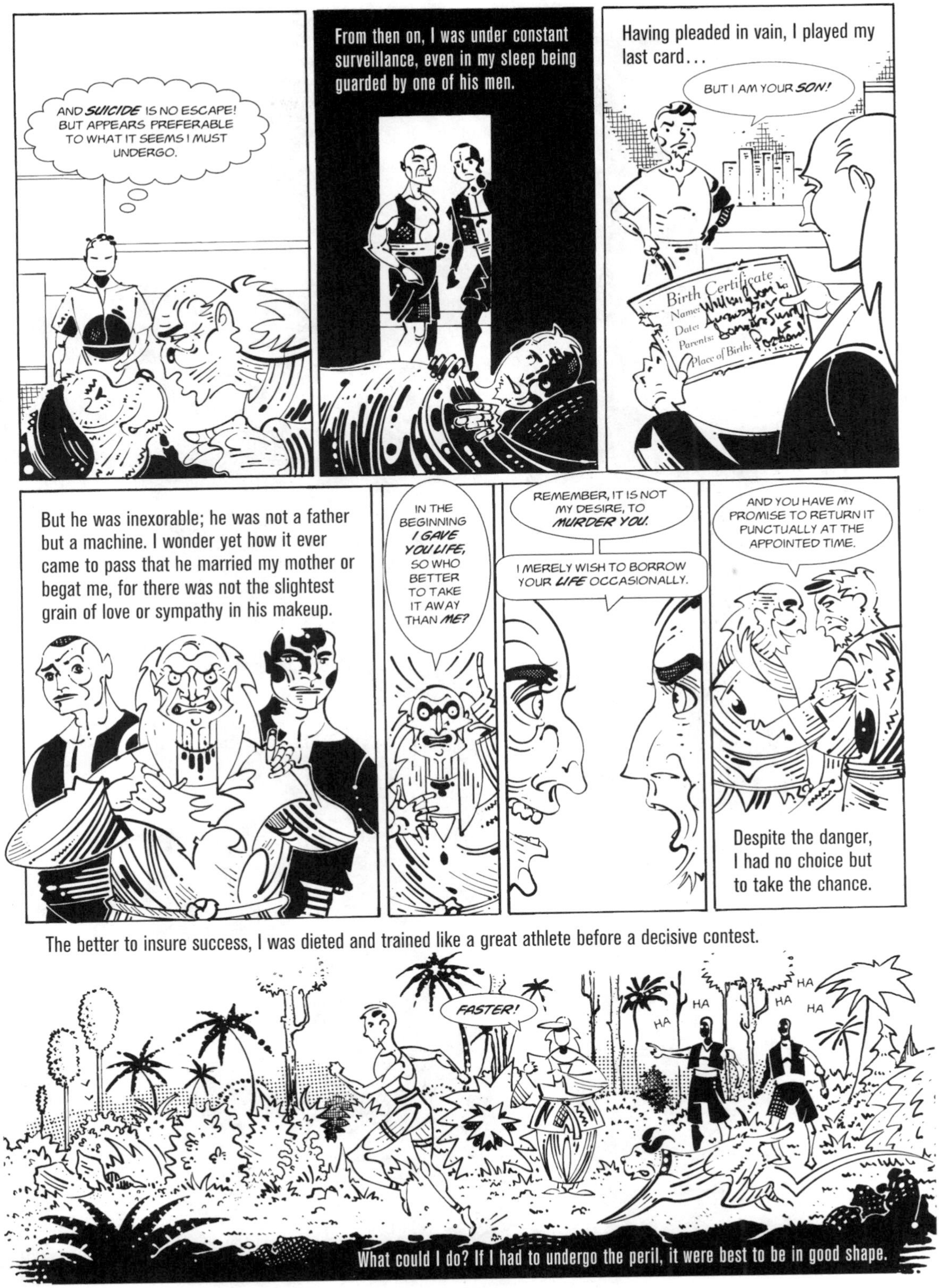
AND SUICIDE IS NO ESCAPE! BUT APPEARS PREFERABLE TO WHAT IT SEEMS I MUST UNDERGO.
From then on, I was under constant surveillance, even in my sleep being guarded by one of his men.
Having pleaded in vain, I played my last card...
BUT I AM YOUR SON!
Birth Certificate
Name:
Date:
Parents:
Place of Birth:
But he was inexorable; he was not a father but a machine. I wonder yet how it ever came to pass that he married my mother or begat me, for there was not the slightest grain of love or sympathy in his makeup.
IN THE BEGINNING I GAVE YOU LIFE, SO WHO BETTER TO TAKE IT AWAY THAN ME?
REMEMBER, IT IS NOT MY DESIRE, TO MURDER YOU.
I MERELY WISH TO BORROW YOUR LIFE OCCASIONALLY.
AND YOU HAVE MY PROMISE TO RETURN IT PUNCTUALLY AT THE APPOINTED TIME.
Despite the danger, I had no choice but to take the chance.
The better to insure success, I was dieted and trained like a great athlete before a decisive contest.
FASTER!
HA
HA
HA
HA
HA
What could I do? If I had to undergo the peril, it were best to be in good shape.

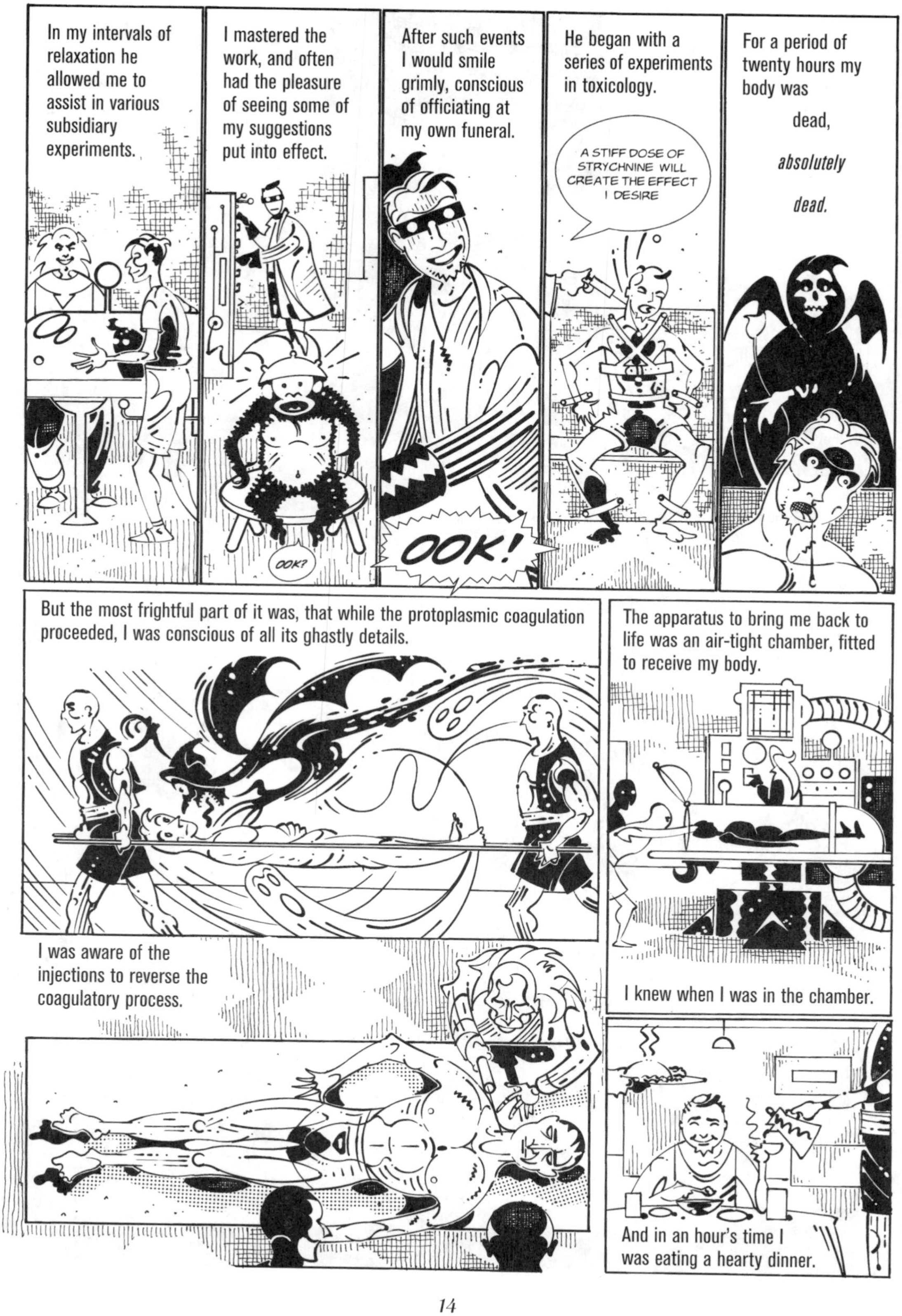
In my intervals of relaxation he allowed me to assist in various subsidiary experiments.
I mastered the work, and often had the pleasure of seeing some of my suggestions put into effect.
OOK?
After such events I would smile grimly, conscious of officiating at my own funeral.
OOK!
He began with a series of experiments in toxicology.
A STIFF DOSE OF STRYCHNINE WILL CREATE THE EFFECT I DESIRE
For a period of twenty hours my body was
dead,
absolutely
dead.
But the most frightful part of it was, that while the protoplasmic coagulation proceeded, I was conscious of all its ghastly details.
The apparatus to bring me back to life was an air-tight chamber, fitted to receive my body.
I knew when I was in the chamber.
I was aware of the injections to reverse the coagulatory process.
And in an hour's time I was eating a hearty dinner.

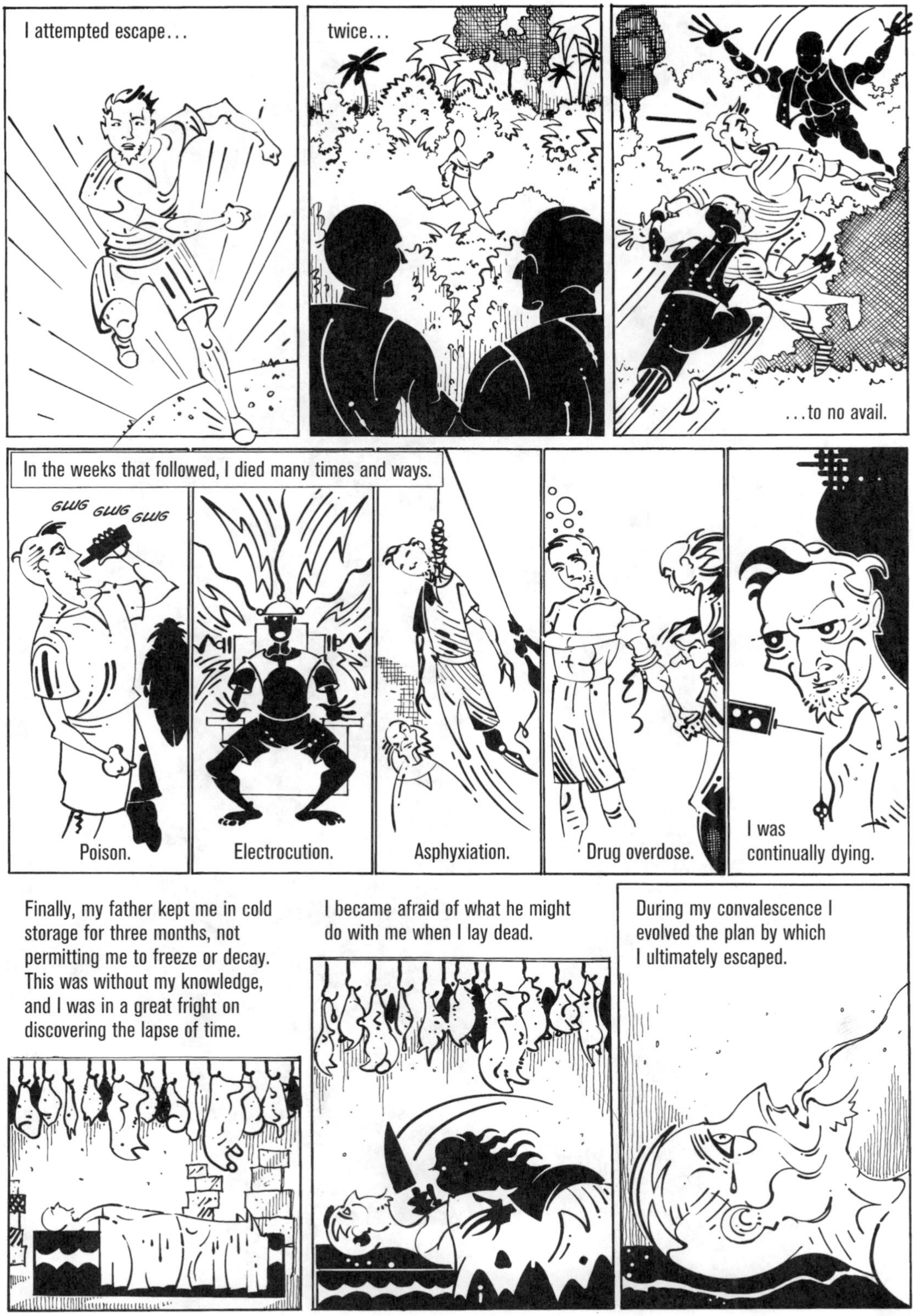
I attempted escape…
twice…
…to no avail.
In the weeks that followed, I died many times and ways.
GLUG GLUG GLUG
Poison.
Electrocution.
Asphyxiation.
Drug overdose.
I was continually dying.
Finally, my father kept me in cold storage for three months, not permitting me to freeze or decay. This was without my knowledge, and I was in a great fright on discovering the lapse of time.
I became afraid of what he might do with me when I lay dead.
During my convalescence I evolved the plan by which I ultimately escaped.

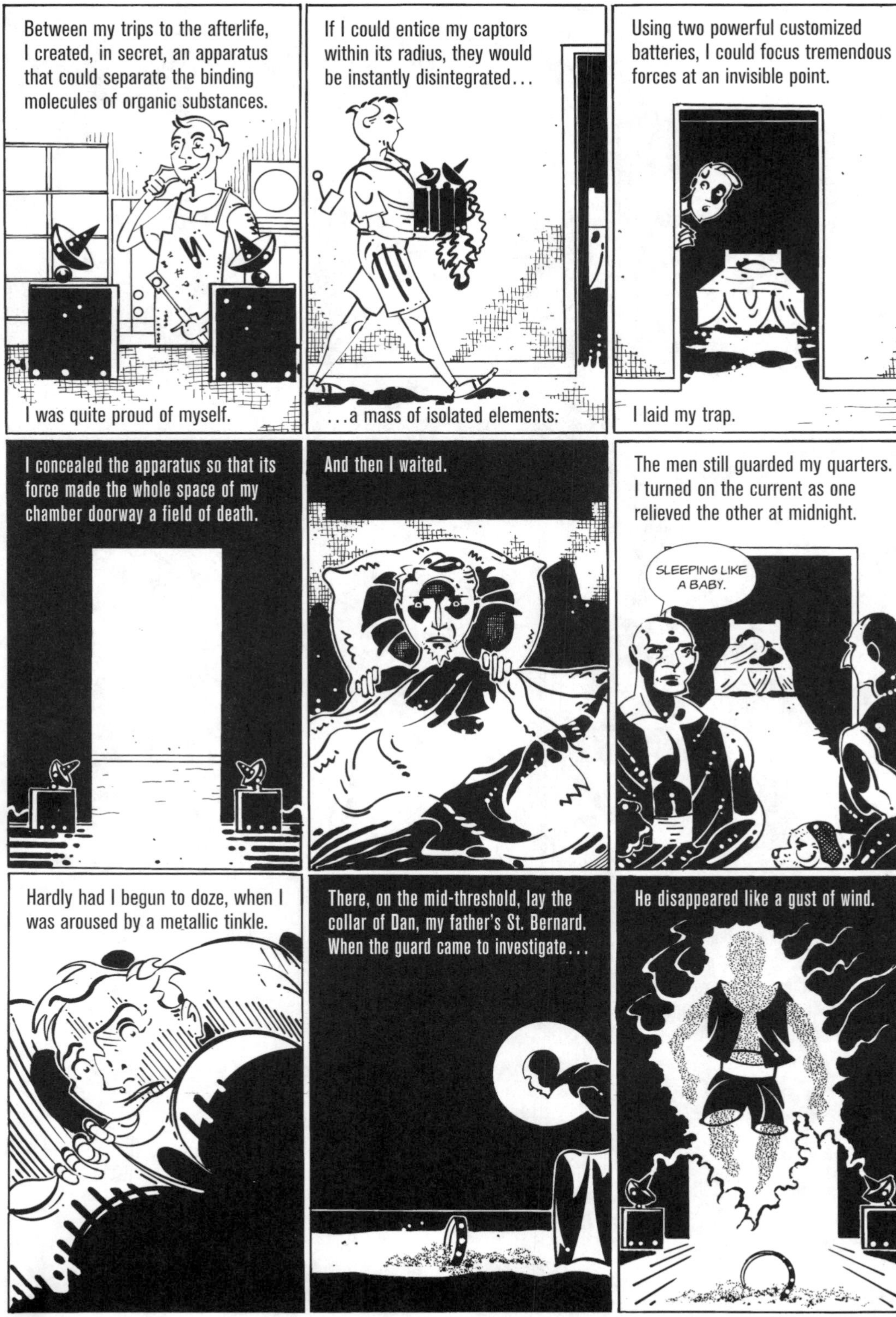
Between my trips to the afterlife, I created, in secret, an apparatus that could separate the binding molecules of organic substances.
I was quite proud of myself.
If I could entice my captors within its radius, they would be instantly disintegrated...
...a mass of isolated elements.
Using two powerful customized batteries, I could focus tremendous forces at an invisible point.
I laid my trap.
I concealed the apparatus so that its force made the whole space of my chamber doorway a field of death.
And then I waited.
The men still guarded my quarters. I turned on the current as one relieved the other at midnight.
SLEEPING LIKE A BABY.
Hardly had I begun to doze, when I was aroused by a metallic tinkle.
There, on the mid-threshold, lay the collar of Dan, my father's St. Bernard. When the guard came to investigate...
He disappeared like a gust of wind.

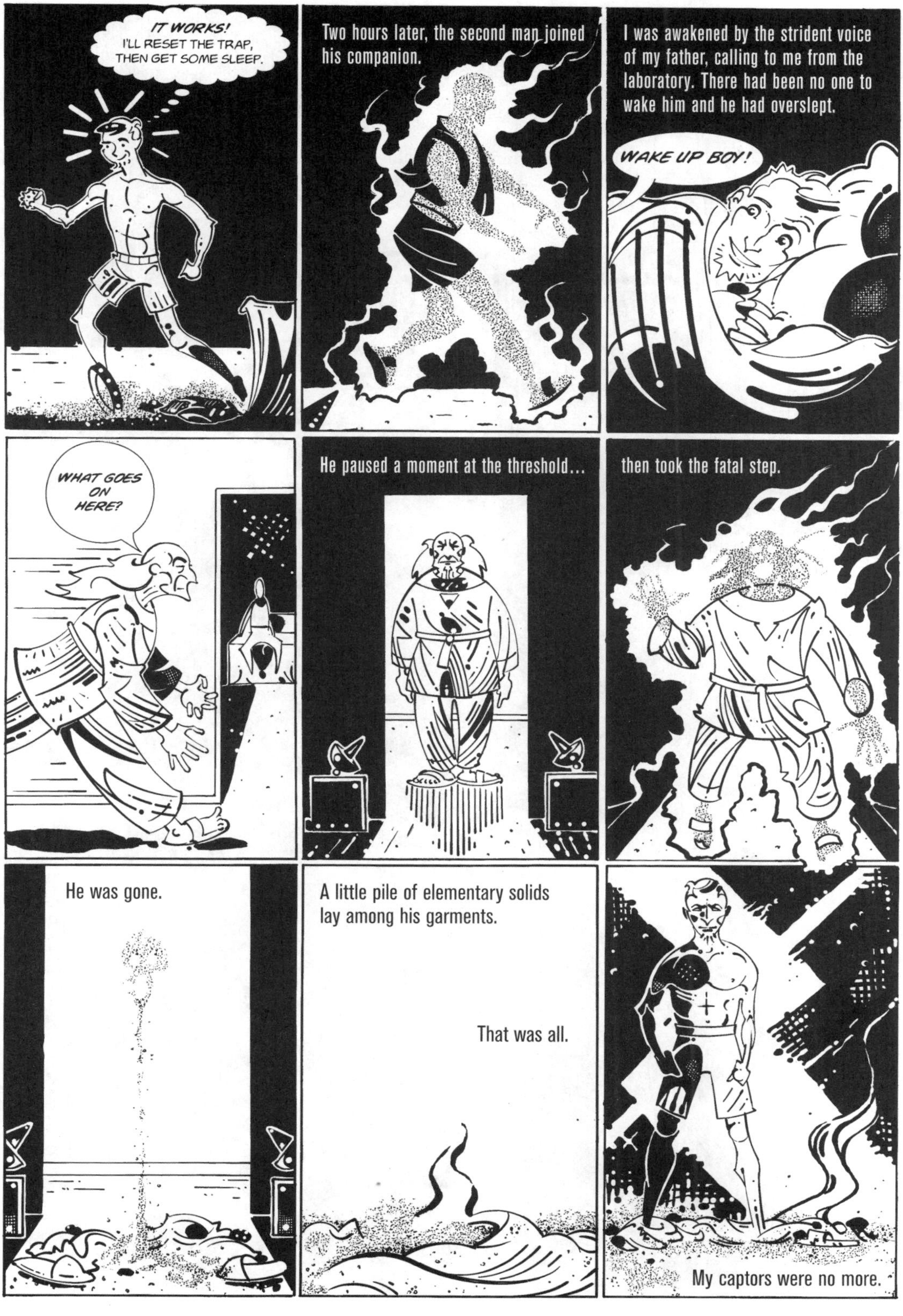
IT WORKS!
I'LL RESET THE TRAP, THEN GET SOME SLEEP.
Two hours later, the second man joined his companion.
I was awakened by the strident voice of my father, calling to me from the laboratory. There had been no one to wake him and he had overslept.
WAKE UP BOY!
WHAT GOES ON HERE?
He paused a moment at the threshold...
then took the fatal step.
He was gone.
A little pile of elementary solids lay among his garments.
That was all.
My captors were no more.

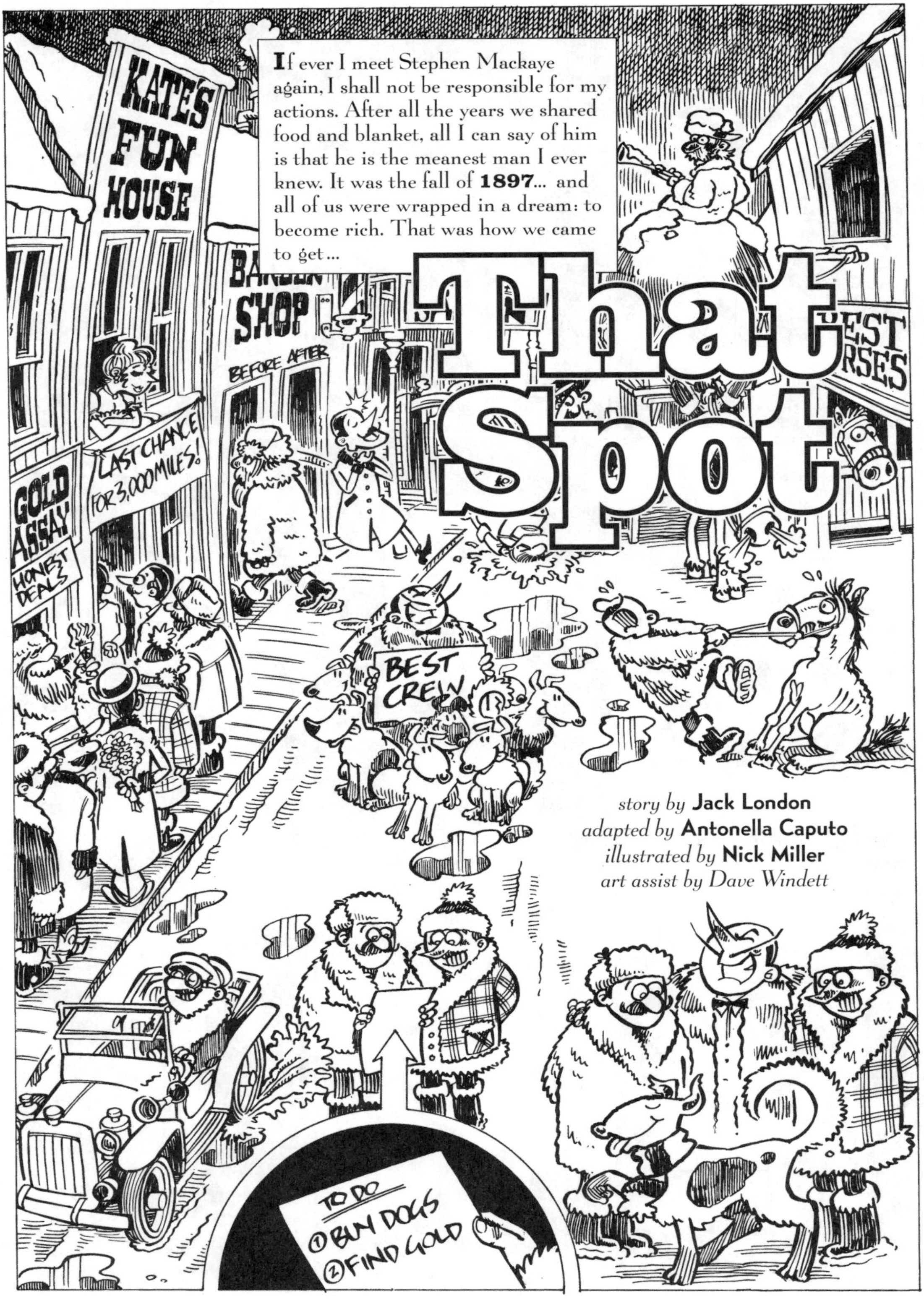
If ever I meet Stephen Mackaye again, I shall not be responsible for my actions. After all the years we shared food and blanket, all I can say of him is that he is the meanest man I ever knew. It was the fall of 1897... and all of us were wrapped in a dream: to become rich. That was how we came to get...
That Spot
KATE'S FUN HOUSE
BARBER SHOP
BEFORE AFTER
LAST CHANCE FOR 3,000 MILES!
GOLD ASSAY
HONEST DEALS
BEST CREW
TO DO
① BUY DOGS
② FIND GOLD
story by Jack London
adapted by Antonella Caputo
illustrated by Nick Miller
art assist by Dave Windett

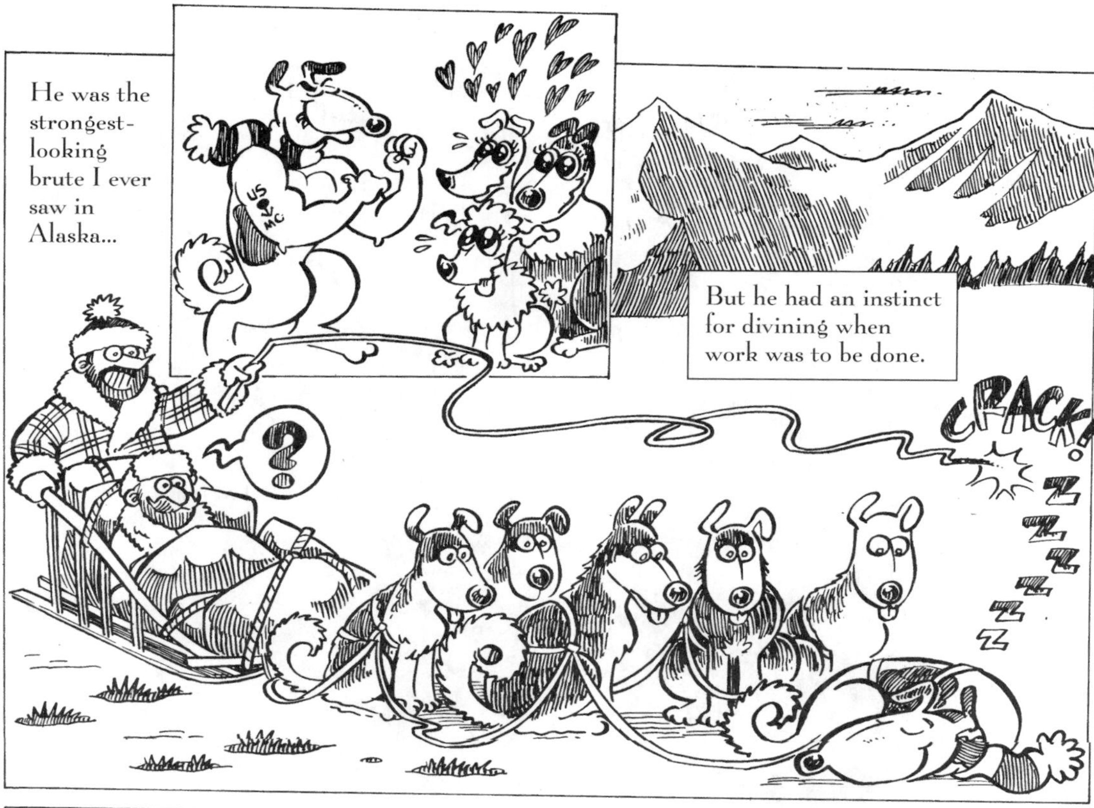
He was the strongest-looking brute I ever saw in Alaska...
US MC
But he had an instinct for divining when work was to be done.
?
CRACK!
Z Z Z Z Z Z

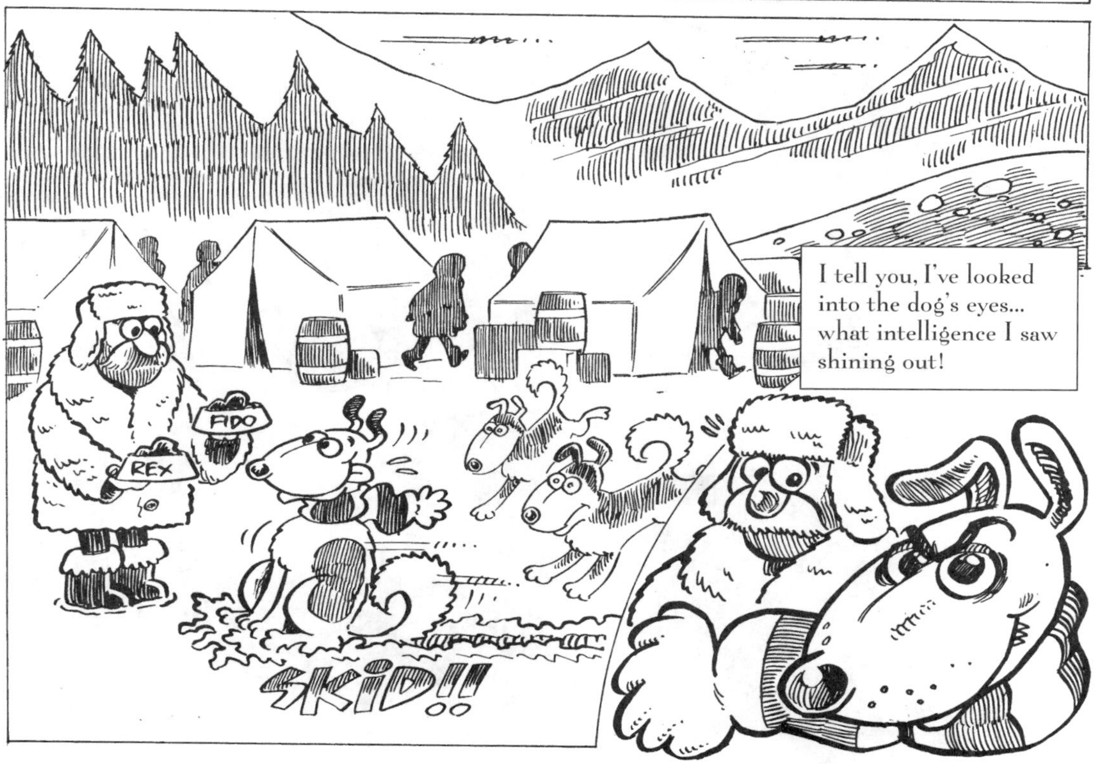
I tell you, I've looked into the dog's eyes... what intelligence I saw shining out!
FIDO
REX
SKID!!

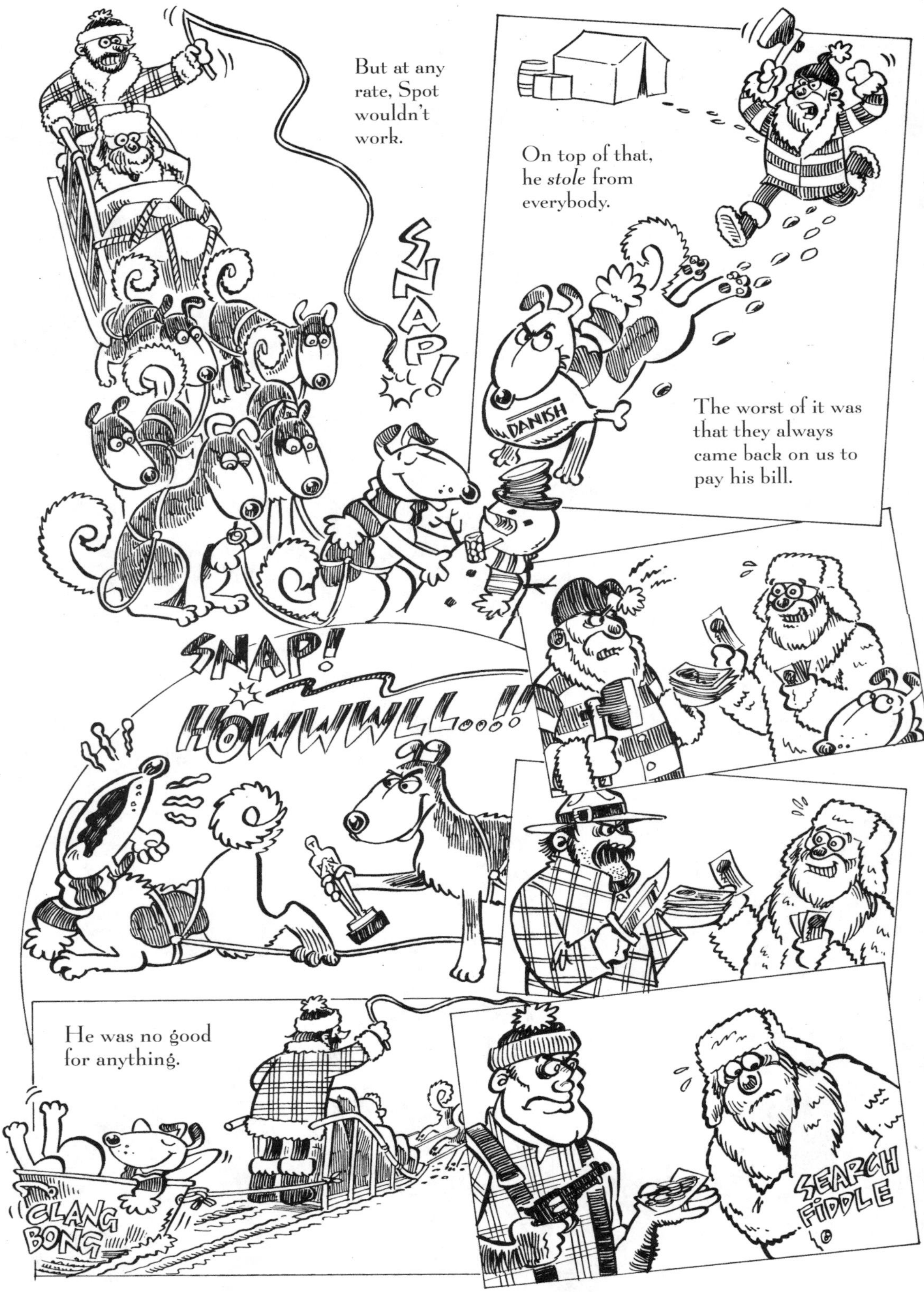
But at any rate, Spot wouldn't work.
SNAP!
On top of that, he *stole* from everybody.
DANISH
The worst of it was that they always came back on us to pay his bill.
SNAP!
HOWWWLL...!!
He was no good for anything.
CLANG
BONG
SEARCH
FIDDLE

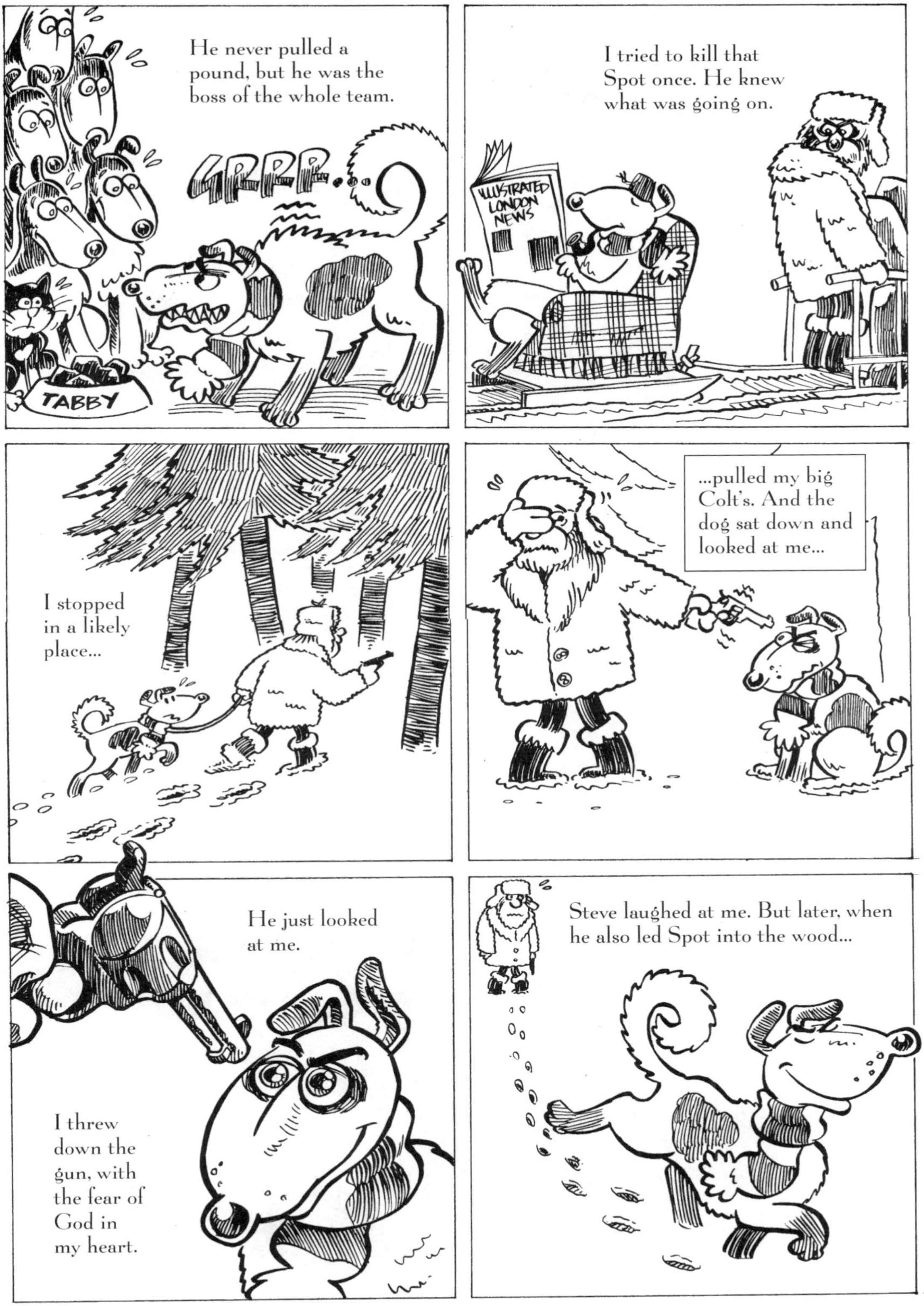
He never pulled a pound, but he was the boss of the whole team.
GRRR...
TABBY
I tried to kill that Spot once. He knew what was going on.
ILLUSTRATED LONDON NEWS
I stopped in a likely place...
...pulled my big Colt's. And the dog sat down and looked at me...
He just looked at me.
I threw down the gun, with the fear of God in my heart.
Steve laughed at me. But later, when he also led Spot into the wood...

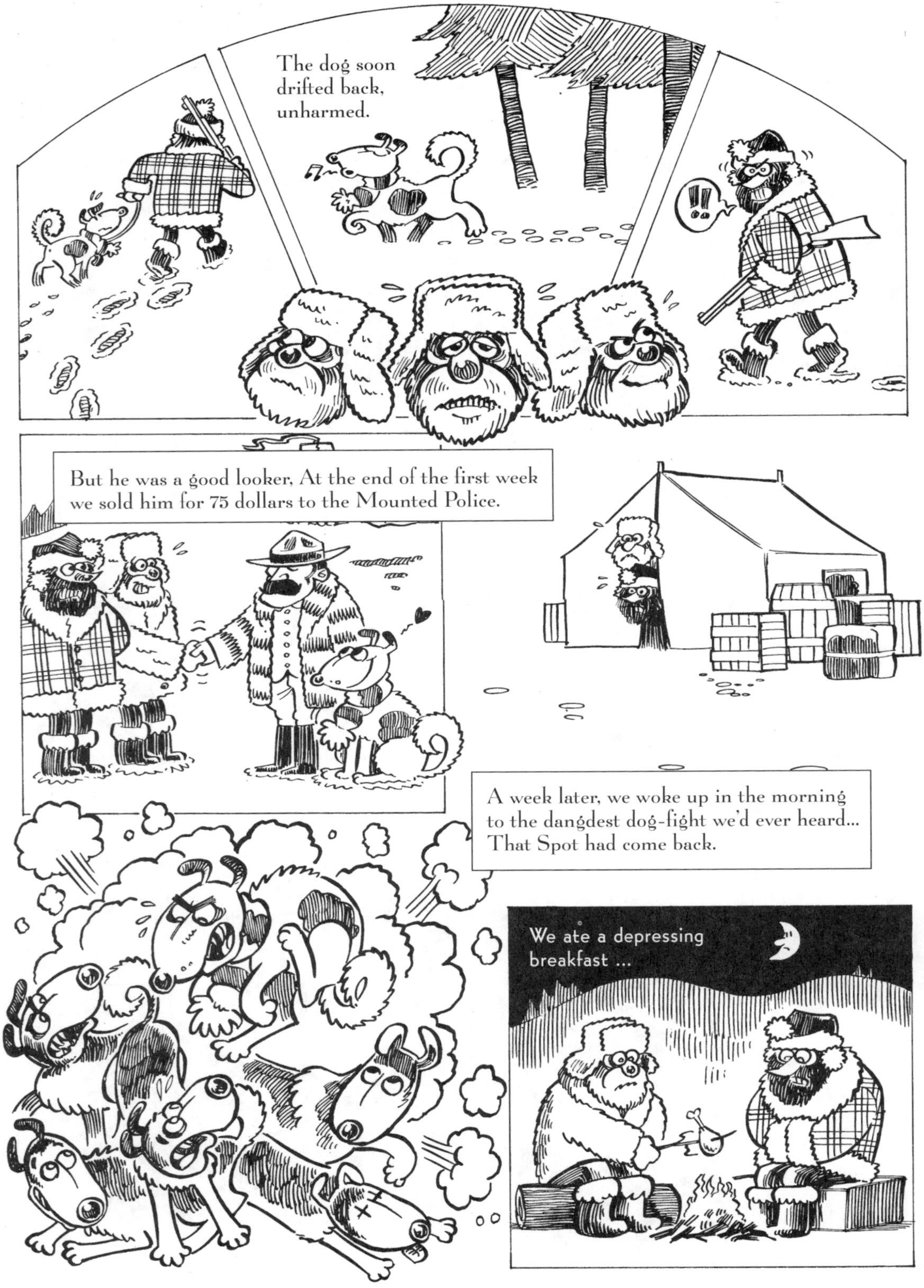
The dog soon drifted back, unharmed.
!!
But he was a good looker, At the end of the first week we sold him for 75 dollars to the Mounted Police.
A week later, we woke up in the morning to the dangdest dog-fight we'd ever heard... That Spot had come back.
We ate a depressing breakfast ...

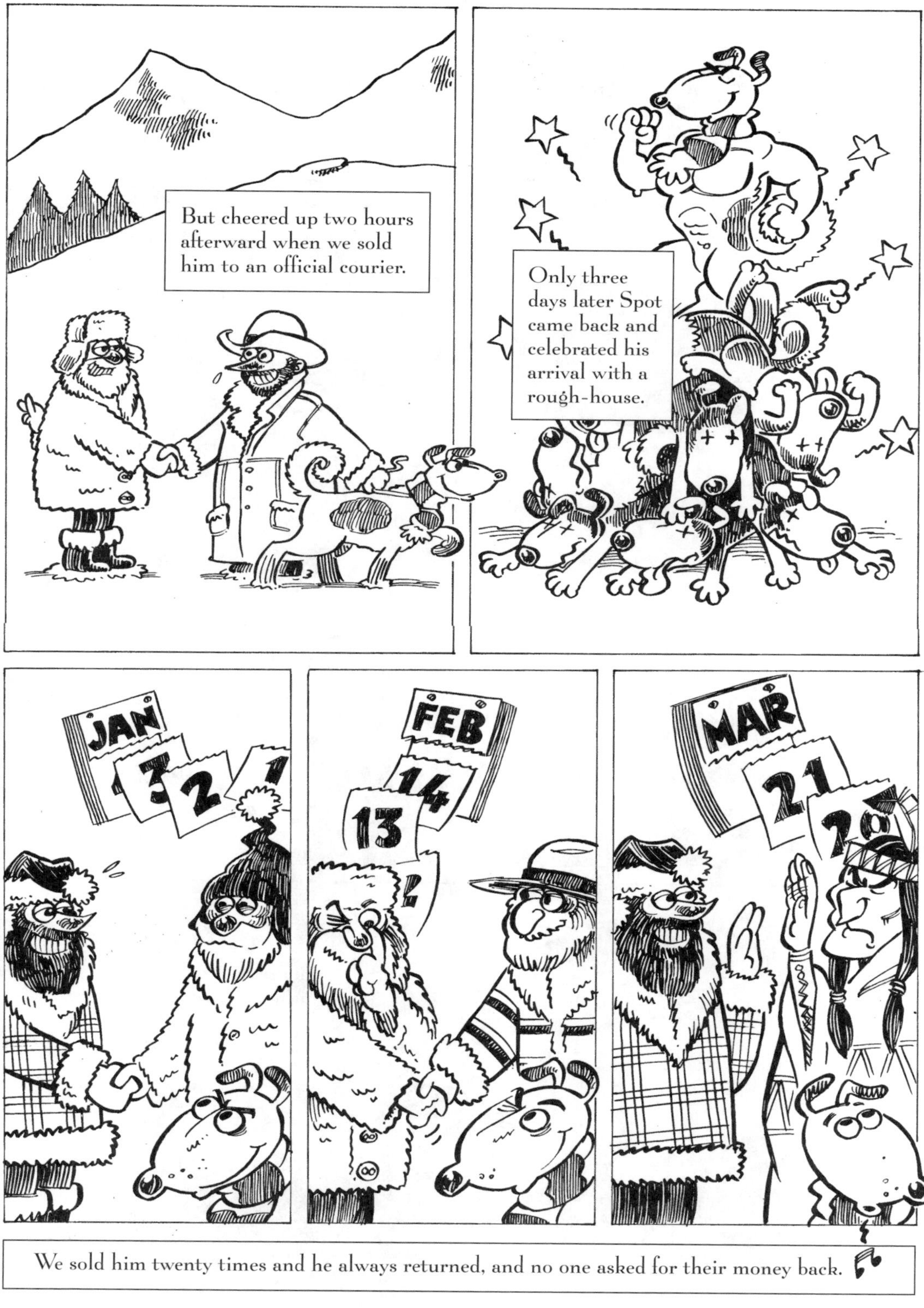
But cheered up two hours afterward when we sold him to an official courier.
Only three days later Spot came back and celebrated his arrival with a rough-house.
JAN
FEB
14
13
MAR
21
We sold him twenty times and he always returned, and no one asked for their money back.

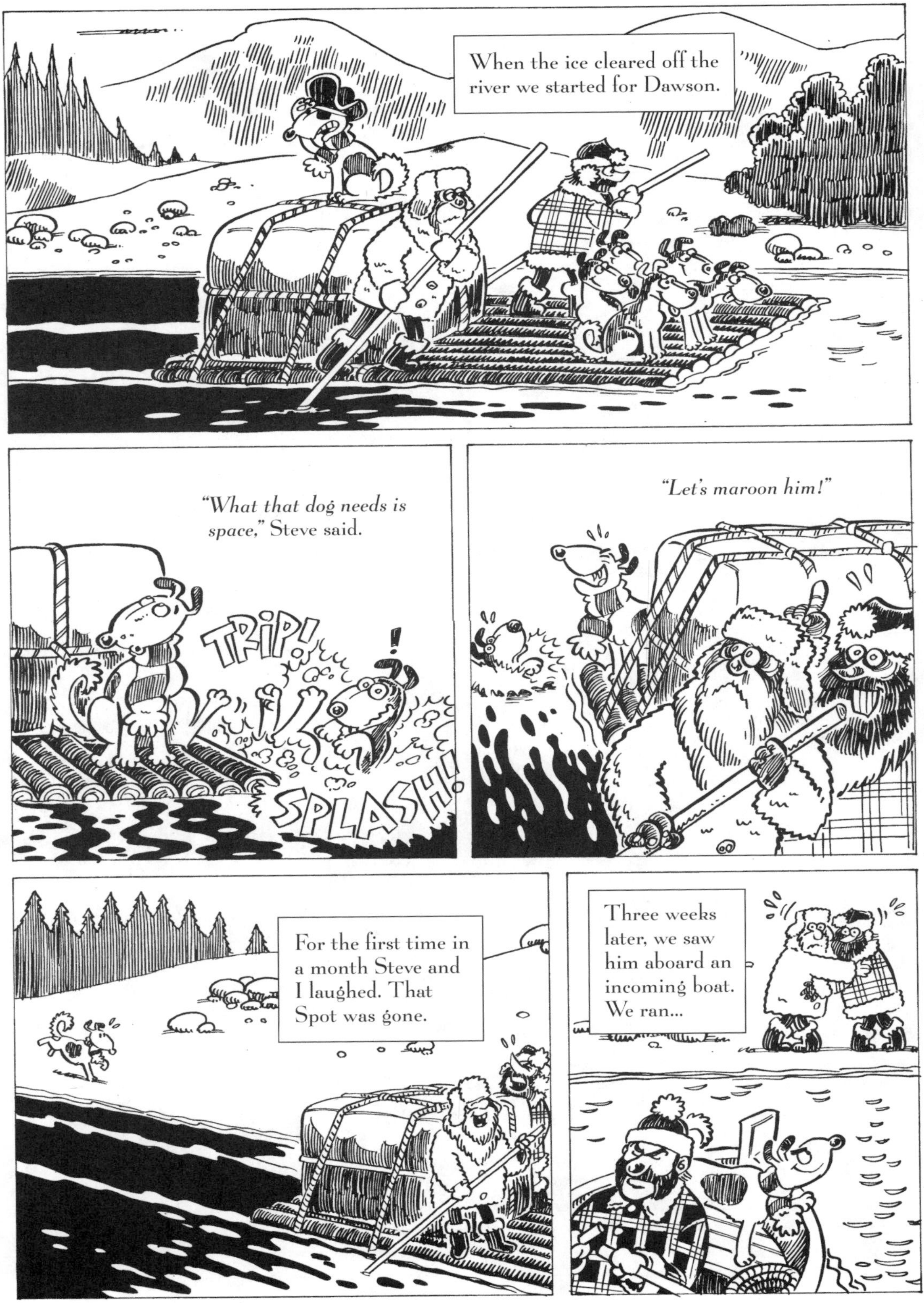
When the ice cleared off the river we started for Dawson.
"What that dog needs is space," Steve said.
TRIP!
!
SPLASH!
"Let's maroon him!"
For the first time in a month Steve and I laughed. That Spot was gone.
Three weeks later, we saw him aboard an incoming boat. We ran...

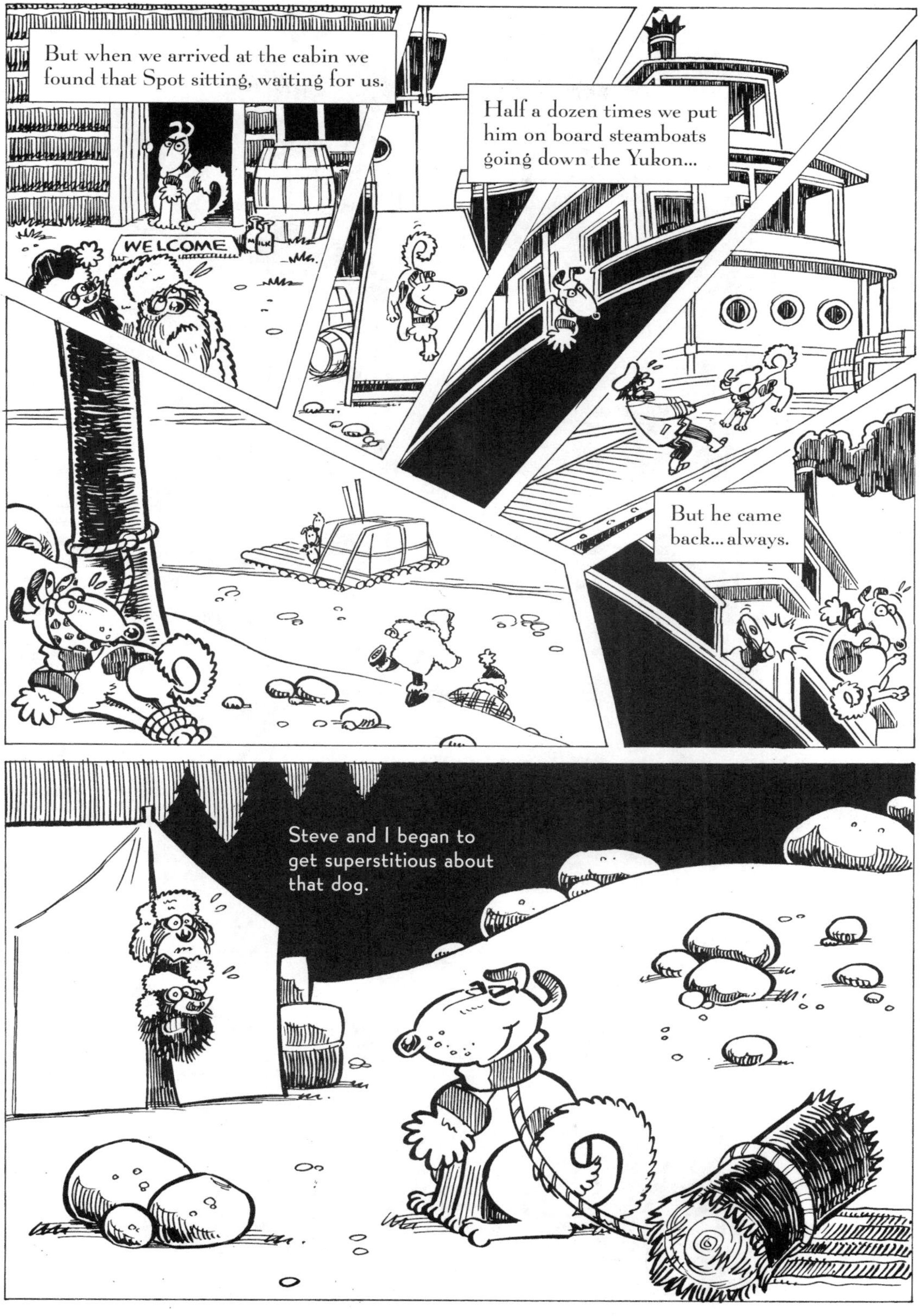
But when we arrived at the cabin we found that Spot sitting, waiting for us.
WELCOME
Half a dozen times we put him on board steamboats going down the Yukon...
But he came back... always.
Steve and I began to get superstitious about that dog.

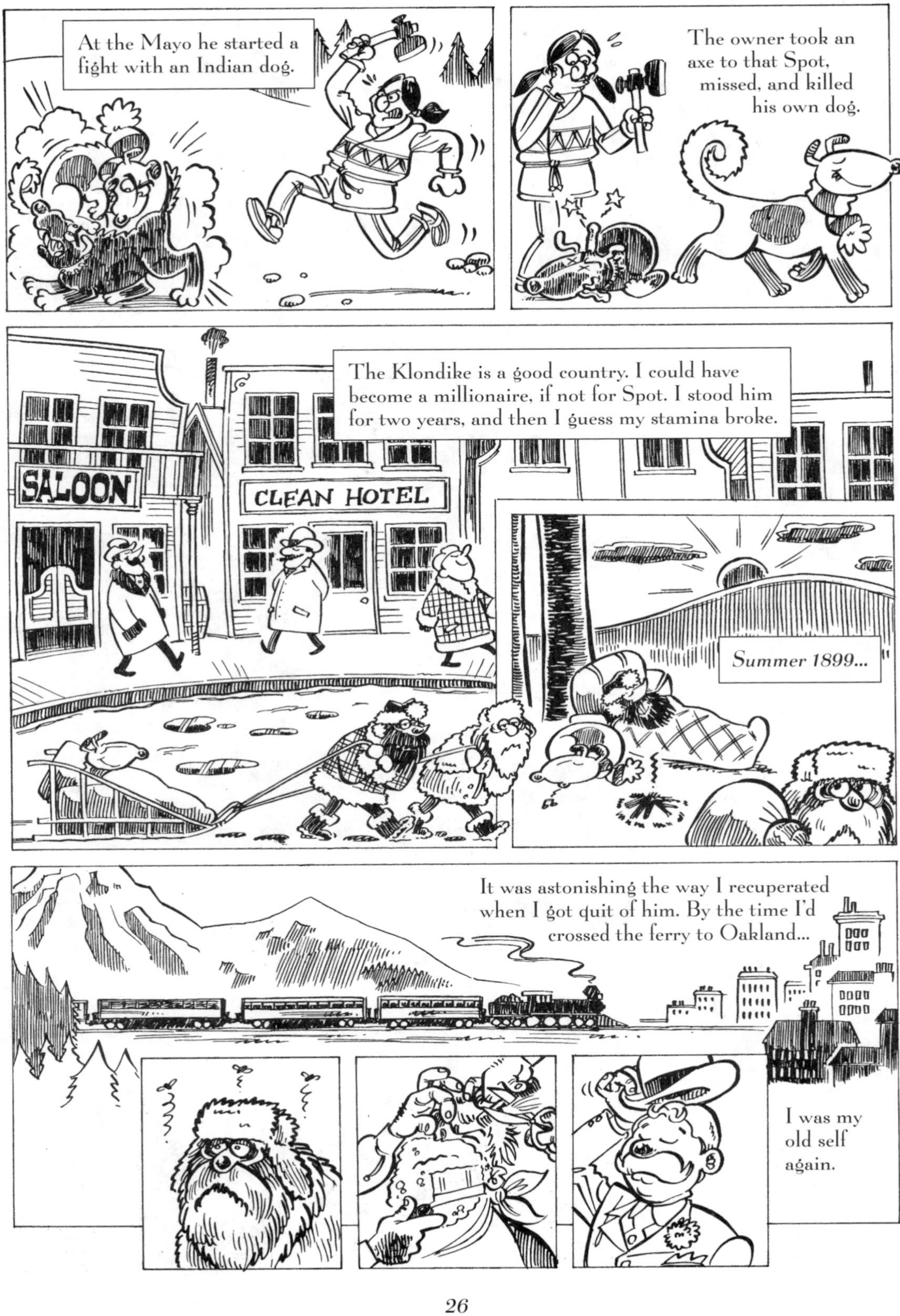
At the Mayo he started a fight with an Indian dog.
The owner took an axe to that Spot, missed, and killed his own dog.
The Klondike is a good country. I could have become a millionaire, if not for Spot. I stood him for two years, and then I guess my stamina broke.
SALOON
CLEAN HOTEL
Summer 1899...
It was astonishing the way I recuperated when I got quit of him. By the time I'd crossed the ferry to Oakland...
I was my old self again.

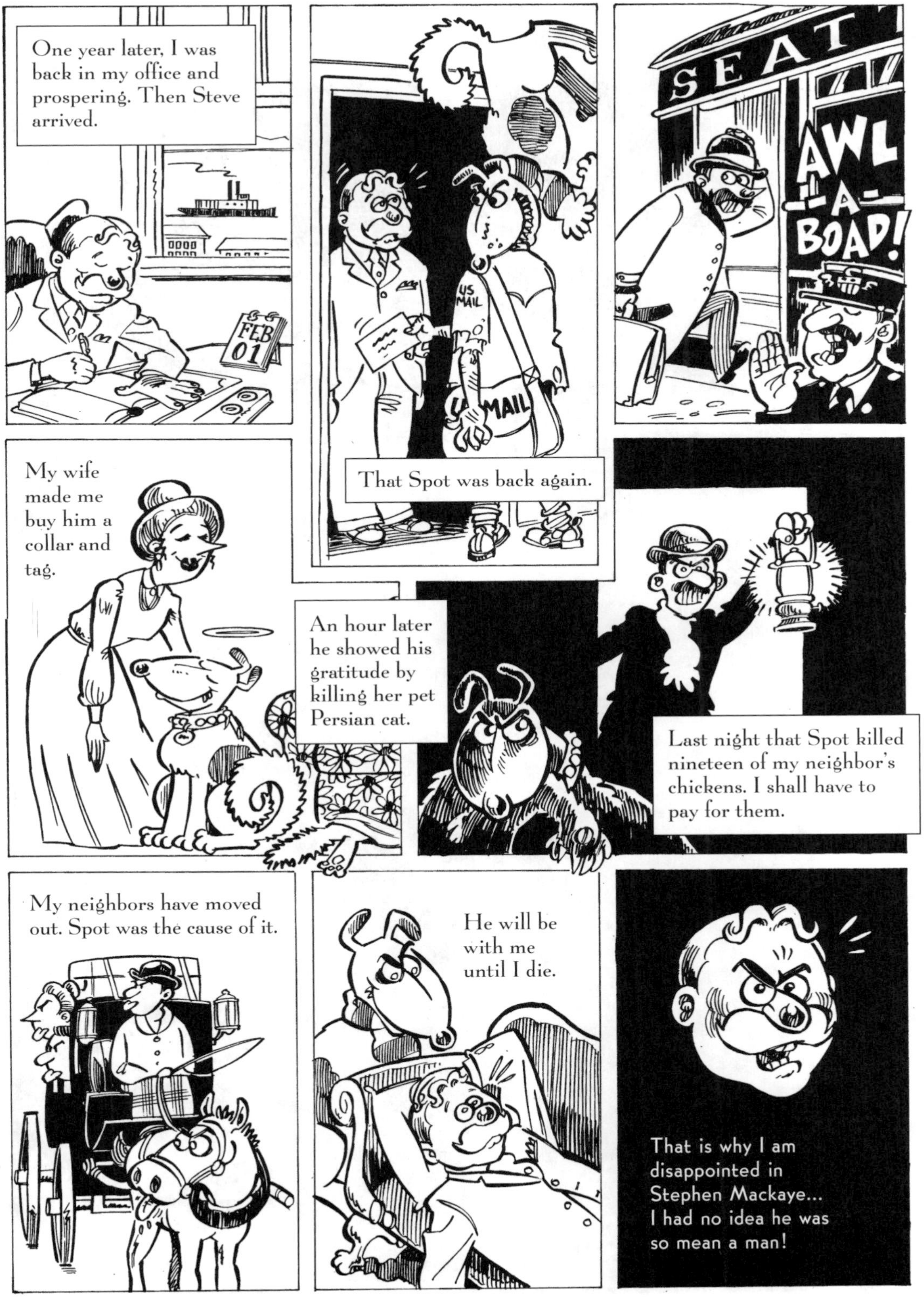
One year later, I was back in my office and prospering. Then Steve arrived.
FEB 01
US MAIL
U MAIL
That Spot was back again.
SEAT
AWL-A-BOAD!
My wife made me buy him a collar and tag.
An hour later he showed his gratitude by killing her pet Persian cat.
Last night that Spot killed nineteen of my neighbor's chickens. I shall have to pay for them.
My neighbors have moved out. Spot was the cause of it.
He will be with me until I die.
That is why I am disappointed in Stephen Mackaye... I had no idea he was so mean a man!

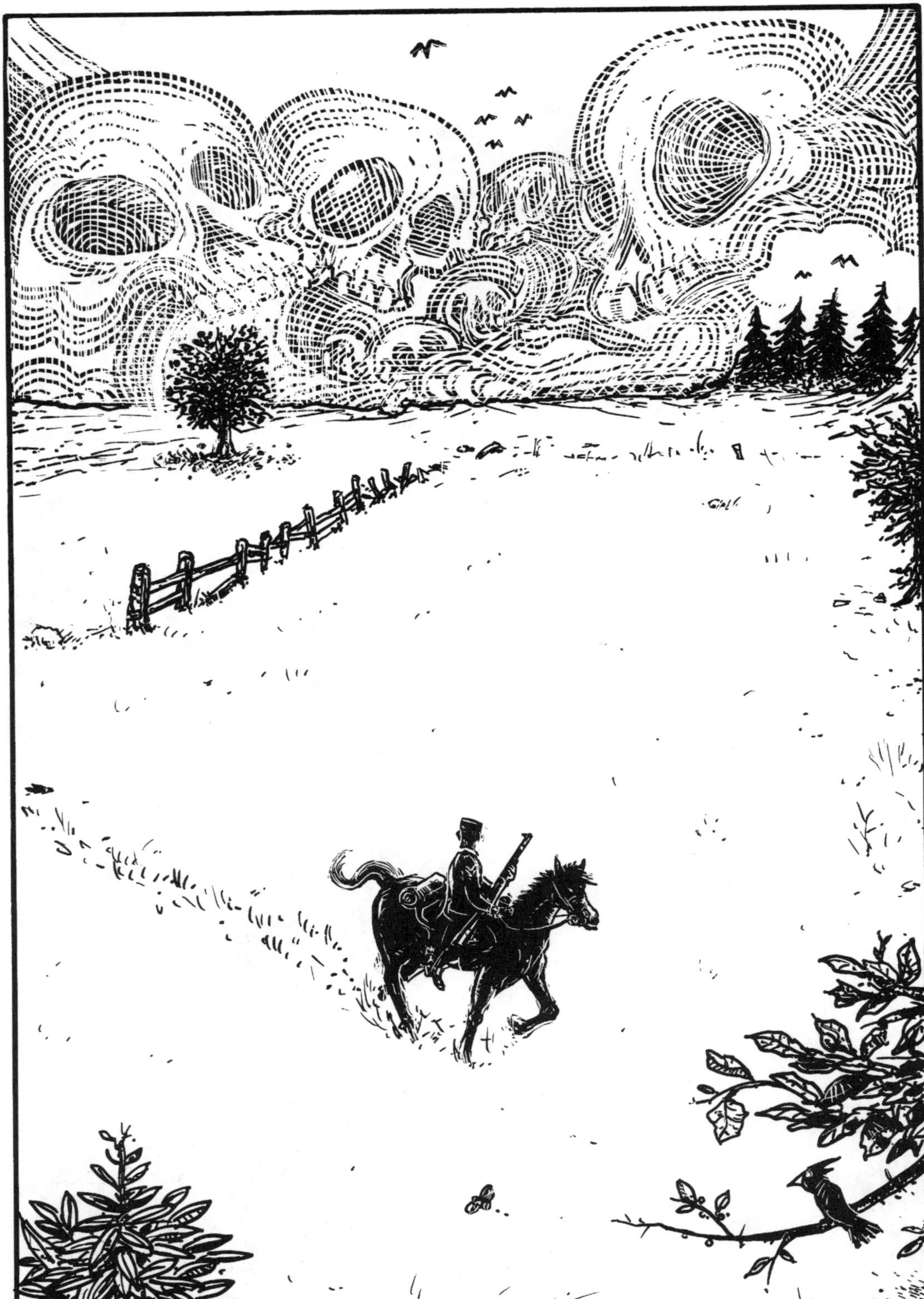

WAR

story by **JACK LONDON**
illustrated by **PETER KUPER**

HE WAS A YOUNG MAN, not more than twenty-four or five, and he might have sat his horse with the careless grace of his youth had he not been so catlike and tense. His black eyes roved everywhere, catching the movements of twigs and branches where small birds hopped, questing ever onward through the changing vistas of trees and brush, and returning always to the clumps of undergrowth on either side. And as he watched, so did he listen, though he rode on in silence, save for the boom of heavy guns from far to the west. This had been sounding monotonously in his ears for hours, and only its cessation could have aroused his notice. For he had business closer to hand. Across his saddle-bow was balanced a carbine.

So tensely was he strung, that a bunch of quail, exploding into flight from under his horse's nose, startled him to such an extent that automatically, instantly, he had reined in and fetched the carbine halfway to his shoulder. He grinned sheepishly, recovered himself, and rode on. So tense was he, so bent upon the work he had to do, that the sweat stung his eyes unwiped, and unheeded rolled down his nose and spattered his saddle pommel. The band of his cavalryman's hat was fresh-stained with sweat. The roan horse under him was likewise wet. It was high noon of a breathless day of heat. Even the birds and squirrels did not dare the sun, but sheltered in shady hiding places among the trees.

Man and horse were littered with leaves and dusted with yellow pollen, for the open was ventured no more than was compulsory. They kept to the brush and trees, and invariably the man halted and peered out before crossing a dry glade or naked stretch of upland pasturage. He worked always to the north, though his way was devious, and it was from the north that he seemed most to apprehend that for which he was looking. He was no coward, but his courage was only that of the average civilized man, and he was looking to live, not die.

Up a small hillside he followed a cow-path through such dense scrub that he was forced to dismount and lead his horse. But when the path swung around to the west, he abandoned it and headed to the north again along the oak-covered top of the ridge.

The ridge ended in a steep descent—so steep that he zigzagged back and forth across the face of the slope, sliding and stumbling among the dead leaves and matted vines and keeping a watchful eye on the horse above that threatened to fall down upon him. The sweat ran from him, and the pollen-dust, settling pungently in mouth and nostrils, increased his thirst. Try as he would, nevertheless the descent was noisy, and frequently he stopped, panting in the dry heat and listening for any warning from beneath.

At the bottom he came out on a flat, so densely forested that he could not make out its extent. Here the character of the woods changed, and he was able to remount. Instead of the twisted hillside oaks, tall straight trees, big-trunked and prosperous, rose from the damp fat soil. Only here and there were thickets, easily avoided, while he encountered winding, park-like glades where the cattle had pastured in the days before war had run them off.

His progress was more rapid now, as he came down into the valley, and at the end of half an hour he halted at an ancient rail fence on the edge of a clearing. He did not like the openness of it, yet his path lay across to the fringe of trees that marked the banks of the stream. It was a mere quarter of a mile across that open, but the thought of venturing out in it was repugnant. A rifle, a score of them, a thousand, might lurk in that fringe by the stream.

Twice he essayed to start, and twice he paused. He was appalled by his own loneliness. The pulse of war that beat from the West suggested the companionship of battling thousands; here was naught but silence, and himself, and possible death-dealing bullets from a myriad ambushes. And yet his task was to find what he feared to find. He must on, and on, till somewhere, some time, he encountered another man, or other men, from the other side, scouting, as he was scouting, to make report, as he must make report, of having come in touch.

Changing his mind, he skirted inside the woods for a distance, and again

peeped forth. This time, in the middle of the clearing, he saw a small farmhouse. There were no signs of life. No smoke curled from the chimney, not a barnyard fowl clucked and strutted. The kitchen door stood open, and he gazed so long and hard into the black aperture that it seemed almost that a farmer's wife must emerge at any moment.

He licked the pollen and dust from his dry lips, stiffened himself, mind and body, and rode out into the blazing sunshine. Nothing stirred. He went on past the house, and approached the wall of trees and bushes by the river's bank. One thought persisted maddeningly. It was of the crash into his body of a high-velocity bullet. It made him feel very fragile and defenseless, and he crouched lower in the saddle.

Tethering his horse in the edge of the wood, he continued a hundred yards on foot till he came to the stream. Twenty feet wide it was, without perceptible current, cool and inviting, and he was very thirsty. But he waited inside his screen of leafage, his eyes fixed on the screen on the opposite side. To make the wait endurable, he sat down, his carbine resting on his knees. The minutes passed, and slowly his tenseness relaxed. At last he decided there was no danger; but just as he prepared to part the bushes and bend down to the water, a movement among the opposite bushes caught his eye.

It might be a bird. But he waited. Again there was an agitation of the bushes, and then, so suddenly that it almost startled a cry from him, the bushes parted and a face peered out. It was a face covered with several weeks' growth of ginger-colored beard. The eyes were blue and wide apart, with laughter-wrinkles in the corners that showed despite the tired and anxious expression of the whole face.

All this he could see with microscopic clearness, for the distance was no more than twenty feet. And all this he saw in

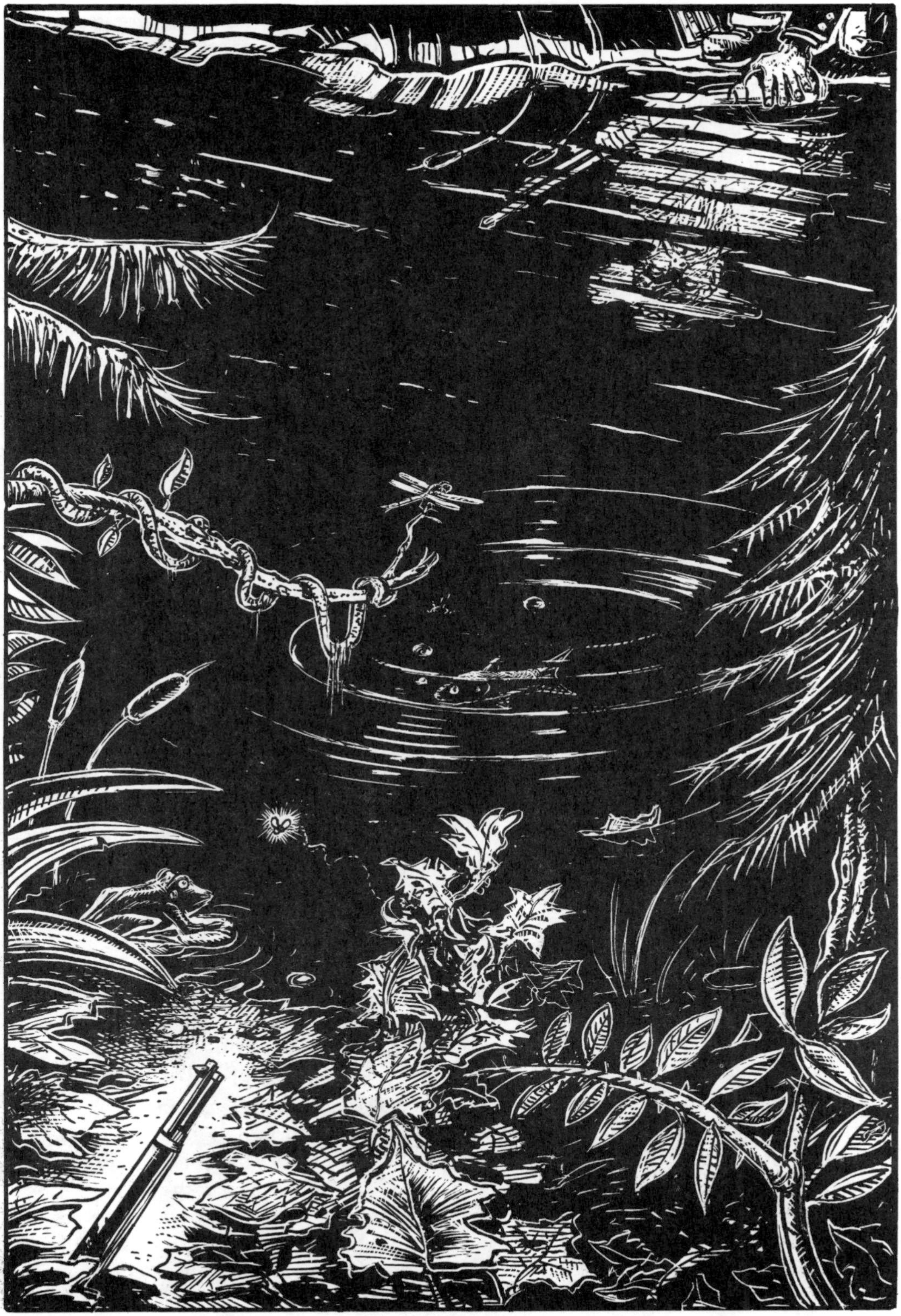

such brief time, that he saw it as he lifted his carbine to his shoulder. He glanced along the sights, and knew that he was gazing upon a man who was as good as dead. It was impossible to miss at such point-blank range.

But he did not shoot. Slowly he lowered the carbine and watched. A hand, clutching a water-bottle, became visible and the ginger beard bent downward to fill the bottle. He could hear the gurgle of the water. Then arm and bottle and ginger beard disappeared behind the closing bushes. A long time he waited, when, with thirst unslaked, he crept back to his horse, rode slowly across the sun-washed clearing, and passed into the shelter of the woods beyond.

TWO

ANOTHER DAY, HOT AND BREATHLESS. A deserted farmhouse, large, with many out-buildings and an orchard, standing in a clearing. From the woods, on a roan horse, carbine across pommel, rode the young man with the quick black eyes. He breathed with relief as he gained the house. That a fight had taken place here earlier in the season was evident. Clips and empty cartridges, tarnished with verdigris, lay on the ground, which, while wet, had been torn up by the hoofs of horses. Hard by the kitchen garden were graves, tagged and numbered. From the oak tree by the kitchen door, in tattered, weatherbeaten garments, hung the bodies of two men. The faces, shriveled and defaced, bore no likeness to the faces of men. The roan horse snorted beneath them, and the rider caressed and soothed it and tied it farther away.

Entering the house, he found the interior a wreck. He trod on empty cartridges as he walked from room to room to reconnoiter from the windows. Men had camped and slept everywhere, and on the floor of one room he came upon stains unmistakable where the wounded had been laid down.

Again outside, he led the horse around behind the barn and invaded the orchard. A dozen trees were burdened with ripe apples. He filled his pockets, eating while he picked. Then a thought came to him, and he glanced at the sun, calculating the time of his return to camp. He pulled off his shirt, tying the sleeves and making a bag. This he proceeded to fill with apples.

As he was about to mount his horse, the animal suddenly pricked up its ears. The man, too, listened, and heard, faintly, the thud of hoofs on soft earth. He crept to the corner of the barn and peered out. A dozen mounted men, strung out loosely, approaching from the opposite side of the clearing, were only a matter of a hundred yards or so away. They rode on to the house. Some dismounted, while others remained in the saddle as an earnest that their stay would be short. They seemed to be holding a council, for he could hear them talking excitedly in the detested tongue of the alien invader. The time passed, but they seemed unable to reach a decision. He put the carbine away in its boot, mounted, and waited impatiently, balancing the shirt of apples on the pommel.

He heard footsteps approaching, and drove his spurs so fiercely into the roan as to force a surprised groan from the animal as it leaped forward. At the corner of the barn he saw the intruder, a mere boy of nineteen or twenty, jump back to escape being run down. At the same moment the roan swerved and its rider caught a glimpse of the aroused men by the house. Some were springing from their horses, and he could see the rifles going to their shoulders. He passed the kitchen door and the corpses swinging in the shade, compelling his foes to run around the front of the house. A rifle cracked, and a second, but he was going fast, leaning forward, low in the saddle, one hand clutching the shirt of apples, the other guiding the horse.

The top bar of the fence was four feet high, but he knew his roan and leaped it at full career to the accompaniment of several scattered shots. Eight hundred yards straight away were the woods, and the roan was covering the distance with mighty strides. Every man was now firing. pumping their guns so rapidly that he no longer heard individual shots. A bullet went through his hat, but he was unaware, though he did know when another tore through the apples on the pommel. And he winced and ducked even lower when a third bullet, fired low, struck a stone between his horse's legs and ricochetted off through the air, buzzing and humming like some incredible insect.

The shots died down as the magazines were emptied, until, quickly, there was no more shooting. The young man was elated. Through that astonishing fusillade he had come unscathed. He glanced back. Yes, they had emptied their magazines. He could see several reloading. Others were running back behind the house for their horses. As he looked, two already mounted, came back into view around the corner, riding hard. And at the same moment, he saw the man with the unmistakable ginger beard kneel down on the ground, level his gun, and coolly take his time for the long shot.

The young man threw his spurs into the horse, crouched very low, and swerved in his flight in order to distract the other's aim. And still the shot did not come. With each jump of the horse, the woods sprang nearer. They were only two hundred yards away and still the shot was delayed.

And then he heard it, the last thing he was to hear, for he was dead ere he hit the ground in the long crashing fall from the saddle. And they, watching at the house, saw him fall, saw his body bounce when it struck the earth, and saw the burst of red-cheeked apples that rolled about him. They laughed at the unexpected eruption of apples, and clapped their hands in applause of the long shot by the man with the ginger beard.

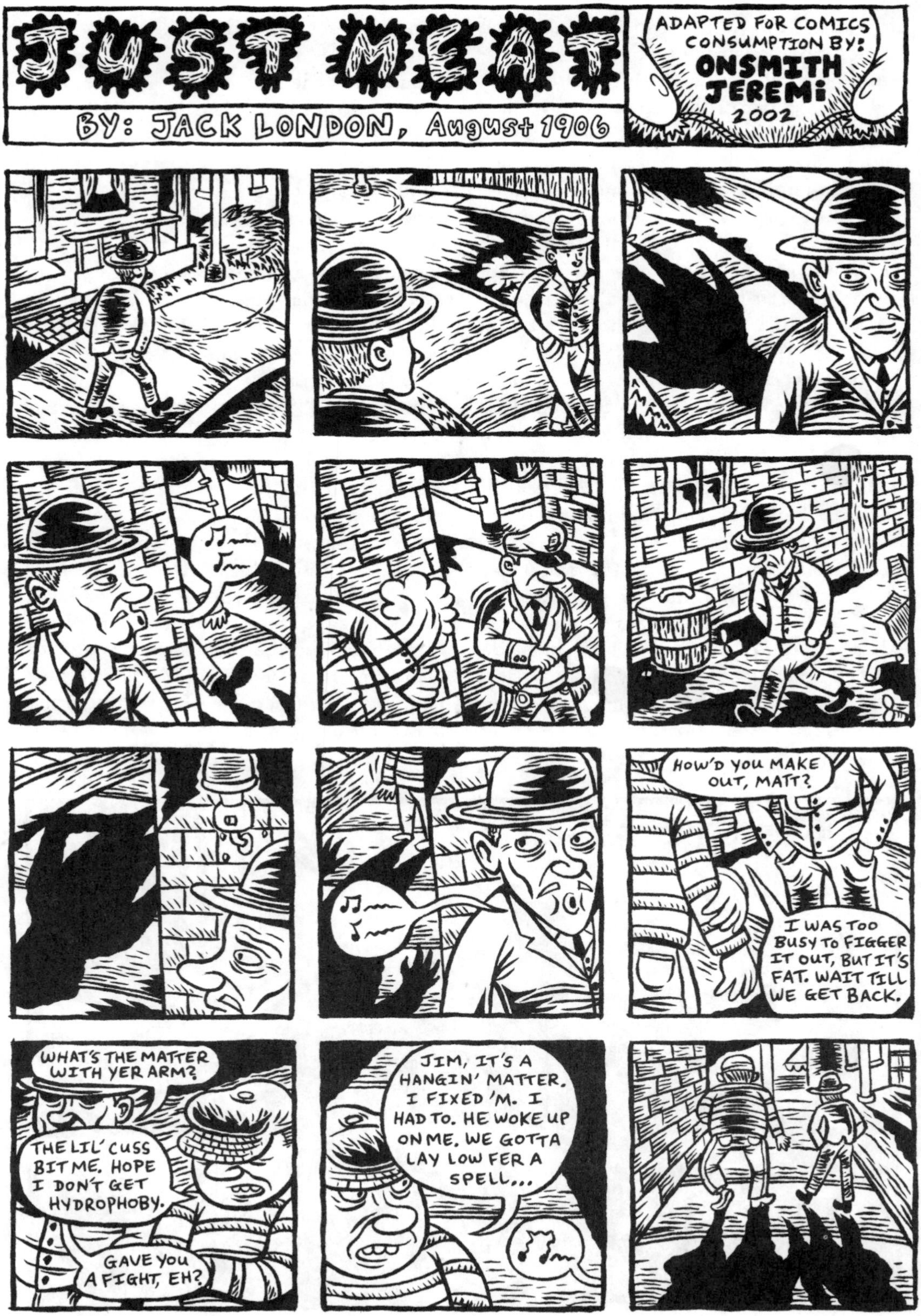
JUST MEAT
BY: JACK LONDON, August 1906
ADAPTED FOR COMICS CONSUMPTION BY:
ONSMITH JEREMI
2002
HOW'D YOU MAKE OUT, MATT?
I WAS TOO BUSY TO FIGGER IT OUT, BUT IT'S FAT. WAIT TILL WE GET BACK.
WHAT'S THE MATTER WITH YER ARM?
THE LIL' CUSS BIT ME. HOPE I DON'T GET HYDROPHOBY.
GAVE YOU A FIGHT, EH?
JIM, IT'S A HANGIN' MATTER. I FIXED 'M. I HAD TO. HE WOKE UP ON ME. WE GOTTA LAY LOW FER A SPELL...

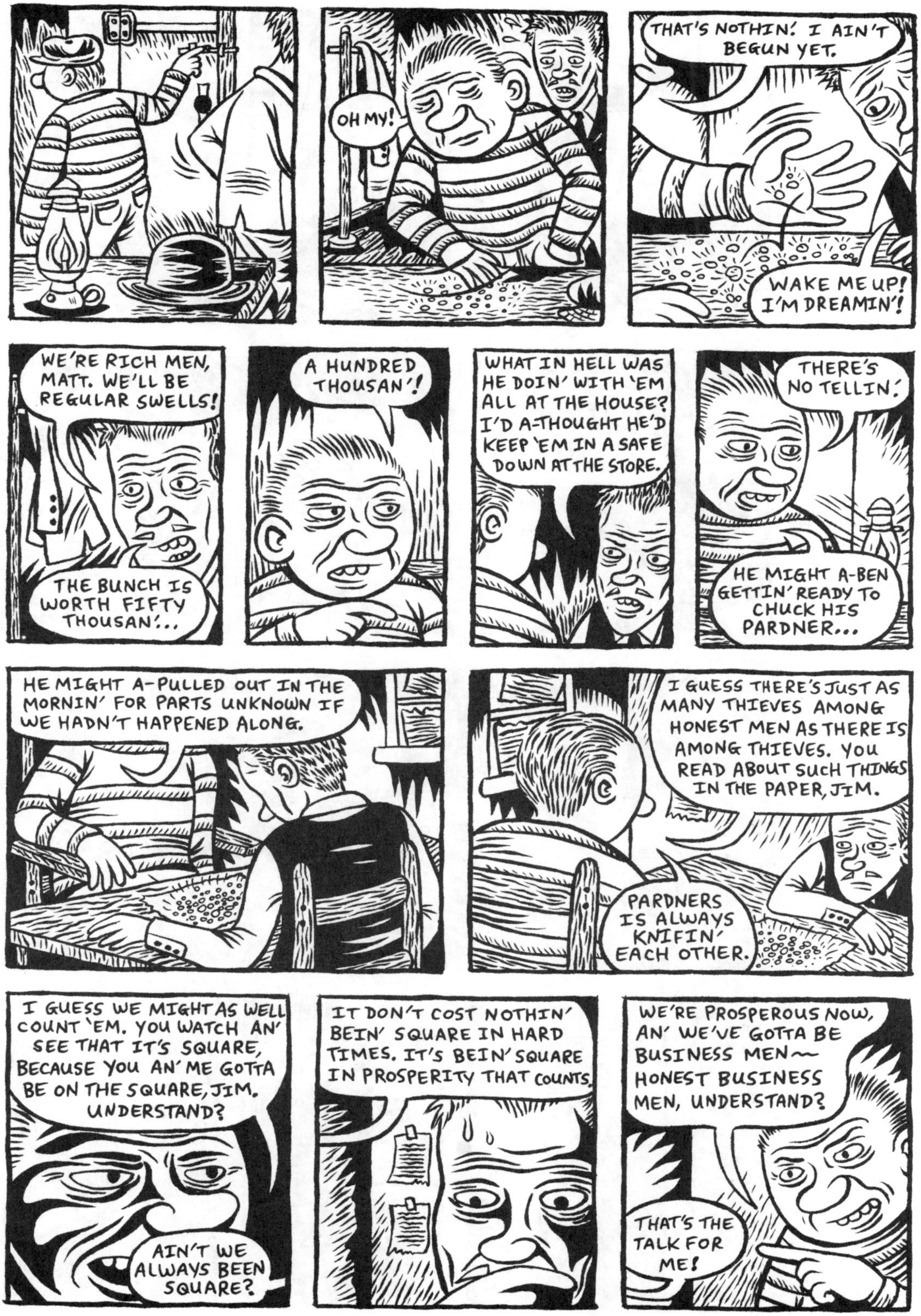
OH MY!
THAT'S NOTHIN'. I AIN'T BEGUN YET.
WAKE ME UP! I'M DREAMIN'!
WE'RE RICH MEN, MATT. WE'LL BE REGULAR SWELLS!
THE BUNCH IS WORTH FIFTY THOUSAN'...
A HUNDRED THOUSAN'!
WHAT IN HELL WAS HE DOIN' WITH 'EM ALL AT THE HOUSE? I'D A-THOUGHT HE'D KEEP 'EM IN A SAFE DOWN AT THE STORE.
THERE'S NO TELLIN'.
HE MIGHT A-BEN GETTIN' READY TO CHUCK HIS PARDNER...
HE MIGHT A-PULLED OUT IN THE MORNIN' FOR PARTS UNKNOWN IF WE HADN'T HAPPENED ALONG.
I GUESS THERE'S JUST AS MANY THIEVES AMONG HONEST MEN AS THERE IS AMONG THIEVES. YOU READ ABOUT SUCH THINGS IN THE PAPER, JIM.
PARDNERS IS ALWAYS KNIFIN' EACH OTHER.
I GUESS WE MIGHT AS WELL COUNT 'EM. YOU WATCH AN' SEE THAT IT'S SQUARE, BECAUSE YOU AN' ME GOTTA BE ON THE SQUARE, JIM. UNDERSTAND?
AIN'T WE ALWAYS BEEN SQUARE?
IT DON'T COST NOTHIN' BEIN' SQUARE IN HARD TIMES. IT'S BEIN' SQUARE IN PROSPERITY THAT COUNTS.
WE'RE PROSPEROUS NOW, AN' WE'VE GOTTA BE BUSINESS MEN~ HONEST BUSINESS MEN, UNDERSTAND?
THAT'S THE TALK FOR ME!

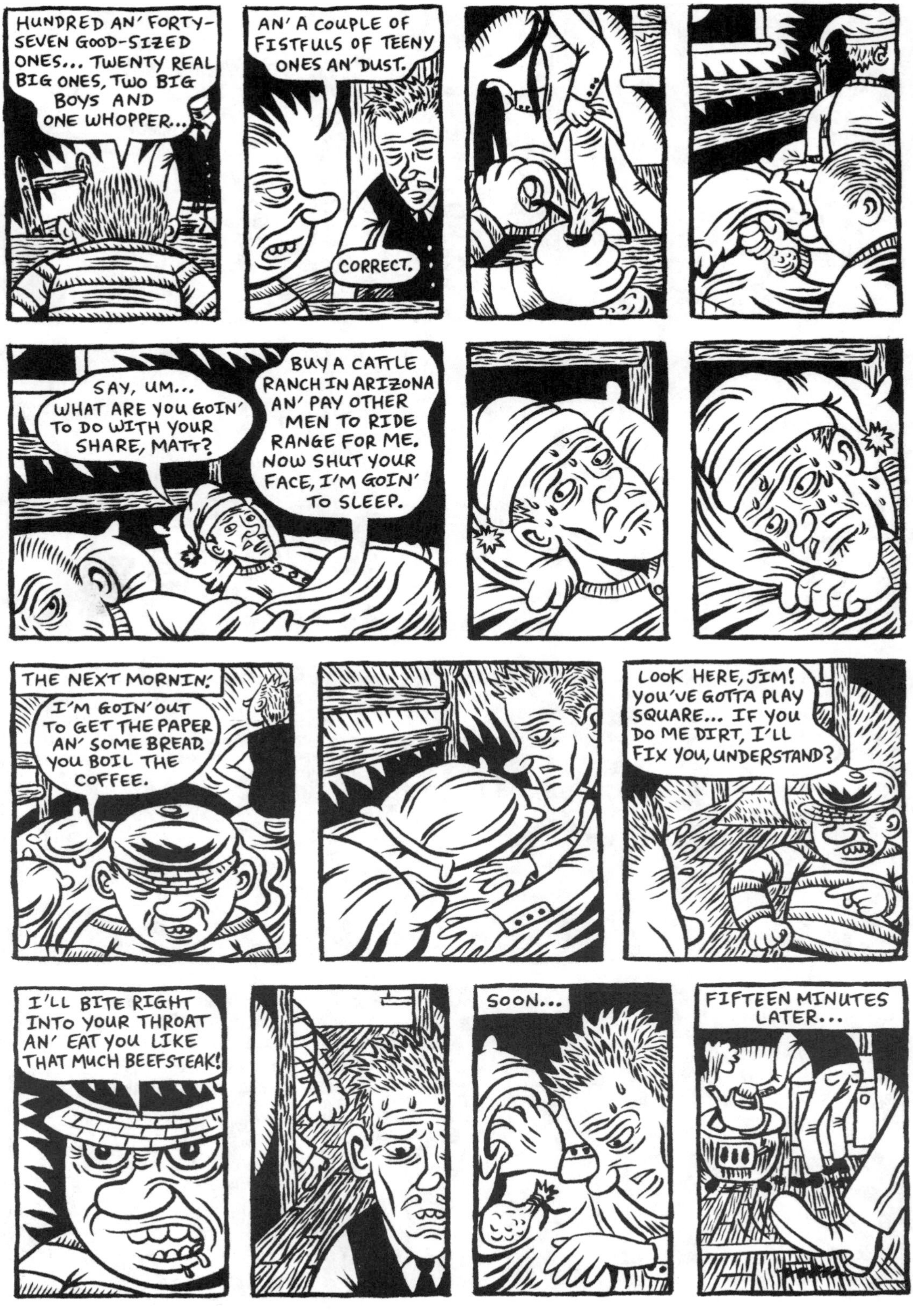
HUNDRED AN' FORTY-SEVEN GOOD-SIZED ONES... TWENTY REAL BIG ONES, TWO BIG BOYS AND ONE WHOPPER...
AN' A COUPLE OF FISTFULS OF TEENY ONES AN' DUST.
CORRECT.
SAY, UM... WHAT ARE YOU GOIN' TO DO WITH YOUR SHARE, MATT?
BUY A CATTLE RANCH IN ARIZONA AN' PAY OTHER MEN TO RIDE RANGE FOR ME. NOW SHUT YOUR FACE, I'M GOIN' TO SLEEP.
THE NEXT MORNIN':
I'M GOIN' OUT TO GET THE PAPER AN' SOME BREAD. YOU BOIL THE COFFEE.
LOOK HERE, JIM! YOU'VE GOTTA PLAY SQUARE... IF YOU DO ME DIRT, I'LL FIX YOU, UNDERSTAND?
I'LL BITE RIGHT INTO YOUR THROAT AN' EAT YOU LIKE THAT MUCH BEEFSTEAK!
SOON...
FIFTEEN MINUTES LATER...

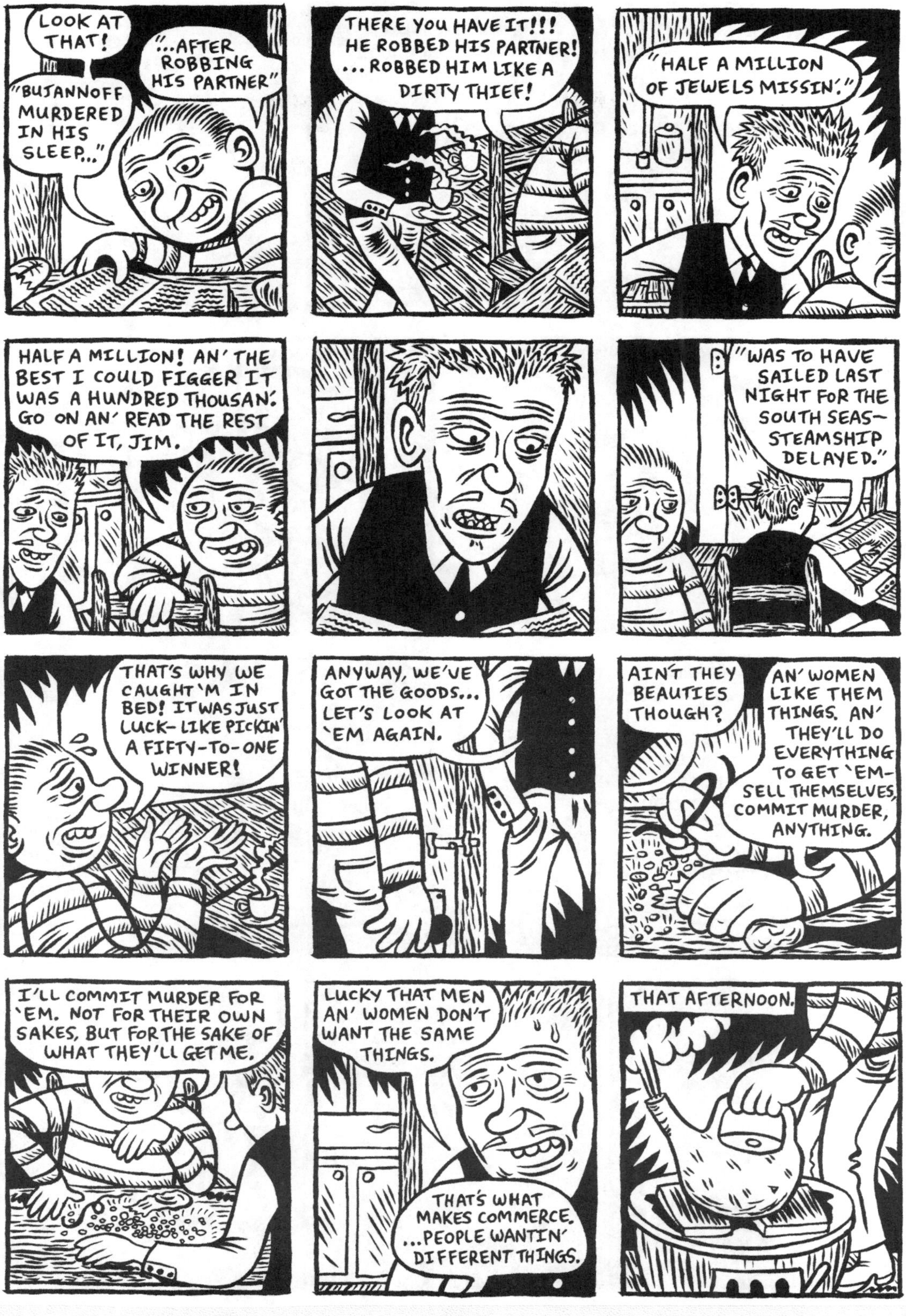
LOOK AT THAT!
"BUJANNOFF MURDERED IN HIS SLEEP..."
"...AFTER ROBBING HIS PARTNER"
THERE YOU HAVE IT!!! HE ROBBED HIS PARTNER! ...ROBBED HIM LIKE A DIRTY THIEF!
"HALF A MILLION OF JEWELS MISSIN'."
HALF A MILLION! AN' THE BEST I COULD FIGGER IT WAS A HUNDRED THOUSAN'. GO ON AN' READ THE REST OF IT, JIM.
"WAS TO HAVE SAILED LAST NIGHT FOR THE SOUTH SEAS— STEAMSHIP DELAYED."
THAT'S WHY WE CAUGHT 'M IN BED! IT WAS JUST LUCK—LIKE PICKIN' A FIFTY-TO-ONE WINNER!
ANYWAY, WE'VE GOT THE GOODS... LET'S LOOK AT 'EM AGAIN.
AIN'T THEY BEAUTIES THOUGH?
AN' WOMEN LIKE THEM THINGS. AN' THEY'LL DO EVERYTHING TO GET 'EM— SELL THEMSELVES, COMMIT MURDER, ANYTHING.
I'LL COMMIT MURDER FOR 'EM. NOT FOR THEIR OWN SAKES, BUT FOR THE SAKE OF WHAT THEY'LL GET ME.
LUCKY THAT MEN AN' WOMEN DON'T WANT THE SAME THINGS.
THAT'S WHAT MAKES COMMERCE. ...PEOPLE WANTIN' DIFFERENT THINGS.
THAT AFTERNOON.

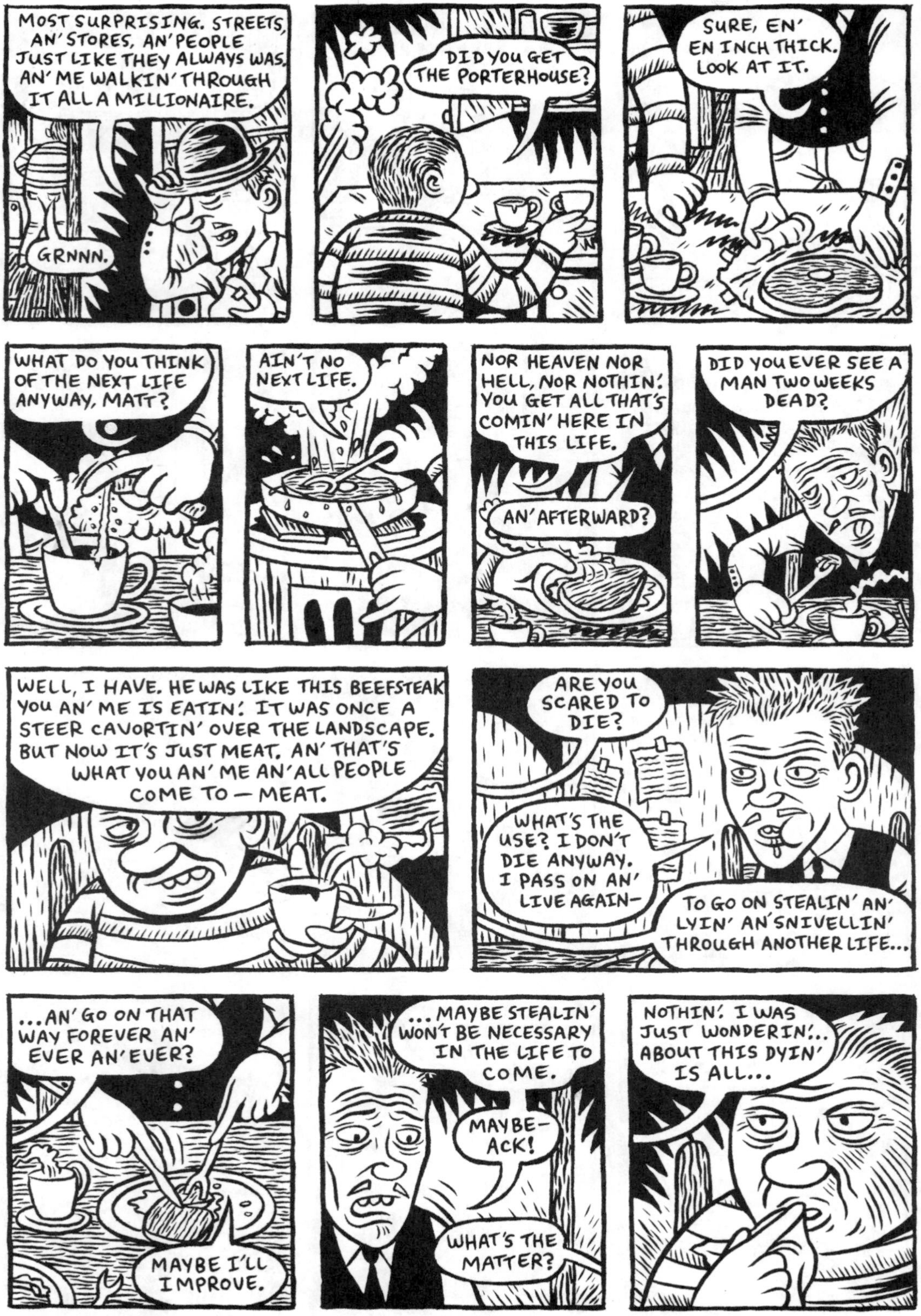
MOST SURPRISING. STREETS, AN' STORES, AN' PEOPLE JUST LIKE THEY ALWAYS WAS, AN' ME WALKIN' THROUGH IT ALL A MILLIONAIRE.
GRNNN.
DID YOU GET THE PORTERHOUSE?
SURE, EN' EN INCH THICK. LOOK AT IT.
WHAT DO YOU THINK OF THE NEXT LIFE ANYWAY, MATT?
AIN'T NO NEXT LIFE.
NOR HEAVEN NOR HELL, NOR NOTHIN'. YOU GET ALL THAT'S COMIN' HERE IN THIS LIFE.
AN' AFTERWARD?
DID YOU EVER SEE A MAN TWO WEEKS DEAD?
WELL, I HAVE. HE WAS LIKE THIS BEEFSTEAK YOU AN' ME IS EATIN'. IT WAS ONCE A STEER CAVORTIN' OVER THE LANDSCAPE. BUT NOW IT'S JUST MEAT. AN' THAT'S WHAT YOU AN' ME AN' ALL PEOPLE COME TO — MEAT.
ARE YOU SCARED TO DIE?
WHAT'S THE USE? I DON'T DIE ANYWAY. I PASS ON AN' LIVE AGAIN—
TO GO ON STEALIN' AN' LYIN' AN' SNIVELLIN' THROUGH ANOTHER LIFE...
...AN' GO ON THAT WAY FOREVER AN' EVER AN' EVER?
MAYBE I'LL IMPROVE.
...MAYBE STEALIN' WON'T BE NECESSARY IN THE LIFE TO COME.
MAYBE-ACK!
WHAT'S THE MATTER?
NOTHIN'. I WAS JUST WONDERIN'... ABOUT THIS DYIN' IS ALL...

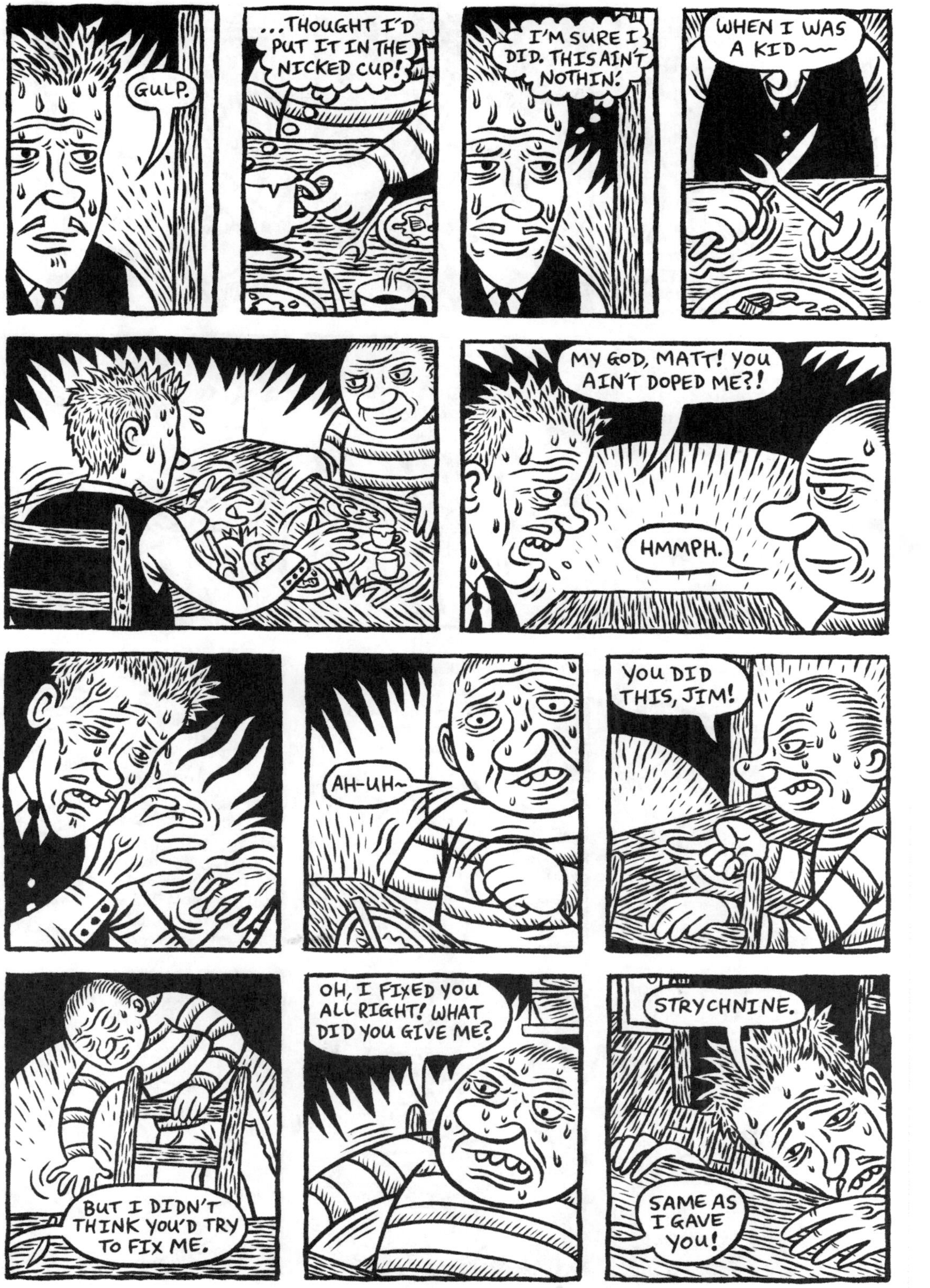
GULP.
...THOUGHT I'D PUT IT IN THE NICKED CUP!
I'M SURE I DID. THIS AIN'T NOTHIN'.
WHEN I WAS A KID~~
MY GOD, MATT! YOU AIN'T DOPED ME?!
HMMPH.
AH-UH~
YOU DID THIS, JIM!
BUT I DIDN'T THINK YOU'D TRY TO FIX ME.
OH, I FIXED YOU ALL RIGHT! WHAT DID YOU GIVE ME?
STRYCHNINE.
SAME AS I GAVE YOU!

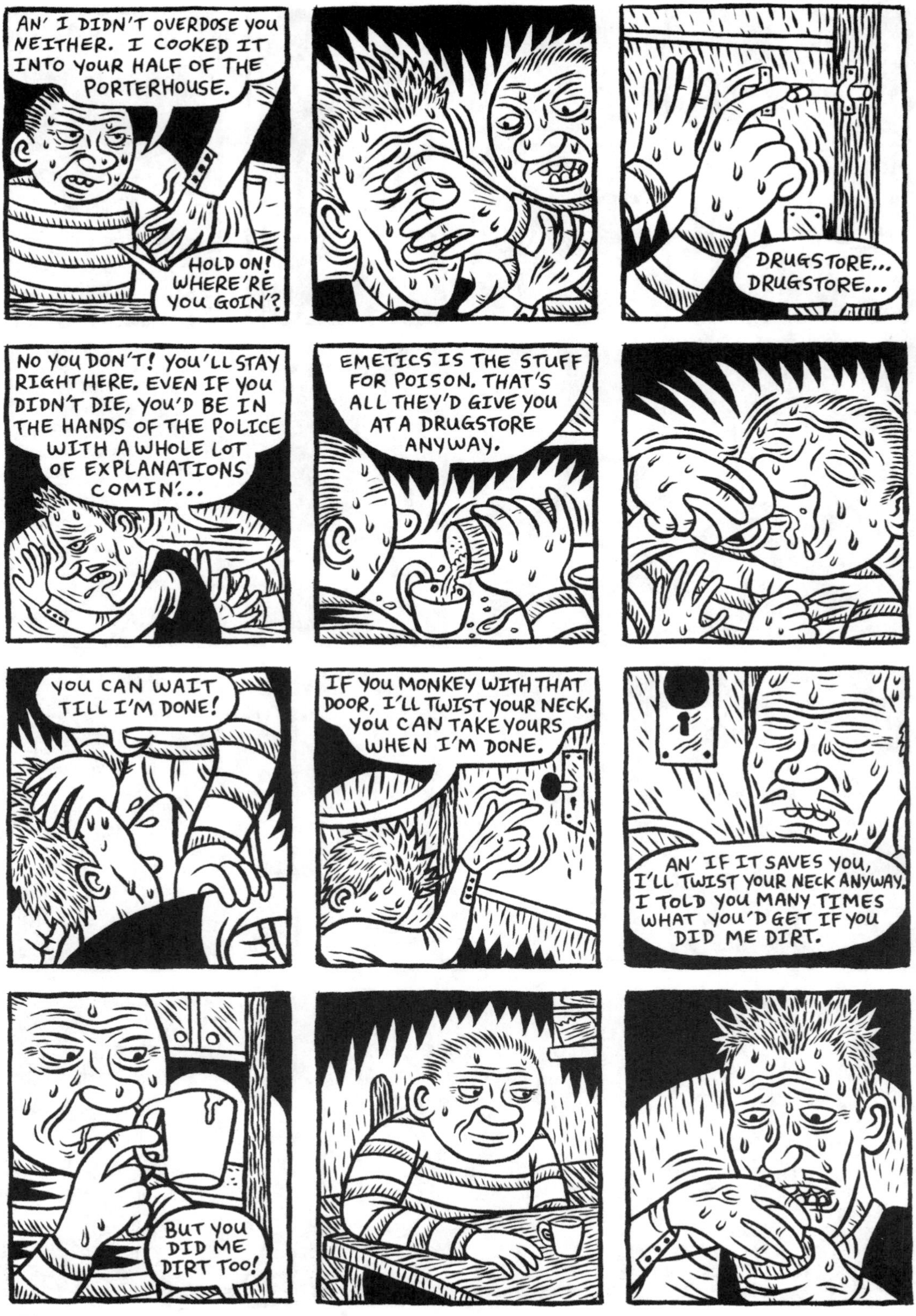
AN' I DIDN'T OVERDOSE YOU NEITHER. I COOKED IT INTO YOUR HALF OF THE PORTERHOUSE.
HOLD ON! WHERE'RE YOU GOIN'?
DRUGSTORE... DRUGSTORE...
NO YOU DON'T! YOU'LL STAY RIGHT HERE. EVEN IF YOU DIDN'T DIE, YOU'D BE IN THE HANDS OF THE POLICE WITH A WHOLE LOT OF EXPLANATIONS COMIN'...
EMETICS IS THE STUFF FOR POISON. THAT'S ALL THEY'D GIVE YOU AT A DRUGSTORE ANYWAY.
YOU CAN WAIT TILL I'M DONE!
IF YOU MONKEY WITH THAT DOOR, I'LL TWIST YOUR NECK. YOU CAN TAKE YOURS WHEN I'M DONE.
AN' IF IT SAVES YOU, I'LL TWIST YOUR NECK ANYWAY. I TOLD YOU MANY TIMES WHAT YOU'D GET IF YOU DID ME DIRT.
BUT YOU DID ME DIRT TOO!

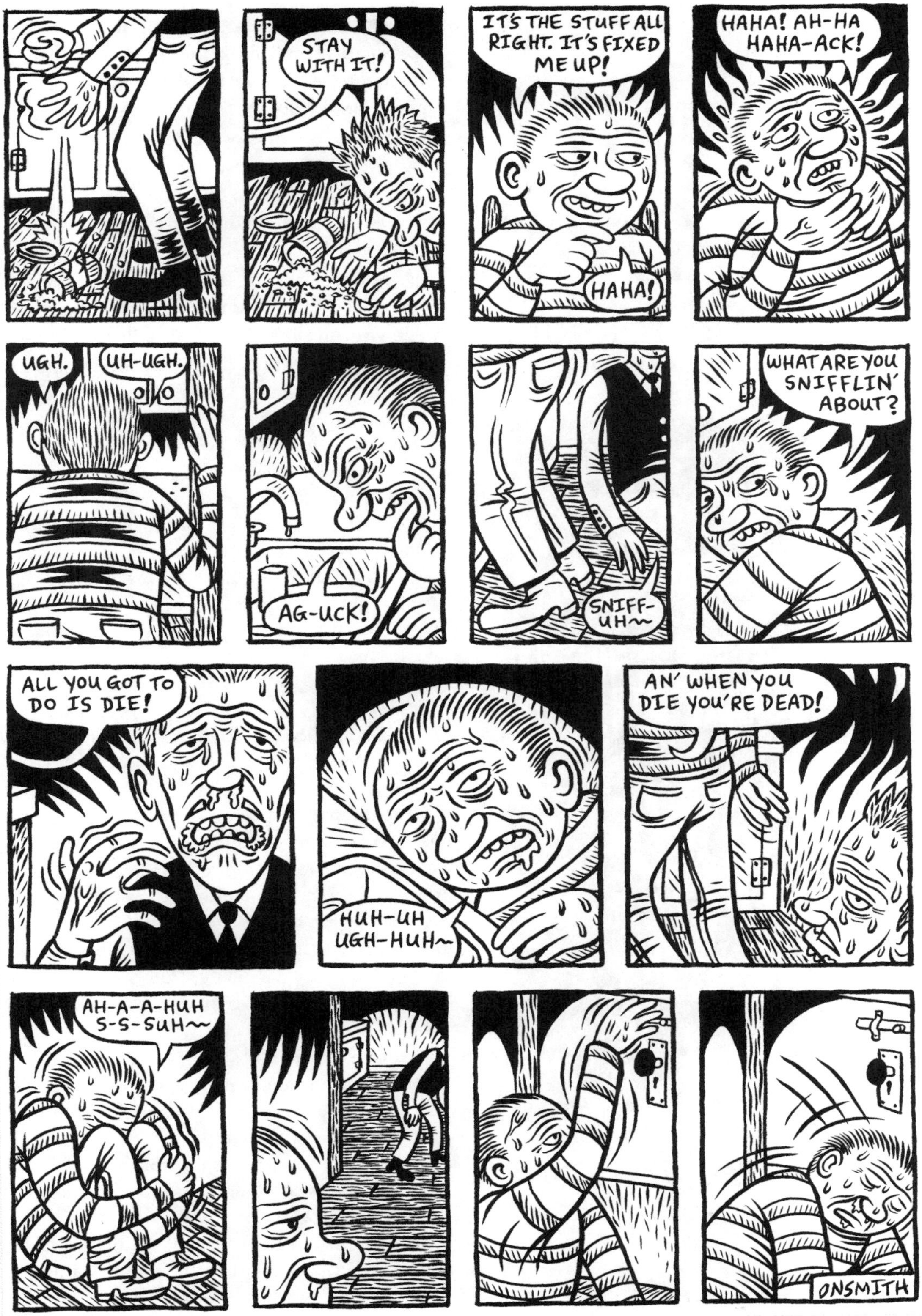
STAY WITH IT!
IT'S THE STUFF ALL RIGHT. IT'S FIXED ME UP!
HAHA!
HAHA! AH-HA HAHA-ACK!
UGH.
UH-UGH.
AG-UCK!
SNIFF-UH~
WHAT ARE YOU SNIFFLIN' ABOUT?
ALL YOU GOT TO DO IS DIE!
HUH-UH UGH-HUH~
AN' WHEN YOU DIE YOU'RE DEAD!
AH-A-A-HUH S-S-SUH~
ONSMITH

TO KILL A MAN

story by **JACK LONDON**

edited by *Tom Pomplun*

illustrated by **KOSTAS ARONIS**

SHE MOVED FAMILIARLY through the big rooms and wide halls, seeking vainly the half-finished book of verse she had mislaid. When she turned on the lights in the drawing room, she disclosed herself clad in a sweeping negligee gown of soft rose-colored stuff. Her massed yellow hair had not yet been taken down. She was delicately, gracefully beautiful, with slender, oval face, red lips, a faint color in the cheeks, and blue eyes of the chameleon sort that will stare wide with the innocence of childhood, go hard and gray and brilliantly cold, or flame up in hot willfulness and mastery.

She turned the lights off and passed out and down the hall toward the morning room. At the entrance she paused and listened. From farther on had come, not a noise, but an impression of movement. She wondered what servant could be prowling about. Not the butler, who was notorious for retiring early. Nor could it be her maid, whom she had permitted to go that evening.

Passing on to the dining room, she felt her way to the light switch and pressed. As the blaze of light flashed on, she stepped back and cried out. It was a mere "Oh!" and it was not loud.

Facing her, flat against the wall, was a man. In his hand, pointed toward her, was a revolver. He was a medium-sized man, roughly clad, brown-eyed, and swarthy with sunburn. He seemed very cool. There was no wobble to the revolver and it was directed toward her stomach from his hip.

"Oh," she said. "I beg your pardon. You startled me. What do you want?"

"I reckon I want to get out," he answered, with a humorous twitch to the lips. "If you'll kindly show me the door I'll cause no trouble and sure vamoose."

"But what are you doing here?" she demanded, her voice touched with the sharpness of one used to authority.

"Plain robbing, Miss, that's all. I came snooping around to see what I could gather up. I thought you wan't to home, seein' as I

saw you pull out with your old man in an
auto. I reckon that must a ben your pa, and
you're Miss Setliffe."

Mrs. Setliffe saw his mistake, appreciated
the naïve compliment, and decided not to
undeceive him.

"I didn't know he had a daughter, but I
reckon you must be her. And now, I'd sure
be obliged if you'd show me the way out."

"But why should I? You are a burglar."

"I come to make a raise outa old Setliffe,
and not to be robbing women-folks," he re-
torted. "If you get outa the way, I reckon I
can find my own way out."

Mrs. Setliffe was a keen woman, and she
felt that from such a man there was little to
fear. From his speech she knew he was not
of the cities, and she seemed to sense the
wider, homelier air of large spaces.

"Suppose I screamed?" she queried
curiously. "Suppose I made an outcry for
help? You couldn't shoot me?...a woman?"

He answered slowly and thoughtfully, as
if working out a difficult problem. "I reckon,
then, I'd have to choke you and maul you
some bad."

"A woman?"

"I'd sure have to," he answered, and she
saw his mouth set grimly.

"You see, Miss, I can't afford to go to
jail. There's a friend of mine waitin' for me
out West. He's in a hole, and I've got to
help him out." The mouth shaped even more
grimly. "I guess I could choke you without
hurting you much to speak of."

Her eyes took on a baby stare of innocent incredulity as she watched him.

"I never met a burglar before," she assured him, "and I can't begin to tell you
how interested I am."

"I'm not a burglar, Miss. Not a real one,"
he hastened to add. "It looks like it, but
it's the first time I ever tackled such a
job. I needed the money bad. Besides, I
kind of look on it like collecting what's
coming to me."

"I don't understand," she smiled encour-
agingly. "You came here to rob, and to rob
is to take what is not yours."

"Yes, and no, in this here particular case.
But I reckon I'd better be going now."

He started for the door of the dining
room, but she interposed, and a very beautiful obstacle she made of herself. His left hand
went out as if to grip her, then hesitated.

"There!" she cried triumphantly. "I knew
you wouldn't."

The man was embarrassed.

"I ain't never manhandled a woman yet,"
he explained, "and it don't come easy. But I
sure will, if you set to screaming."

"Won't you stay a few minutes?" she
urged. "I should like to hear you explain how
burglary is collecting what is coming to you."

He looked at her admiringly.

"I always thought women were scairt of
robbers," he confessed. "But you don't seem
none."

She laughed gaily.

"There are robbers and robbers, you
know. I am not afraid of you, because I am
confident you are not the sort of creature
that would harm a woman. Come, talk with
me a while. Nobody will disturb us. I am all
alone. My—father caught the night train to
New York. The servants are all asleep. Per-
haps you will have something to drink?"

He hesitated, and did not reply; but she
could see the admiration for her growing in
his eyes.

"You've sure got the spunk," he declared,
for the first time lowering the weapon and
letting it hang at his side. "There ain't many
women, or men either. who'd treat a man
with a gun the way you're treating me."

She smiled her pleasure in the compliment, and her face was very earnest as she
said, "That is because you are too decent-
looking a man to be a robber. Come, put
away that nasty revolver and let us talk it
over. If you are in bad luck you should go
to work."

"Not in this burg," he commented bit-
terly. "I've walked two inches off the bottom
of my legs trying to find a job."

"Come, you must tell me all about it
while I get that drink for you. What will it
be? Whisky?"

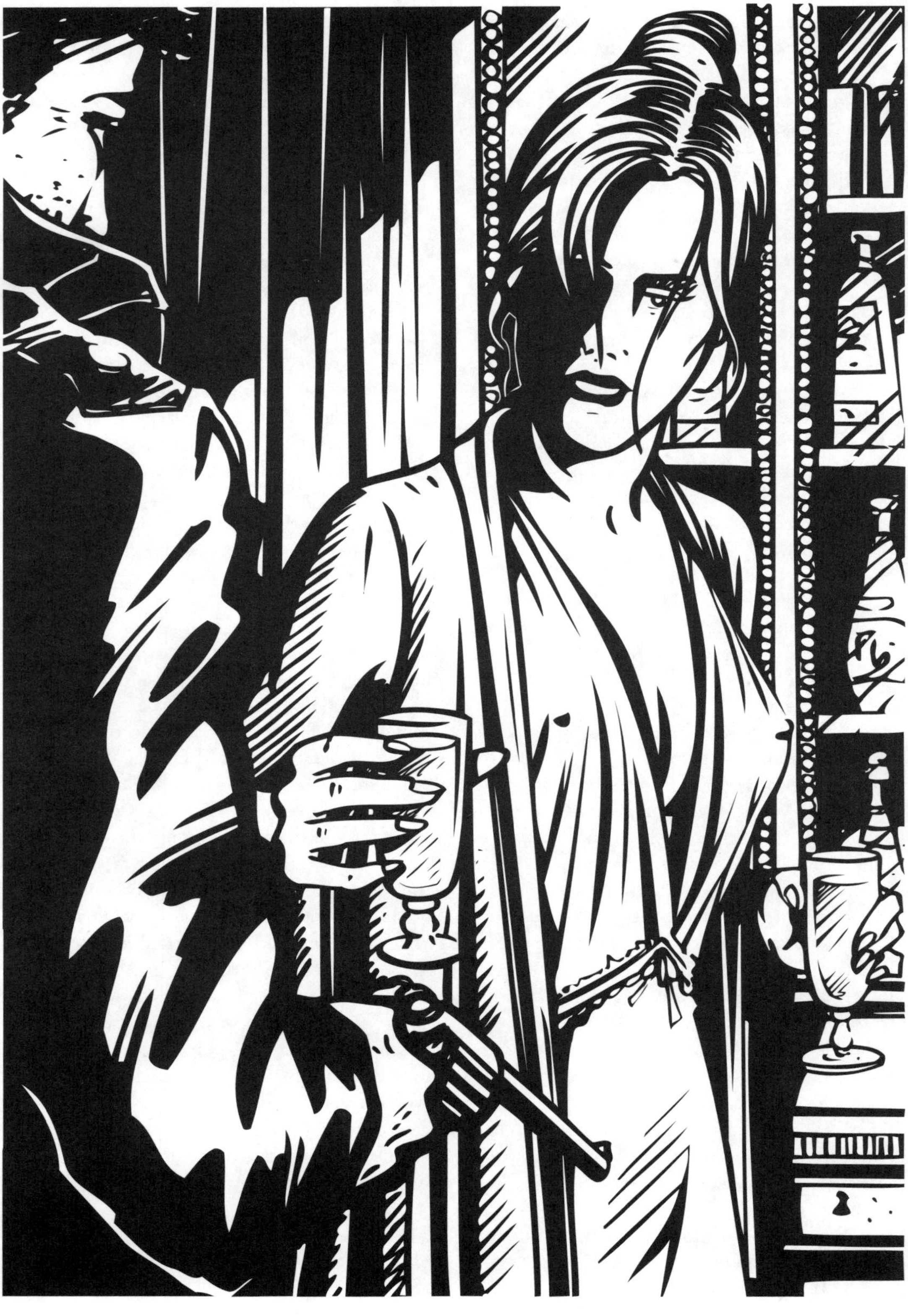

"Yes, ma'am," he said, as he followed her, though he still carried the big revolver at his side.

She filled a glass for him at the sideboard.

"I promised to drink with you," she said hesitatingly. "But I don't like whisky. I prefer sherry."

She lifted the sherry bottle tentatively for his consent.

"Sure," he answered, with a nod. "Whisky's a man's drink. I never like to see women at it. Wine's more their stuff."

She raised her glass to his, her eyes meltingly sympathetic.

"Here's to finding you a good position— you are a drinking man?" It was half a question, half a challenge.

"No, ma'am, not to speak of. But there is times when a good stiff jolt lands on the right spot kerchunk, and this is sure one of them. And now, thanking you for your kindness, ma'am, I'll just be a pulling along."

But Mrs. Setliffe did not want to lose her burglar. There was a thrill about the present situation that delighted her. Also, farther back in her consciousness glimmered the thought of an audience of admiring friends.

"You haven't explained how burglary, in your case, is merely collecting what is your own," she said. "Come, sit down, and tell me about it here at the table."

She maneuvered for her own seat, and placed him across the corner from her. His alertness had not deserted him, as she noted, and his eyes roved sharply about, returning always with smoldering admiration to hers, but never resting long. Nor had he relinquished the revolver, which lay at the corner of the table between them, the butt close to his right hand.

But this man from the West did not know that under the table, close to her foot, was the push button of an electric bell. He had never heard of such a contrivance, and his keenness and wariness went for naught.

"It's like this, Miss," he began, in response to her urging. "Old Setliffe done me up in a little deal once. It was raw, but it worked. Anything will work full and legal when it's got few hundred million behind it. He don't know me from Adam. I'm only one of thousands that have been done up by your pa, that's all.

"You see, ma'am, I had a little hole in the ground—a dinky, one-horse outfit of a mine. And when the Setliffe crowd shook down Idaho, and reorganized the smelter trust, and roped in the rest of the landscape, and put through the big hydraulic scheme at Twin Pines, I was scratched off the card before the first heat. And so, tonight, being broke and my friend needing me bad, I just dropped around to make a raise outa your pa. Seeing as it kinda was coming to me."

"Granting all that you say is so," she said, "it does not make house-breaking any the less house-breaking. You couldn't make such a defense in a court of law."

"I know that," he confessed meekly. "What's right ain't always legal. When times is hard and they ain't no work, men get desperate. And then the other men who've got something to be robbed of get desperate, too, and they just sure soak it to the other fellows. If I got caught, I reckon I wouldn't get a mite less than ten years. That's why I'm hankering to be on my way."

"No; wait." She lifted a detaining hand, at the same time removing her foot from the bell, which she had been pressing intermittently. "Something must be done for you. You are a young man, and you are just at the beginning of a bad start. If you begin by attempting to collect what you think is coming to you, later on you will be collecting what you are perfectly sure isn't coming to you. And you know what the end will be. Instead of this, we must find something honorable for you to do."

"I need the money now," he replied doggedly. "It's not for myself, but for that friend I told you about. He's in a peck of trouble, and he's got to get his lift now or not at all."

"I can find you a position," she said quickly. "And—yes, the very thing!—I'll lend you the money you want to send to your

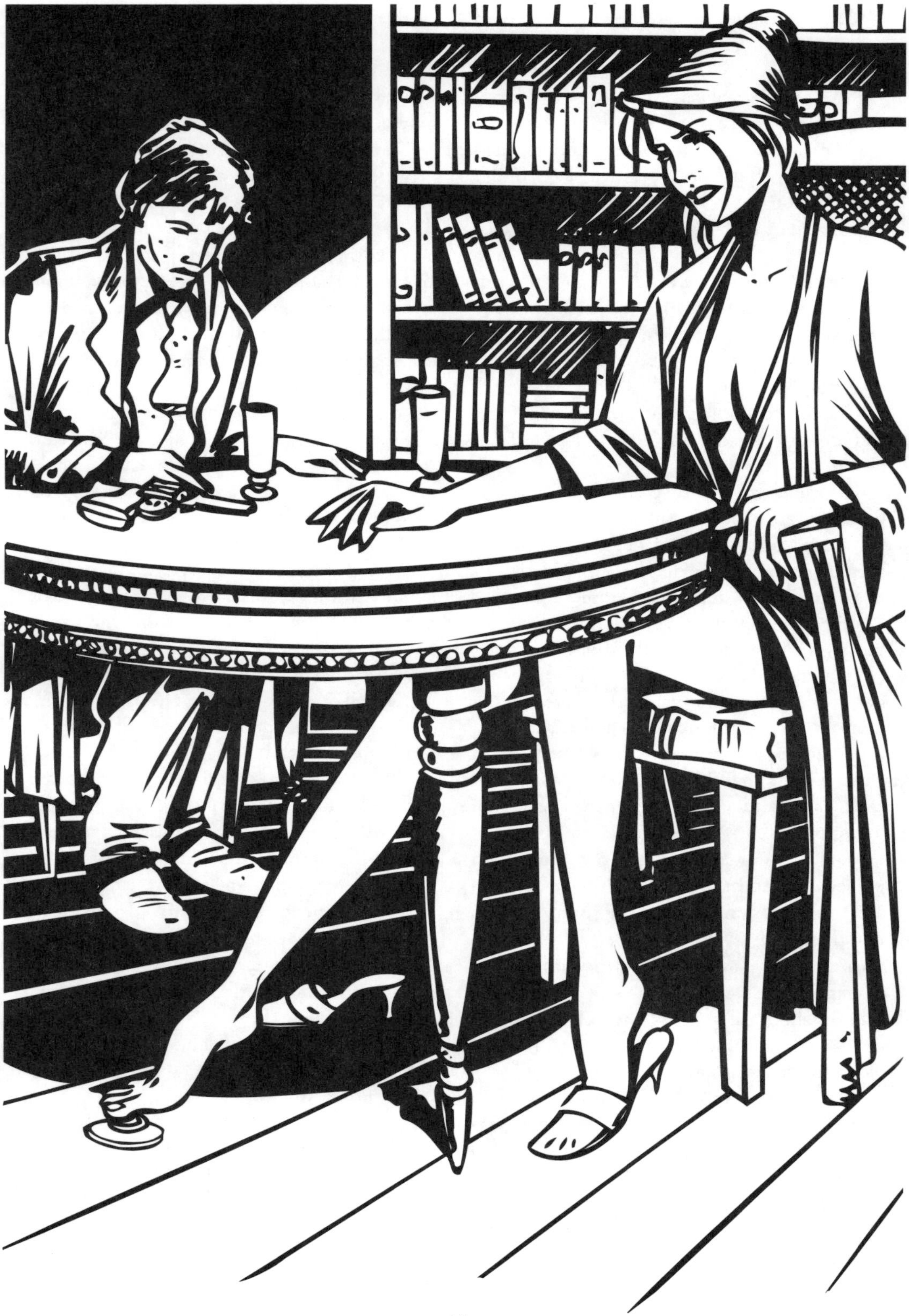

friend. This you can pay back out of your salary."

"About three hundred would do," he said slowly. "I'd work my fingers off for a year for that, and my keep, and a few cents to buy Bull Durham with."

"Ah! You smoke! I never thought of it."

Her hand went out over the revolver toward his hand, as she pointed to the tell-tale yellow stain on his fingers. At the same time her eyes measured the nearness of her own hand and of his to the weapon. She ached to grip it in one swift movement. She was sure she could do it, and yet she was not sure; and so it was that she refrained as she withdrew her hand.

"Won't you smoke?" she invited.

"I'm 'most dying to."

"Then do so. I don't mind. I really like it—cigarettes, I mean."

With his left hand he dipped into his side pocket, brought out a loose wheat-straw paper and shifted it to his right hand close by the revolver. Again he dipped, transferring to the paper a pinch of brown, flaky tobacco. Then he proceeded, both hands just over the revolver, to roll the cigarette.

"From the way you hover close to that nasty weapon, you seem to be afraid of me," she challenged.

"I sure beg your pardon, ma'am," he said. "I reckon my nervousness ain't complimentary."

As he spoke, he drew his right hand from the table, and after lighting the cigarette, dropped it by his side.

"Thank you for your confidence," she breathed softly, resolutely keeping her eyes from measuring the distance to the revolver, and keeping her foot pressed firmly on the bell.

"About that three hundred," he began. "I can telegraph it West tonight. And I'll agree to work a year for it and my keep."

"You will earn more than that. I can promise seventy-five dollars a month at the least. Do you know horses?"

His face lighted up and his eyes sparkled.

"We have a stock farm, and there's room for just such a man as you. Will you take it?"

"Will I, ma'am?" His voice was rich with gratitude. "Show me to it. I'll dig right in tomorrow. And I can sure promise you'll never be sorry for lending Hughie Luke a hand in his trouble. If you'll give me the address of that stock farm of yours, and the railroad fare, I'll head for it first thing in the morning."

Throughout the conversation she had never relaxed her attempts on the bell. And she had been divided between objurgation of the stupid, heavy-sleeping butler and doubt if the bell were in order.

"I am so glad," she said; "so glad that you are willing. But you will first have to trust me while I go upstairs for my purse."

She saw the doubt flicker momentarily in his eyes. But before she could extract consent, a slight muffled jar from the distance came to her ear. She knew it for the swing-door of the butler's pantry.

"What was that?" the robber demanded.

For answer, her left hand flashed out to the revolver and brought it back.

"Sit down!" she commanded sharply, in a voice new to him. "Don't move. Keep your hands on the table."

She had taken a lesson from him. Instead of holding the heavy weapon extended, the butt of it and her forearm rested on the table, the muzzle pointed at his chest. And he, looking coolly and obeying her commands, saw that the revolver did not wobble, nor the hand shake, and he was thoroughly conversant with the size of hole the soft-nosed bullets could make. He had eyes, not for her, but for the hammer, which had risen under the pressure of her forefinger on the trigger.

"I reckon I'd best warn you that that there trigger-pull is filed dreadful fine. Don't press too hard, or you'll make a pretty mess all over your nice floor."

A door opened behind him, and he heard somebody enter the room. But he did not turn his head. He was looking at her, and he found it the face of another woman—hard, cold, pitiless yet brilliant in its beauty.

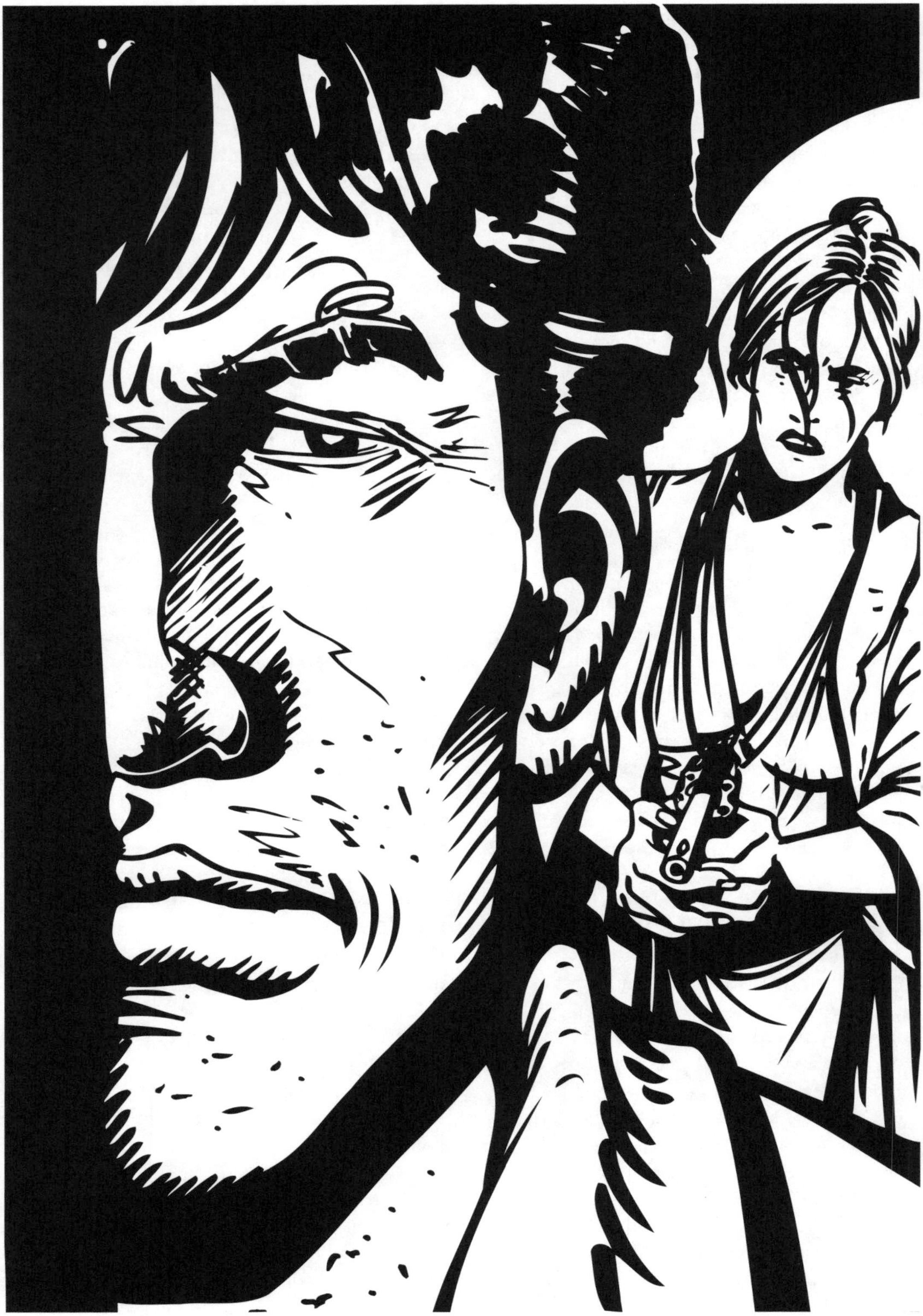

"Thomas," she commanded, "go to the telephone and call the police. Why were you so long in answering?"

"I came as soon as I heard the bell, madam," was the answer.

The butler slippered out of the room, and the man and the woman sat on, gazing into each other's eyes. To her it was an experience keen with enjoyment, and in her mind was the gossip of her crowd, and she saw notes in the society weeklies of the beautiful young Mrs. Setliffe capturing an armed robber single-handed.

"When you get that sentence you mentioned," she said coldly, "you will have time to meditate upon what a fool you have been, taking other persons' property and threatening women with revolvers. Now tell the truth. You haven't any friend in trouble. All that you told me was lies."

He did not reply. Though his eyes were upon her, what he saw was the wide sun-washed spaces of the West, where men and women were bigger than the rotten denizens of the thrice rotten cities of the East.

"Go on. Why don't you lie some more? Why don't you beg to be let off?"

"I might," he answered, licking his dry lips. "I might ask to be let off if..."

"If what?" she demanded peremptorily, as he paused.

"I was trying to think of a word you reminded me of. As I was saying, I might if you was a decent woman."

Her face paled.

"Be careful," she warned.

"You don't dast kill me," he sneered. "You're sure bad, but the trouble with you is that you're weak in your badness. It ain't much to kill a man, but you ain't got it in you."

"Be careful of what you say," she repeated. "Or else, I warn you, it will go hard with you. It can be seen to whether your sentence is light or heavy."

"Will you kindly answer one question, ma'am?" the man said. "That servant said something about a bell. I watched you like a cat, and you sure rung no bell."

"It was under the table, you poor fool. I pressed it with my foot."

"Thank you, ma'am. I reckoned I'd seen your kind before, and now I sure know I have. I spoke to you true and trusting, and all the time you was lying like hell to me."

She laughed mockingly.

"Go on. Say what you wish. It is very interesting."

"You made eyes at me, looking soft and kind, playing up all the time the fact that you wore skirts instead of pants—and all the time with your foot on the bell under the table. Well, there's some consolation. I'd sooner be poor Hughie Luke, doing his ten years, than be in your skin. Ma'am, hell is full of women like you."

There was silence for a space, in which the man, never taking his eyes from her, studying her, was making up his mind.

"Go on," she urged. "Say something."

"Yes, ma'am, I'll say something. I'll sure say something. Do you know what I'm going to do? I'm going to get right up from this chair and walk out that door. And you ain't going to pull that gun off either. It takes guts to shoot a man, and you sure ain't got them. Now get ready and see if you can pull that trigger."

Keeping his eyes fixed on her, he pushed back the chair and slowly stood erect. The hammer rose halfway.

"Pull harder," he advised. "It ain't half up yet. Go on and pull it and kill a man, spatter his brains out on the floor, or slap a hole into him the size of your fist. That's what killing a man means."

The hammer lowered gently. The man turned his back and walked slowly to the door. She swung the revolver around so that it bore on his back. Twice again the hammer came up halfway and was reluctantly eased down.

At the door the man turned for a moment before passing on. A sneer was on his lips. He spoke to her in a low voice, almost drawling, but in it was the quintessence of all loathing, as he called her a name unspeakable and vile.

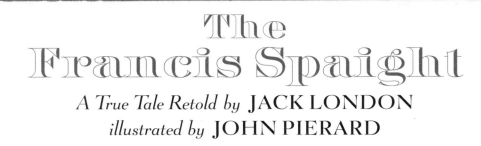

The Francis Spaight

A True Tale Retold by **JACK LONDON**

illustrated by **JOHN PIERARD**

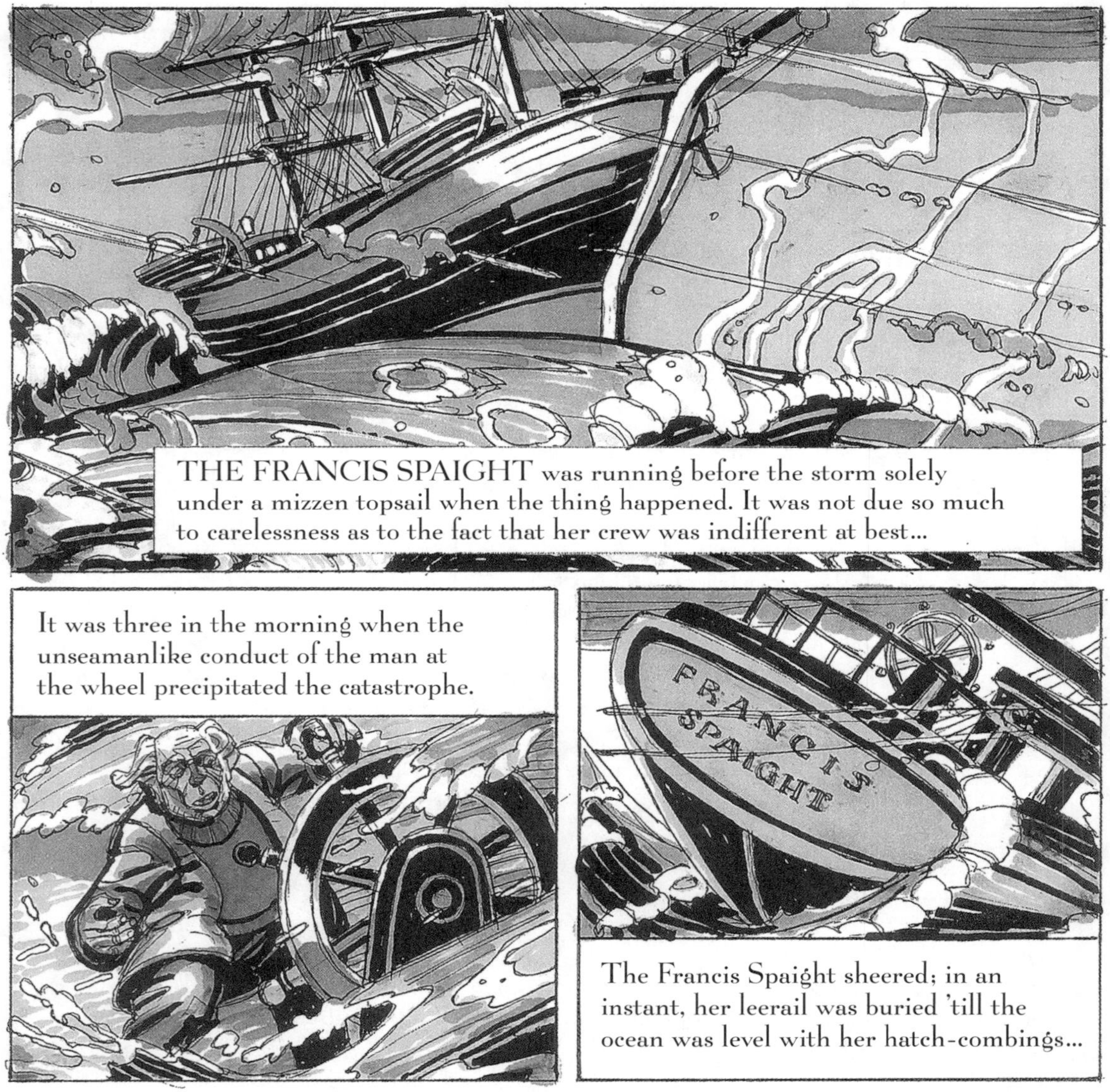
THE FRANCIS SPAIGHT was running before the storm solely under a mizzen topsail when the thing happened. It was not due so much to carelessness as to the fact that her crew was indifferent at best...
It was three in the morning when the unseamanlike conduct of the man at the wheel precipitated the catastrophe.
FRANCIS SPAIGHT
The Francis Spaight sheered; in an instant, her leerail was buried 'till the ocean was level with her hatch-combings...

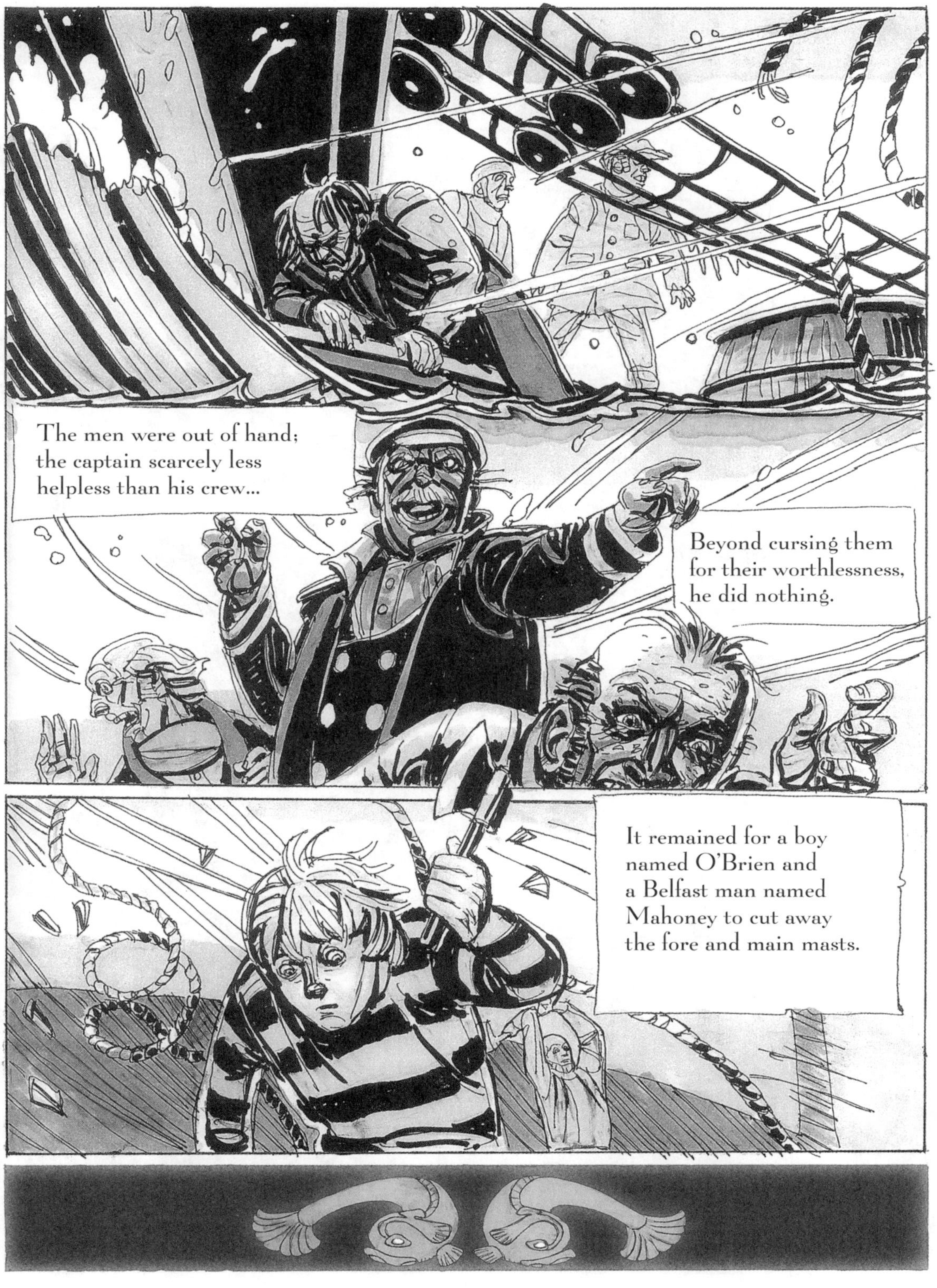
The men were out of hand; the captain scarcely less helpless than his crew...
Beyond cursing them for their worthlessness, he did nothing.
It remained for a boy named O'Brien and a Belfast man named Mahoney to cut away the fore and main masts.

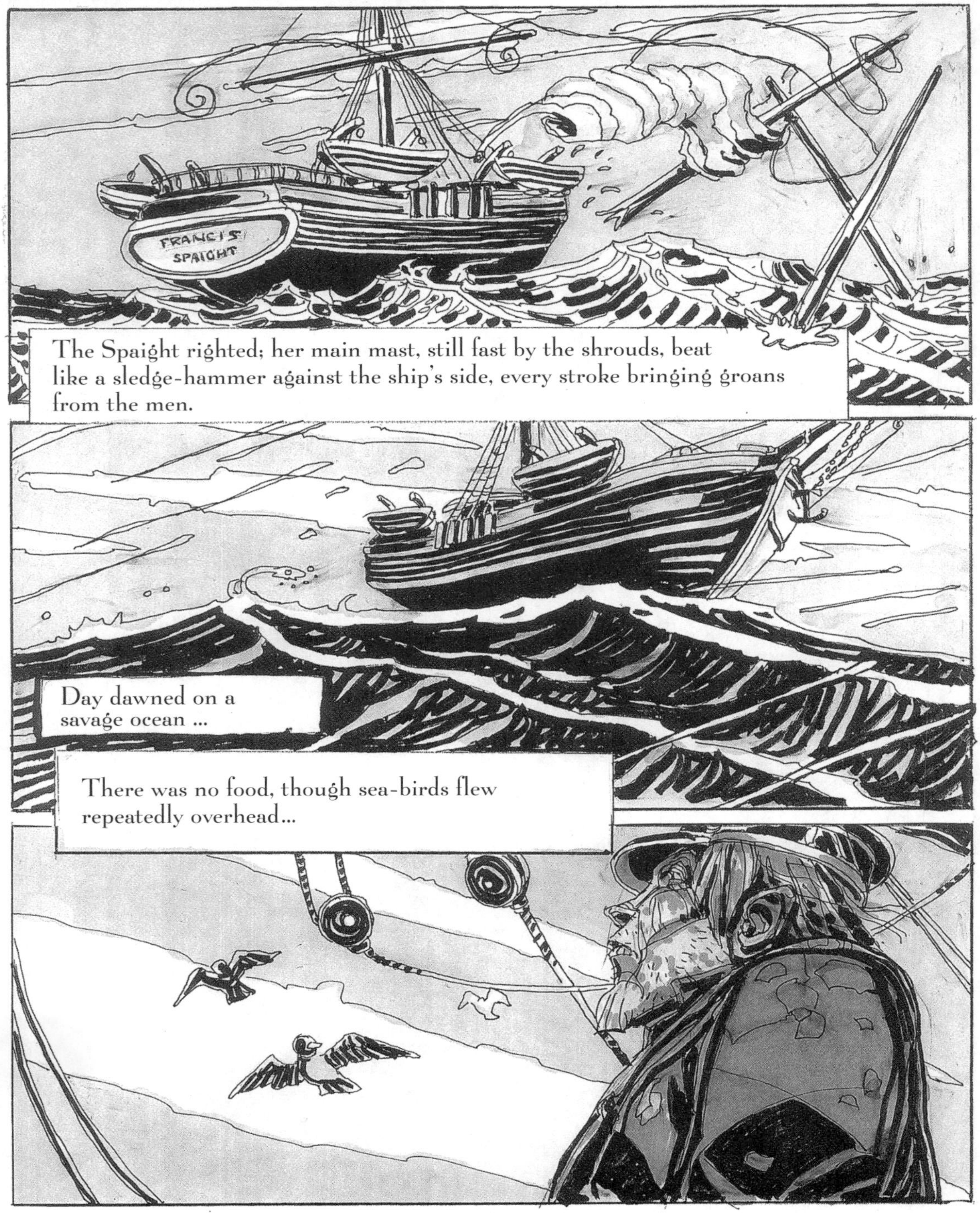
FRANCIS SPAIGHT
The Spaight righted; her main mast, still fast by the shrouds, beat like a sledge-hammer against the ship's side, every stroke bringing groans from the men.
Day dawned on a savage ocean ...
There was no food, though sea-birds flew repeatedly overhead...

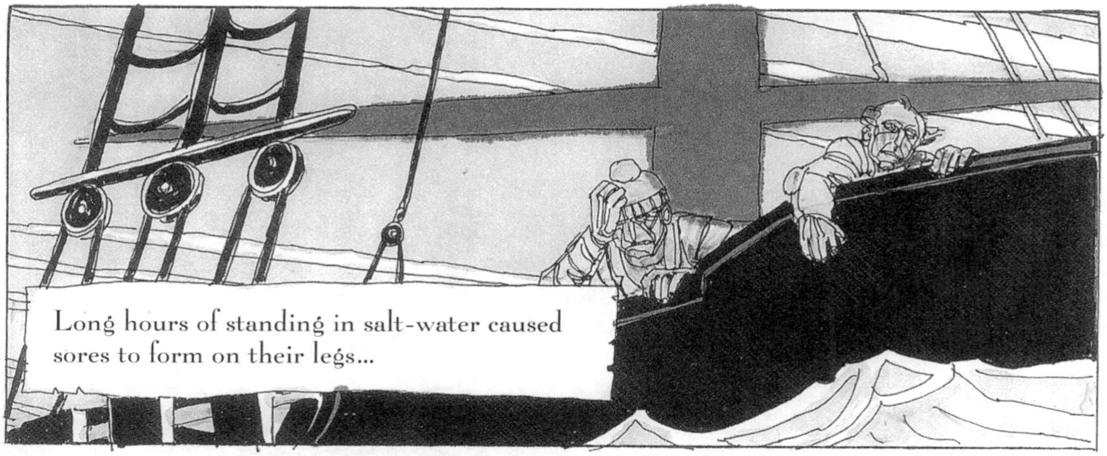
Long hours of standing in salt-water caused sores to form on their legs...

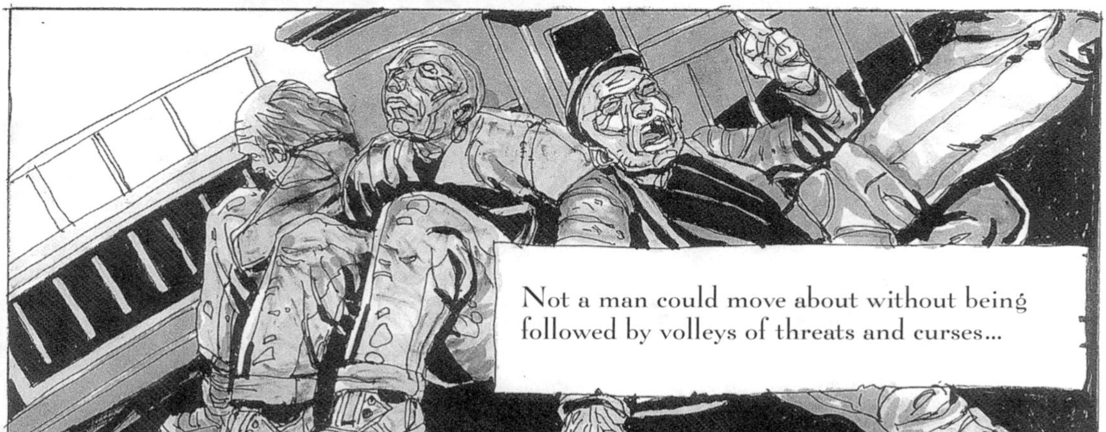
Not a man could move about without being followed by volleys of threats and curses...

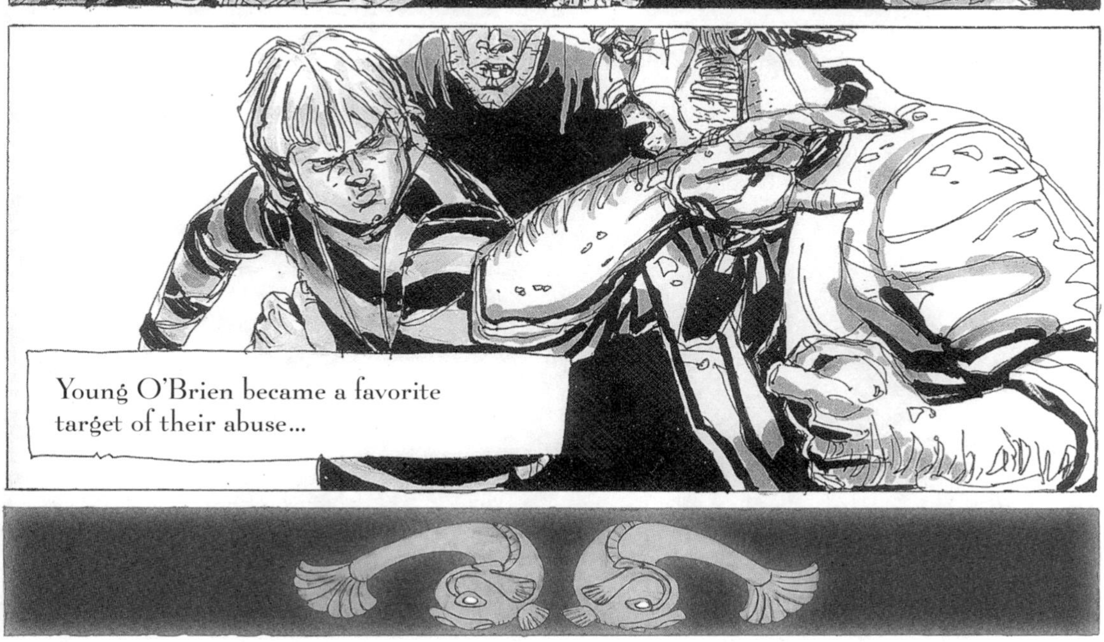
Young O'Brien became a favorite target of their abuse...

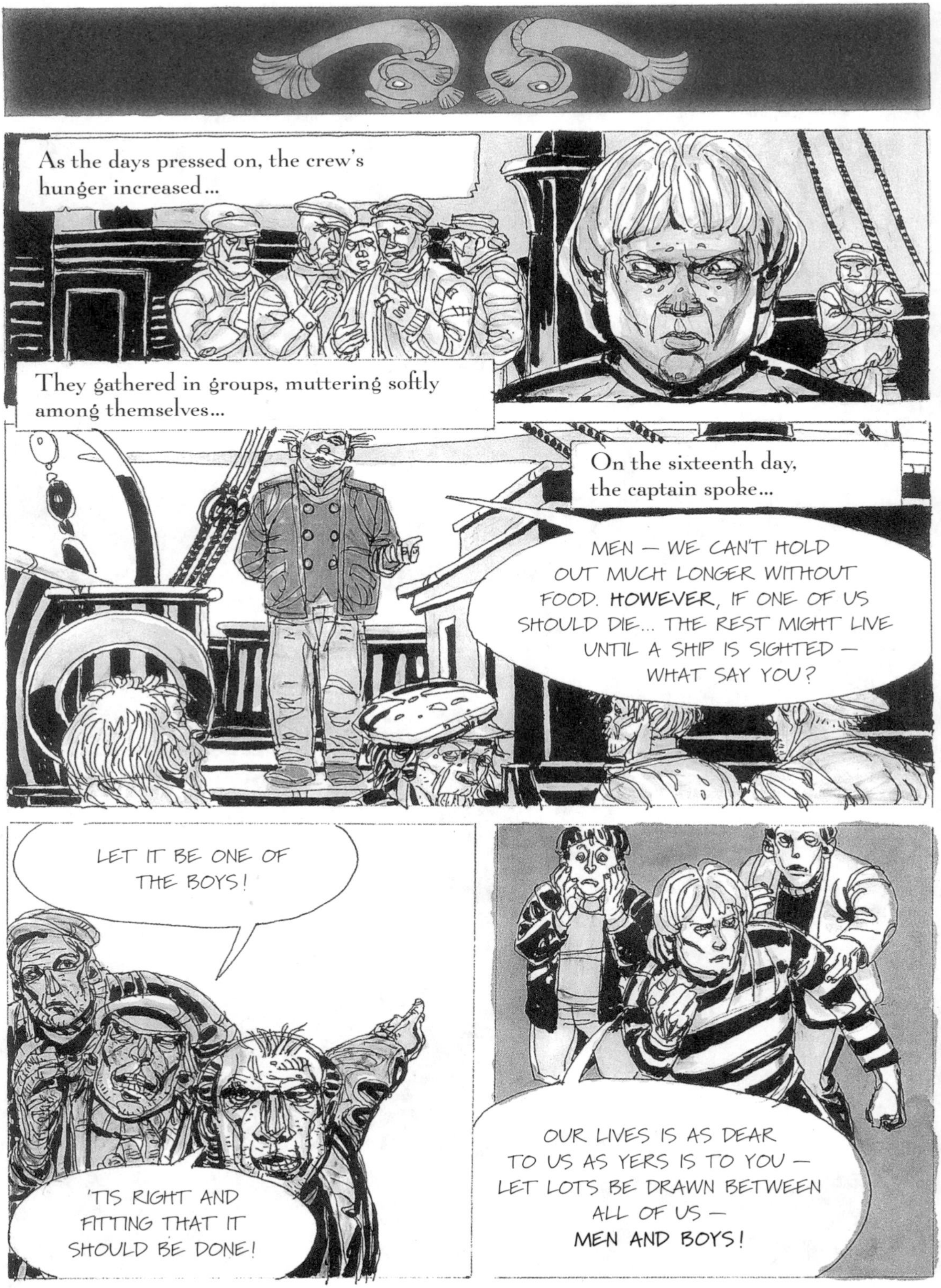
As the days pressed on, the crew's hunger increased...
They gathered in groups, muttering softly among themselves...
On the sixteenth day, the captain spoke...
MEN — WE CAN'T HOLD OUT MUCH LONGER WITHOUT FOOD. HOWEVER, IF ONE OF US SHOULD DIE... THE REST MIGHT LIVE UNTIL A SHIP IS SIGHTED — WHAT SAY YOU?
LET IT BE ONE OF THE BOYS!
'TIS RIGHT AND FITTING THAT IT SHOULD BE DONE!
OUR LIVES IS AS DEAR TO US AS YERS IS TO YOU — LET LOTS BE DRAWN BETWEEN ALL OF US — MEN AND BOYS!

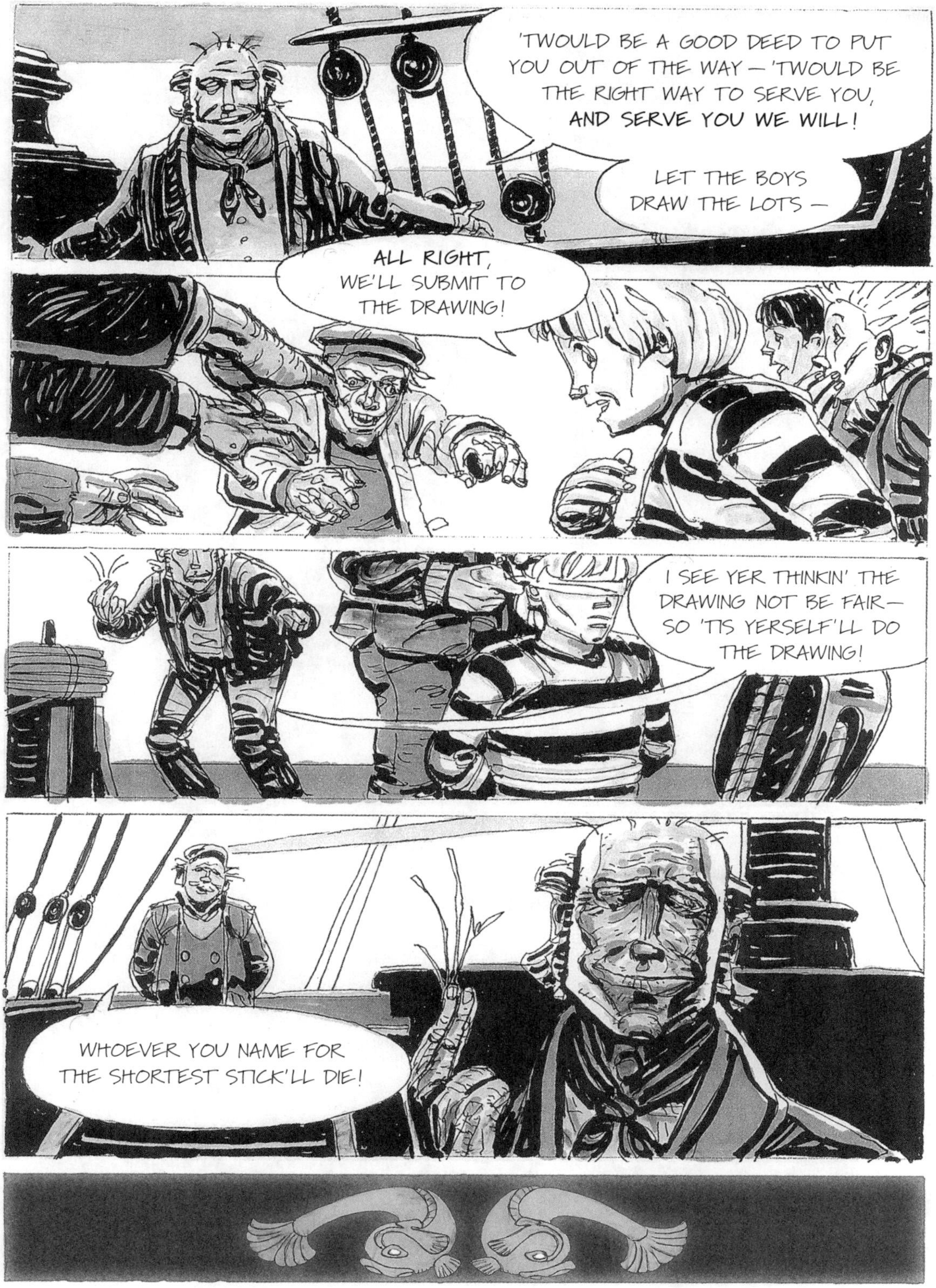
'TWOULD BE A GOOD DEED TO PUT YOU OUT OF THE WAY — 'TWOULD BE THE RIGHT WAY TO SERVE YOU, **AND SERVE YOU WE WILL!**
LET THE BOYS DRAW THE LOTS —
ALL RIGHT, WE'LL SUBMIT TO THE DRAWING!
I SEE YER THINKIN' THE DRAWING NOT BE FAIR— SO 'TIS YERSELF'LL DO THE DRAWING!
WHOEVER YOU NAME FOR THE SHORTEST STICK'LL DIE!

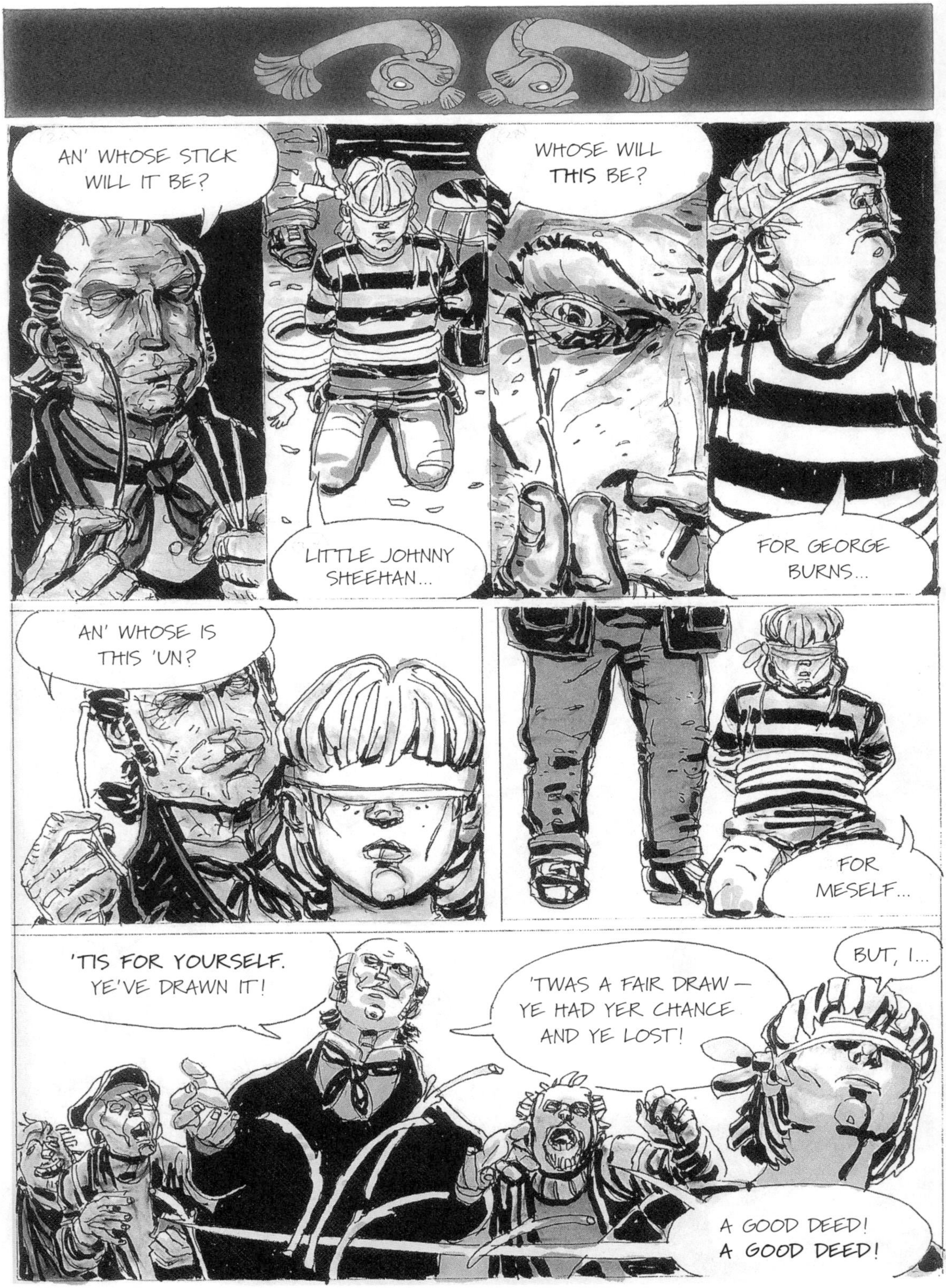
AN' WHOSE STICK WILL IT BE?
LITTLE JOHNNY SHEEHAN...
WHOSE WILL THIS BE?
FOR GEORGE BURNS...
AN' WHOSE IS THIS 'UN?
FOR MESELF...
'TIS FOR YOURSELF. YE'VE DRAWN IT!
'TWAS A FAIR DRAW— YE HAD YER CHANCE AND YE LOST!
BUT, I...
A GOOD DEED! A GOOD DEED!

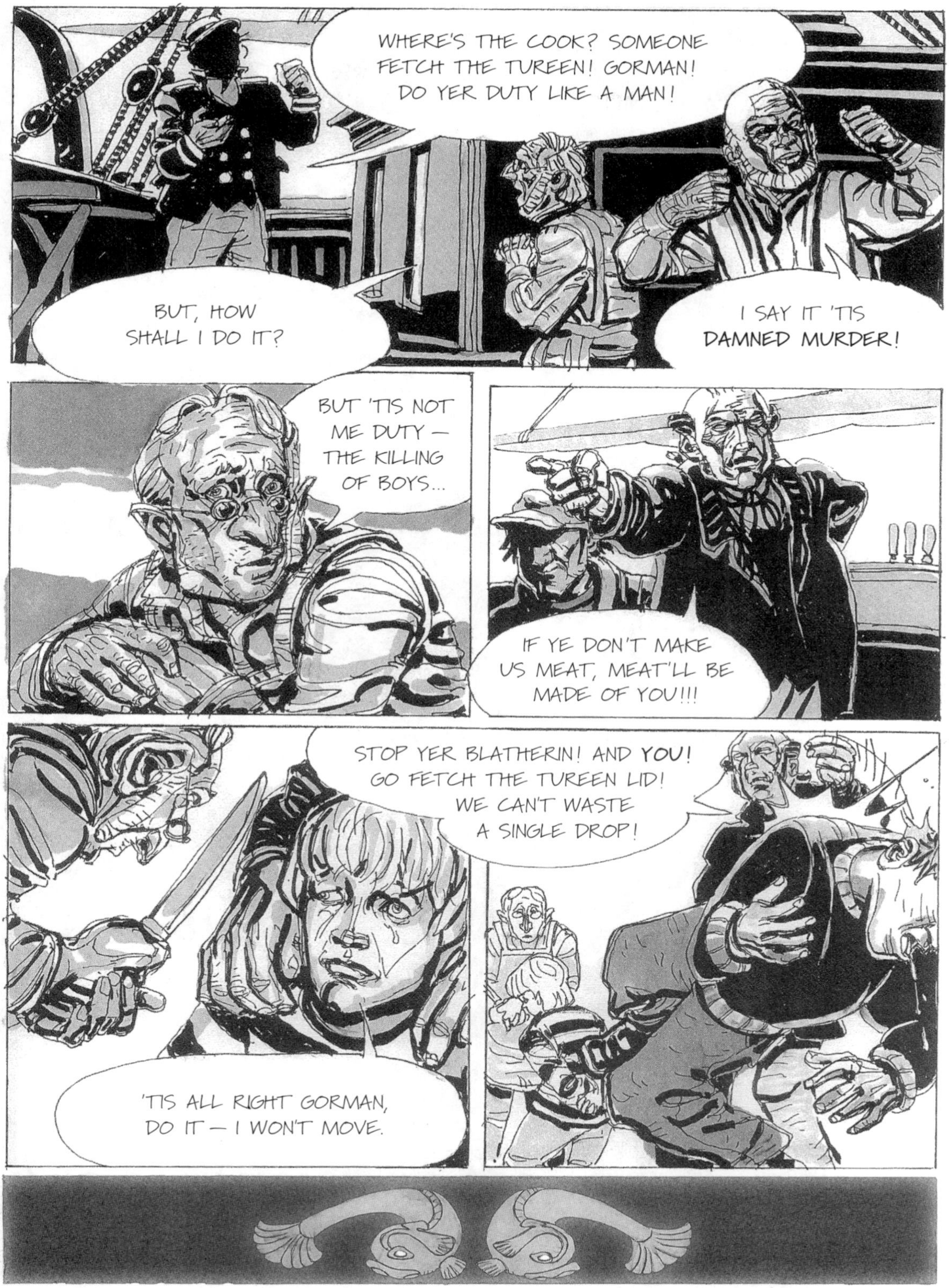
WHERE'S THE COOK? SOMEONE FETCH THE TUREEN! GORMAN! DO YER DUTY LIKE A MAN!
BUT, HOW SHALL I DO IT?
I SAY IT 'TIS DAMNED MURDER!
BUT 'TIS NOT ME DUTY — THE KILLING OF BOYS...
IF YE DON'T MAKE US MEAT, MEAT'LL BE MADE OF YOU!!!
STOP YER BLATHERIN! AND YOU! GO FETCH THE TUREEN LID! WE CAN'T WASTE A SINGLE DROP!
'TIS ALL RIGHT GORMAN, DO IT — I WON'T MOVE.

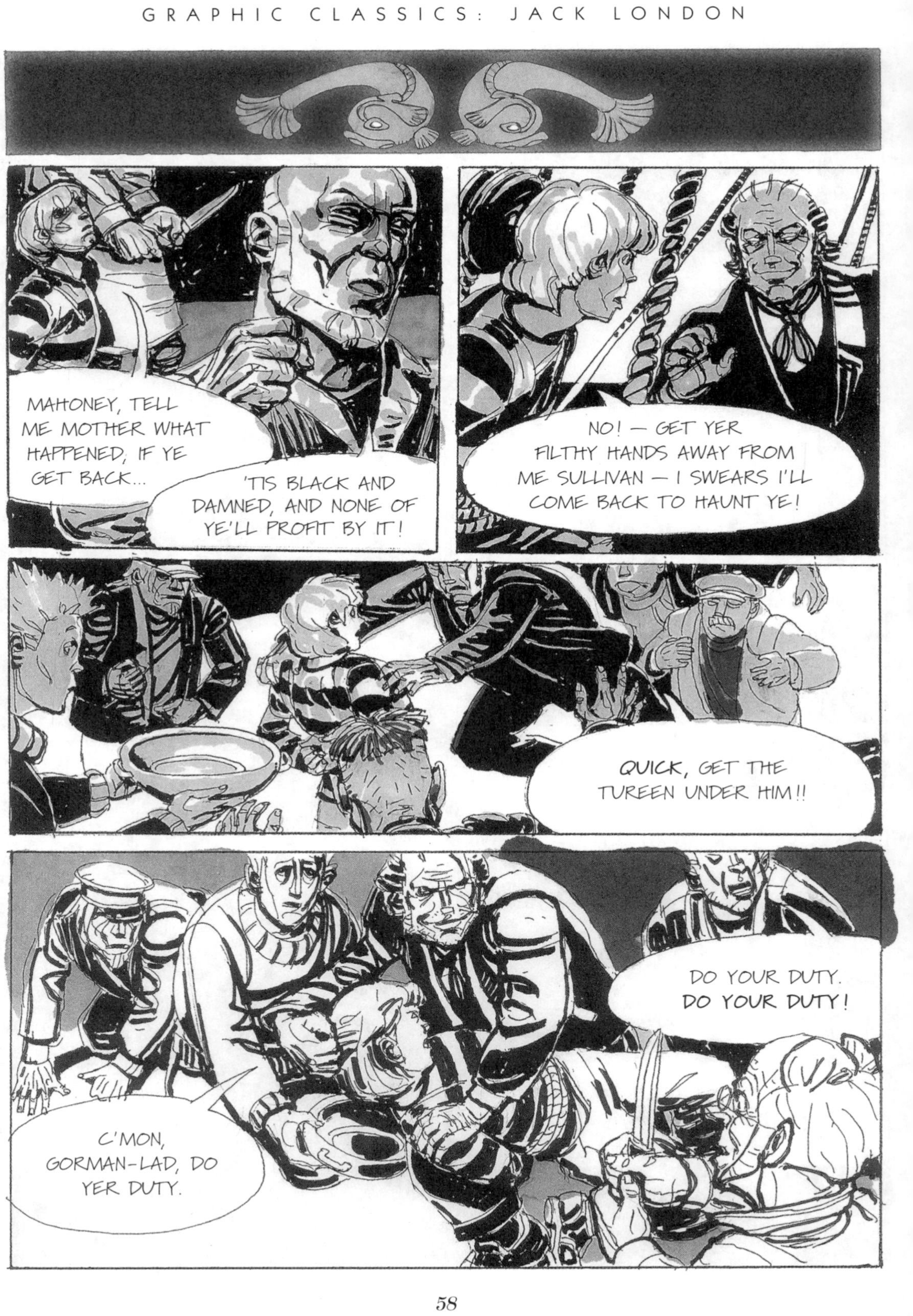
MAHONEY, TELL ME MOTHER WHAT HAPPENED, IF YE GET BACK...
'TIS BLACK AND DAMNED, AND NONE OF YE'LL PROFIT BY IT!
NO! — GET YER FILTHY HANDS AWAY FROM ME SULLIVAN — I SWEARS I'LL COME BACK TO HAUNT YE!
QUICK, GET THE TUREEN UNDER HIM!!
DO YOUR DUTY. DO YOUR DUTY!
C'MON, GORMAN-LAD, DO YER DUTY.

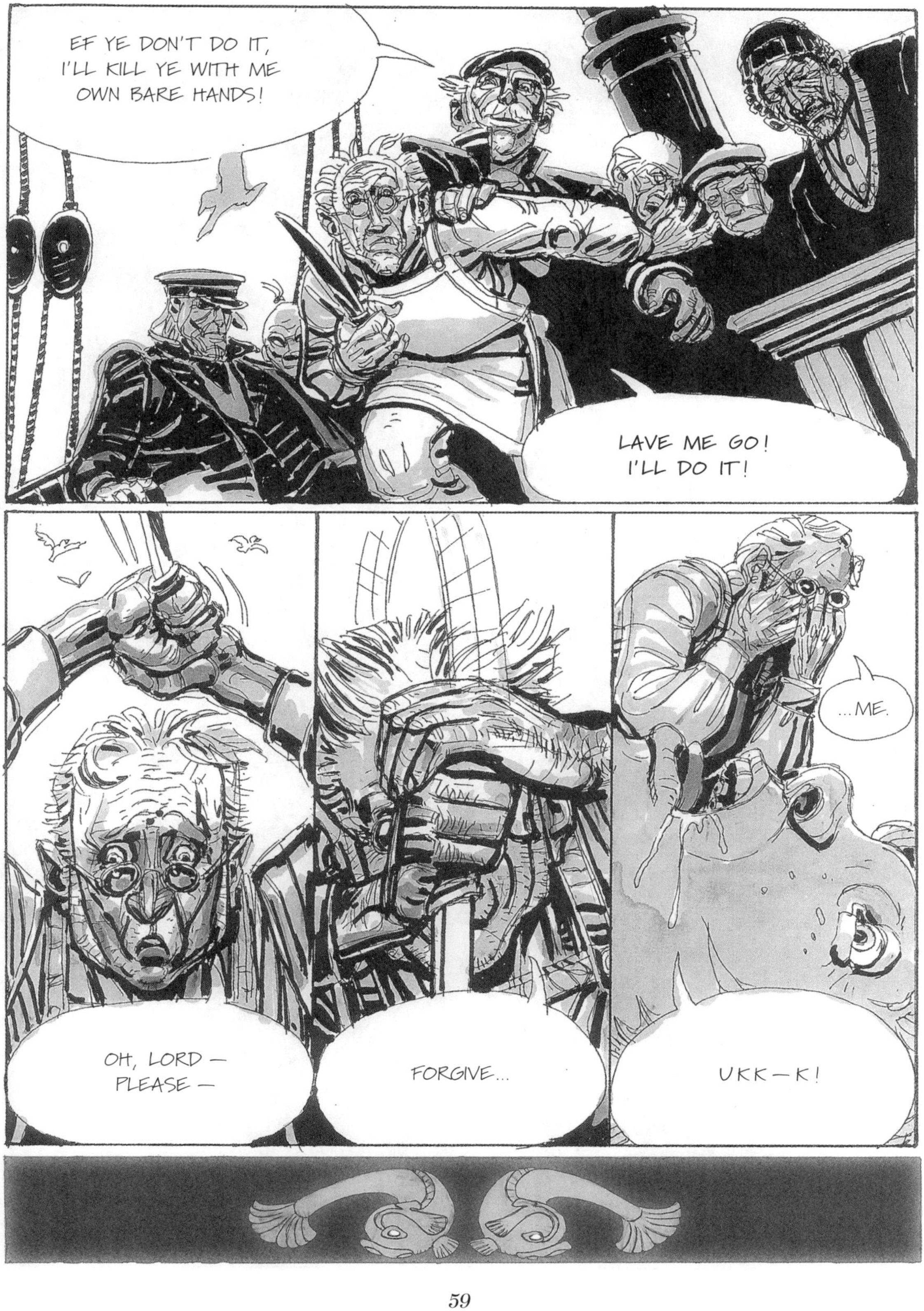
EF YE DON'T DO IT, I'LL KILL YE WITH ME OWN BARE HANDS!
LAVE ME GO! I'LL DO IT!
OH, LORD — PLEASE —
FORGIVE...
...ME.
UKK—K!

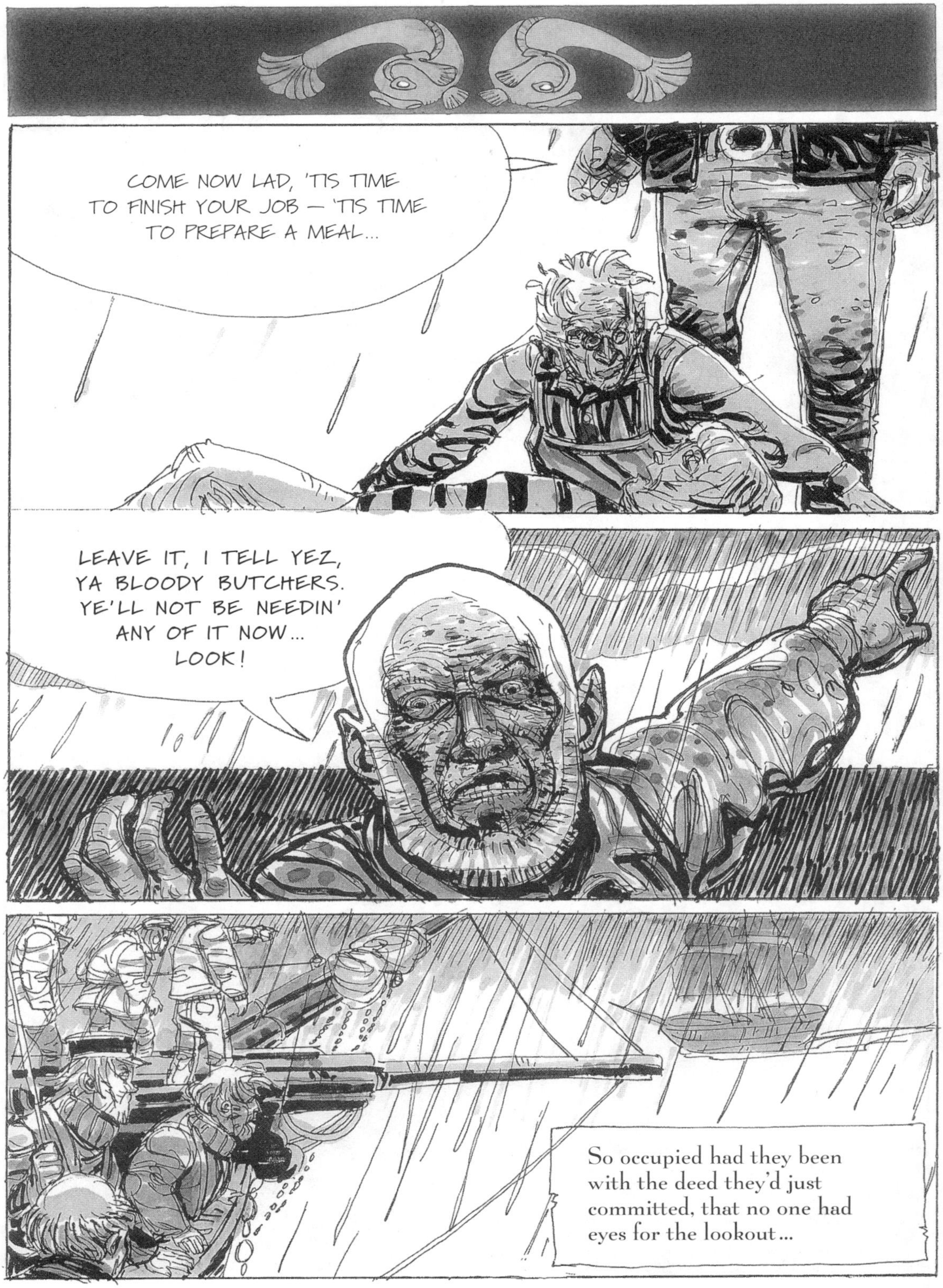
COME NOW LAD, 'TIS TIME TO FINISH YOUR JOB — 'TIS TIME TO PREPARE A MEAL...
LEAVE IT, I TELL YEZ, YA BLOODY BUTCHERS. YE'LL NOT BE NEEDIN' ANY OF IT NOW... LOOK!
So occupied had they been with the deed they'd just committed, that no one had eyes for the lookout...

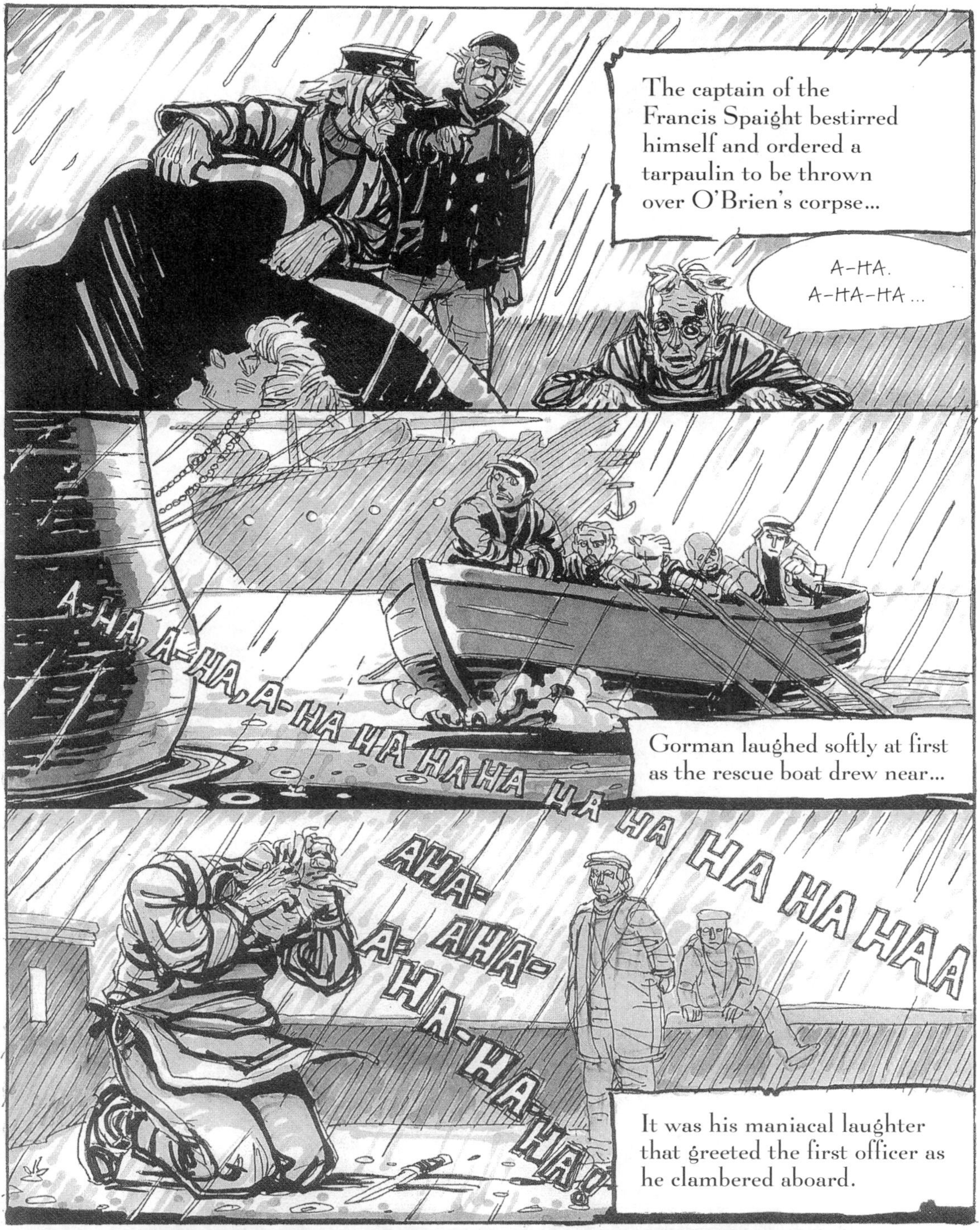
The captain of the Francis Spaight bestirred himself and ordered a tarpaulin to be thrown over O'Brien's corpse...
A-HA.
A-HA-HA...
A-HA, A-HA, A-HA HA HA HAHA HA
Gorman laughed softly at first as the rescue boat drew near...
HA HA HA HA HA HAA
AHA-
AHA-
A-
HA-
HA-
HA-
HA-
HA!
It was his maniacal laughter that greeted the first officer as he clambered aboard.

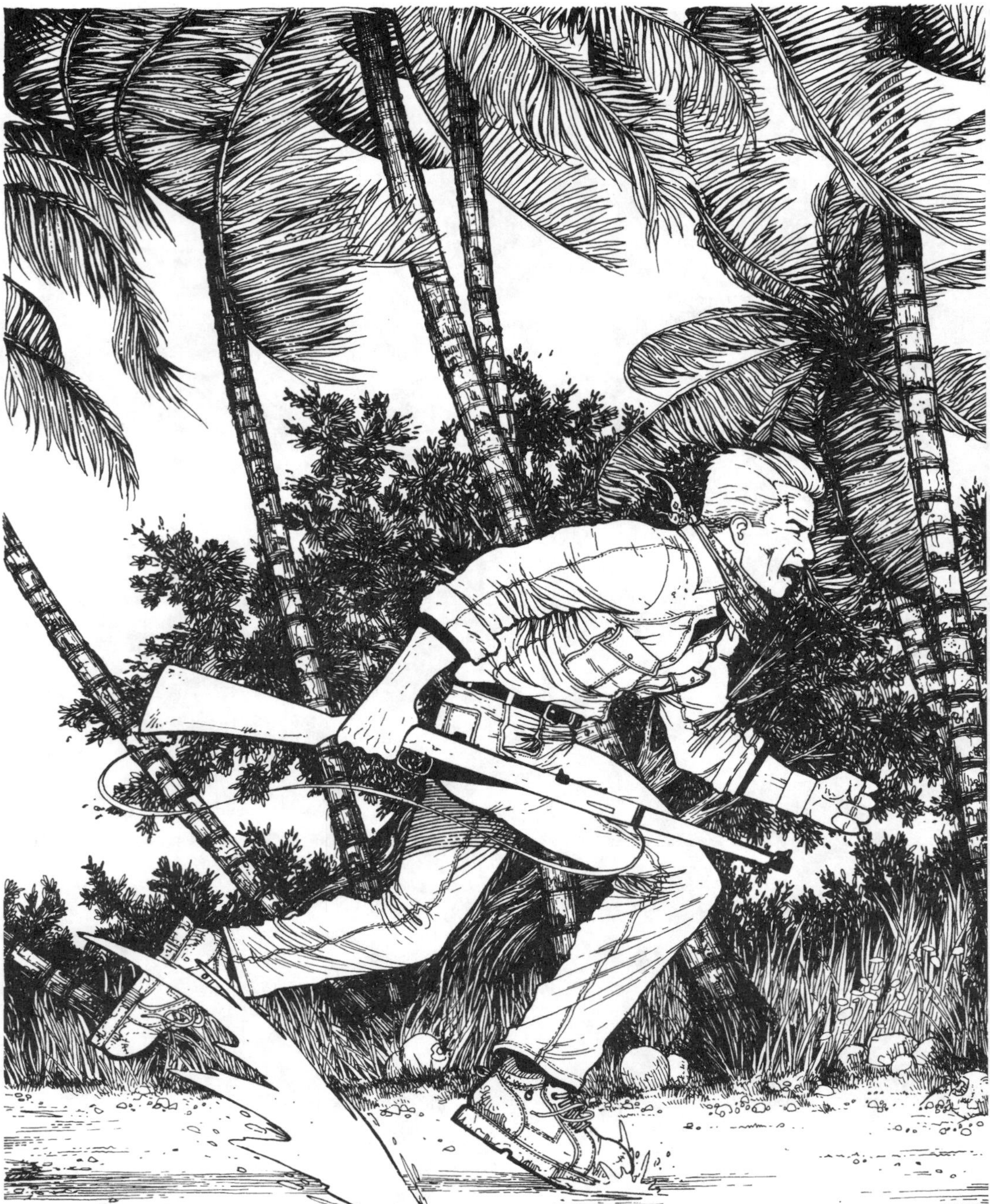
·ALANGUILAN· 2003

MODERN DUELLING

story by **JACK LONDON**
illustrated by **GERRY ALANGUILAN**

Barely had Sheldon reached the Balesuna, when he heard the faint report of a distant rifle and knew it was the signal of Tudor, giving notice that he had reached the Berande, turned about, and was coming back. Sheldon fired his rifle into the air in answer, and in turn proceeded to advance. He moved as in a dream, absent-mindedly keeping to the open beach. The thing was so preposterous that he had to struggle to realize it, and he reviewed in his mind the conversation with Tudor, trying to find some clue to the common-sense of what he was doing. He did not want to kill Tudor. Because that man had blundered in his lovemaking was no reason that he, Sheldon, should take his life. Then what was it all about? True, the fellow had insulted Joan by his subsequent remarks and been knocked down for it, but because he had knocked him down was no reason that he should now try to kill him.

In this fashion, he covered a quarter of the distance between the two rivers, when it dawned upon him that Tudor was not on the beach at all. Of course not. He was advancing, according to the terms of the agreement, in the shelter of the coconut trees. Sheldon promptly swerved to the left to seek similar shelter, when the faint crack of a rifle came to his ears, and almost immediately the bullet, striking the hard sand a hundred feet beyond him, ricochetted and whined onward in a second flight, convincing him that preposterous and unreal as it was, it was, nevertheless, sober fact. It had been intended for him. Yet even then it was hard to believe. He glanced over the familiar landscape and at the sea, dimpling in the light but steady breeze. From the direction of Tulagi he could see the white sails of a schooner laying a tack across toward Berande. Down the beach a horse was grazing, and he idly wondered where the others were. The smoke rising from the copra-drying caught his eyes, which roved on over the barracks, the tool-houses, the boat-sheds, and the bungalow, and came to rest on Joan's little grass house in the corner of the compound.

Keeping now to the shelter of the trees, he went forward another quarter of a mile. If Tudor had advanced with equal speed, they should have come together at that point, and Sheldon concluded that the other was circling. The difficulty was to locate him. The rows of trees, running at right angles, enabled him to see along only one narrow avenue at a time. His enemy might be coming along the next avenue, or the next, to right or left. He might be a hundred feet away or half a mile. Sheldon plodded on, and decided that the old stereotyped duel was far simpler and easier than this protracted hide-and-seek affair. He, too, tried circling, in the hope of cutting the other's circle; but, without catching a glimpse of him, he finally emerged upon a fresh clearing where the young trees, waist-high, afforded little shelter and less hiding. Just as he emerged, stepping out a pace, a rifle cracked to his right, and though he did not hear the bullet in passing, the thud of it came to his ears when it struck a palm trunk farther on.

He sprang back into the protection of the larger trees. Twice he had exposed himself and been fired at, while he had failed to catch a single glimpse of his antagonist. A slow anger began to burn in him. It was deucedly unpleasant, he decided, this being peppered at; and non-sensical as it really was, it was none the less deadly serious. There was no avoiding the issue, no firing in the air and getting over with it as in the old-fashioned duel. This mutual manhunt must keep up until one got the other. And if one neglected a chance to get the other, that increased the other's chance to get him. There could be no false sentiment about it. Tudor had been a cunning devil when he proposed this sort of duel, Sheldon concluded, as he began to work along cautiously in the direction of the last shot.

When he arrived at the spot, Tudor was gone, and only his footprints remained, pointing out the course he had taken into the depths of the plantation. Once, ten minutes later, he caught a glimpse of Tudor, a hundred yards away, crossing the same avenue as himself but going in the opposite direction. His rifle half leaped to his shoulder, but the other was gone. More in whim than in hope of result, grinning to himself as he did so, Sheldon raised his automatic pistol and in two seconds sent eight shots scattering through the trees in the direction in which Tudor had disap-peared. Wishing he had a shotgun, Sheldon dropped to the ground behind a tree, slipped a fresh clip up the hollow butt of the pistol, threw a cartridge into the chamber, shoved the safety catch into place, and reloaded the empty clip.

It was but a short time after that that Tudor tried the same trick on him, the bul-lets pattering about him like spiteful rain, thudding into the palm trunks, or glancing off in whining ricochets. The last bullet of all, making a double ricochet from two different trees and losing most of its mo-mentum, struck Sheldon a sharp blow on

the forehead and dropped at his feet. He was partly stunned for the moment, but on investigation found no greater harm than a nasty lump that soon rose to the size of a pigeon's egg.

The hunt went on. Once, coming to the edge of the grove near the bungalow, he saw the house-boys and the cook, clus-tered on the back veranda and peering curiously among the trees, talking and laughing with one another. Another time he came upon a working gang busy at hoeing weeds. They scarcely noticed him when he came up, though they knew thoroughly well what was going on. It was no affair of theirs that the enigmatical white men should be out trying to kill each other, and whatever interest in the proceedings might be theirs, they were careful to conceal it from Sheldon. He told them to continue hoeing weeds in a distant and out-of-the-way corner, and went on with the pursuit of Tudor.

Tiring of the endless circling, Sheldon tried once more to advance directly on his foe, but the latter was too crafty, taking ad-vantage of his boldness to fire a couple of shots at him and slipping away on some changed and continually changing course. For an hour, they dodged and turned and twisted back and forth and around and hunted each other among the orderly palms. They caught fleeting glimpses of each other and chanced flying shots which were without result. On a grassy shelter behind a tree, Sheldon came upon where Tudor had rested and smoked a cigarette. The pressed grass showed where he had sat. To one side lay the cigarette stump and the charred match which had lighted it. In front lay a scattering of bright metal-lic fragments. Sheldon recognized their significance. Tudor was notching his steel-jacketed bullets, or cutting them blunt, so that they would spread on striking – in short, he was making them into the vicious dumdum prohibited in modern warfare. Sheldon knew now what would happen to him if a bullet struck his body. It would leave a tiny hole where it entered, but the hole where it emerged would be the size of a saucer.

He decided to give up the pursuit, and lay down in the grass, protected right and left by the row of palms, with, on either hand, the long avenue extending. This he could watch. Tudor would have to come to him or else there would be no termination of the affair. He wiped the sweat from his face and tied the handkerchief around his neck to keep off the stinging gnats that lurked in the grass. Never had he felt so great a disgust for the thing called "adventure." Joan had been bad enough, with her Baden-Powell and long-barrelled Colt's; but here was this newcomer, also looking for adventure and finding it in no other way than by lugging a peace-loving planter into an absurd and preposterous bushwhacking duel. If ever adventure was well damned, it was by Sheldon, sweating in the windless grass and fighting gnats, the while he kept close watch up and down the avenue.

Then Tudor came. Sheldon happened to be looking in his direction at the moment he came into view, peering quickly up and down the avenue before he stepped into the open. Midway he stopped, as if debating what course to pursue. He made a splendid mark, facing his concealed enemy at two hundred yards' distance. Sheldon aimed at the center of his chest, then deliberately shifted the aim to his right shoulder, and, with the thought, "that will put him out of business," pulled the trigger. The bullet, driving with momentum sufficient to perforate a man's body a mile distant, struck Tudor with such force as to pivot him, whirling him half around by the shock of its impact and knocking him down.

"Hope I haven't killed the beggar," Sheldon muttered aloud, springing to his feet and running forward.

A hundred feet away, all anxiety on that score was relieved by Tudor, who made shift with his left hand and from his automatic pistol hurled a rain of bullets all around Sheldon. The latter dodged behind a palm trunk, counting the shots, and when the eighth had been fired, he rushed in on the wounded man. He kicked the pistol out of the other's hand and then sat down on him in order to keep him down.

"Be quiet," he said. "I've got you, so there's no use struggling." Tudor still attempted to struggle and to throw him off.

"Keep quiet, I tell you," Sheldon commanded. "I'm satisfied with the outcome, and you've got to be. So you might as well give in and call this affair closed."

Tudor reluctantly relaxed.

"Rather funny, isn't it, these modern duels?" Sheldon grinned down at him as he removed his weight. "Not a bit dignified. If you'd struggled a moment longer, I'd have rubbed your face in the earth. I've a good mind to do it anyway, just to teach you that duelling has gone out of fashion. Now, let us see to your injuries."

"You only got me that last," Tudor grunted sullenly, "lying in ambush like —"

"Like a savage. Precisely. You've caught the idea, old man." Sheldon ceased his mocking and stood up. "You lie there quietly until I send back some of the men to carry you in. You're not seriously hurt, and it's lucky for you I didn't follow your example. If you had been struck with one of your own bullets, a carriage and pair would have been none too large to drive through the hole it would have made. As it is, you're drilled clean — a nice little perforation. All you need is antiseptic washing and dressing and you'll be around in a month. Now take it easy, and I'll send a stretcher for you."

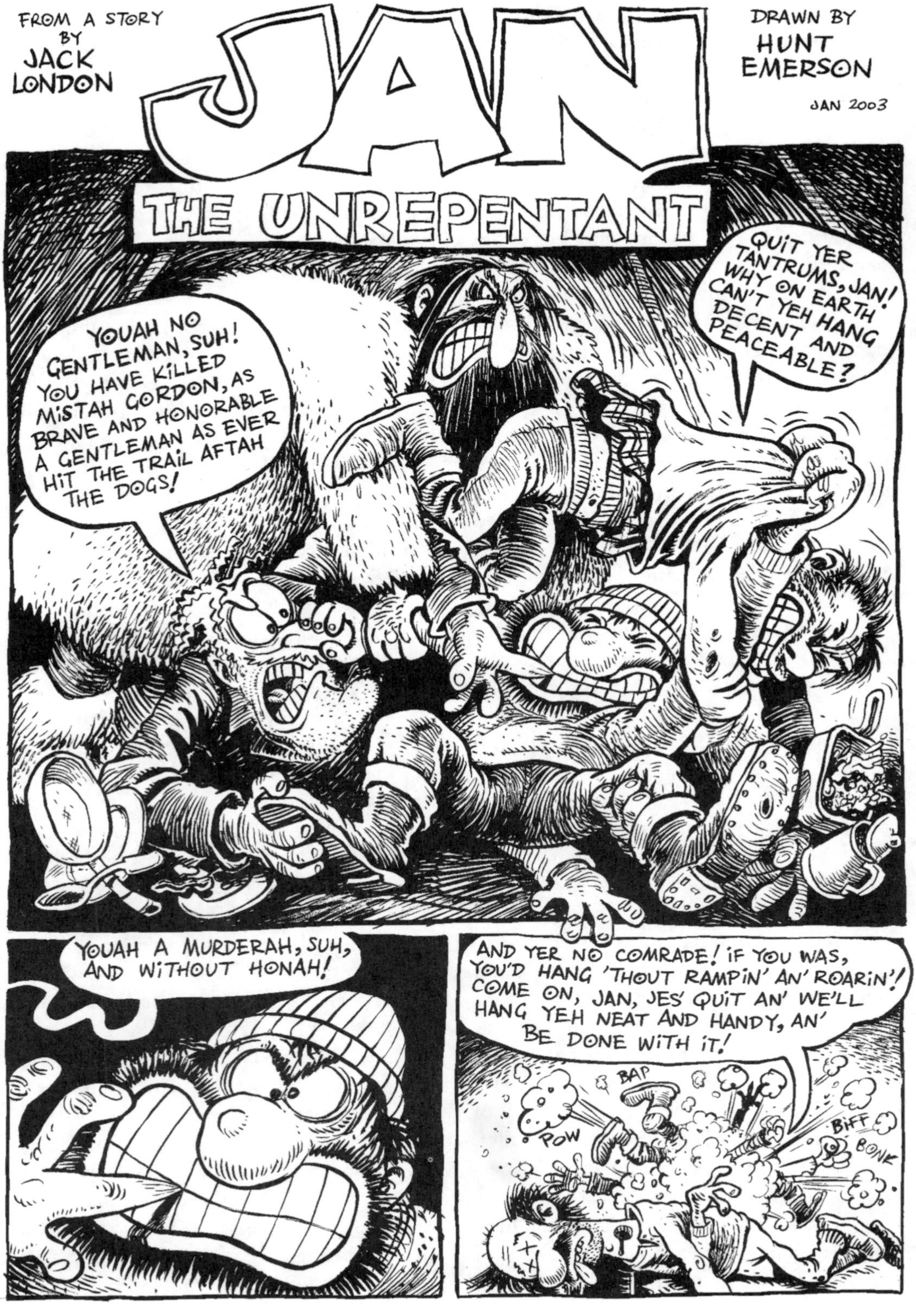
FROM A STORY BY JACK LONDON
JAN THE UNREPENTANT
DRAWN BY HUNT EMERSON
JAN 2003
YOUAH NO GENTLEMAN, SUH! YOU HAVE KILLED MISTAH GORDON, AS BRAVE AND HONORABLE A GENTLEMAN AS EVER HIT THE TRAIL AFTAH THE DOGS!
QUIT YER TANTRUMS, JAN! WHY ON EARTH CAN'T YEH HANG DECENT AND PEACEABLE?
YOUAH A MURDERAH, SUH, AND WITHOUT HONAH!
AND YER NO COMRADE! IF YOU WAS, YOU'D HANG 'THOUT RAMPIN' AN' ROARIN'! COME ON, JAN, JES' QUIT AN' WE'LL HANG YEH NEAT AND HANDY, AN' BE DONE WITH IT!
BAP
POW
BIFF
BONK

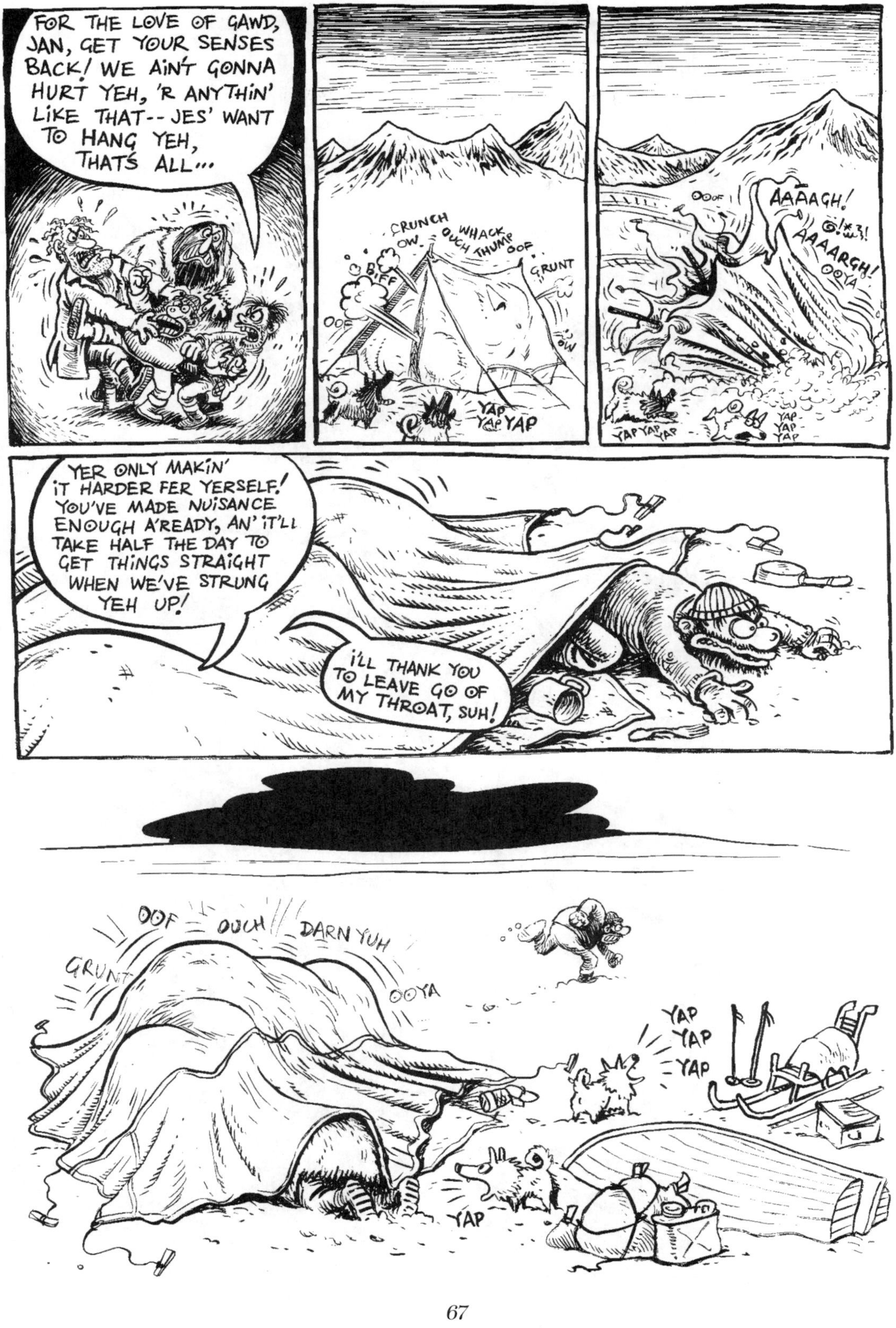
FOR THE LOVE OF GAWD, JAN, GET YOUR SENSES BACK! WE AIN'T GONNA HURT YEH, 'R ANYTHIN' LIKE THAT-- JES' WANT TO HANG YEH, THAT'S ALL...
CRUNCH
WHACK
OW
OUCH
THUMP
OOF
BIFF
GRUNT
OOF
OW
YAP YAP YAP
OOF
AAAAGH!
AAAARGH!
OOYA
YAP YAP YAP
YAP YAP YAP
YER ONLY MAKIN' IT HARDER FER YERSELF! YOU'VE MADE NUISANCE ENOUGH A'READY, AN' IT'LL TAKE HALF THE DAY TO GET THINGS STRAIGHT WHEN WE'VE STRUNG YEH UP!
I'LL THANK YOU TO LEAVE GO OF MY THROAT, SUH!
OOF
OUCH
DARN YUH
GRUNT
OOYA
YAP
YAP
YAP
YAP

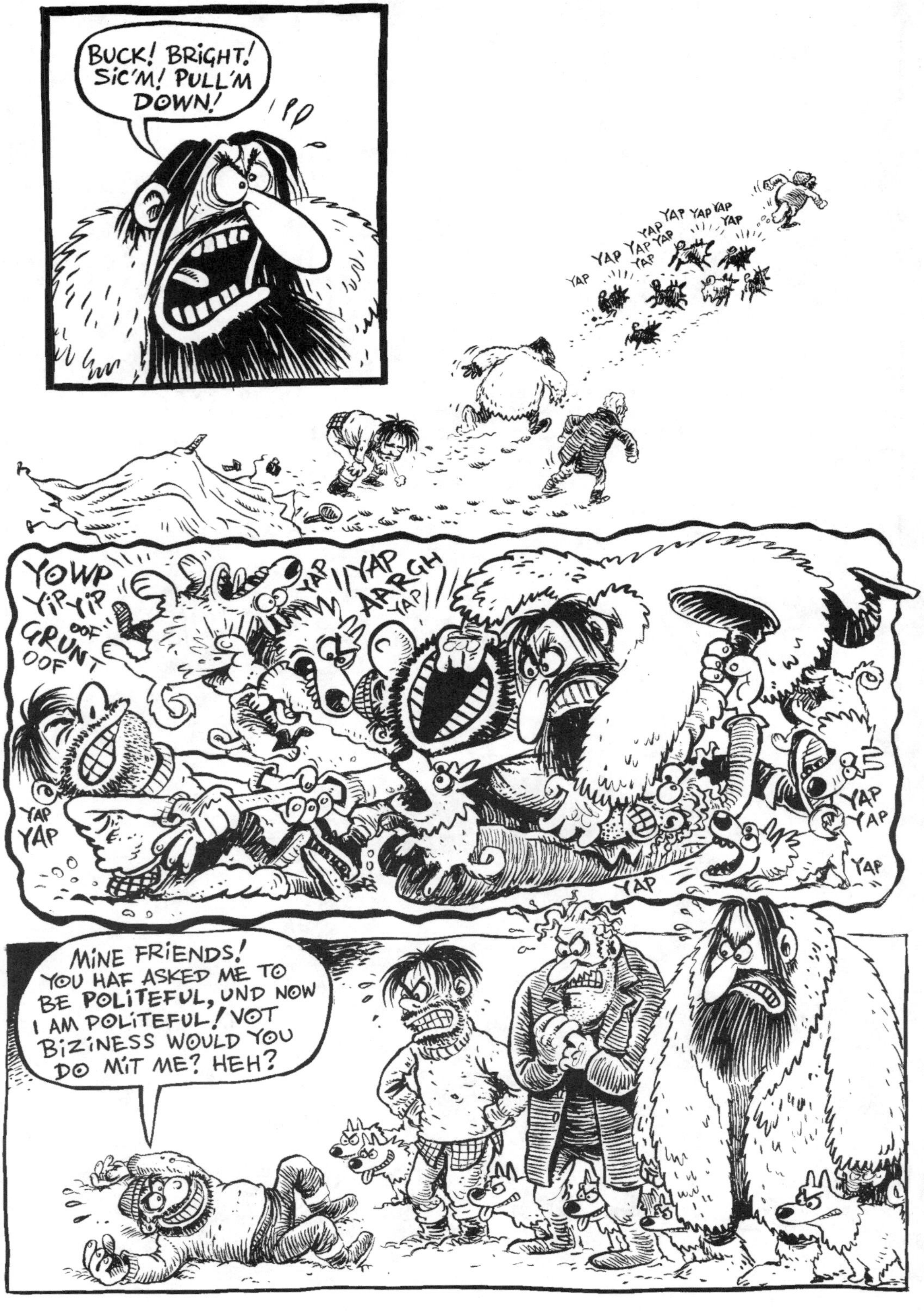
BUCK! BRIGHT! SIC'M! PULL'M DOWN!
YAP YAP YAP YAP YAP YAP YAP YAP YAP YAP YAP
YOWP
YIP YIP
GRUNT
OOF
OOF
YAP
YAP
AARGH
YAP
YAP YAP
YAP YAP
YAP
YAP
MINE FRIENDS! YOU HAF ASKED ME TO BE POLITEFUL, UND NOW I AM POLITEFUL! VOT BIZINESS WOULD YOU DO MIT ME? HEH?

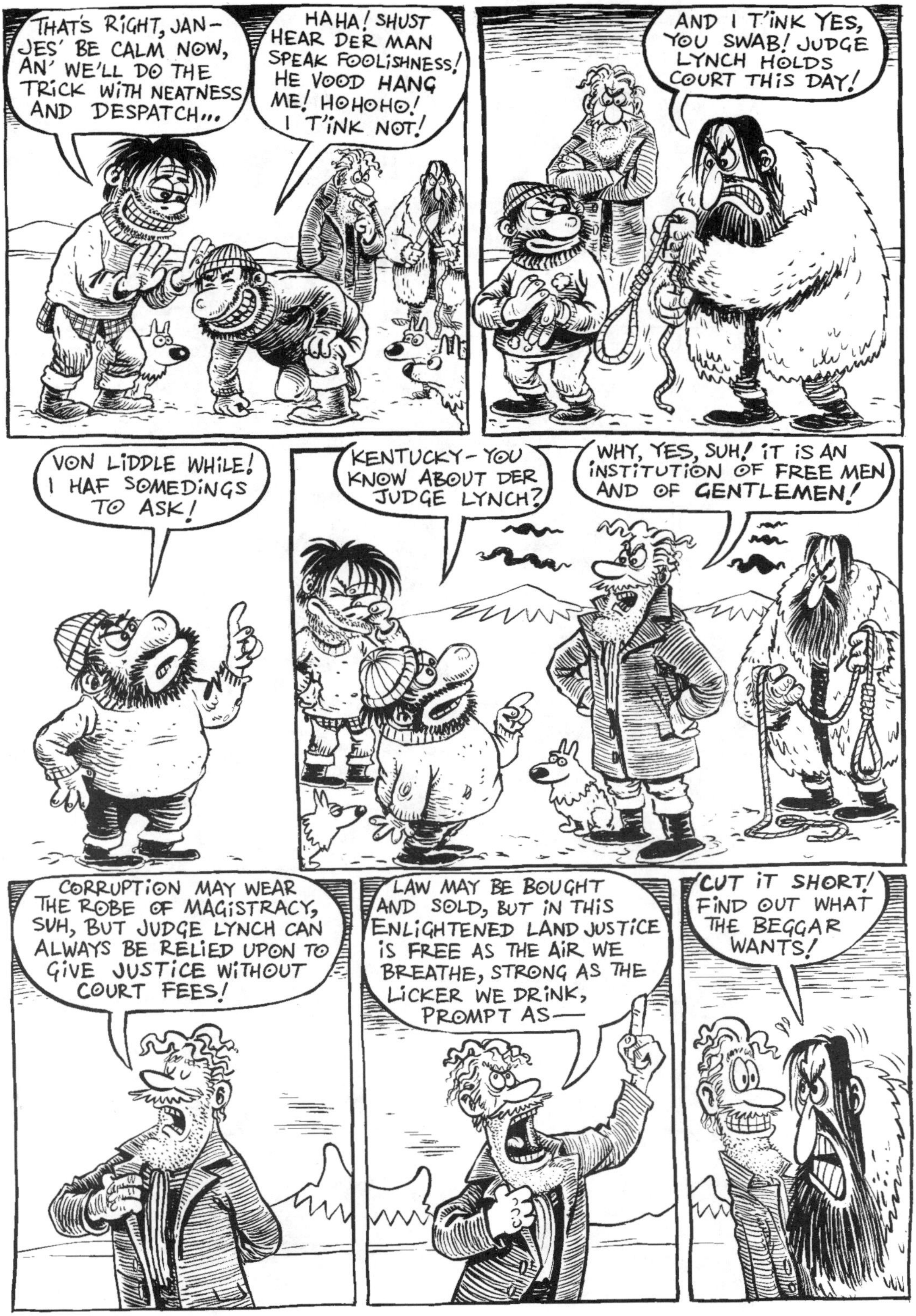
THAT'S RIGHT, JAN— JES' BE CALM NOW, AN' WE'LL DO THE TRICK WITH NEATNESS AND DESPATCH...
HAHA! SHUST HEAR DER MAN SPEAK FOOLISHNESS! HE VOOD HANG ME! HOHOHO! I T'INK NOT!
AND I T'INK YES, YOU SWAB! JUDGE LYNCH HOLDS COURT THIS DAY!
VON LIDDLE WHILE! I HAF SOMEDINGS TO ASK!
KENTUCKY— YOU KNOW ABOUT DER JUDGE LYNCH?
WHY, YES, SUH! IT IS AN INSTITUTION OF FREE MEN AND OF GENTLEMEN!
CORRUPTION MAY WEAR THE ROBE OF MAGISTRACY, SUH, BUT JUDGE LYNCH CAN ALWAYS BE RELIED UPON TO GIVE JUSTICE WITHOUT COURT FEES!
LAW MAY BE BOUGHT AND SOLD, BUT IN THIS ENLIGHTENED LAND JUSTICE IS FREE AS THE AIR WE BREATHE, STRONG AS THE LICKER WE DRINK, PROMPT AS—
CUT IT SHORT! FIND OUT WHAT THE BEGGAR WANTS!

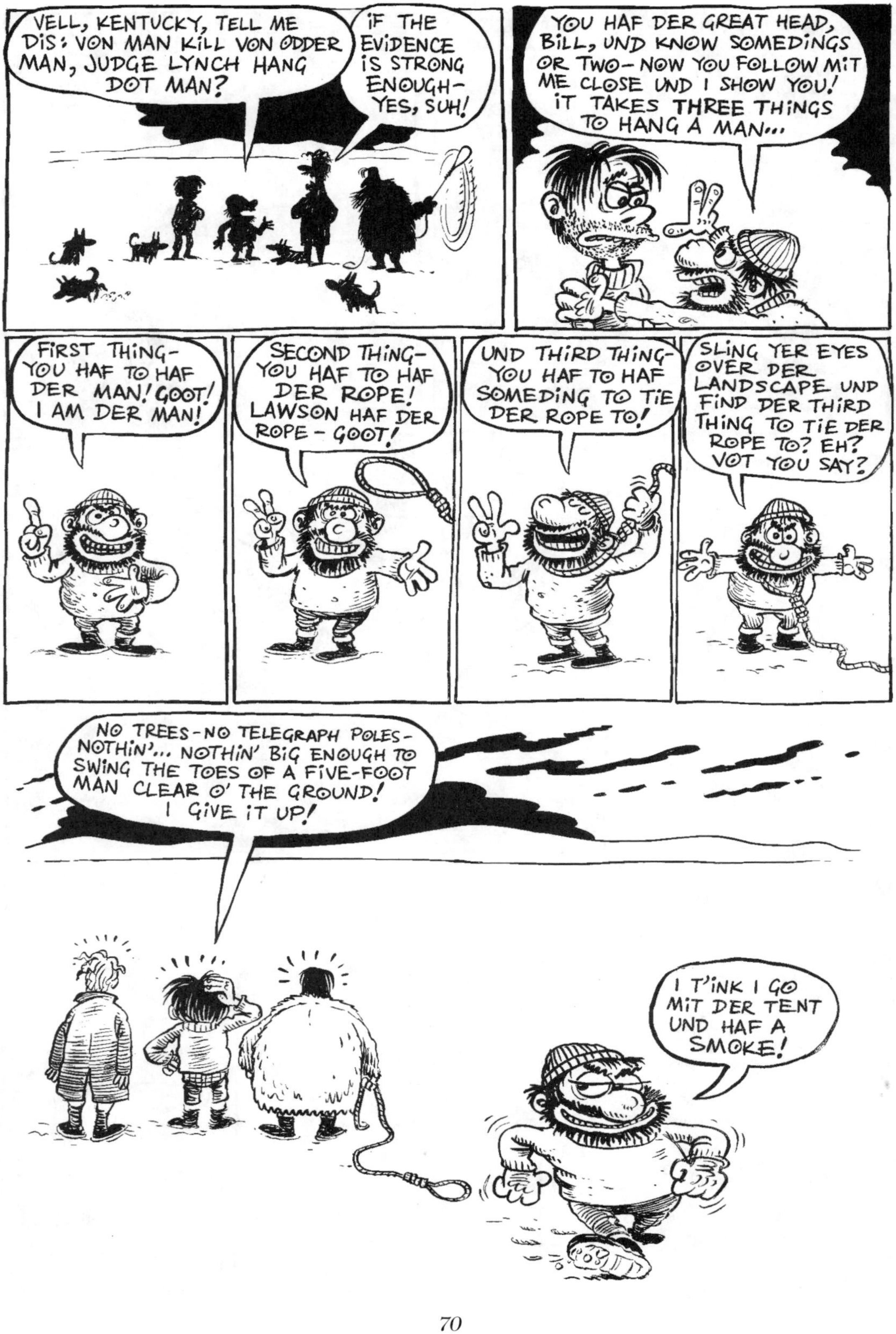
VELL, KENTUCKY, TELL ME DIS: VON MAN KILL VON ODDER MAN, JUDGE LYNCH HANG DOT MAN?
IF THE EVIDENCE IS STRONG ENOUGH- YES, SUH!
YOU HAF DER GREAT HEAD, BILL, UND KNOW SOMEDINGS OR TWO- NOW YOU FOLLOW MIT ME CLOSE UND I SHOW YOU! IT TAKES THREE THINGS TO HANG A MAN...
FIRST THING- YOU HAF TO HAF DER MAN! GOOT! I AM DER MAN!
SECOND THING- YOU HAF TO HAF DER ROPE! LAWSON HAF DER ROPE - GOOT!
UND THIRD THING- YOU HAF TO HAF SOMEDING TO TIE DER ROPE TO!
SLING YER EYES OVER DER LANDSCAPE UND FIND DER THIRD THING TO TIE DER ROPE TO? EH? VOT YOU SAY?
NO TREES-NO TELEGRAPH POLES- NOTHIN'... NOTHIN' BIG ENOUGH TO SWING THE TOES OF A FIVE-FOOT MAN CLEAR O' THE GROUND! I GIVE IT UP!
I T'INK I GO MIT DER TENT UND HAF A SMOKE!

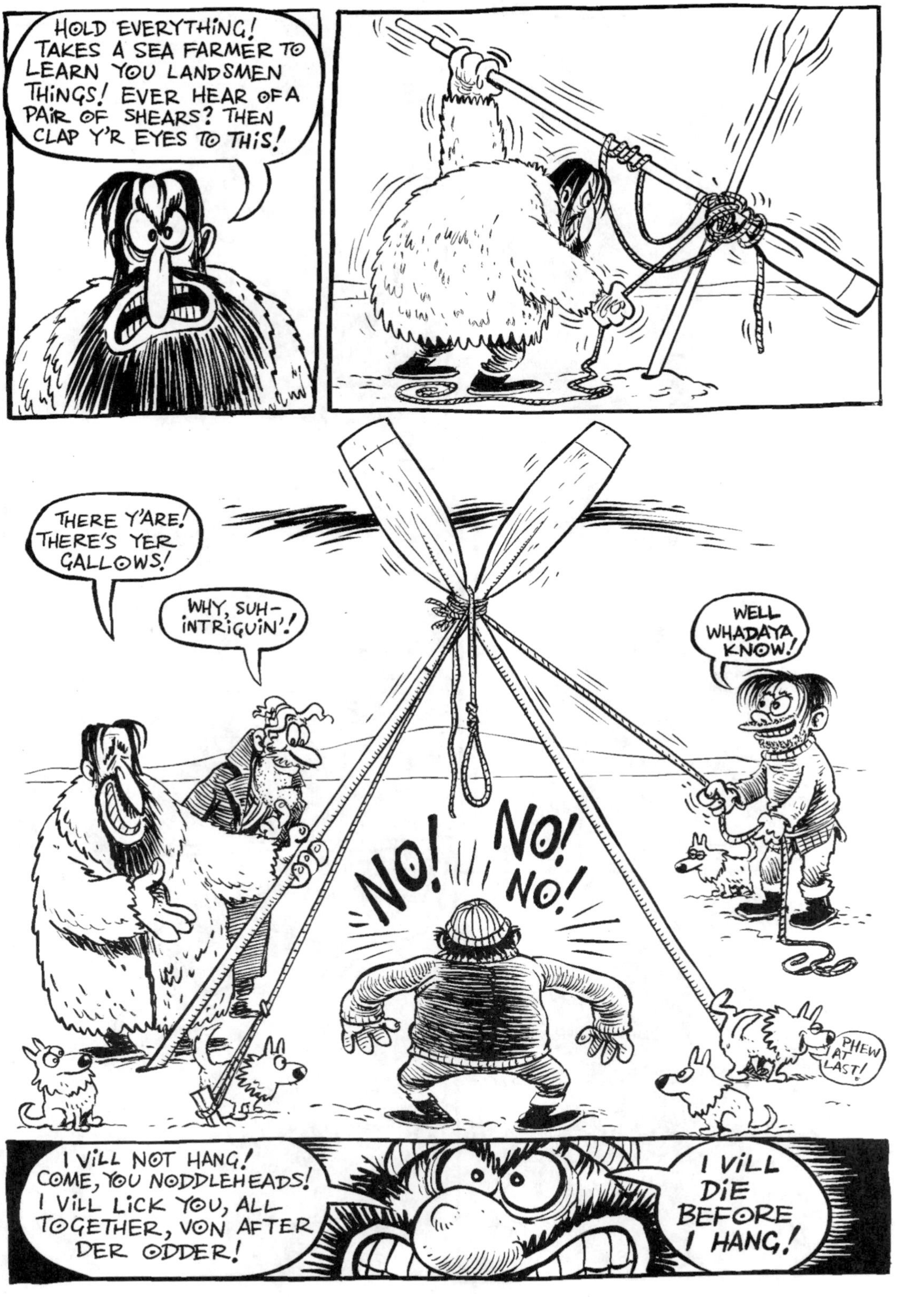
HOLD EVERYTHING! TAKES A SEA FARMER TO LEARN YOU LANDSMEN THINGS! EVER HEAR OF A PAIR OF SHEARS? THEN CLAP Y'R EYES TO THIS!
THERE Y'ARE! THERE'S YER GALLOWS!
WHY, SUH- INTRIGUIN'!
WELL WHADAYA KNOW!
NO! NO! NO!
PHEW AT LAST!
I VILL NOT HANG! COME, YOU NODDLEHEADS! I VILL LICK YOU, ALL TOGETHER, VON AFTER DER ODDER!
I VILL DIE BEFORE I HANG!

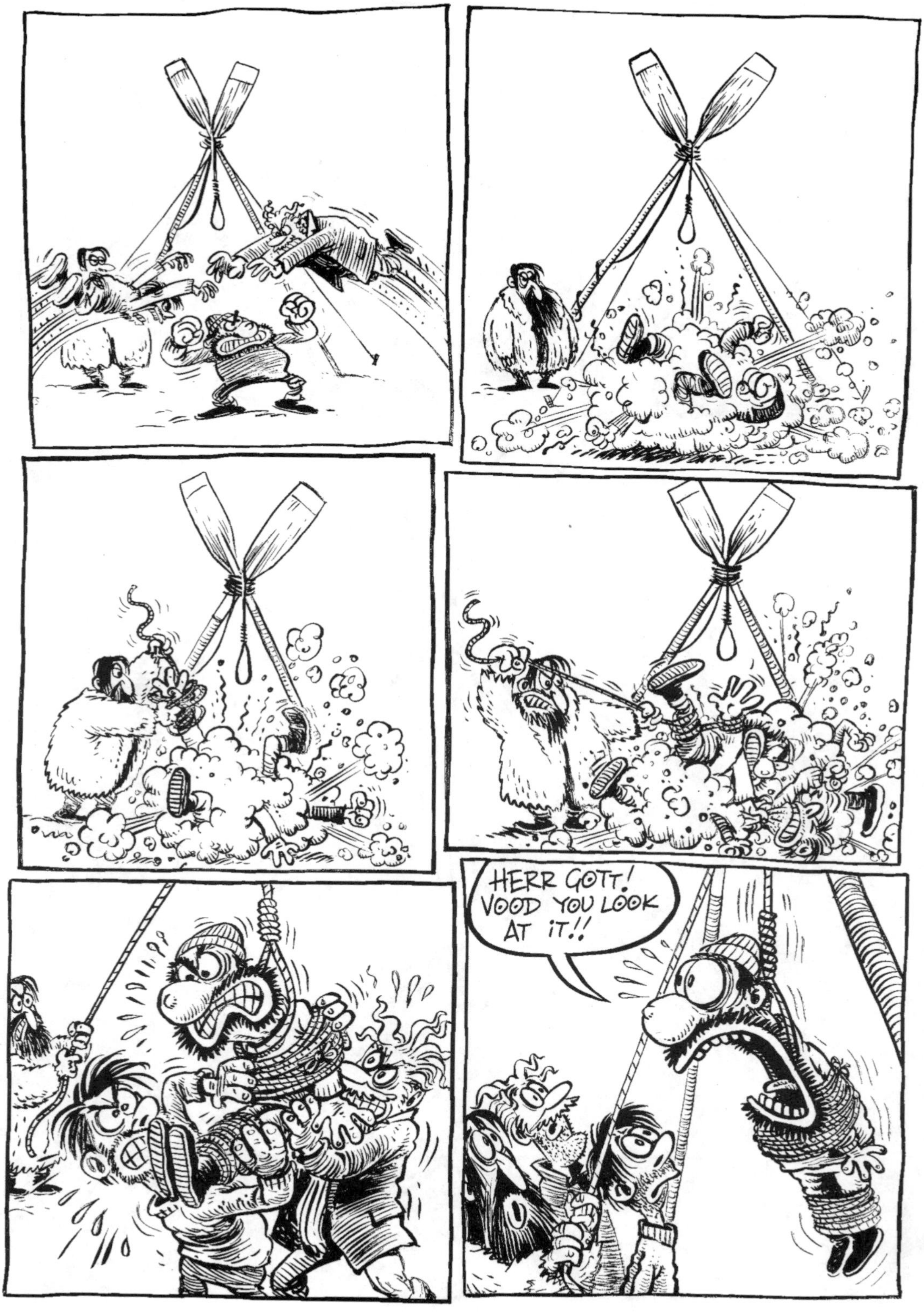
HERR GOTT!
VOOD YOU LOOK
AT IT!!

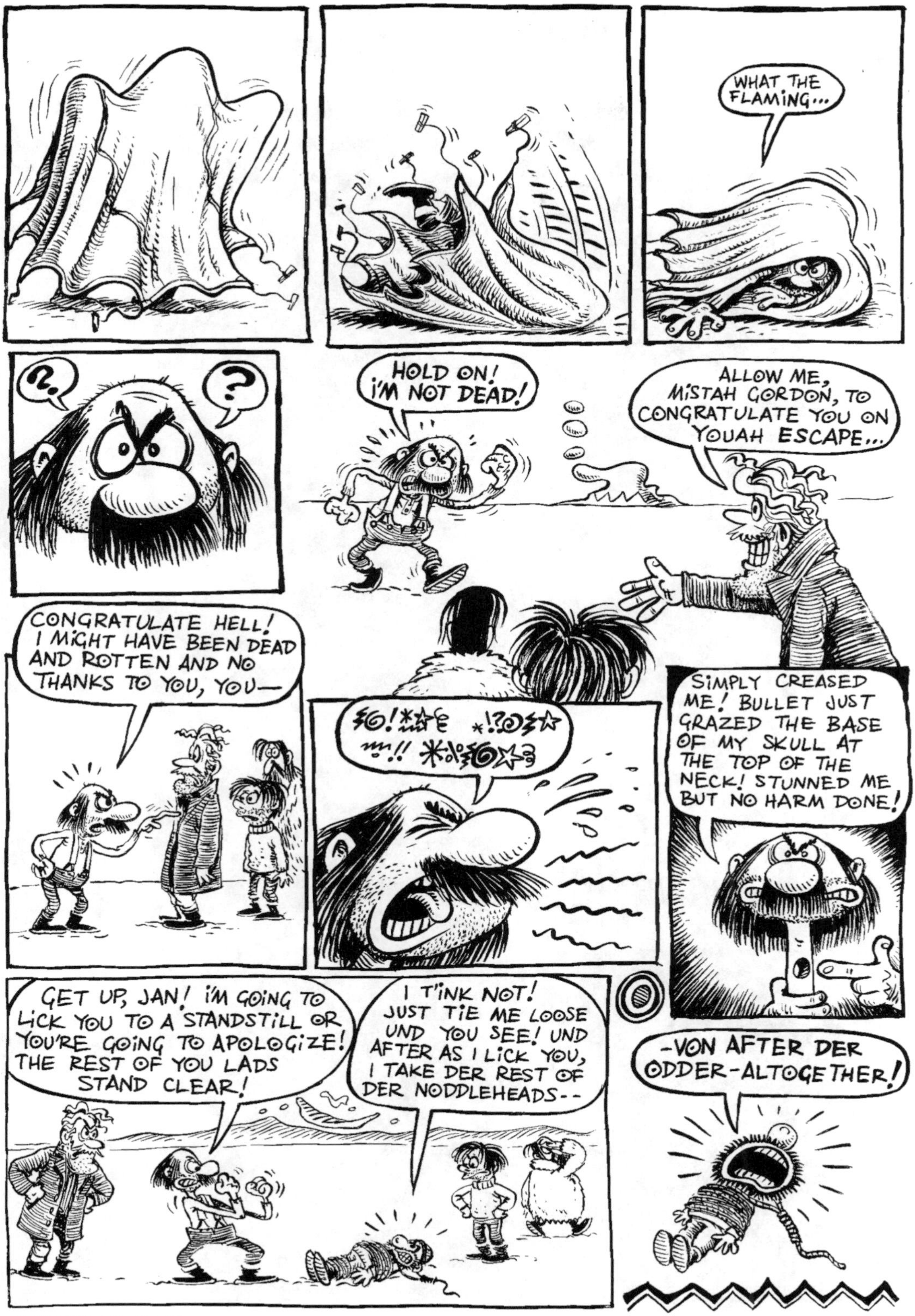
WHAT THE FLAMING...
HOLD ON! I'M NOT DEAD!
ALLOW ME, MISTAH GORDON, TO CONGRATULATE YOU ON YOUAH ESCAPE...
CONGRATULATE HELL! I MIGHT HAVE BEEN DEAD AND ROTTEN AND NO THANKS TO YOU, YOU—
SIMPLY CREASED ME! BULLET JUST GRAZED THE BASE OF MY SKULL AT THE TOP OF THE NECK! STUNNED ME BUT NO HARM DONE!
GET UP, JAN! I'M GOING TO LICK YOU TO A STANDSTILL OR YOU'RE GOING TO APOLOGIZE! THE REST OF YOU LADS STAND CLEAR!
I T'INK NOT! JUST TIE ME LOOSE UND YOU SEE! UND AFTER AS I LICK YOU, I TAKE DER REST OF DER NODDLEHEADS--
-VON AFTER DER ODDER-ALTOGETHER!

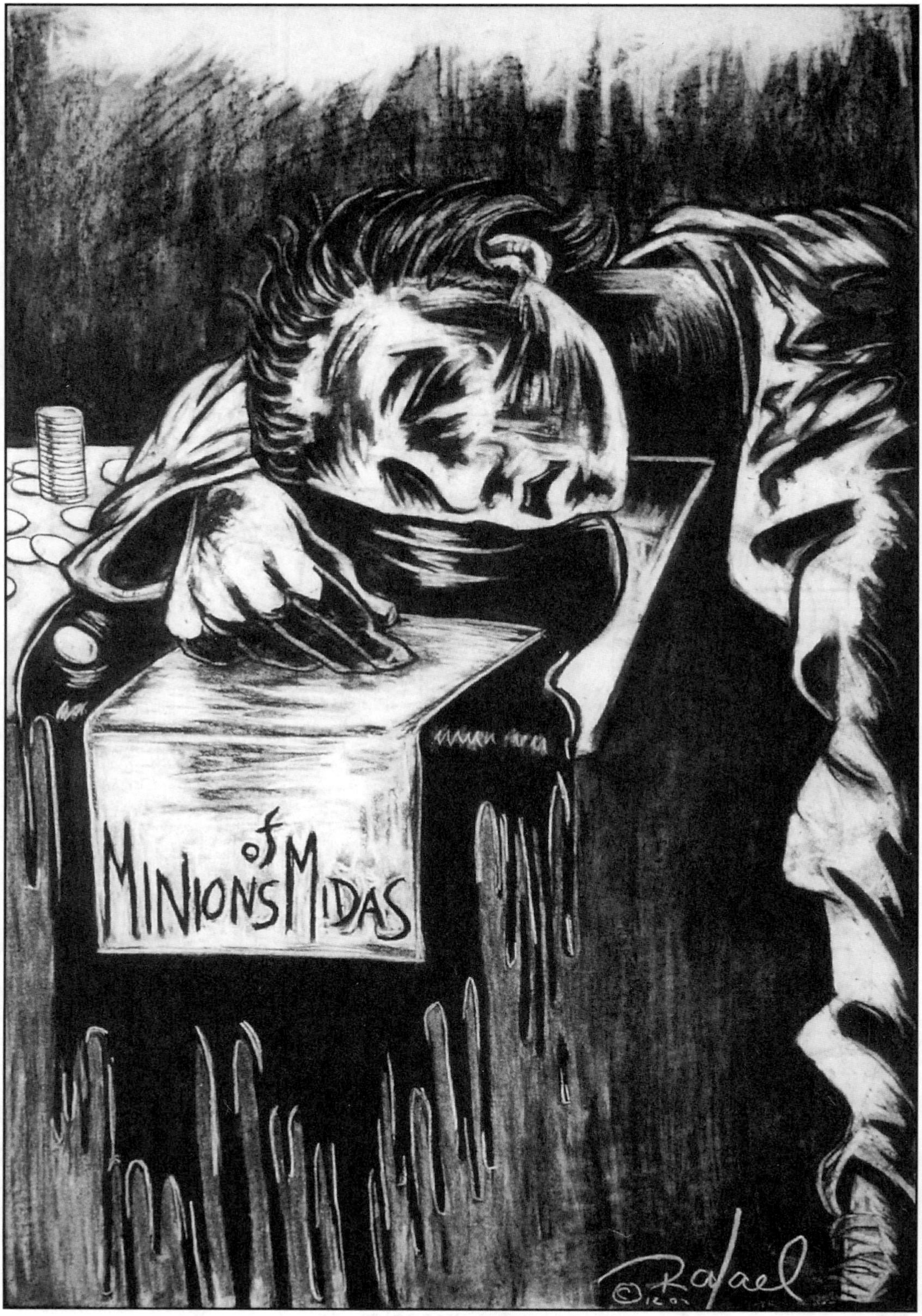
MINIONS of MIDAS
©12.02 Rafael

THE MINIONS OF MIDAS

by JACK LONDON

adapted by Tom Pomplun

illustrated by RAFAEL AVILA

WADE ATSHELER is dead—dead by his own hand. Young, handsome, with an assured position as the right-hand man of Eben Hale, the great street-railway magnate, there could be no reason for him to complain of fortune's favors. Yet we had watched his smooth brow furrow and corrugate as under some burdensome care or devouring sorrow.

When Eben Hale died, whose confidential secretary he was—nay, well-nigh adopted son and full business partner—he no longer came among us. Not, as I now know, that our company was distasteful to him, but because his trouble had so grown that he could not respond to our happiness nor find surcease with us. Why this should be so we could not at the time understand, for when Eben Hale's will was probated, the world learned that he was sole heir to his employer's many millions, and it was expressly stipulated that this great inheritance was given to him without qualification. Not a share of stock, not a penny of cash, was bequeathed to the dead man's relatives. As for his direct family, one astounding clause expressly stated that Wade Atsheler was to dispense to Eben Hale's wife and sons and daughters whatever moneys his judgement dictated, at whatever times he deemed advisable. Needless to state, this inexplicable will was a wonder; but the expectant public was disappointed in that no contest was made.

It was only the other day that Eben Hale was laid away in his stately marble mausoleum. And now Wade Atsheler is dead. I have just received through the mail a letter from him, posted, evidently, but a short hour before he hurled himself into eternity. This letter, which lies before me, is a narrative in his own handwriting, linking together numerous newspaper clippings and facsimiles of letters. He has begged me, as a warning to society against a most frightful and diabolical danger which threatens its very existence, to make public the terrible series of tragedies in which he has been innocently concerned. I herewith append the final words of Wade Atsheler:

Dear John,

It was in August, 1899, just after my return from my summer vacation, that the blow fell. We did not know it at the time; we had not yet learned to school our minds to such awful possibilities. Mr. Hale opened the letter, read it, and tossed it upon my desk with a laugh. When I had looked it over, I also laughed, saying, "Some ghastly joke, Mr. Hale, and one in very poor taste." Find here the letter in question.

OFFICE OF THE M. OF M. August 17, 1899
MR. EBEN HALE, Money Baron

Dear Sir,

We desire you to obtain from your vast holdings, IN CASH, the sum of twenty million dollars. This we require you to pay over to us, or to our agents. We are members of that intellectual proletariat, the increasing numbers of which mark in red lettering the last days of the nineteenth century. We have, from a thorough study of economics, decided to enter upon this business, and we hope our dealings with you may be pleasant and satisfactory.

Pray attend while we explain our views more fully. At the base of the present system of society is to be found the property right. And this right of the individual to hold property is demonstrated, in the last analysis, to rest solely upon MIGHT. The old-time Feudal Baronage ravaged the world with fire and sword; the modern Money Baronage exploits the world by applying economic forces. We, the M. of M., are not content to become wage slaves. The great trusts and business combinations prevent us from rising to the place among you which our intellects qualify us to occupy. Why? Because we are without capital. We are of the unwashed, but with this difference: our brains are of the best, and we have no foolish ethical nor social scruples. As wage slaves we could not save a sum of money sufficient to cope with the great aggregations of massed capital which now exist. Nevertheless, we have entered the arena.

When you have agreed to our terms, insert a suitable notice in the agony column of the "Morning Blazer." We shall then acquaint you with our plan for transferring the sum mentioned. Do this some time prior to October 1st. If you do not, in order to show that we are in earnest we shall on that date kill a man on East Thirty-ninth Street. This man you do not know; nor do we. We are simply a business proposition. You may save this man's life if you agree to our conditions and act in time.

There was once a king cursed with a golden touch. His name we have taken to do duty as our official seal.

We beg to remain,
THE MINIONS OF MIDAS

I leave it to you, dear John, why should we not have laughed over such a preposterous communication? The idea was too grotesque to be taken seriously. Mr. Hale said he would preserve it as a literary curiosity, and shoved it away in a pigeonhole. Then we forgot its existence until, on the 1st of October, going over the morning mail, we read the following:

OFFICE OF THE **M. OF M.**, October 1, 1899
MR. EBEN HALE, Money Baron

Dear Sir,

   Your victim has met his fate. An hour ago, on East Thirty-ninth Street, a workingman was thrust through the heart with a knife. Ere you read this his body will be lying at the Morgue. Go and look upon your handiwork. On October 14th, in token of our earnestness in this matter, and in case you do not relent, we shall kill a policeman on or near the corner of Polk Street and Clermont Avenue.

Very cordially,
THE MINIONS OF MIDAS

Again Mr. Hale laughed. His mind was full of a prospective deal, and so he went on dictating to the stenographer, never giving it a second thought. But somehow, I know not why, a heavy depression fell upon me. What if it were not a joke, I asked myself, and turned involuntarily to the morning paper. There it was, a paltry half-dozen lines tucked away in a corner:

> Shortly after five o'clock this morning, on East Thirty-ninth Street, a laborer named Pete Lascalle, while on his way to work, was stabbed to the heart by an unknown assailant, who escaped by running. The police have been unable to discover any motive for the murder.

"Impossible!" was Mr. Hale's rejoinder, when I had read the item aloud; but late in the afternoon, he asked me to acquaint the police with the affair. I had the pleasure of being laughed at in the Inspector's private office, although I went away with the assurance that they would look into it and that the vicinity of Polk and Clermont would be doubly patrolled on the night mentioned. There it dropped, till the two weeks had sped by, when the following note came to us through the mail:

OFFICE OF THE **M. OF M.** October 15, 1899
MR. EBEN HALE, Money Baron

Dear Sir,

   Your second victim has fallen on the scheduled time. We are in no
hurry; but to increase the pressure we shall henceforth **kill** weekly.
To protect ourselves we shall hereafter inform you of the event but
a little prior to or simultaneously with the deed.

Trusting this finds you in good health,
THE MINIONS OF MIDAS

This time Mr. Hale took up the paper, and read to me this account:

A DASTARDLY CRIME

Joseph Donahue, assigned only last night to special patrol duty, was shot
through the brain and instantly killed. The tragedy was enacted in the
full glare of the street lights on the corner of Polk Street and Clermont
Avenue. The police have so far been unable to obtain the slightest clue.

*Barely had he finished when the police arrived. The Inspector confidently
assured us that all would soon be straightened out and the assassins run to
earth. In the meantime he thought it well to set guards for the protection
of Mr. Hale and myself. After a week, this telegram was received:*

OFFICE OF THE **M. OF M.** October 21, 1899
MR. EBEN HALE, Money Baron

Dear Sir,

   We are sorry to note how completely you have misunderstood us.
You have seen fit to surround yourself with armed guards, as though
we were common criminals, apt to break in upon you and wrest away
by force your twenty millions. Believe us, this is farthest from our
intention. We would not hurt you for the world. Your death means
nothing to us. If it did, rest assured that we would not hesitate a
moment in destroying you. Dismiss your guards now, and cut down your
expenses. Within minutes of the time you receive this a nurse will
have been choked to death in Brentwood Park. The body may be found
in the shrubbery lining the path which leads off from the bandstand.

Cordially yours,
THE MINIONS OF MIDAS

The next instant Mr. Hale was at the telephone, warning the Inspector of the impending murder. The Inspector excused himself in order to despatch men to the scene. Fifteen minutes later he rang us up and informed us that the body had been discovered, yet warm, in the place indicated. That evening the papers teemed with headlines denouncing the brutality of the deed and complaining about the laxity of the police.

Mr. Hale refused to surrender. But week by week came the notification and death of some person, innocent of evil, but just as much killed by us as though we had done it with our own hands. A word from Mr. Hale and the slaughter would have ceased. But he hardened his heart and waited, the lines deepening, the mouth and eyes growing sterner and firmer, and the face aging with the hours.

Mr. Hale was grit clear through. He disbursed at the rate of one hundred thousand per week for secret service. Our agents swarmed everywhere, in all guises, penetrating all classes of society. Hundreds of suspects were jailed, and at various times thousands of suspicious persons were under surveillance, but nothing tangible came to light. With its communications the M. of M. continually changed its method of delivery. And every messenger they sent us was arrested forthwith. But these inevitably proved to be innocent individuals, while their descriptions of the persons who had employed them for the errand never tallied. On the last day of December we received this notification:

OFFICE OF THE **M. OF M.**, December 31, 1899
MR. EBEN HALE, Money Baron

Dear Sir,

Pursuant of our policy, with which we flatter ourselves you are already well versed, we beg to state that we shall give a passport from this Vale of Tears to Inspector Bying, with whom, because of our attentions, you have become so well acquainted. It is his custom to be in his private office at this hour. Even as you read this he breathes his last.

Cordially yours,
THE MINIONS OF MIDAS

I dropped the letter and sprang to the telephone. Great was my relief when I heard the Inspector's hearty voice. But, even as he spoke, his voice died away in the receiver to a gurgling sob, and I heard faintly the crash of a falling body. Then a strange voice sent me the regards of the M. of M., and broke the switch. Like a flash I called up the Central Police. I then held the line, and a few minutes later received the intelligence that he had been found bathed in his own blood and breathing his last. There were no eyewitnesses, and no trace was discoverable of the murderer.

Whereupon Mr. Hale increased his secret service till a quarter of a million flowed weekly from his coffers. He was determined to win out. It was the principle, he affirmed, that he was fighting for, not the gold. The police departments of all the great cities cooperated in the unearthing of the M. of M., and every government agent was on the alert. But all in vain. The Minions of Midas carried on their damnable work unhampered.

But while he fought to the last, Mr. Hale could not wash his hands of the blood with which they were dyed. A word from him and the slaughter would have ceased. But he refused to give that word. He insisted that the integrity of society was assailed, and that it was manifestly just that a few should be martyred for the ultimate welfare of the many. Nevertheless, he sank into deeper and deeper gloom. Babies were ruthlessly killed, children, aged men; and not only were these murders local, but they were distributed over the country. In the middle of February, as we sat in the library, there came a knock at the door. On responding to it I found, lying on the carpet of the corridor, the following missive:

OFFICE OF THE M. OF M., February 15, 1900
MR. EBEN HALE, Money Baron

Dear Sir,
    Does not your soul cry out upon the red harvest it is reaping? Perhaps we have been too abstract in conducting our business. Let us now be concrete. Miss Adelaide Laidlaw is the daughter of your old friend, Judge Laidlaw. She is your daughter's closest friend, and at present is visiting her. When your eyes have read thus far her visit will have terminated.

Very cordially,
THE MINIONS OF MIDAS

My God! did we not instantly realize the terrible import! We rushed to her apartment. The door was locked, but we crashed it down by hurling ourselves against it. There she lay, smothered with pillows torn from the couch, the flush of life yet on her flesh, the body still flexible and warm.

Late that night Mr. Hale summoned me to him, and before God did pledge me most solemnly to stand by him and not to compromise, even if all kith and kin were destroyed.

The next day I was surprised at his cheerfulness. I had thought he would be deeply shocked by this last tragedy, but all day he was high-spirited, as though at last he had found a way out of the frightful difficulty. The next morning we found him dead in his bed, a peaceful smile upon his careworn face.

Barely had I left that chamber of death, when—but too late—the following extraordinary letter was received:

OFFICE OF THE **M.** of **M.**, February 17, 1900.
MR. EBEN HALE, Money Baron:

Dear Sir,

You will pardon our intrusion, we hope, so closely upon the sad event of day before yesterday; but what we wish to say may be of the utmost importance to you. It is in our mind that you may attempt to escape us in death. But we wish to inform you that even this one way is barred. Note this: WE ARE PART AND PARCEL OF YOUR POSSESSIONS. WITH YOUR **MILLIONS** WE PASS DOWN TO YOUR HEIRS AND ASSIGNS FOREVER.

We are the inevitable. We are the culmination of industrial and social wrong. We turn upon the society that has created us. We are the creatures of a perverse social selection. We meet force with force. We believe in the survival of the fittest. You have crushed your wage slaves into the dirt and you have survived. The captains of war, at your command, have shot down like dogs your employees in a score of bloody strikes. By such means you have endured. We do not grumble at the result, for we acknowledge and have our being in the same natural law. And now the question has arisen: UNDER THE PRESENT SOCIAL ENVIRONMENT, WHICH OF US SHALL SURVIVE? We believe we are the fittest. You believe you are the fittest. We leave the eventuality to time and law.

Cordially yours,
THE MINIONS OF MIDAS

John, do you wonder now that I shunned pleasure and avoided friends? But why explain? Surely this narrative will make everything clear. Three weeks ago Adelaide Laidlaw died. Since then I have waited in hope and fear. Yesterday the will was probated and made public. Today I was notified that a woman of the middle class would be killed in Golden Gate Park, in faraway San Francisco.

It is useless. I cannot struggle against the inevitable. I have been faithful to Mr. Hale and have worked hard. Why my faithfulness should have been thus rewarded I cannot understand. I have willed the many millions I lately received to their rightful owners. Let the stalwart sons of Eben Hale work out their own salvation. Ere you read this I shall have passed on. The Minions of Midas are all-powerful. The police are impotent. I have learned from them that other millionnaires have been likewise persecuted—how many is not known, for when one yields to the M. of M., his mouth is thenceforth sealed. Those who have not yielded are even now reaping their scarlet harvest. The grim game is being played out. The Federal Government can do nothing. I also understand that similar organizations have made their appearance in Europe. Society is shaken to its foundations. Principalities and powers are as brands ripe for the burning. Instead of the masses against the classes, it is a class against the classes. We, the guardians of human progress, are being singled out and struck down. Law and order have failed.

The officials have begged me to keep this secret. I have done so, but can do so no longer. I shall do my duty before I leave this world by informing it of its peril. Do you, John, as my last request, make this public. The fate of humanity rests in your hand. Let the press strike off millions of copies; let the electric currents sweep it round the world; wherever men meet and speak, let them speak of it in fear and trembling. And then, when thoroughly aroused, let society arise in its might and cast out this abomination.

Yours, in long farewell,
Wade Atsheler

THE LEOPARD MAN'S STORY

by
JACK LONDON

adapted & illustrated by
RICK GEARY

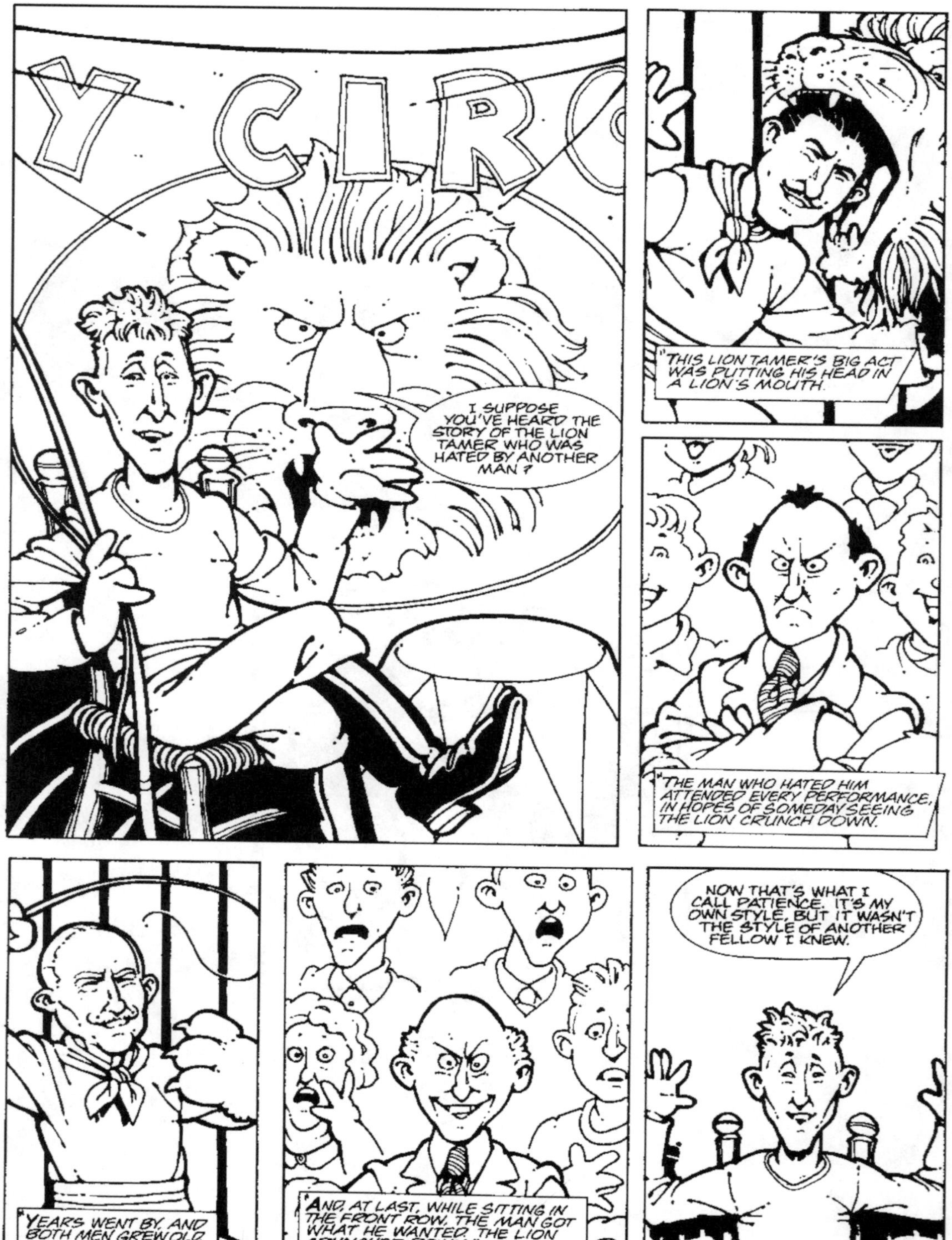

I SUPPOSE YOU'VE HEARD THE STORY OF THE LION TAMER WHO WAS HATED BY ANOTHER MAN ?
"THIS LION TAMER'S BIG ACT WAS PUTTING HIS HEAD IN A LION'S MOUTH.
"THE MAN WHO HATED HIM ATTENDED EVERY PERFORMANCE, IN HOPES OF SOMEDAY SEEING THE LION CRUNCH DOWN.
"YEARS WENT BY, AND BOTH MEN GREW OLD.
"AND, AT LAST, WHILE SITTING IN THE FRONT ROW, THE MAN GOT WHAT HE WANTED. THE LION CRUNCHED DOWN."
NOW THAT'S WHAT I CALL PATIENCE. IT'S MY OWN STYLE, BUT IT WASN'T THE STYLE OF ANOTHER FELLOW I KNEW.

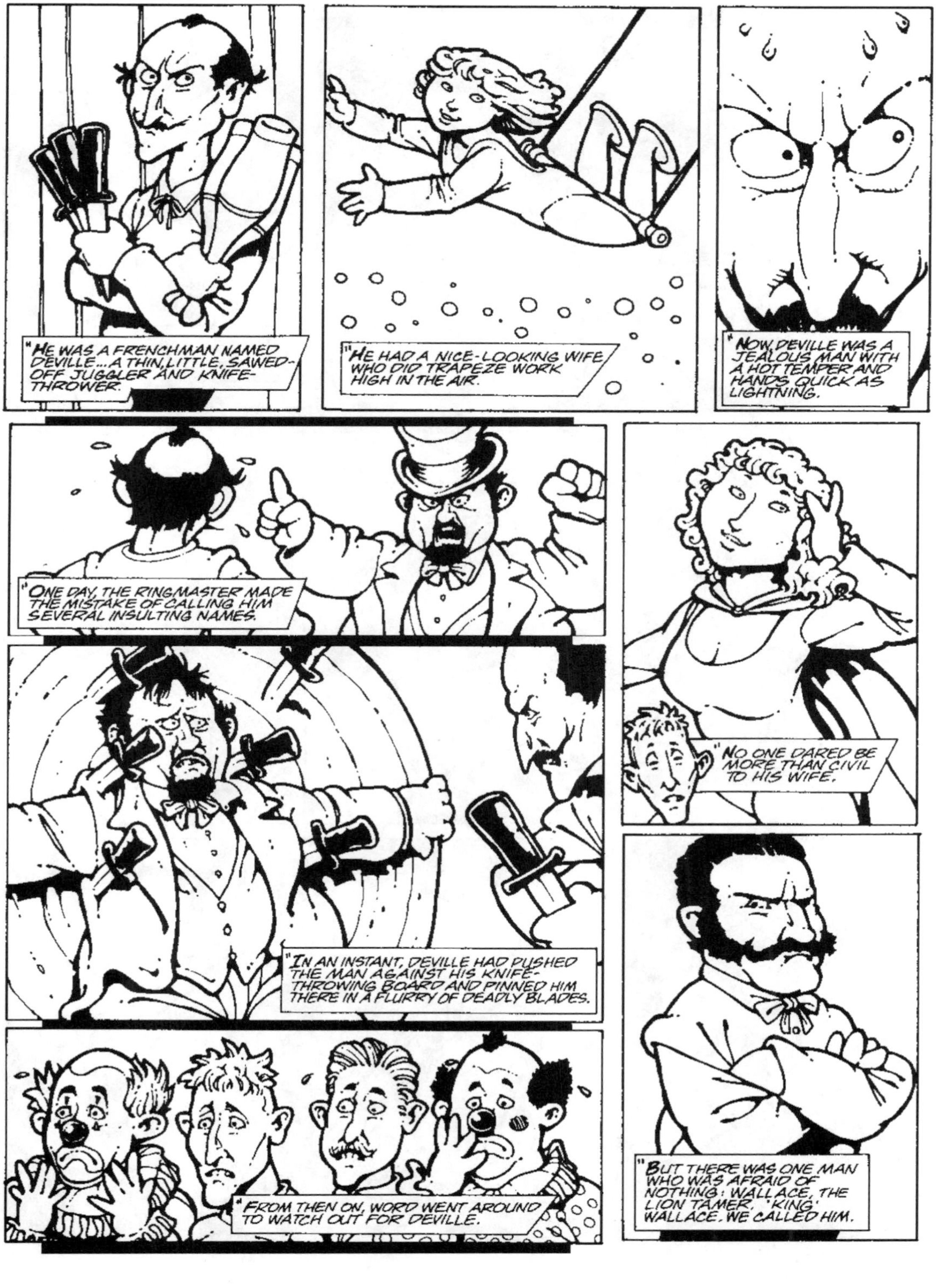
"HE WAS A FRENCHMAN NAMED DEVILLE... A THIN, LITTLE, SAWED-OFF JUGGLER AND KNIFE-THROWER.
"HE HAD A NICE-LOOKING WIFE WHO DID TRAPEZE WORK HIGH IN THE AIR.
"NOW, DEVILLE WAS A JEALOUS MAN WITH A HOT TEMPER AND HANDS QUICK AS LIGHTNING.
"ONE DAY, THE RINGMASTER MADE THE MISTAKE OF CALLING HIM SEVERAL INSULTING NAMES.
"NO ONE DARED BE MORE THAN CIVIL TO HIS WIFE.
"IN AN INSTANT, DEVILLE HAD PUSHED THE MAN AGAINST HIS KNIFE-THROWING BOARD AND PINNED HIM THERE IN A FLURRY OF DEADLY BLADES.
"FROM THEN ON, WORD WENT AROUND TO WATCH OUT FOR DEVILLE.
"BUT THERE WAS ONE MAN WHO WAS AFRAID OF NOTHING: WALLACE, THE LION TAMER. 'KING' WALLACE, WE CALLED HIM.

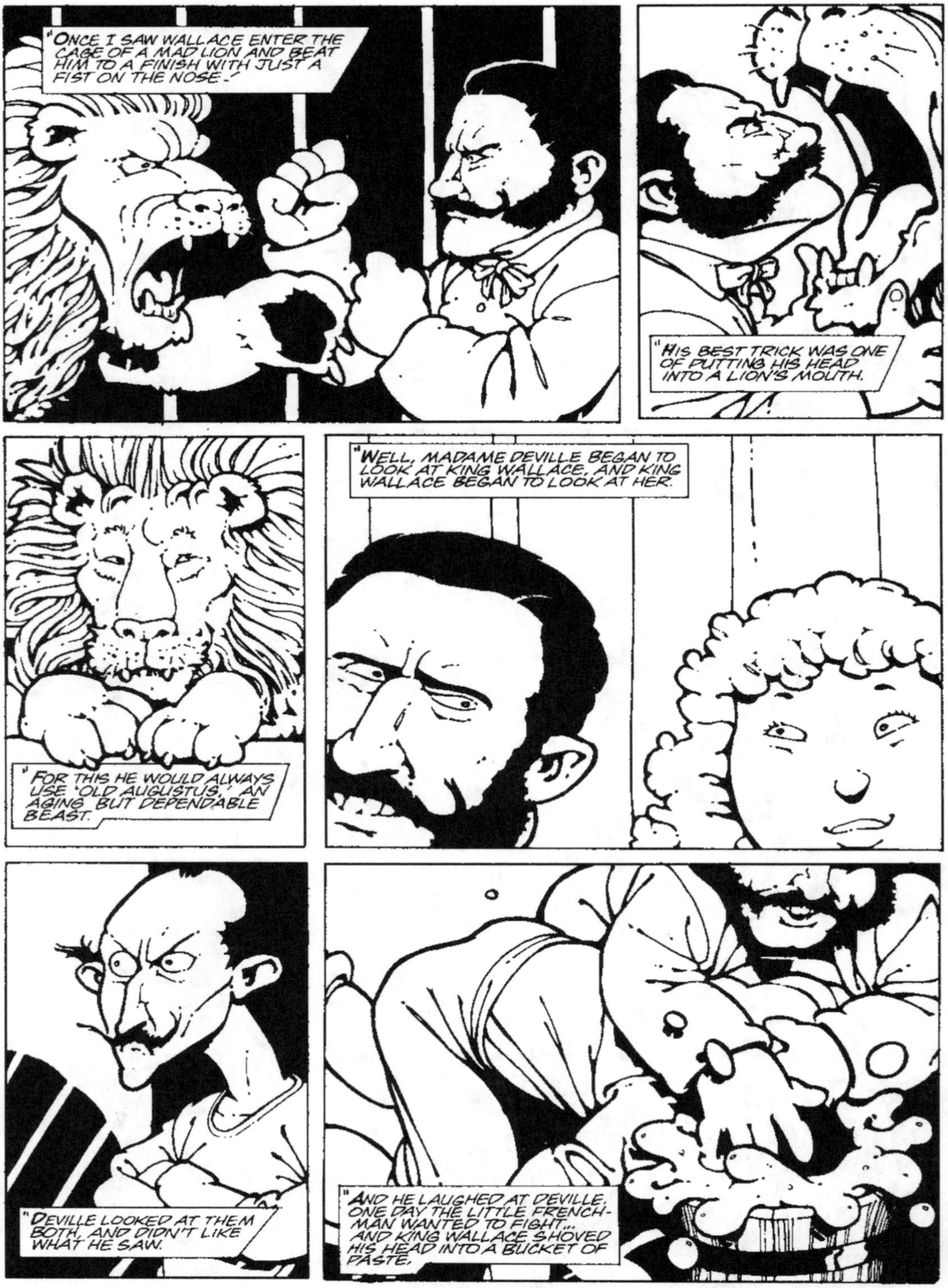
"ONCE I SAW WALLACE ENTER THE CAGE OF A MAD LION AND BEAT HIM TO A FINISH WITH JUST A FIST ON THE NOSE.-
"HIS BEST TRICK WAS ONE OF PUTTING HIS HEAD INTO A LION'S MOUTH.
"FOR THIS HE WOULD ALWAYS USE 'OLD AUGUSTUS,' AN AGING BUT DEPENDABLE BEAST.
"WELL, MADAME DEVILLE BEGAN TO LOOK AT KING WALLACE, AND KING WALLACE BEGAN TO LOOK AT HER.
"DEVILLE LOOKED AT THEM BOTH, AND DIDN'T LIKE WHAT HE SAW.
"AND HE LAUGHED AT DEVILLE. ONE DAY THE LITTLE FRENCH-MAN WANTED TO FIGHT... AND KING WALLACE SHOVED HIS HEAD INTO A BUCKET OF PASTE.

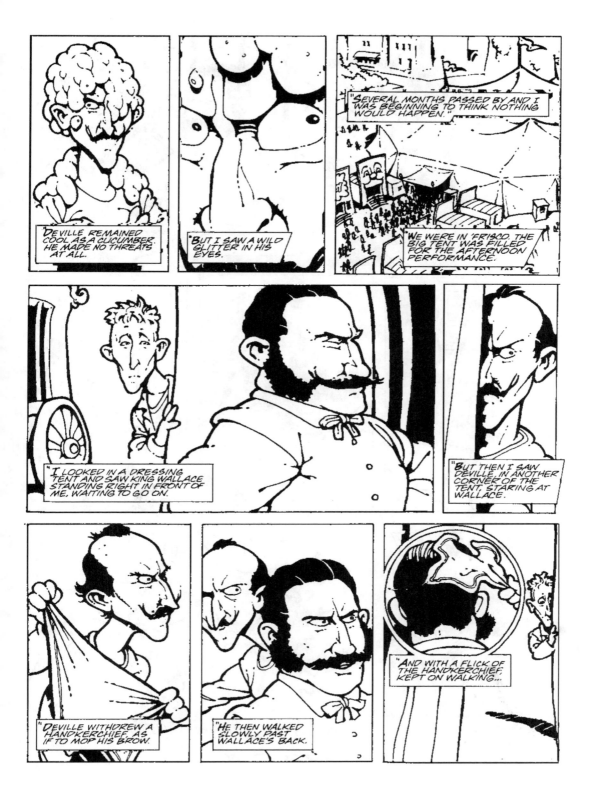

"DEVILLE REMAINED COOL AS A CUCUMBER. HE MADE NO THREATS AT ALL.

"BUT I SAW A WILD GLITTER IN HIS EYES.

"SEVERAL MONTHS PASSED BY AND I WAS BEGINNING TO THINK NOTHING WOULD HAPPEN."

WE WERE IN 'FRISCO. THE BIG TENT WAS FILLED FOR THE AFTERNOON PERFORMANCE.

"I LOOKED IN A DRESSING TENT AND SAW KING WALLACE STANDING RIGHT IN FRONT OF ME, WAITING TO GO ON.

"BUT THEN I SAW DEVILLE, IN ANOTHER CORNER OF THE TENT, STARING AT WALLACE.

"DEVILLE WITHDREW A HANDKERCHIEF, AS IF TO MOP HIS BROW.

"HE THEN WALKED SLOWLY PAST WALLACE'S BACK.

"AND WITH A FLICK OF THE HANDKERCHIEF, KEPT ON WALKING...

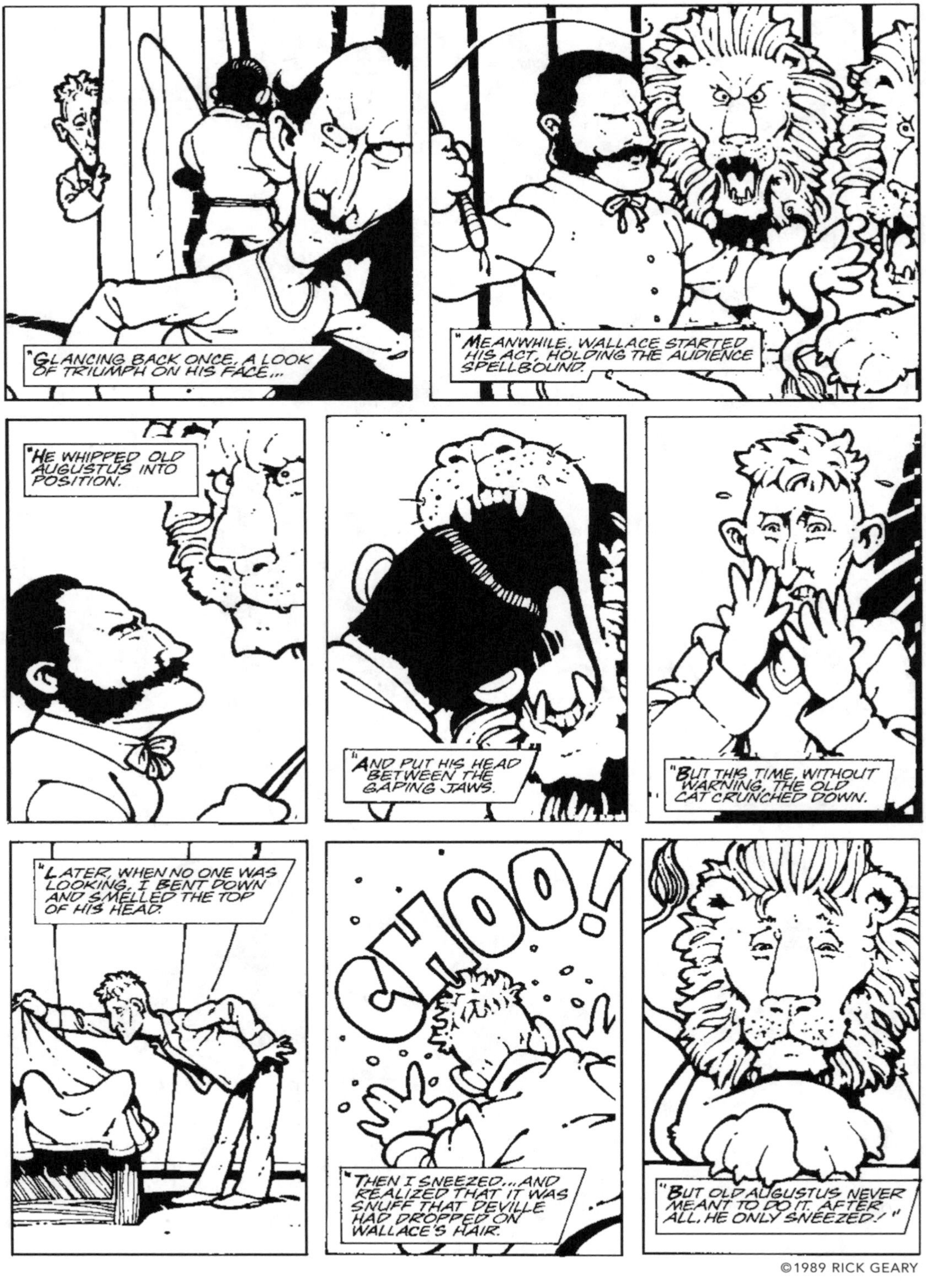
"GLANCING BACK ONCE, A LOOK OF TRIUMPH ON HIS FACE...
"MEANWHILE, WALLACE STARTED HIS ACT, HOLDING THE AUDIENCE SPELLBOUND.
"HE WHIPPED OLD AUGUSTUS INTO POSITION.
"AND PUT HIS HEAD BETWEEN THE GAPING JAWS.
"BUT THIS TIME, WITHOUT WARNING, THE OLD CAT CRUNCHED DOWN.
"LATER, WHEN NO ONE WAS LOOKING, I BENT DOWN AND SMELLED THE TOP OF HIS HEAD.
CHOO!
"THEN I SNEEZED... AND REALIZED THAT IT WAS SNUFF THAT DEVILLE HAD DROPPED ON WALLACE'S HAIR.
"BUT OLD AUGUSTUS NEVER MEANT TO DO IT. AFTER ALL, HE ONLY SNEEZED!"

The Handsome Cabin Boy

story by
JACK LONDON

adapted by
TRINA ROBBINS

illustrated by
ANNE TIMMONS

©2003 ANNE TIMMONS & TRINA ROBBINS

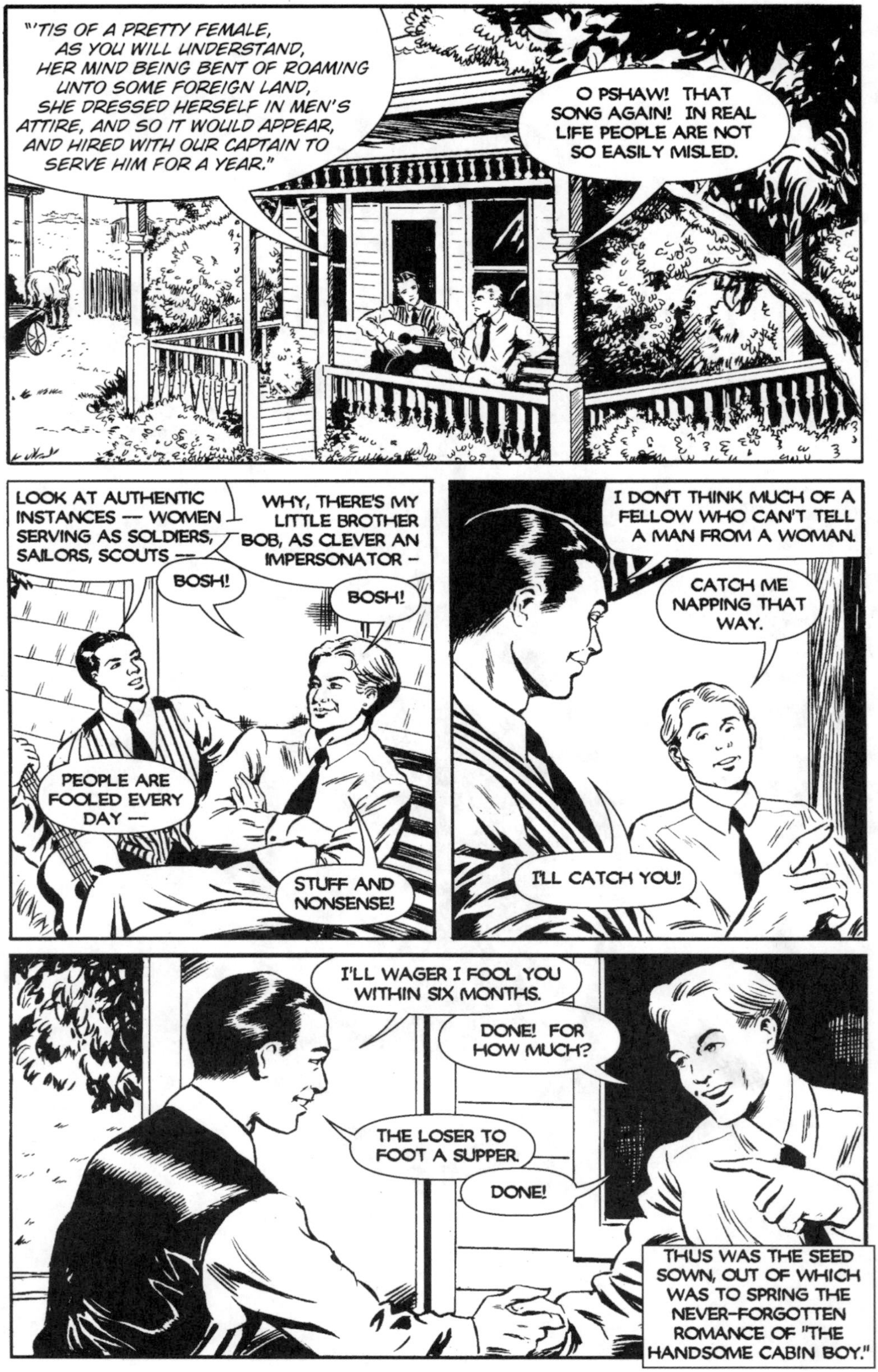
"'TIS OF A PRETTY FEMALE, AS YOU WILL UNDERSTAND, HER MIND BEING BENT OF ROAMING UNTO SOME FOREIGN LAND, SHE DRESSED HERSELF IN MEN'S ATTIRE, AND SO IT WOULD APPEAR, AND HIRED WITH OUR CAPTAIN TO SERVE HIM FOR A YEAR."
O PSHAW! THAT SONG AGAIN! IN REAL LIFE PEOPLE ARE NOT SO EASILY MISLED.
LOOK AT AUTHENTIC INSTANCES — WOMEN SERVING AS SOLDIERS, SAILORS, SCOUTS —
BOSH!
WHY, THERE'S MY LITTLE BROTHER BOB, AS CLEVER AN IMPERSONATOR –
BOSH!
PEOPLE ARE FOOLED EVERY DAY —
STUFF AND NONSENSE!
I DON'T THINK MUCH OF A FELLOW WHO CAN'T TELL A MAN FROM A WOMAN.
CATCH ME NAPPING THAT WAY.
I'LL CATCH YOU!
I'LL WAGER I FOOL YOU WITHIN SIX MONTHS.
DONE! FOR HOW MUCH?
THE LOSER TO FOOT A SUPPER.
DONE!
THUS WAS THE SEED SOWN, OUT OF WHICH WAS TO SPRING THE NEVER-FORGOTTEN ROMANCE OF "THE HANDSOME CABIN BOY."

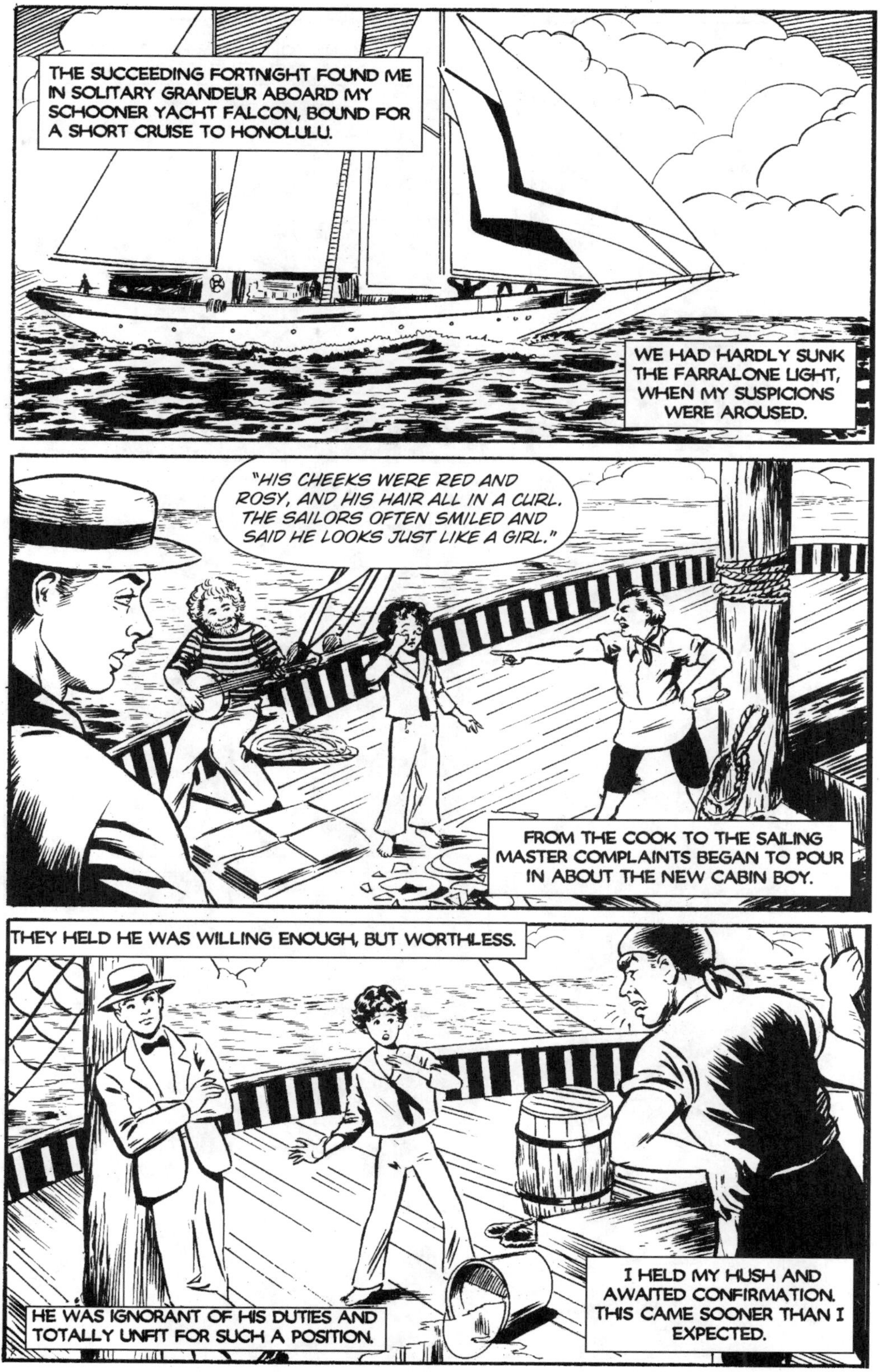
THE SUCCEEDING FORTNIGHT FOUND ME IN SOLITARY GRANDEUR ABOARD MY SCHOONER YACHT FALCON, BOUND FOR A SHORT CRUISE TO HONOLULU.
WE HAD HARDLY SUNK THE FARRALONE LIGHT, WHEN MY SUSPICIONS WERE AROUSED.
"HIS CHEEKS WERE RED AND ROSY, AND HIS HAIR ALL IN A CURL. THE SAILORS OFTEN SMILED AND SAID HE LOOKS JUST LIKE A GIRL."
FROM THE COOK TO THE SAILING MASTER COMPLAINTS BEGAN TO POUR IN ABOUT THE NEW CABIN BOY.
THEY HELD HE WAS WILLING ENOUGH, BUT WORTHLESS.
HE WAS IGNORANT OF HIS DUTIES AND TOTALLY UNFIT FOR SUCH A POSITION.
I HELD MY HUSH AND AWAITED CONFIRMATION. THIS CAME SOONER THAN I EXPECTED.

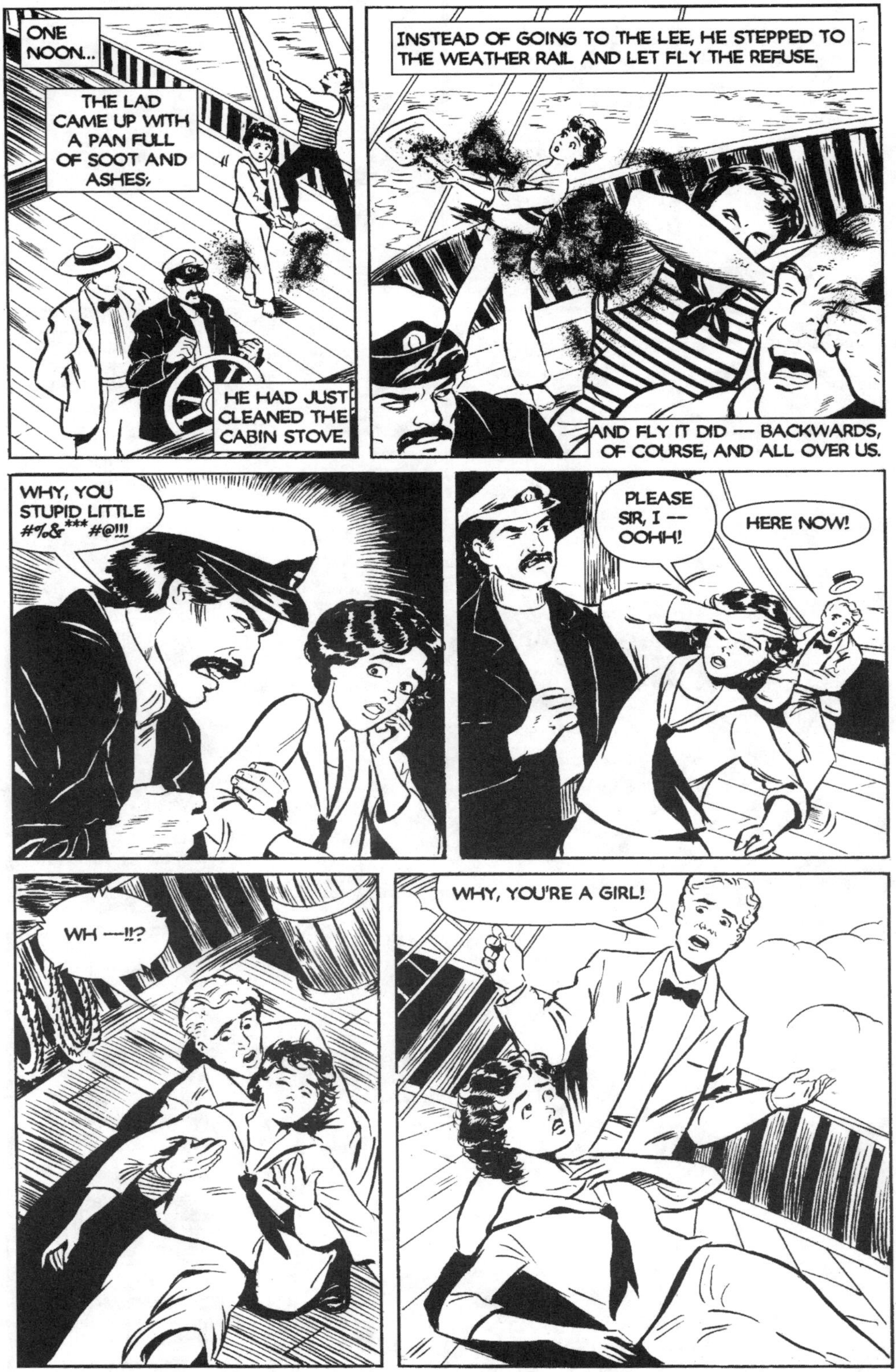
ONE NOON...
THE LAD CAME UP WITH A PAN FULL OF SOOT AND ASHES;
HE HAD JUST CLEANED THE CABIN STOVE.
INSTEAD OF GOING TO THE LEE, HE STEPPED TO THE WEATHER RAIL AND LET FLY THE REFUSE.
AND FLY IT DID — BACKWARDS, OF COURSE, AND ALL OVER US.
WHY, YOU STUPID LITTLE #%&*** #@!!!
PLEASE SIR, I — OOHH!
HERE NOW!
WH —!!?
WHY, YOU'RE A GIRL!

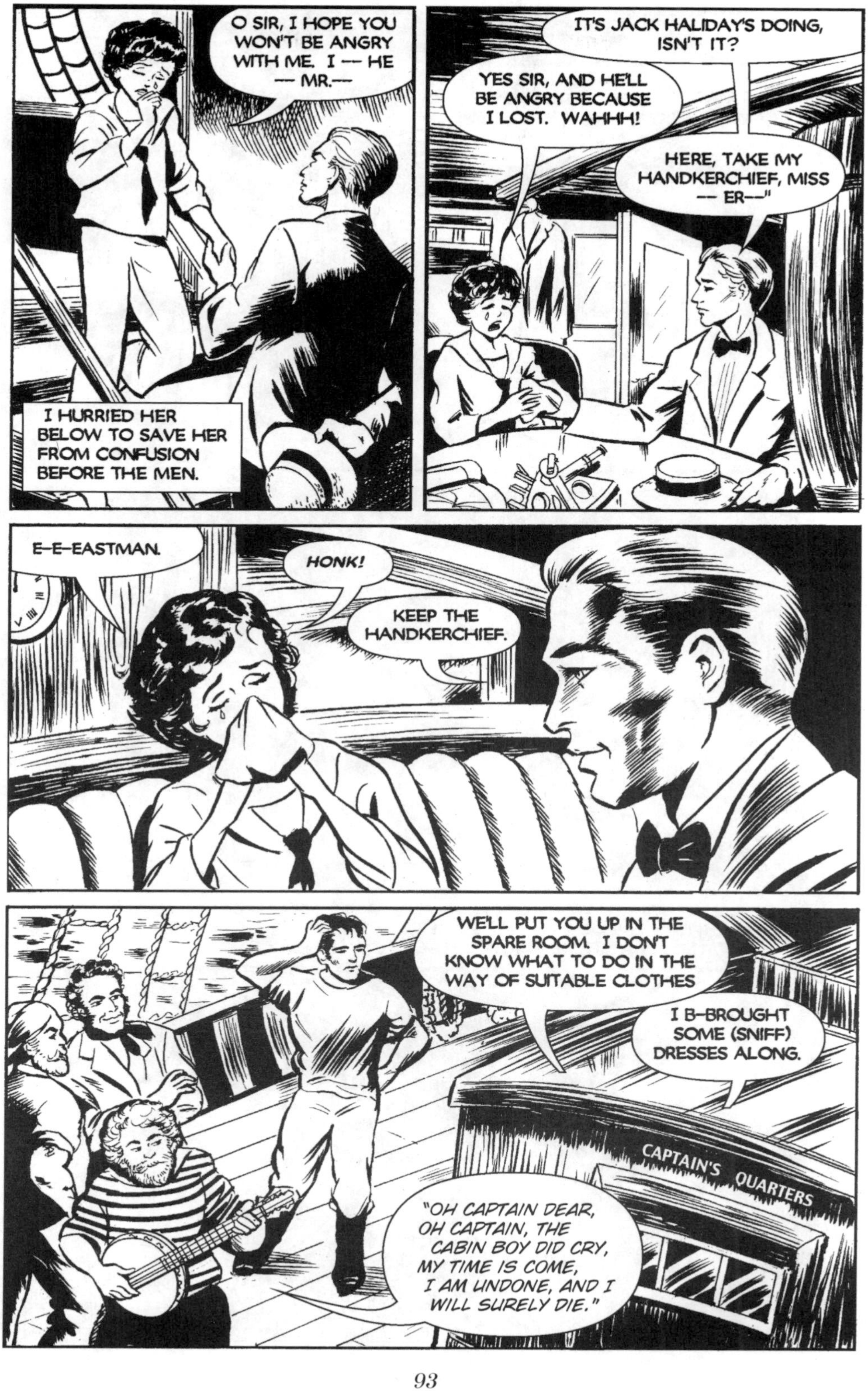
O SIR, I HOPE YOU WON'T BE ANGRY WITH ME. I -- HE -- MR.--
I HURRIED HER BELOW TO SAVE HER FROM CONFUSION BEFORE THE MEN.
IT'S JACK HALIDAY'S DOING, ISN'T IT?
YES SIR, AND HE'LL BE ANGRY BECAUSE I LOST. WAHHH!
HERE, TAKE MY HANDKERCHIEF, MISS -- ER--"
E-E-EASTMAN.
HONK!
KEEP THE HANDKERCHIEF.
WE'LL PUT YOU UP IN THE SPARE ROOM. I DON'T KNOW WHAT TO DO IN THE WAY OF SUITABLE CLOTHES
I B-BROUGHT SOME (SNIFF) DRESSES ALONG.
CAPTAIN'S QUARTERS
"OH CAPTAIN DEAR, OH CAPTAIN, THE CABIN BOY DID CRY, MY TIME IS COME, I AM UNDONE, AND I WILL SURELY DIE."

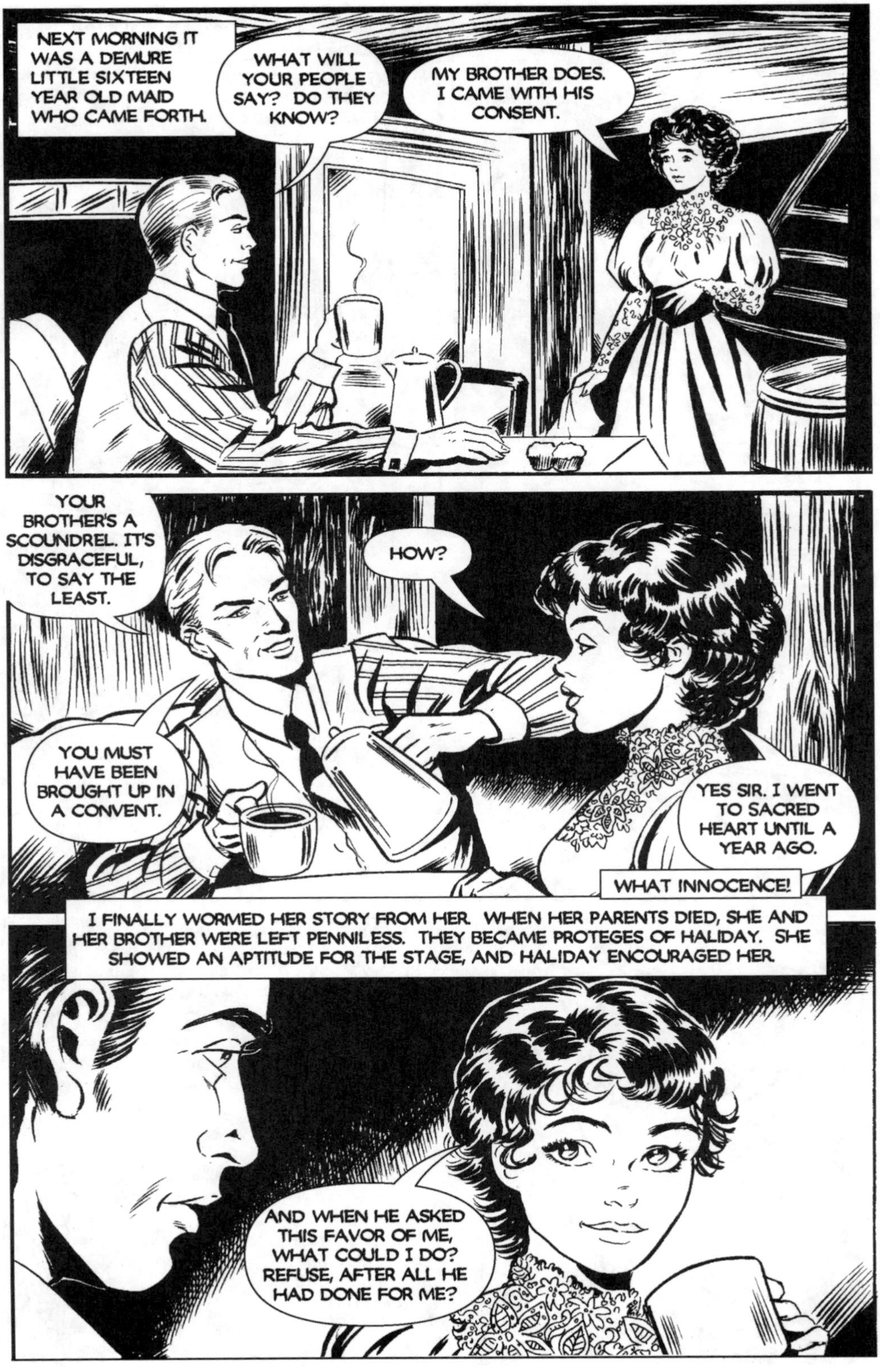
NEXT MORNING IT WAS A DEMURE LITTLE SIXTEEN YEAR OLD MAID WHO CAME FORTH.
WHAT WILL YOUR PEOPLE SAY? DO THEY KNOW?
MY BROTHER DOES. I CAME WITH HIS CONSENT.
YOUR BROTHER'S A SCOUNDREL. IT'S DISGRACEFUL, TO SAY THE LEAST.
HOW?
YOU MUST HAVE BEEN BROUGHT UP IN A CONVENT.
YES SIR. I WENT TO SACRED HEART UNTIL A YEAR AGO.
WHAT INNOCENCE!
I FINALLY WORMED HER STORY FROM HER. WHEN HER PARENTS DIED, SHE AND HER BROTHER WERE LEFT PENNILESS. THEY BECAME PROTEGES OF HALIDAY. SHE SHOWED AN APTITUDE FOR THE STAGE, AND HALIDAY ENCOURAGED HER.
AND WHEN HE ASKED THIS FAVOR OF ME, WHAT COULD I DO? REFUSE, AFTER ALL HE HAD DONE FOR ME?

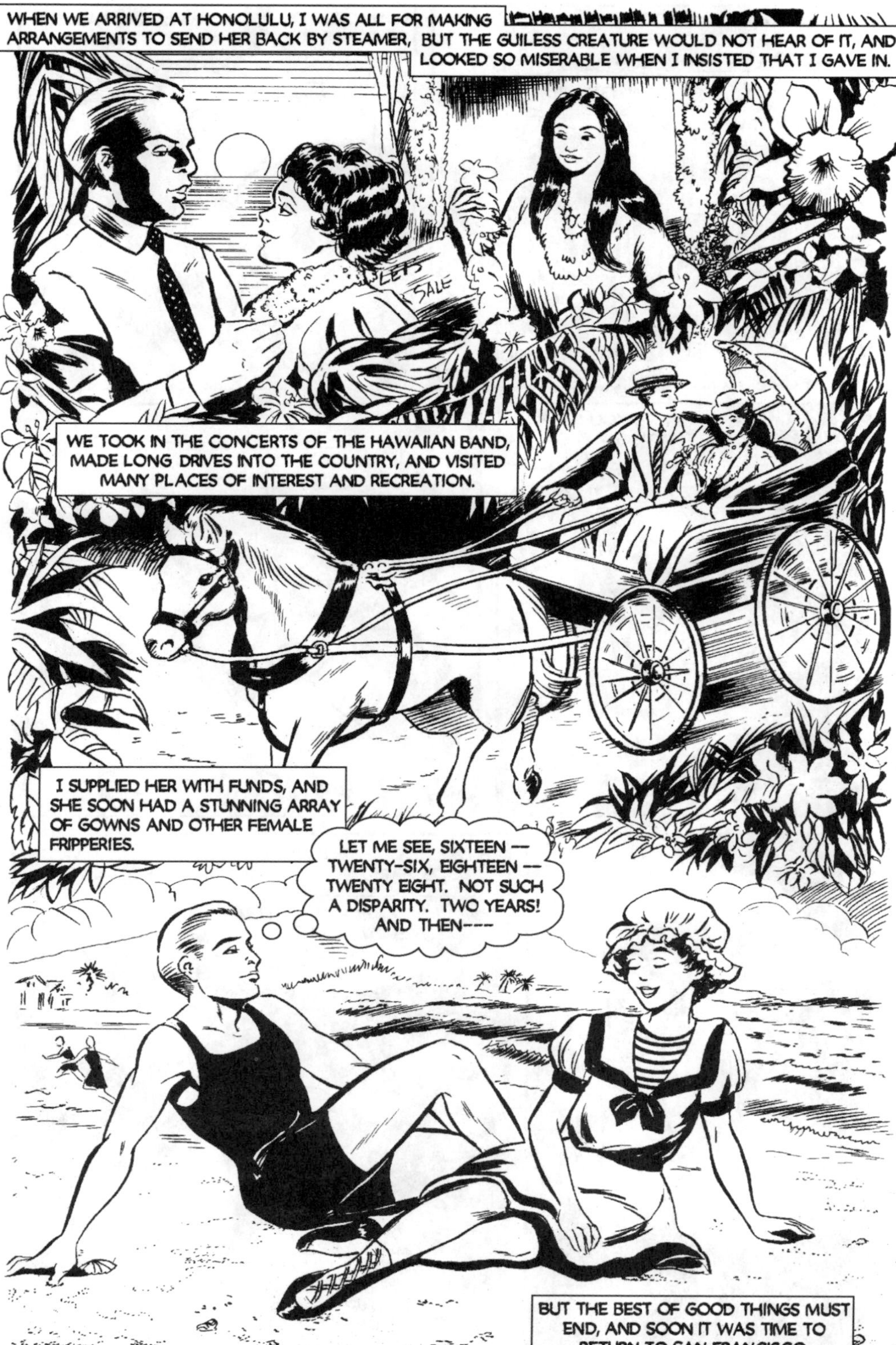
WHEN WE ARRIVED AT HONOLULU, I WAS ALL FOR MAKING ARRANGEMENTS TO SEND HER BACK BY STEAMER,
BUT THE GUILESS CREATURE WOULD NOT HEAR OF IT, AND LOOKED SO MISERABLE WHEN I INSISTED THAT I GAVE IN.
WE TOOK IN THE CONCERTS OF THE HAWAIIAN BAND, MADE LONG DRIVES INTO THE COUNTRY, AND VISITED MANY PLACES OF INTEREST AND RECREATION.
I SUPPLIED HER WITH FUNDS, AND SHE SOON HAD A STUNNING ARRAY OF GOWNS AND OTHER FEMALE FRIPPERIES.
LET ME SEE, SIXTEEN -- TWENTY-SIX, EIGHTEEN -- TWENTY EIGHT. NOT SUCH A DISPARITY. TWO YEARS! AND THEN---
BUT THE BEST OF GOOD THINGS MUST END, AND SOON IT WAS TIME TO RETURN TO SAN FRANCISCO.

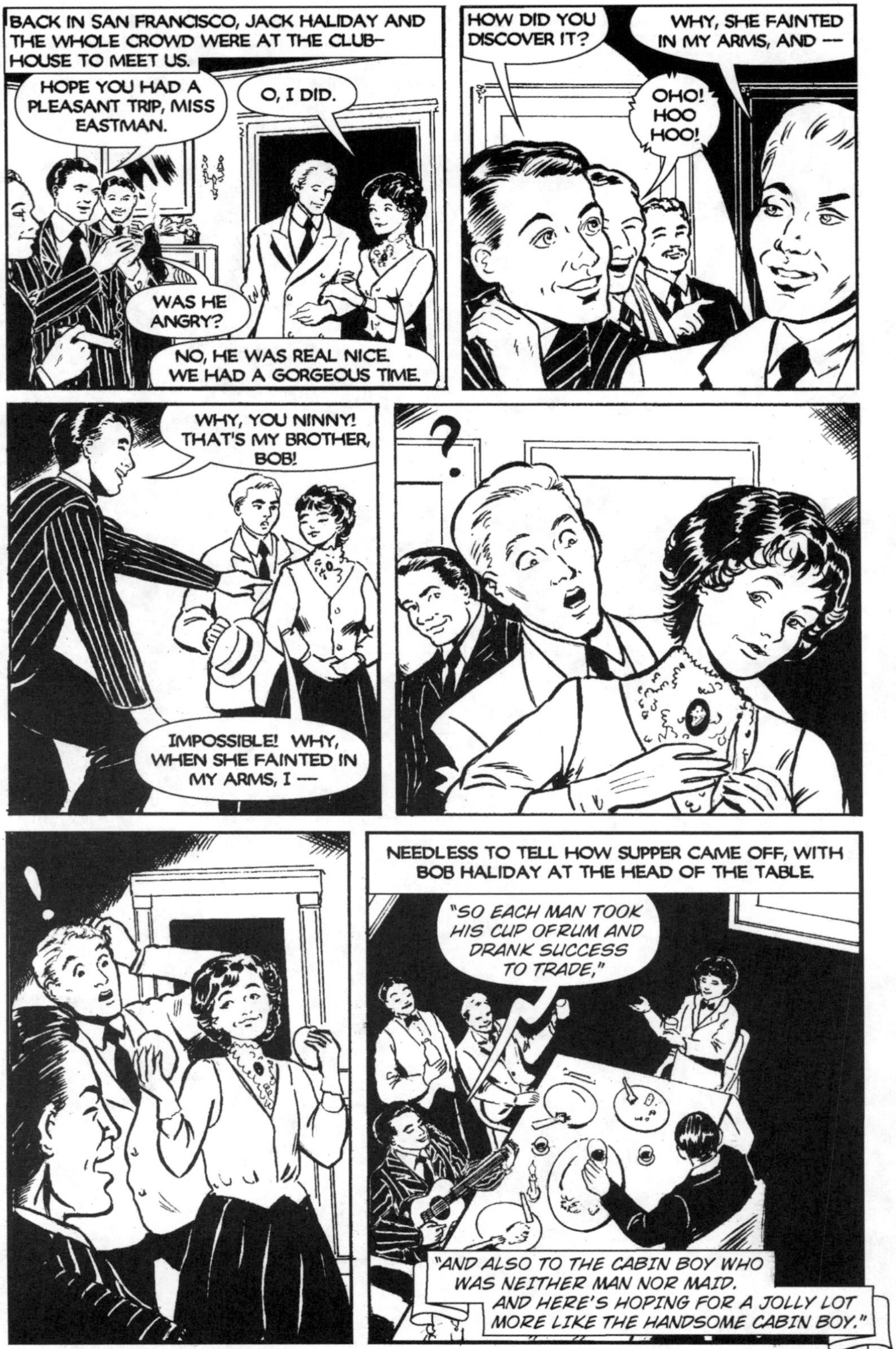
BACK IN SAN FRANCISCO, JACK HALIDAY AND THE WHOLE CROWD WERE AT THE CLUB-HOUSE TO MEET US.
HOPE YOU HAD A PLEASANT TRIP, MISS EASTMAN.
O, I DID.
WAS HE ANGRY?
NO, HE WAS REAL NICE. WE HAD A GORGEOUS TIME.
HOW DID YOU DISCOVER IT?
WHY, SHE FAINTED IN MY ARMS, AND —
OHO! HOO HOO!
WHY, YOU NINNY! THAT'S MY BROTHER, BOB!
IMPOSSIBLE! WHY, WHEN SHE FAINTED IN MY ARMS, I —
?
!
NEEDLESS TO TELL HOW SUPPER CAME OFF, WITH BOB HALIDAY AT THE HEAD OF THE TABLE.
"SO EACH MAN TOOK HIS CUP OFRUM AND DRANK SUCCESS TO TRADE,"
"AND ALSO TO THE CABIN BOY WHO WAS NEITHER MAN NOR MAID.
AND HERE'S HOPING FOR A JOLLY LOT MORE LIKE THE HANDSOME CABIN BOY."

The Handsome Cabin Boy

Traditional Sea Chantey

'Tis of a pret-ty fe- male, as you will un- der stand, Her mind being bent of

ro- a- ming un- to some for- eign land, She dressed her- self in men's at- tire or

so it does ap- pear, And hi- red with our cap- tain to serve him for a year.

The captain's wife, she being on board, she seemed in great joy,
To think her husband had engaged such a handsome cabin boy.
And now and then she'd slip him a kiss, and she would 'a liked to toy,
But was the captain found out the secret of the handsome cabin boy.

His cheeks were red and rosy, and his hair all in a curl.
The sailors often smiled and said, "he looks just like a girl."
But eating of the captain's biscuit, her color did destroy,
And the waist did swell of pretty Nell, the handsome cabin boy.

It was in the Bay of Biscayne, our gallant ship did plough.
One night among the sailors was a fearful flurry and row.
They tumbled from their hammocks, for sleep it did destroy.
They swore about the groaning of the handsome cabin boy.

"Oh captain dear, oh captain", the cabin boy did cry,
"My time is come, I am undone, and I will surely die."
The doctor came a-runnin', and smilin' at the fun,
To think a sailor lad should have a daughter or a son.

The sailors, when they saw the joke, they all did stand and stare.
The child belonged to none of them, they solemnly did swear.
The captain's wife she says to him "My dear I wish you joy,
For it's either you or me's betrayed the handsome cabin boy."

So each man took his cup of rum, and drank success to trade,
And also to the cabin boy, who was neither man nor maid.
"Here's hoping wars don't rise again, our sailors to destroy,
And here's hoping for a jolly lot more like the handsome cabin boy."

TOLD IN THE DROOLING WARD

story by

JACK LONDON

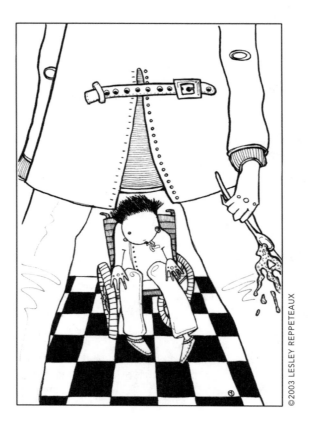

illustrated by

LESLEY REPPETEAUX

Me? I'm not a drooler. I'm the assistant. I don't know what Miss Jones or Miss Kelsey could do without me. There are fifty-five low-grade droolers in this ward, and how could they ever all be fed if I wasn't around? I like to feed droolers. They don't make trouble. They can't. Something's wrong with most of their legs and arms, and they can't talk. They're very low-grade. I can walk, and talk, and do things. You must be careful with the droolers and not feed them too fast. Then they choke. Miss Jones says I'm an expert. When a new nurse comes I show her how to do it. It's funny watching a new nurse try to feed them. She goes at it so slow and careful that supper time would be around before she finished shoving down their breakfast. Then I show her, because I'm an expert. Doctor Dalrymple says I am, and he ought to know. A drooler can eat twice as fast if you know how to make him.

My name's Tom. I'm twenty-eight years old. Everybody knows me in the institution. This is an institution, you know. It belongs to the State of California and is run by politics. I know. I've been here a long time. Everybody trusts me. I run errands all over the place, when I'm not busy with the droolers. I like droolers. It makes me think how lucky I am that I ain't a drooler.

I like it here in the Home. I don't like the outside. I know. I've been around a bit, and run away, and adopted. Me for the Home, and for the drooling ward best of all. I don't look like a drooler, do I? You can tell the difference soon as you look at me. I'm an assistant, expert assistant. That's going some for a feeb. Feeb? Oh, that's feeble-minded. I thought you knew. We're all feebs in here.

But I'm a high-grade feeb. Doctor Dalrymple says I'm too smart to be in the Home, but I never let on. It's a pretty good place. And I don't throw fits like lots of the feebs. You see that house up there through the trees. The high-grade epilecs all live in it by themselves. They're stuck up because they ain't just ordinary feebs. They call it the club house, and they say they're just as good as anybody outside, only they're sick. I don't like them much. They laugh at me, when they ain't busy throwing fits. But I don't care. I never have to be scared about falling down and busting my head. Sometimes they run around in circles trying to find a place to sit down quick, only they don't. Low-grade epilecs are disgusting, and high-grade epilecs put on airs. I'm glad I ain't an epilec. There ain't anything to them. They just talk big, that's all.

Miss Kelsey says I talk too much. But I talk sense, and that's more than the other feebs do. Doctor Dalrymple says I have the gift of language. I know it. You ought to hear me talk when I'm by myself, or when I've got a drooler to listen. Sometimes I think I'd like to be a politician, only it's too much trouble. They're all great talkers; that's how they hold their jobs.

Nobody's crazy in this institution. They're just feeble in their minds. Let me tell you something funny. There's about a dozen high-grade girls that set the tables in the big dining room. Sometimes when they're done ahead of time, they all sit down in chairs in a circle and talk. I sneak up to the door and listen, and I nearly die to keep from laughing. Do you want to know what they talk? It's like this. They don't say a word for a long time. And then one says, "Thank God I'm not feeble-minded." And all the rest nod their heads and look pleased. And then nobody says anything for a time. After which the next girl in the circle says, "Thank God I'm not feeble-minded," and they nod their heads all over again. And it goes on around the circle, and they never say anything else. Now they're real feebs, ain't they? I leave it to you. I'm not that kind of a feeb, thank God.

Sometimes I don't think I'm a feeb at all. I play in the band and read music. We're all supposed to be feebs in the band except the leader. He's crazy. We know it, but we never talk about it except amongst ourselves. His job is politics, too, and we don't want him to lose it. I play the drum. They can't get along without me in this institution. I was sick once, so I know. It's a wonder the drooling ward didn't break down while I was in hospital.

I could get out of here if I wanted to. I'm not so feeble as some might think. But I don't let on. I have too good a time. Besides, everything would run down if I went away. I'm afraid some time they'll find out I'm not a feeb and send me out into the world to earn my own living. I know the world, and I don't like it. The Home is fine enough for me.

You see how I grin sometimes. I can't help that. But I can put it on a lot. I'm not bad, though. I look at myself in the glass. My mouth

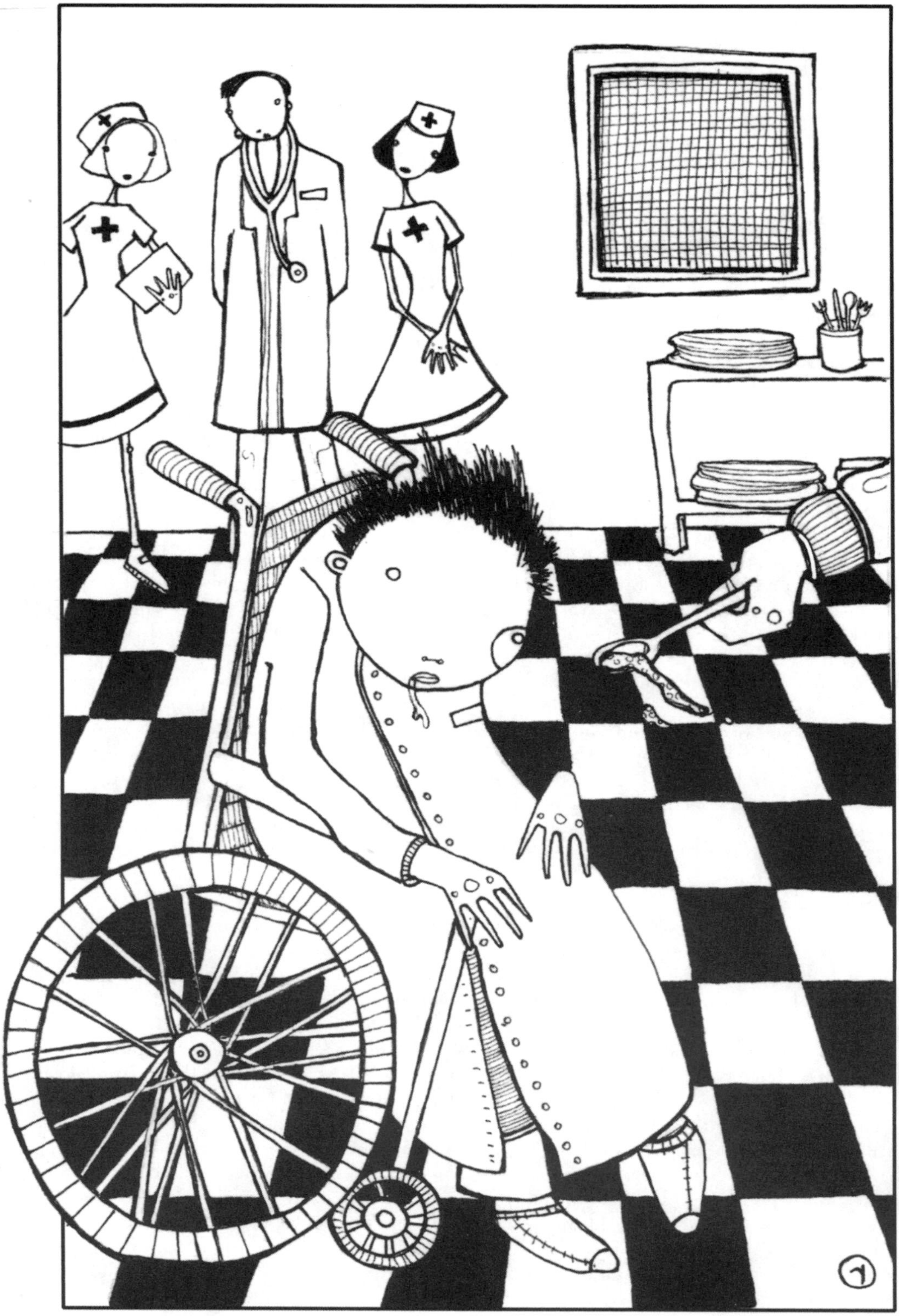

is funny, I know that, and it lops down, and my teeth are bad. You can tell a feeb anywhere by looking at his mouth and teeth. But that doesn't prove I'm a feeb. It's just because I'm lucky that I look like one.

I know a lot. If I told you all I know, you'd be surprised. But when I don't want to know, or when they want me to do something I don't want to do, I just let my mouth lop down and laugh and make foolish noises. I watch the foolish noises made by the low-grades, and I can fool anybody. And I know a lot of foolish noises. Miss Kelsey called me a fool the other day. She was very angry, and that was where I fooled her.

Miss Kelsey asked me once why I don't write a book about feebs. I was telling her what was the matter with little Albert. He's a drooler, you know, and I can always tell the way he twists his left eye what's the matter with him. So I was explaining it to Miss Kelsey, and, because she didn't know, it made her mad. But some day, mebbe, I'll write that book. Only it's so much trouble. Besides, I'd sooner talk.

Do you know what a micro is? It's the kind with the little heads no bigger than your fist. They're usually droolers, and they live a long time. The hydros don't drool. They have the big heads, and they're smarter. But they never grow up. They always die. I never look at one without thinking he's going to die. Sometimes, when I'm feeling lazy, or the nurse is mad at me, I wish I was a drooler with nothing to do and somebody to feed me. But I guess I'd sooner talk and be what I am.

Only yesterday Doctor Dalrymple said to me, "Tom," he said, "just don't know what I'd do without you." And he ought to know, seeing as he's had the bossing of a thousand feebs for going on two years. Doctor Whatcomb was before him. They get appointed, you know. It's politics. I've seen a whole lot of doctors here in my time. I was here before any of them. I've been in this institution twenty-five years. No, I've got no complaints. The institution couldn't be run better.

It's a snap to be a high-grade feeb. Just look at Doctor Dalrymple. He has troubles. He holds his job by politics. You bet we high-graders talk politics. We know all about it, and it's bad. An institution like this oughtn't to be run on politics. Look at Doctor Dalrymple. He's been here two years and learned a lot.

Then politics will come along and throw him out and send a new doctor who don't know anything about feebs.

I've been acquainted with just thousands of nurses in my time. Some of them are nice. But they come and go. Most of the women get married. Sometimes I think I'd like to get married. I spoke to Doctor Whatcomb about it once, but he told me he was very sorry, because feebs ain't allowed to get married. I've been in love. She was a nurse, I won't tell you her name. She had blue eyes, and yellow hair, and a kind voice, and she liked me. She told me so. And she always told me to be a good boy. And I was, too, until afterward, and then I ran away. You see, she went off and got married, and she didn't tell me about it.

I guess being married ain't what it's cracked up to be. Doctor Anglin and his wife used to fight. I've seen them. And once I heard her call him a feeb. Now nobody has a right to call anybody a feeb that ain't. Dr. Anglin got awful mad when she called him that. But he didn't last long. Politics drove him out, and Doctor Mandeville came. He didn't have a wife. I heard him talking one time with the engineer. The engineer and his wife fought like cats and dogs, and that day Doctor Mandeville told him he was damn glad he wasn't tied to no petticoats. A petticoat is a skirt. I knew what he meant, if I was a feeb. But never let on. You hear lots when you don't let on.

I've seen a lot in my time. Once I was adopted, and went away on the railroad over forty miles to live with a man named Peter Bopp and his wife. They had a ranch. Doctor Anglin said I was strong and bright, and I said I was, too. That was because I wanted to be adopted. And Peter Bopp said he'd give me a good home, and the lawyers fixed up the papers.

But I soon made up my mind that a ranch was no place for me. Mrs. Bopp was scared to death of me and wouldn't let me sleep in the house. They fixed up the woodshed and made me sleep there. I had to get up at four o'clock and feed the horses, and milk cows, and carry the milk to the neighbours. They called it chores, but it kept me going all day. I chopped wood, and cleaned chicken houses, and weeded vegetables, and did most everything on the place. I never had any fun. I hadn't no time.

Let me tell you one thing. I'd sooner feed mush and milk to feebs than milk cows with the frost on the ground. Mrs. Bopp was scared to let me play with her children. And I was scared, too. They used to make faces at me when nobody was looking, and call me "Looney." Everybody called me Looney Tom. And the other boys in the neighbourhood threw rocks at me. You never see anything like that in the Home here. The feebs are better behaved.

Mrs. Bopp used to pinch me and pull my hair when she thought I was too slow, and I only made foolish noises and went slower. She said I'd be the death of her some day. I left the boards off the old well in the pasture, and the pretty new calf fell in and got drowned. Then Peter Bopp said he was going to give me a licking. He did, too. He took a strap halter and went at me. It was awful. I'd never had a licking in my life. They don't do such things in the Home, which is why I say the Home is the place for me.

I know the law, and I knew he had no right to lick me with a strap halter. That was being cruel, and the guardianship papers said he mustn't be cruel. I didn't say anything. I just waited, which shows you what kind of a feeb I am. I waited a long time, and got slower, and made more foolish noises; but he wouldn't send me back to the Home, which was what I wanted. But one day, it was the first of the month, Mrs. Brown gave me three dollars, which was for her milk bill with Peter Bopp. That was in the morning. When I brought the milk in the evening I was to bring back the receipt. But I didn't. I just walked down to the station, bought a ticket like any one, and rode on the train back to the Home. That's the kind of a feeb I am.

Doctor Anglin was gone then, and Doctor Mandeville had his place. I walked right into his office. He didn't know me. "Hello," he said, "this ain't visiting day." "I ain't a visitor," I said. "I'm Tom. I belong here." Then he whistled and showed he was surprised. I told him all about it, and showed him the marks of the strap halter, and he got madder and madder all the time and said he'd attend to Mr. Peter Bopp's case.

And mebbe you think some of them little droolers weren't glad to see me.

I walked right into the ward. There was a new nurse feeding little Albert. "Hold on," I said. "That ain't the way. Don't you see how he's twisting that left eye? Let me show you." Mebbe she thought I was a new doctor, for she just gave me the spoon, and I guess I filled

little Albert up with the most comfortable meal he'd had since I went away. Droolers ain't bad when you understand them. I heard Miss Jones tell Miss Kelsey once that I had an amazing gift in handling droolers.

Some day, mebbe, I'm going to talk with Doctor Dalrymple and get him to give me a declaration that I ain't a feeb. Then I'll get him to make me a real assistant in the drooling ward, with forty dollars a month and my board. And then I'll marry Miss Jones and live right on here. And if she won't have me, I'll marry Miss Kelsey or some other nurse. There's lots of them that want to get married. And I won't care if my wife gets mad and calls me a feeb. What's the good? And I guess when one's learned to put up with droolers a wife won't be much worse.

I didn't tell you about when I ran away. I hadn't no idea of such a thing, and it was Charley and Joe who put me up to it. They're high-grade epilecs, you know. I'd been up to Doctor Wilson's office with a message, and was going back to the drooling ward, when I saw Charley and Joe hiding around the corner of the gymnasium and making motions to me. I went over to them.

"Hello," Joe said. "How's droolers?"

"Fine," I said. "Had any fits lately?"

That made them mad, and I was going on, when Joe said, "We're running away. Come on."

"What for?" I said.

"We're going up over the top of the mountain," Joe said.

"And find a gold mine," said Charley. "We don't have fits any more. We're cured."

"All right," I said. And we sneaked around back of the gymnasium and in among the trees. Mebbe we walked along about ten minutes, when I stopped.

"What's the matter?" said Joe.

"Wait," I said. "I got to go back."

"What for?" said Joe.

And I said, "To get little Albert."

And they said I couldn't, and got mad. But I didn't care. I knew they'd wait. You see, I've been here twenty-five years, and I know the back trails that lead up the mountain, and Charley and Joe didn't know those trails. That's why they wanted me to come.

So I went back and got little Albert. He can't walk, or talk, or do anything except drool, and I had to carry him in my arms. We went

on past the last hayfield, which was as far as I'd ever gone. Then the woods and brush got so thick, and me not finding any more trail, we followed the cow-path down to a big creek and crawled through the fence which showed where the Home land stopped.

We climbed up the big hill on the other side of the creek. It was all big trees, and no brush, but it was so steep and slippery with dead leaves we could hardly walk. By and by we came to a real bad place. It was forty feet across, and if you slipped you'd fall a thousand feet, or mebbe a hundred. Anyway, you wouldn't fall — just slide. I went across first, carrying little Albert. Joe came next. But Charley got scared right in the middle and sat down.

"I'm going to have a fit," he said.

"No, you're not," said Joe. "Because if you was you wouldn't 'a sat down. You take all your fits standing."

"This is a different kind of a fit," said Charley, beginning to cry.

He shook and shook, but just because he wanted to he couldn't scare up the least kind of a fit.

Joe got mad and used awful language. But that didn't help none. So I talked soft and kind to Charley. That's the way to handle feebs. If you get mad, they get worse. I know. I'm that way myself. That's why I was almost the death of Mrs. Bopp. She got mad.

It was getting along in the afternoon, and I knew we had to be on our way, so I said to

Joe: "Here, stop your cussing and hold Albert. I'll go back and get him."

And I did, too; but he was so scared and dizzy he crawled along on hands and knees while I helped him. When I got him across and took Albert back in my arms, I heard somebody laugh and looked down. And there was a man and woman on horseback looking up at us. He had a gun on his saddle, and it was her who was laughing.

"Who in hell's that?" said Joe, getting scared. "Somebody to catch us?"

"Shut up your cussing," I said to him. "That is the man who owns this ranch and writes books."

"How do you do, Mr. Endicott," I said down to him.

"Hello," he said. "What are you doing here?"

"We're running away," I said.

And he said, "Good luck. But be sure and get back before dark."

"But this is a real running away," I said.

And then both he and his wife laughed.

"All right," he said. "Good luck just the same. But watch out the bears and mountain lions don't get you when it gets dark."

Then they rode away laughing, pleasant like; but I wished he hadn't said that about the bears and mountain lions.

After we got around the hill, I found a trail, and we went much faster. Charley didn't have any more signs of fits, and began laughing and talking about gold mines. The trouble was with little Albert. He was almost as big as me. You see, all the time I'd been calling him little Albert, he'd been growing up. He was so heavy I couldn't keep up with Joe and Charley. I was all out of breath. So I told them they'd have to take turns in carrying him, which they said they wouldn't. Then I said I'd leave them and they'd get lost, and the mountain lions and bears would eat them. Charley looked like he was going to have a fit right there, and Joe said, "Give him to me." And after that we carried him in turn.

We kept right on up that mountain. I don't think there was any gold mine, but we might 'a got to the top and found it, if we hadn't lost the trail, and if it hadn't got dark, and if little Albert hadn't tired us all out carrying him. Lots of feebs are scared of the dark, and Joe said he was going to have a fit right there. Only he didn't. I never saw such an unlucky boy. He never could throw a fit when he wanted to. Some of the feebs can throw fits as quick as a wink.

By and by it got real black, and we were hungry, and we didn't have no fire. You see, they don't let feebs carry matches, and all we could do was just shiver. And we'd never thought about being hungry. You see, feebs always have their food ready for them, and that's why it's better to be a feeb than earning your living in the world.

And worse than everything was the quiet. There was only one thing worse, and it was the noises. There was all kinds of noises every once in a while, with quiet spells in between. I reckon they were rabbits, but they made noises in the brush like wild animals — you know, rustle rustle, thump, bump, crackle crackle, just like that. First Charley got a fit, a real one, and Joe threw a terrible one. I don't mind fits in the Home with everybody around. But out in the woods on a dark night is different. You listen to me, and never go hunting gold mines with epilecs, even if they are high-grade.

I never had such an awful night. When Joe and Charley weren't throwing fits they were making believe, and in the darkness the shivers from the cold which I couldn't see seemed like fits, too. And I shivered so hard I thought I was getting fits myself. And little Albert, with nothing to eat, just drooled and drooled. I never seen him as bad as that before. Why, he twisted that left eye of his until it ought to have

dropped out. I couldn't see it, but I could tell from the movements he made. And Joe just lay and cussed and cussed, and Charley cried and wished he was back in the Home.

We didn't die, and next morning we went right back the way we'd come. And little Albert got awful heavy. Doctor Wilson was mad as could be, and said I was the worst feeb in the institution, along with Joe and Charley. But Miss Striker, who was a nurse in the drooling ward then, just put her arms around me and cried, she was that happy I'd got back. I thought right there that mebbe I'd marry her. But only a month afterward she got married to the plumber that came up from the city to fix the gutter-pipes of the new hospital. And little Albert never twisted his eye for two days, it was that tired.

Next time I run away I'm going right over that mountain. But I ain't going to take epilecs along. They ain't never cured, and when they get scared or excited they throw fits to beat the band. But I'll take little Albert. Somehow I can't get along without him. And, anyway, I ain't going to run away. The drooling ward's a better snap than gold mines, and I hear there's a new nurse coming. Besides, little Albert's bigger than I am now, and I could never carry him over a mountain. And he's growing bigger every day. It's astonishing.

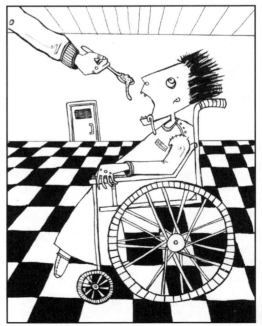

ILLUSTRATIONS ©2003 LESLEY REPPETEAUX

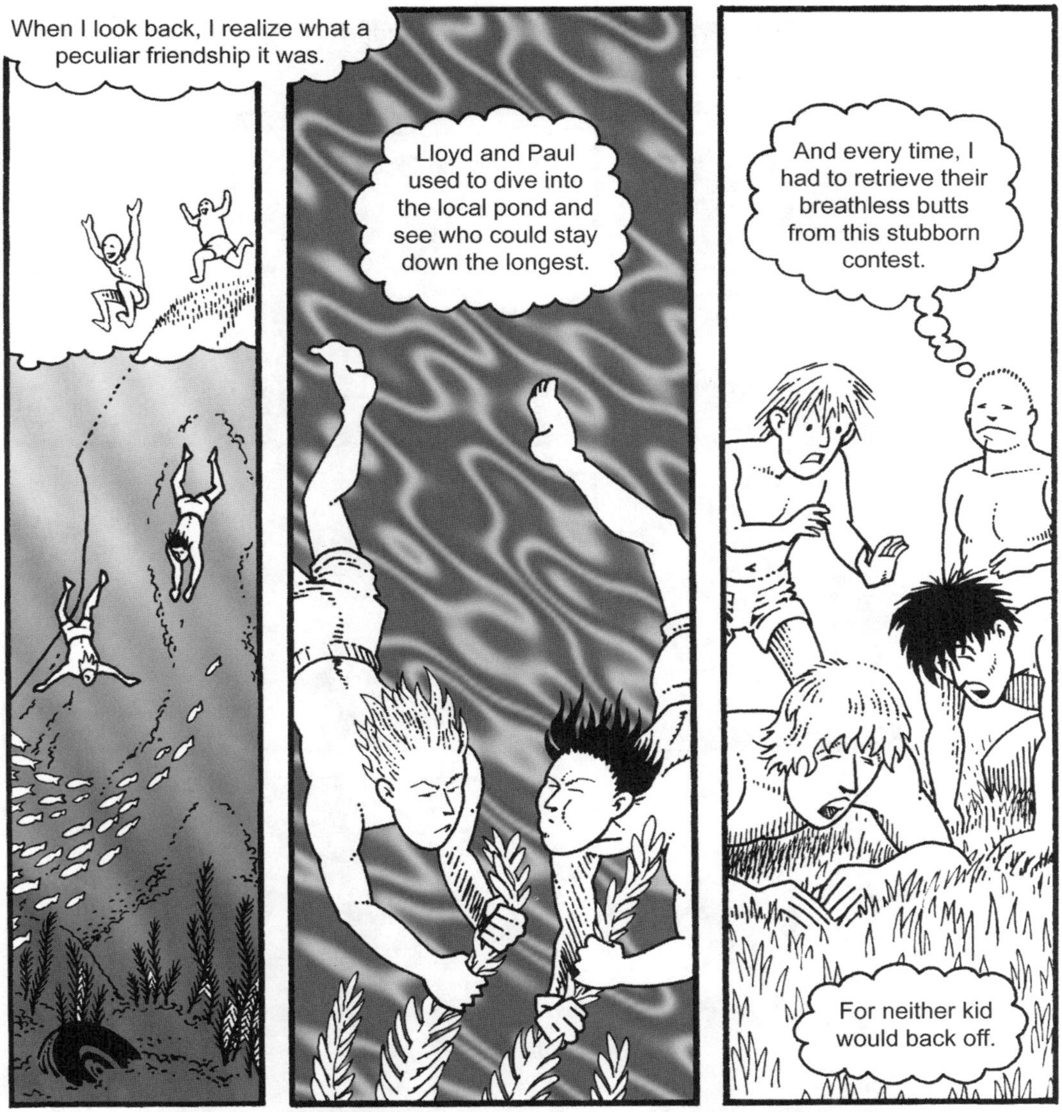
When I look back, I realize what a peculiar friendship it was.
Lloyd and Paul used to dive into the local pond and see who could stay down the longest.
And every time, I had to retrieve their breathless butts from this stubborn contest.
For neither kid would back off.

THE SHADOW AND THE FLASH

story/JACK LONDON visual adaptation/MATT HOWARTH

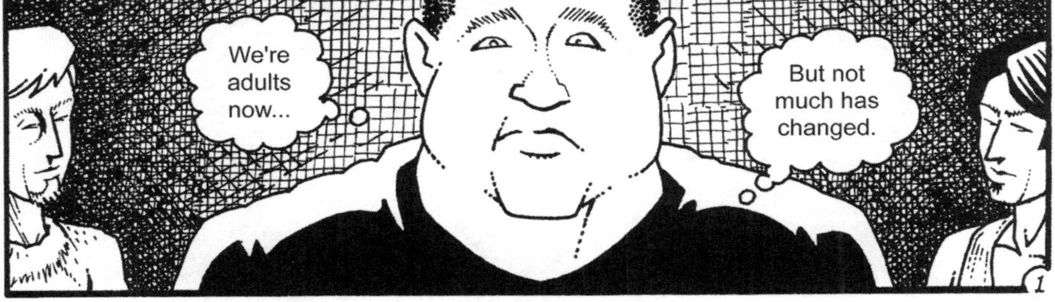
We're adults now...
But not much has changed.

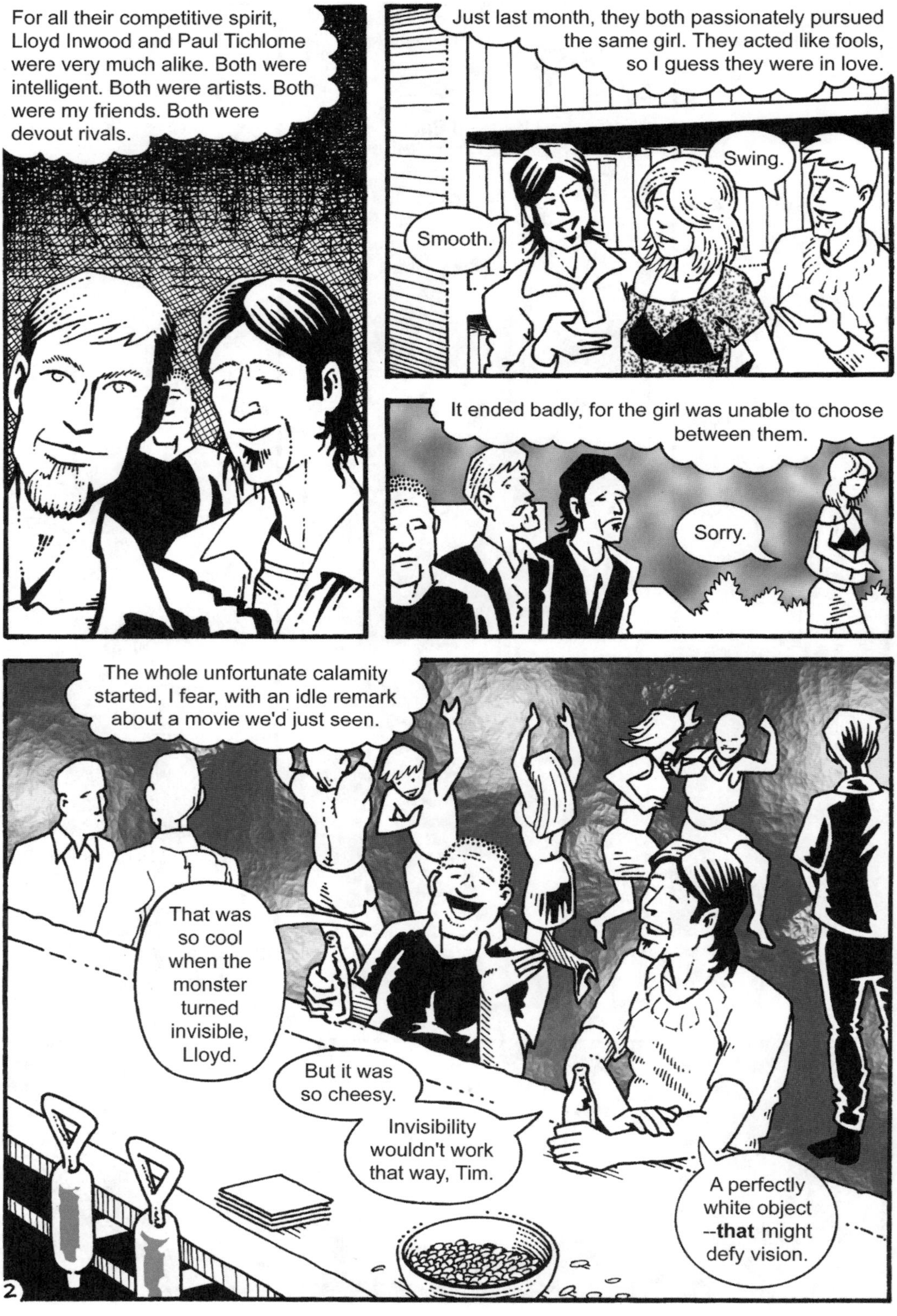
For all their competitive spirit, Lloyd Inwood and Paul Tichlome were very much alike. Both were intelligent. Both were artists. Both were my friends. Both were devout rivals.
Just last month, they both passionately pursued the same girl. They acted like fools, so I guess they were in love.
Smooth.
Swing.
It ended badly, for the girl was unable to choose between them.
Sorry.
The whole unfortunate calamity started, I fear, with an idle remark about a movie we'd just seen.
That was so cool when the monster turned invisible, Lloyd.
But it was so cheesy.
Invisibility wouldn't work that way, Tim.
A perfectly white object --**that** might defy vision.
2

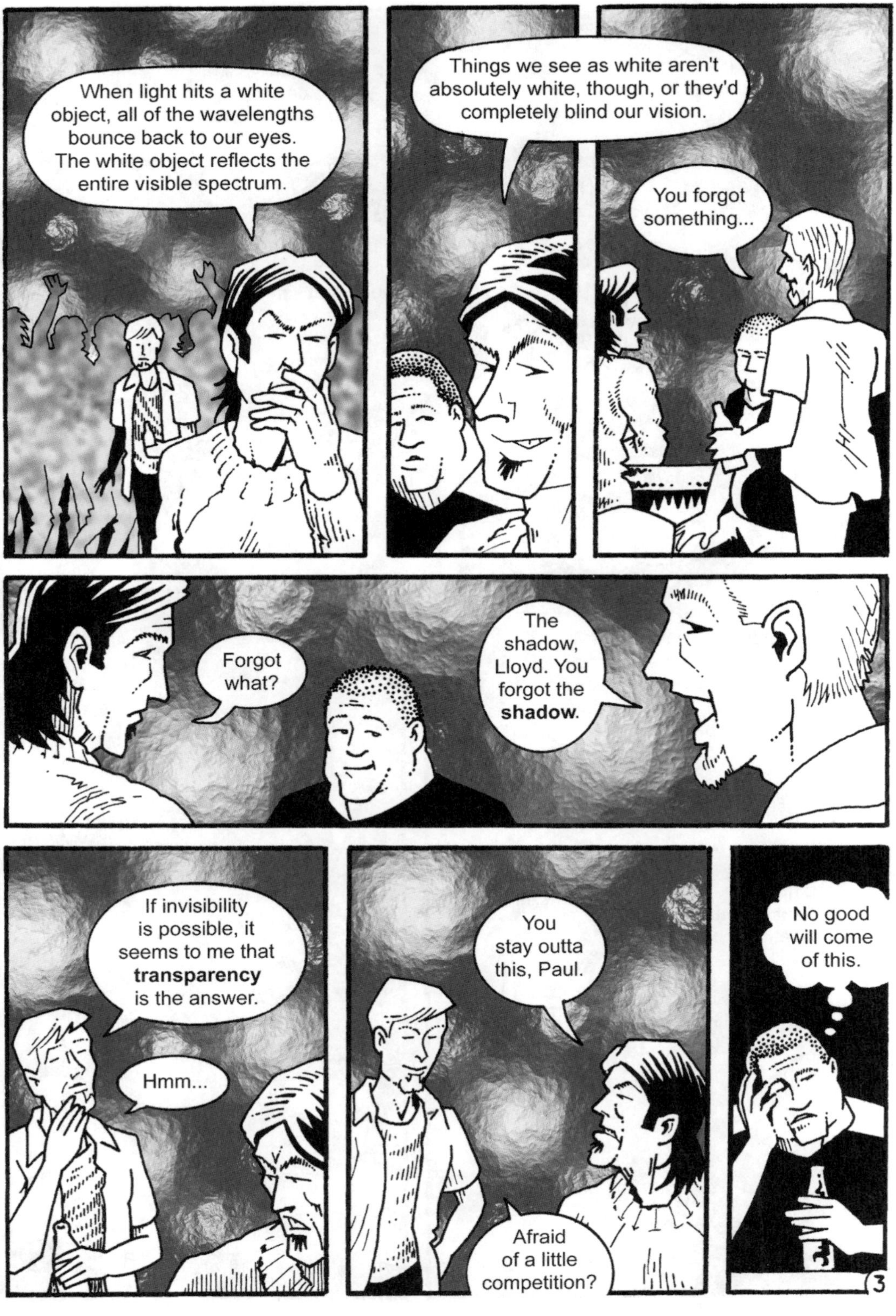
When light hits a white object, all of the wavelengths bounce back to our eyes. The white object reflects the entire visible spectrum.
Things we see as white aren't absolutely white, though, or they'd completely blind our vision.
You forgot something...
Forgot what?
The shadow, Lloyd. You forgot the **shadow**.
If invisibility is possible, it seems to me that **transparency** is the answer.
Hmm...
You stay outta this, Paul.
Afraid of a little competition?
No good will come of this.
3

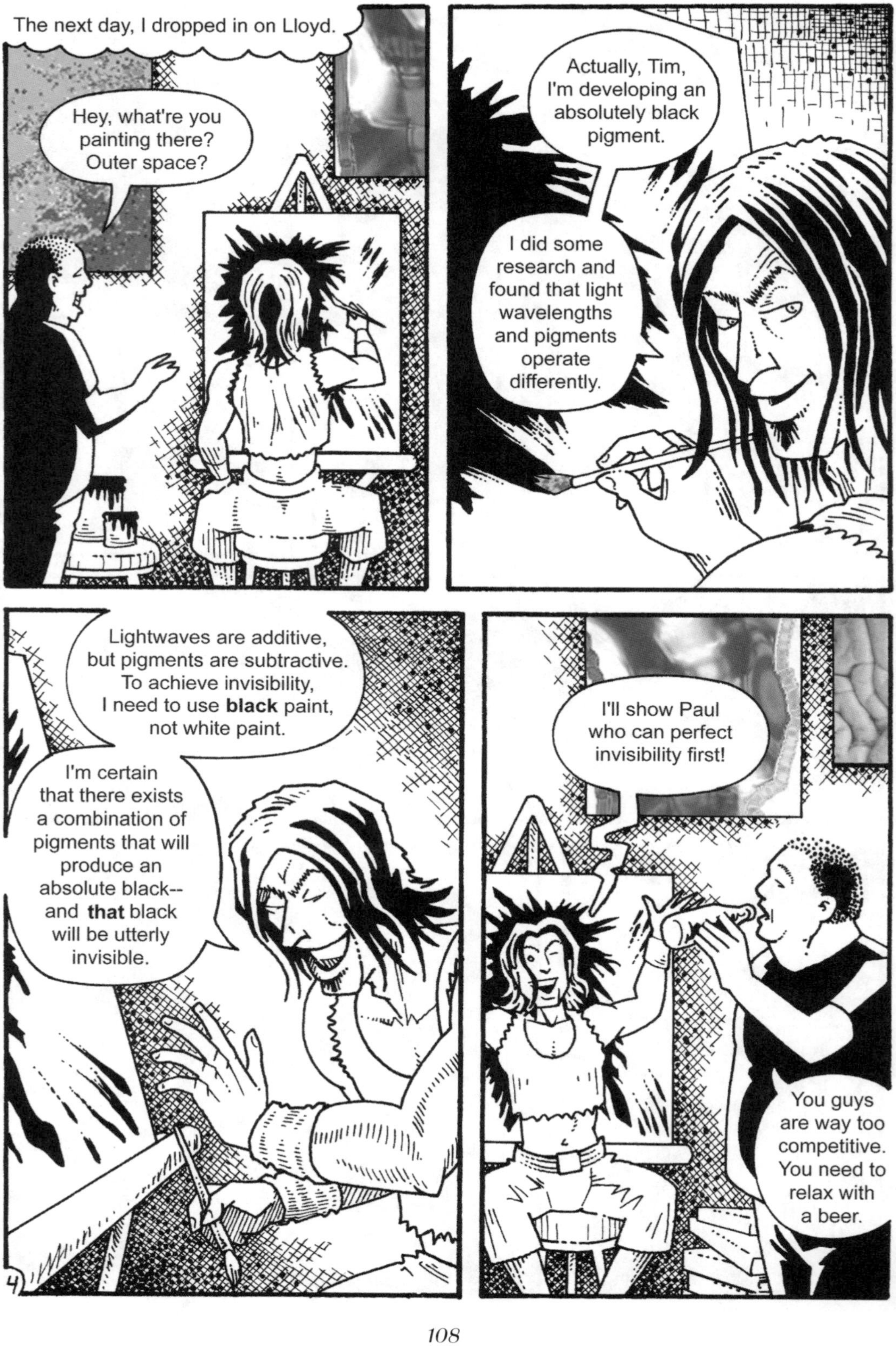
The next day, I dropped in on Lloyd.
Hey, what're you painting there? Outer space?
Actually, Tim, I'm developing an absolutely black pigment.
I did some research and found that light wavelengths and pigments operate differently.
Lightwaves are additive, but pigments are subtractive. To achieve invisibility, I need to use **black** paint, not white paint.
I'm certain that there exists a combination of pigments that will produce an absolute black-- and **that** black will be utterly invisible.
I'll show Paul who can perfect invisibility first!
You guys are way too competitive. You need to relax with a beer.

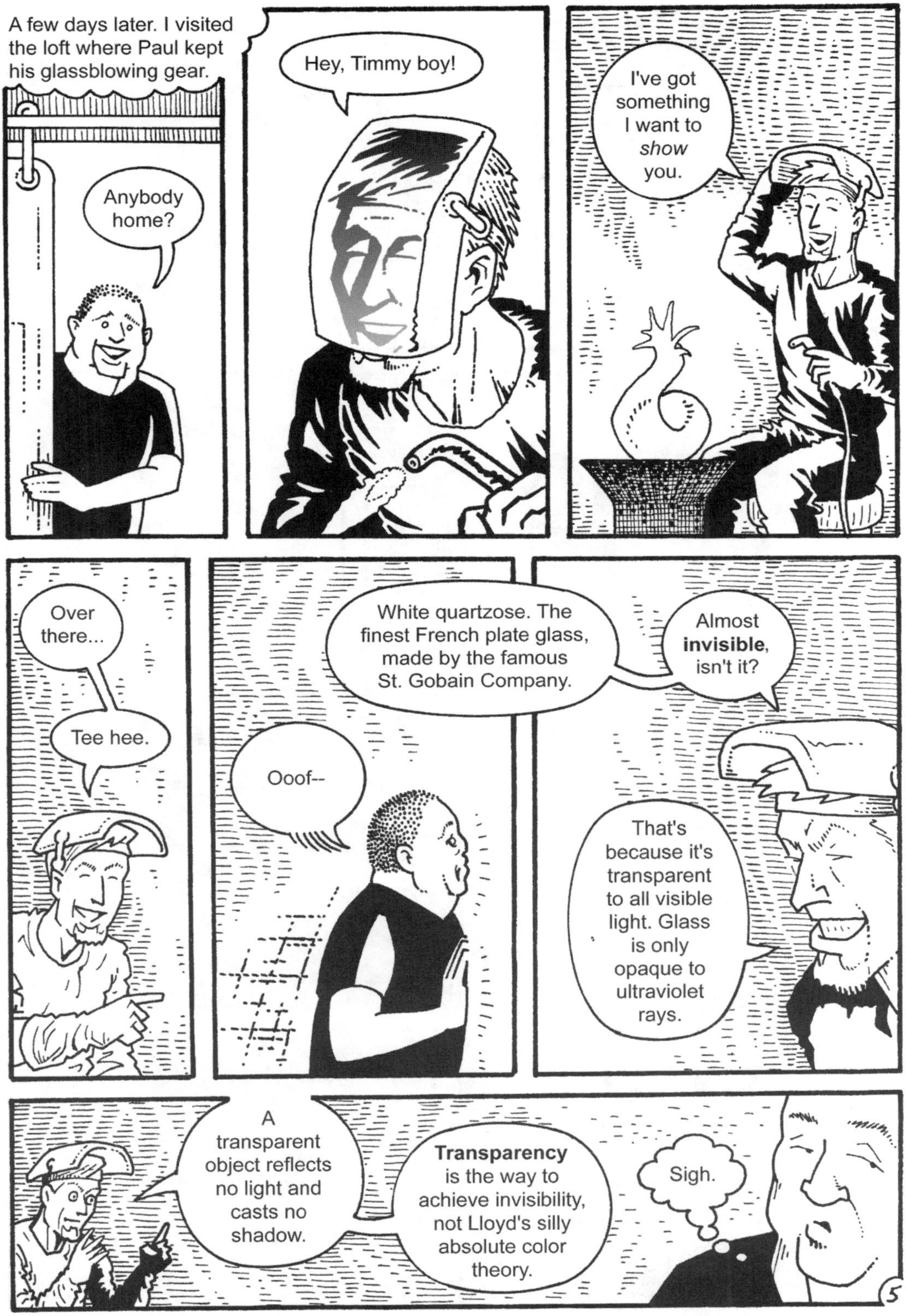
A few days later. I visited the loft where Paul kept his glassblowing gear.
Anybody home?
Hey, Timmy boy!
I've got something I want to *show* you.
Over there...
Tee hee.
White quartzose. The finest French plate glass, made by the famous St. Gobain Company.
Ooof--
Almost **invisible**, isn't it?
That's because it's transparent to all visible light. Glass is only opaque to ultraviolet rays.
A transparent object reflects no light and casts no shadow.
Transparency is the way to achieve invisibility, not Lloyd's silly absolute color theory.
Sigh.
5

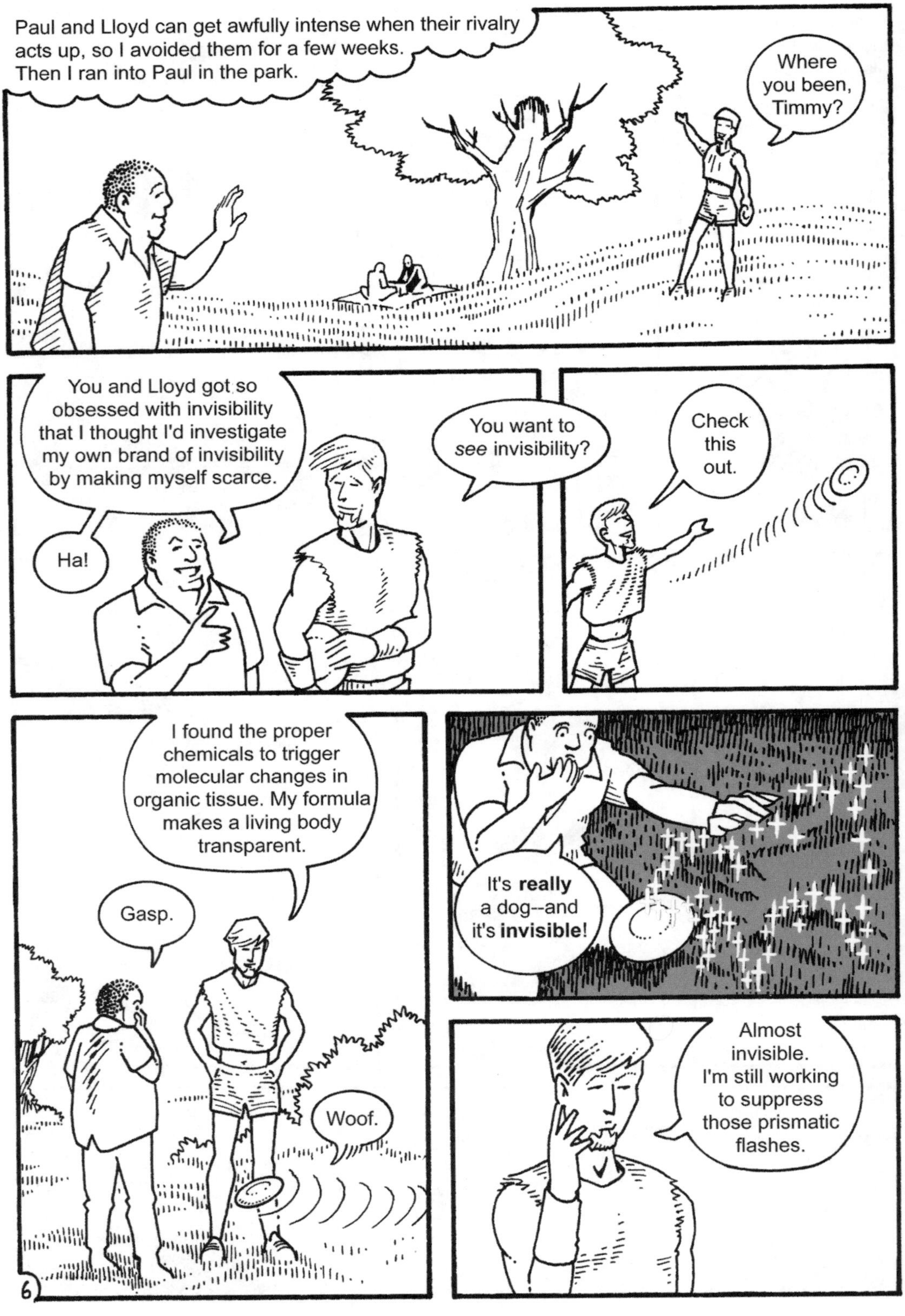
Paul and Lloyd can get awfully intense when their rivalry acts up, so I avoided them for a few weeks. Then I ran into Paul in the park.
Where you been, Timmy?
You and Lloyd got so obsessed with invisibility that I thought I'd investigate my own brand of invisibility by making myself scarce.
Ha!
You want to *see* invisibility?
Check this out.
I found the proper chemicals to trigger molecular changes in organic tissue. My formula makes a living body transparent.
Gasp.
Woof.
It's **really** a dog--and it's **invisible**!
Almost invisible. I'm still working to suppress those prismatic flashes.
6

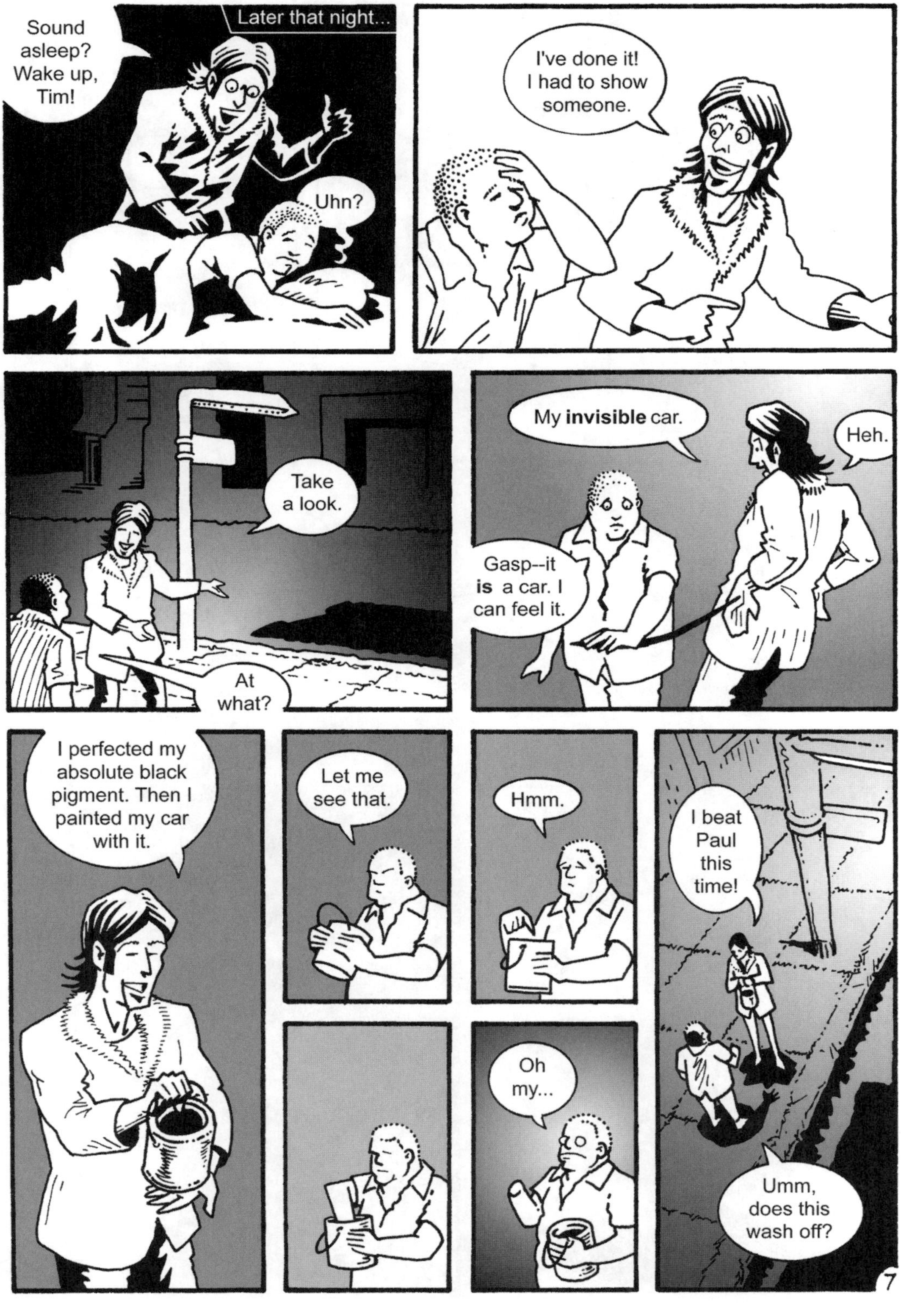
Later that night...
Sound asleep? Wake up, Tim!
Uhn?
I've done it! I had to show someone.
Take a look.
At what?
My **invisible** car.
Heh.
Gasp--it **is** a car. I can feel it.
I perfected my absolute black pigment. Then I painted my car with it.
Let me see that.
Hmm.
Oh my...
I beat Paul this time!
Umm, does this wash off?
7

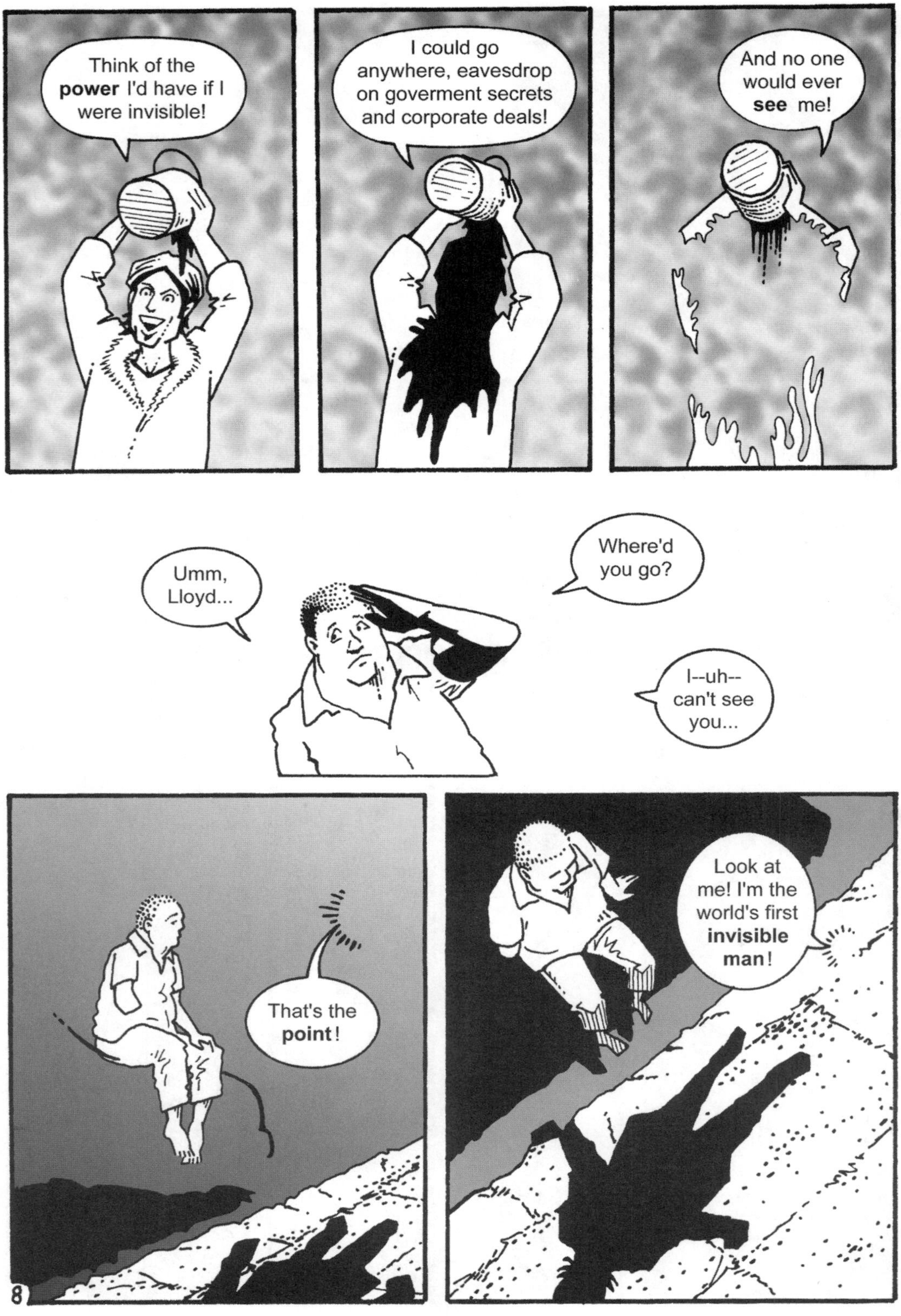
Think of the **power** I'd have if I were invisible!
I could go anywhere, eavesdrop on goverment secrets and corporate deals!
And no one would ever **see** me!
Umm, Lloyd...
Where'd you go?
I--uh-- can't see you...
That's the **point**!
Look at me! I'm the world's first **invisible man**!
8

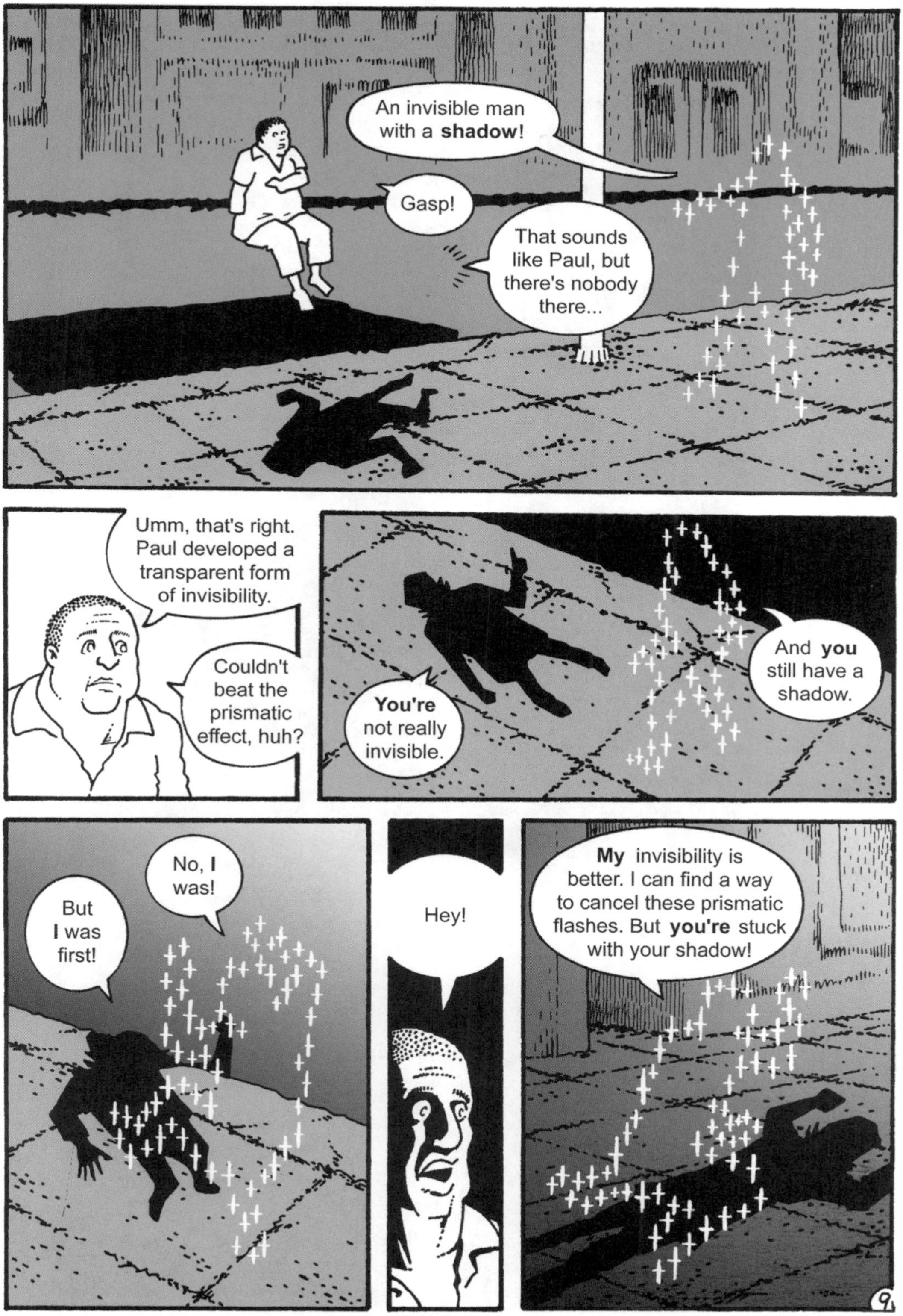
An invisible man with a **shadow**!
Gasp!
That sounds like Paul, but there's nobody there...
Umm, that's right. Paul developed a transparent form of invisibility.
Couldn't beat the prismatic effect, huh?
You're not really invisible.
And **you** still have a shadow.
But **I** was first!
No, **I** was!
Hey!
My invisibility is better. I can find a way to cancel these prismatic flashes. But **you're** stuck with your shadow!
9

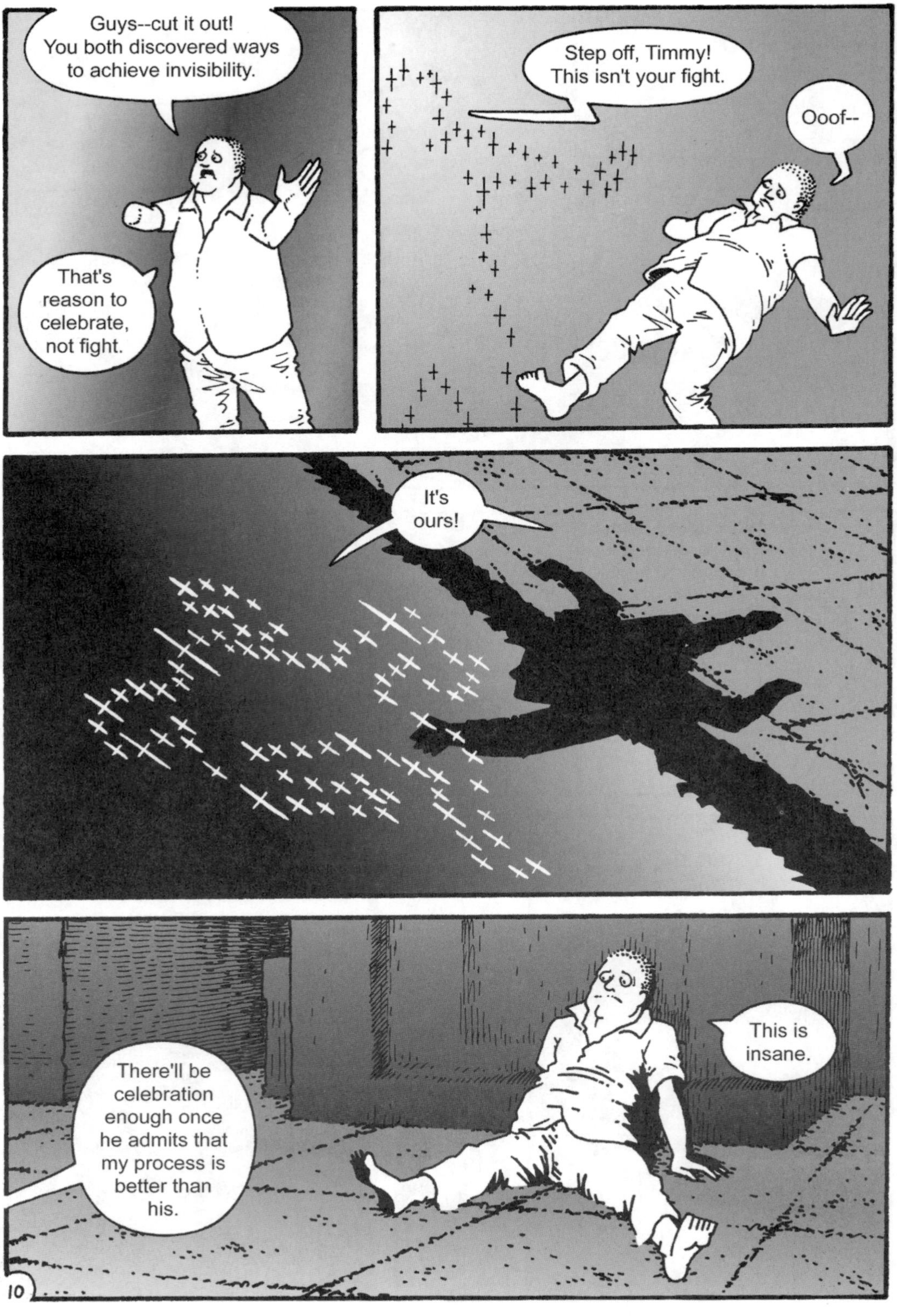
Guys--cut it out! You both discovered ways to achieve invisibility.
That's reason to celebrate, not fight.
Step off, Timmy! This isn't your fight.
Ooof--
It's ours!
This is insane.
There'll be celebration enough once he admits that my process is better than his.
10

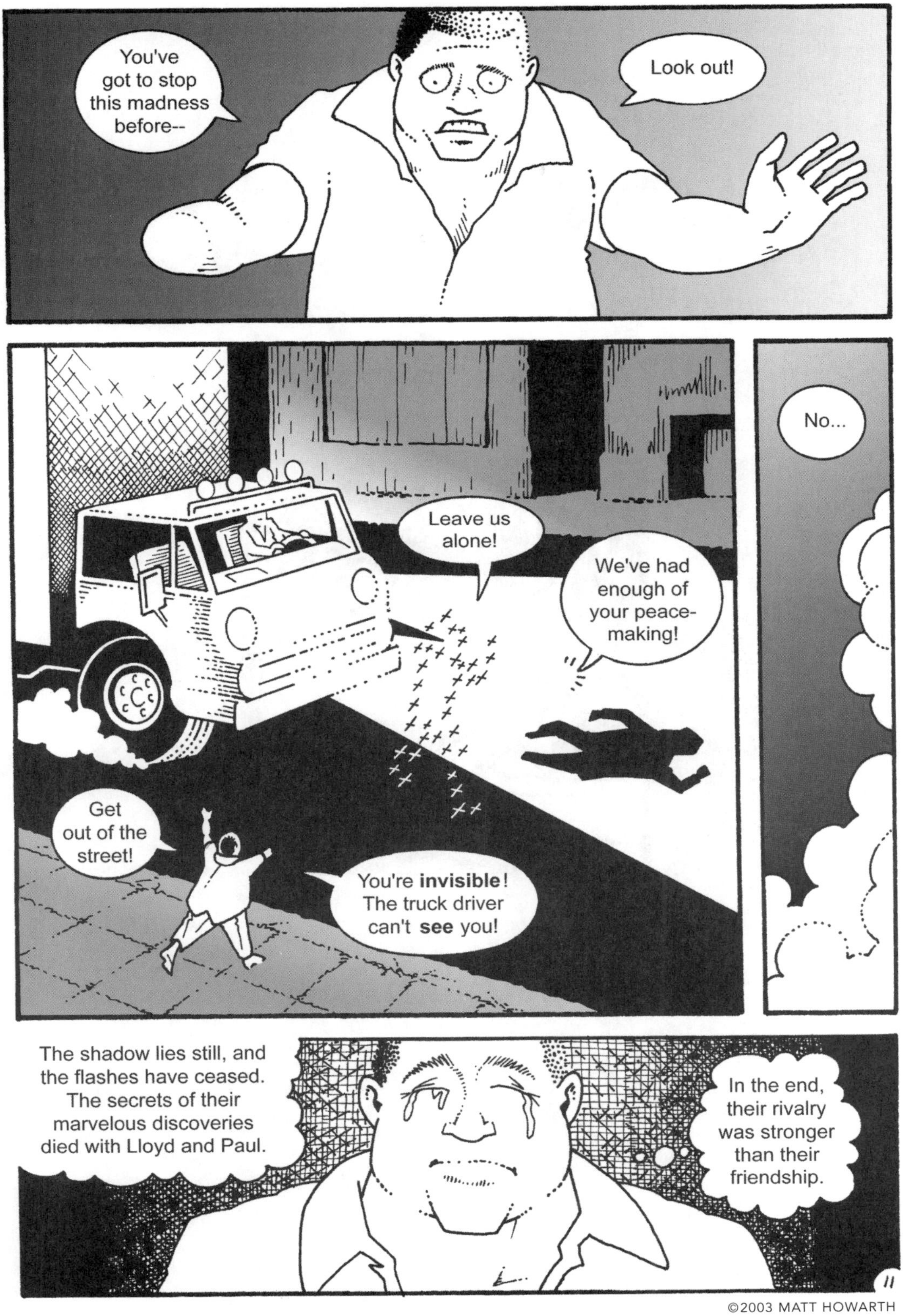
You've got to stop this madness before--
Look out!
Leave us alone!
We've had enough of your peace-making!
Get out of the street!
You're **invisible**! The truck driver can't **see** you!
No...
The shadow lies still, and the flashes have ceased. The secrets of their marvelous discoveries died with Lloyd and Paul.
In the end, their rivalry was stronger than their friendship.
11

MOON-FACE

A STORY OF MORAL ANTIPATHY

by **JACK LONDON**

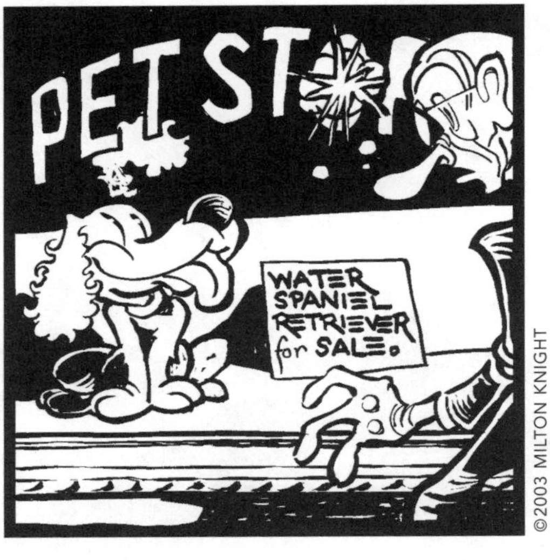
PET ST
WATER
SPANIEL
RETRIEVER
for SALE.
©2003 MILTON KNIGHT

adapted & illustrated by

MILTON KNIGHT

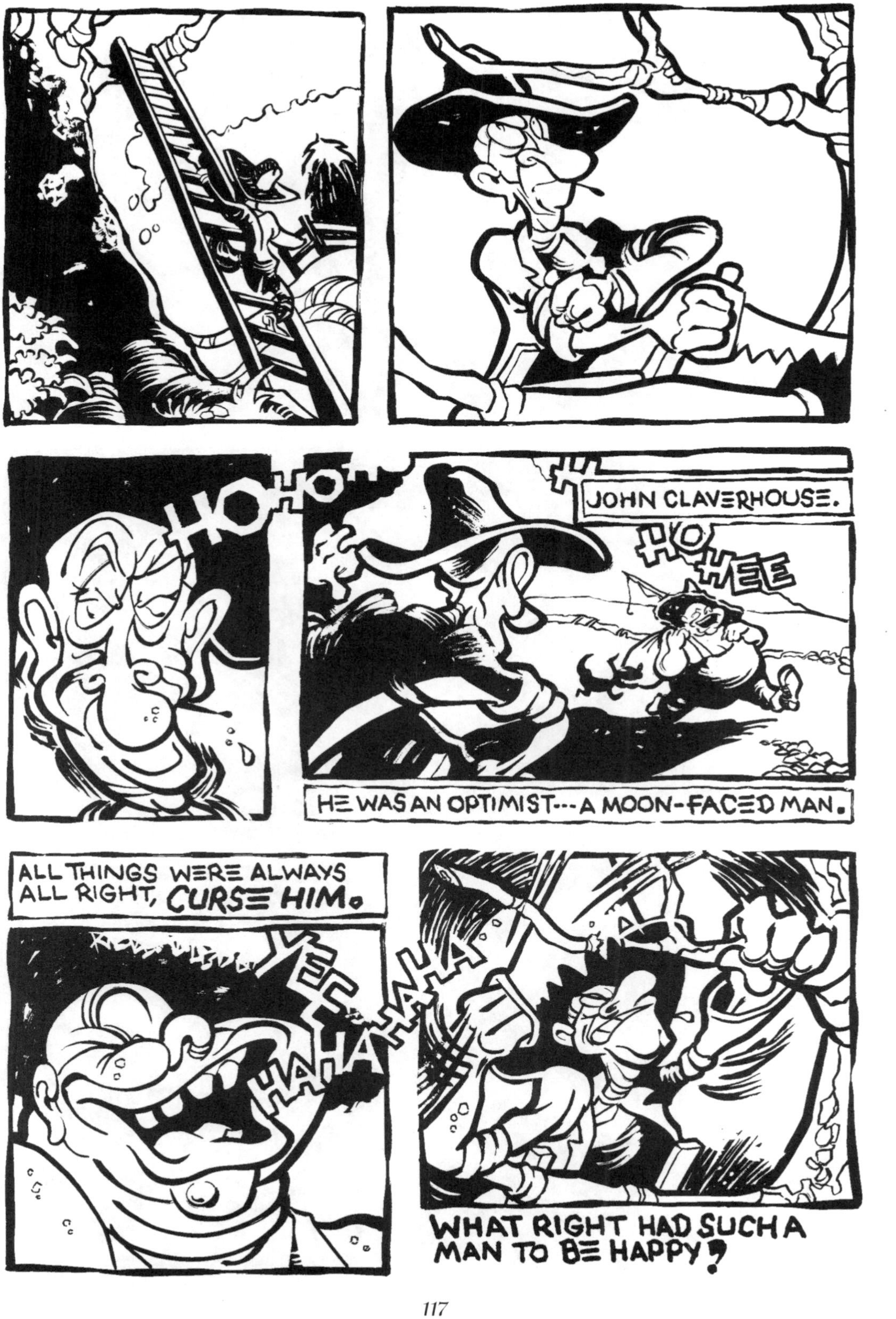
HOHO
JOHN CLAVERHOUSE.
HO HEE
HE WAS AN OPTIMIST--- A MOON-FACED MAN.
ALL THINGS WERE ALWAYS ALL RIGHT, CURSE HIM.
HAHA
WHAT RIGHT HAD SUCH A MAN TO BE HAPPY?

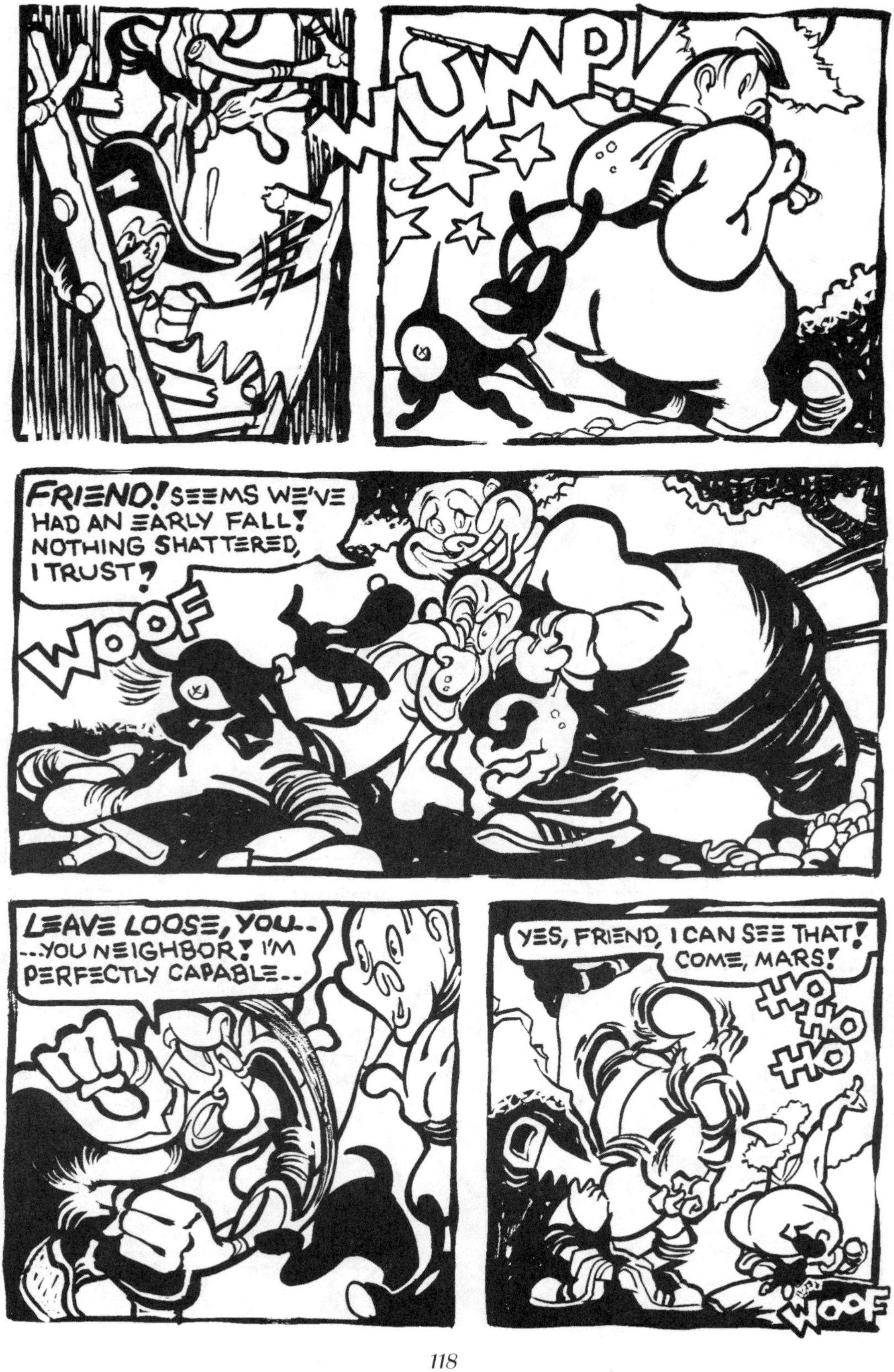
WUMP!
FRIEND! SEEMS WE'VE HAD AN EARLY FALL! NOTHING SHATTERED, I TRUST?
WOOF
LEAVE LOOSE, YOU.. ...YOU NEIGHBOR! I'M PERFECTLY CAPABLE..
YES, FRIEND, I CAN SEE THAT! COME, MARS!
HO HO HO HO
WOOF

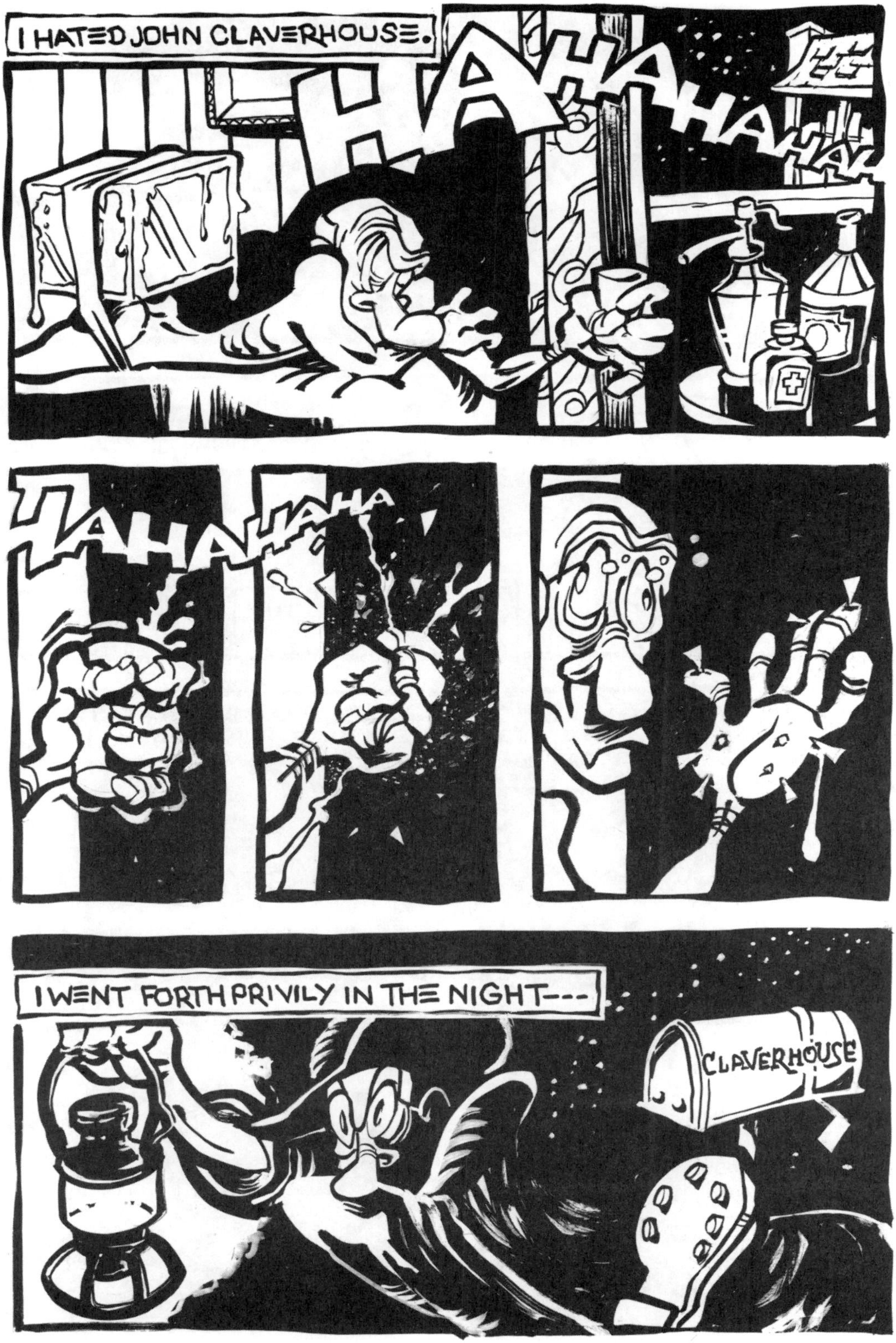
I HATED JOHN CLAVERHOUSE.
HAHAHAHAHAK
HAHAHAHAHA
I WENT FORTH PRIVILY IN THE NIGHT---
CLAVERHOUSE

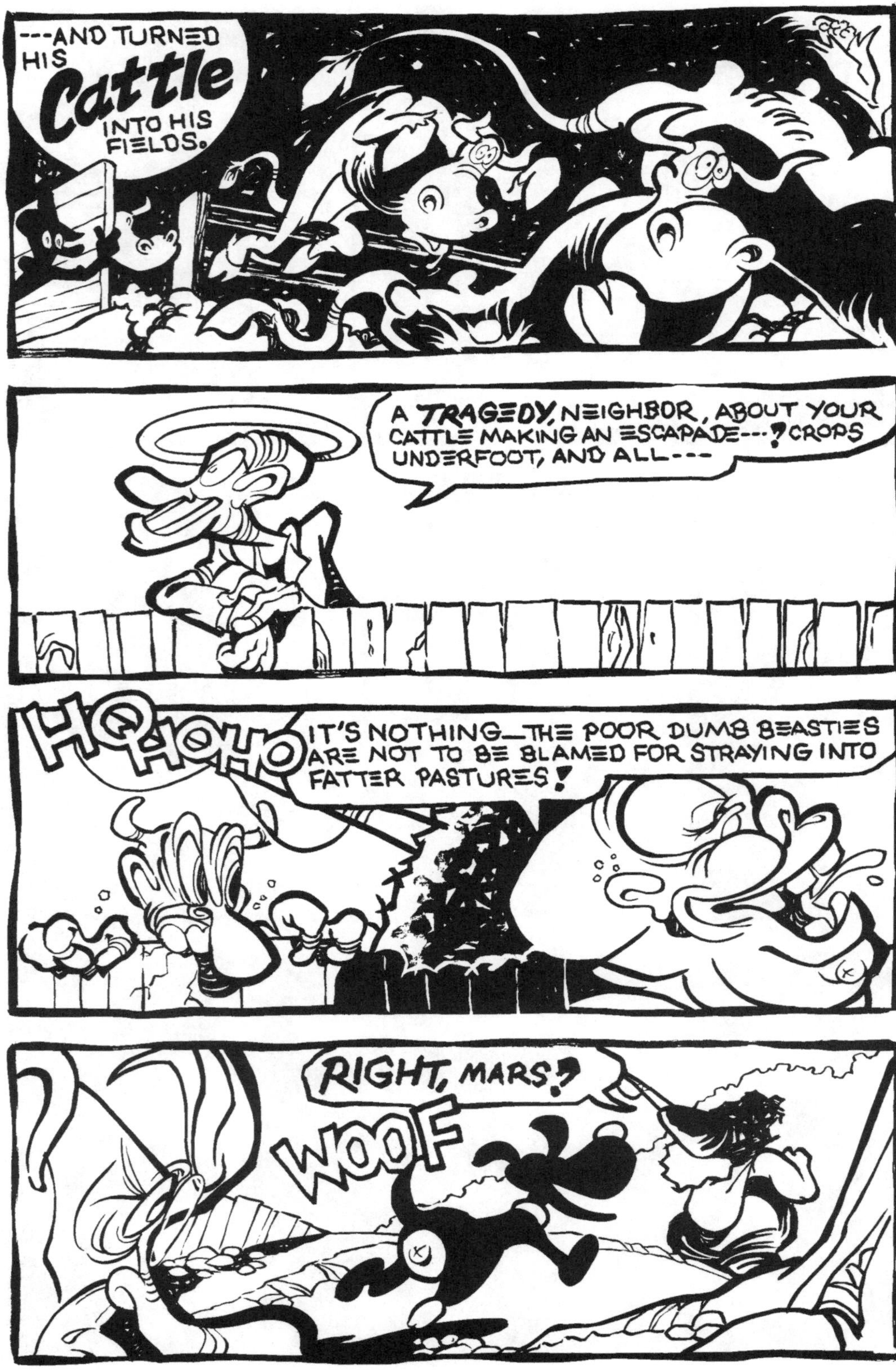
---AND TURNED HIS Cattle INTO HIS FIELDS.
A TRAGEDY, NEIGHBOR, ABOUT YOUR CATTLE MAKING AN ESCAPADE---? CROPS UNDERFOOT, AND ALL---
HOHOHO
IT'S NOTHING—THE POOR DUMB BEASTIES ARE NOT TO BE BLAMED FOR STRAYING INTO FATTER PASTURES!
RIGHT, MARS?
WOOF

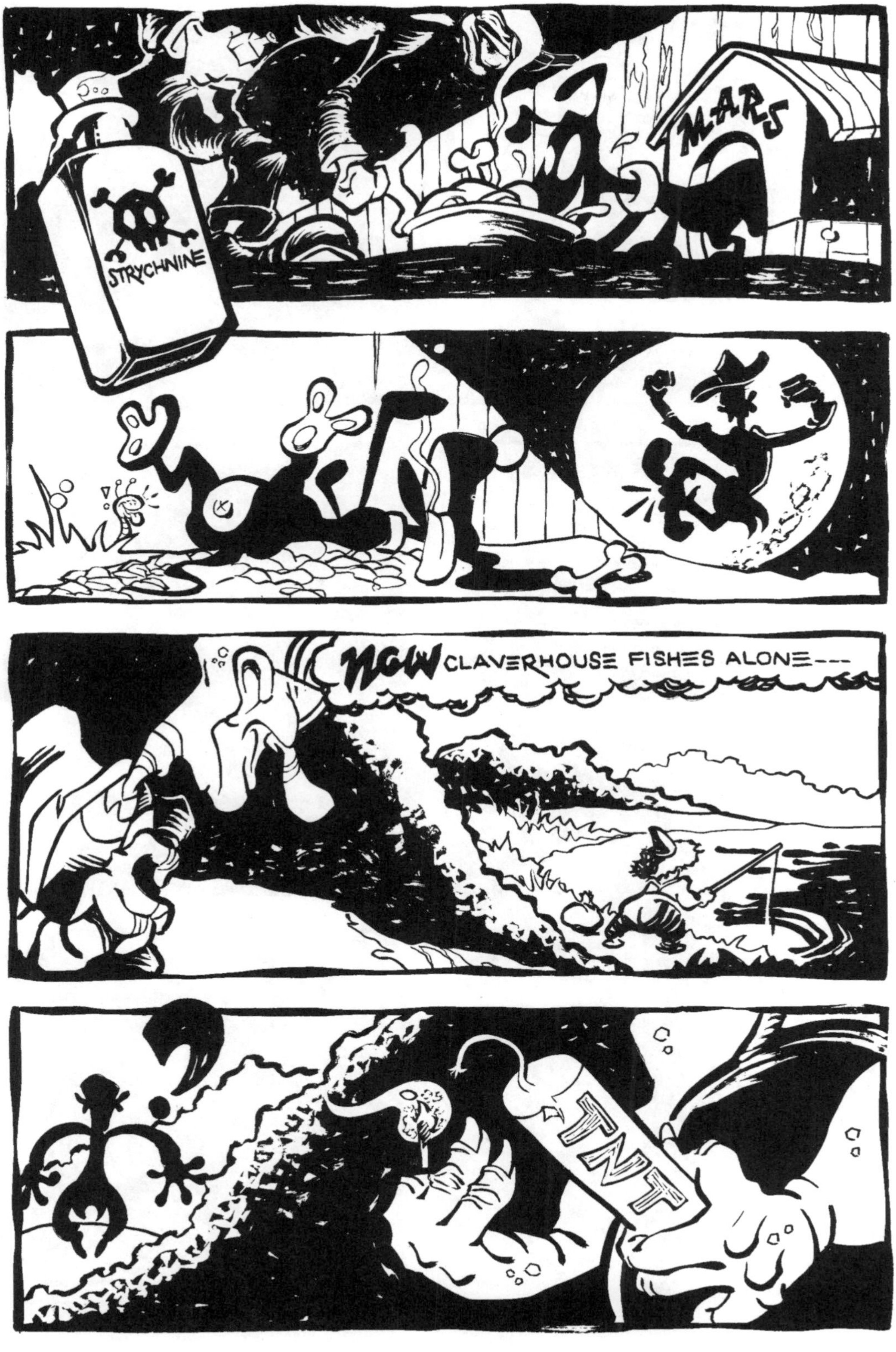
MARS
STRYCHNINE
NOW CLAVERHOUSE FISHES ALONE---
TNT

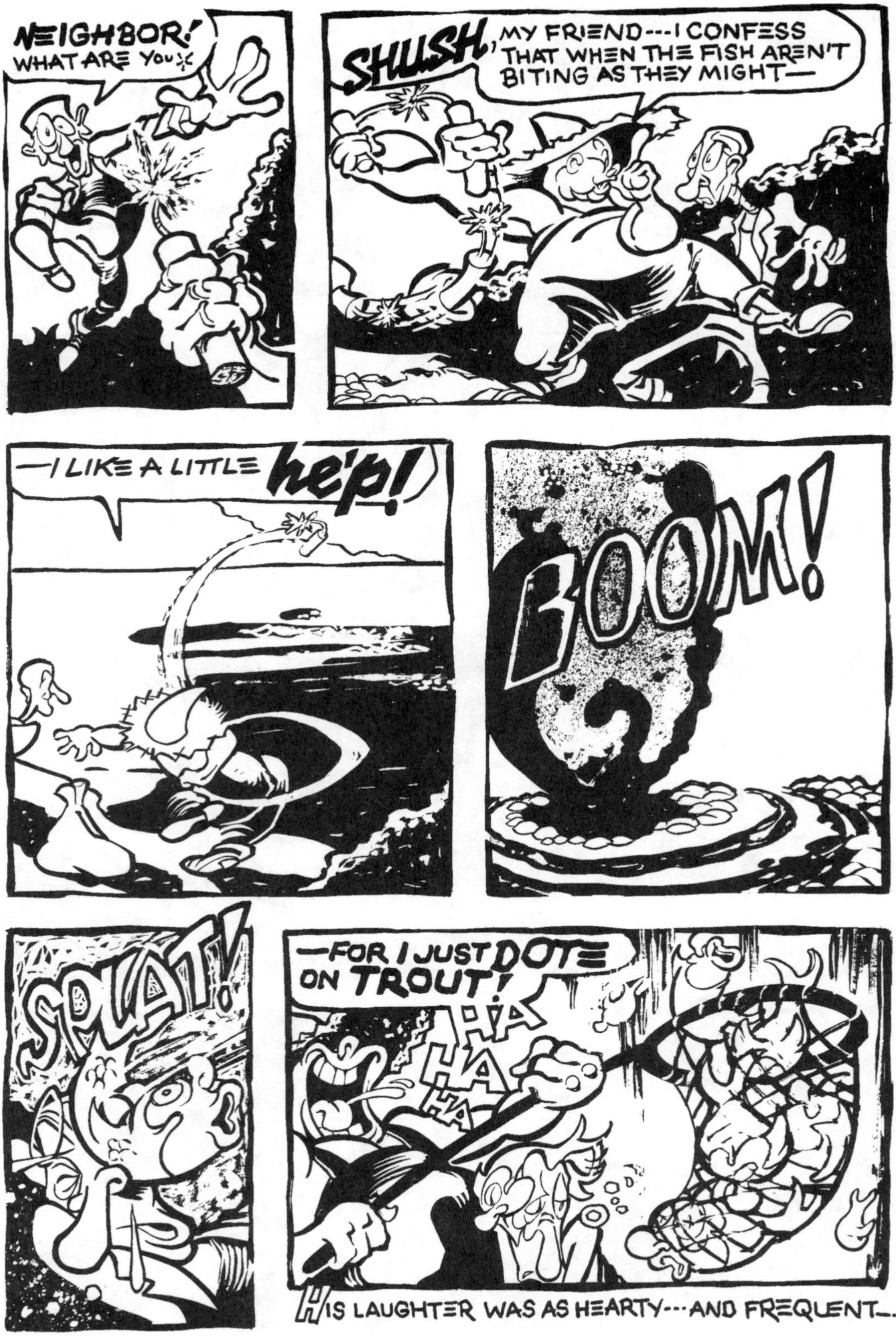
NEIGHBOR! WHAT ARE YOU*
SHUSH, MY FRIEND---I CONFESS THAT WHEN THE FISH AREN'T BITING AS THEY MIGHT—
—I LIKE A LITTLE he'p!
BOOM!
SPLAT!
—FOR I JUST DOTE ON TROUT!
HA HA HA
HIS LAUGHTER WAS AS HEARTY---AND FREQUENT..

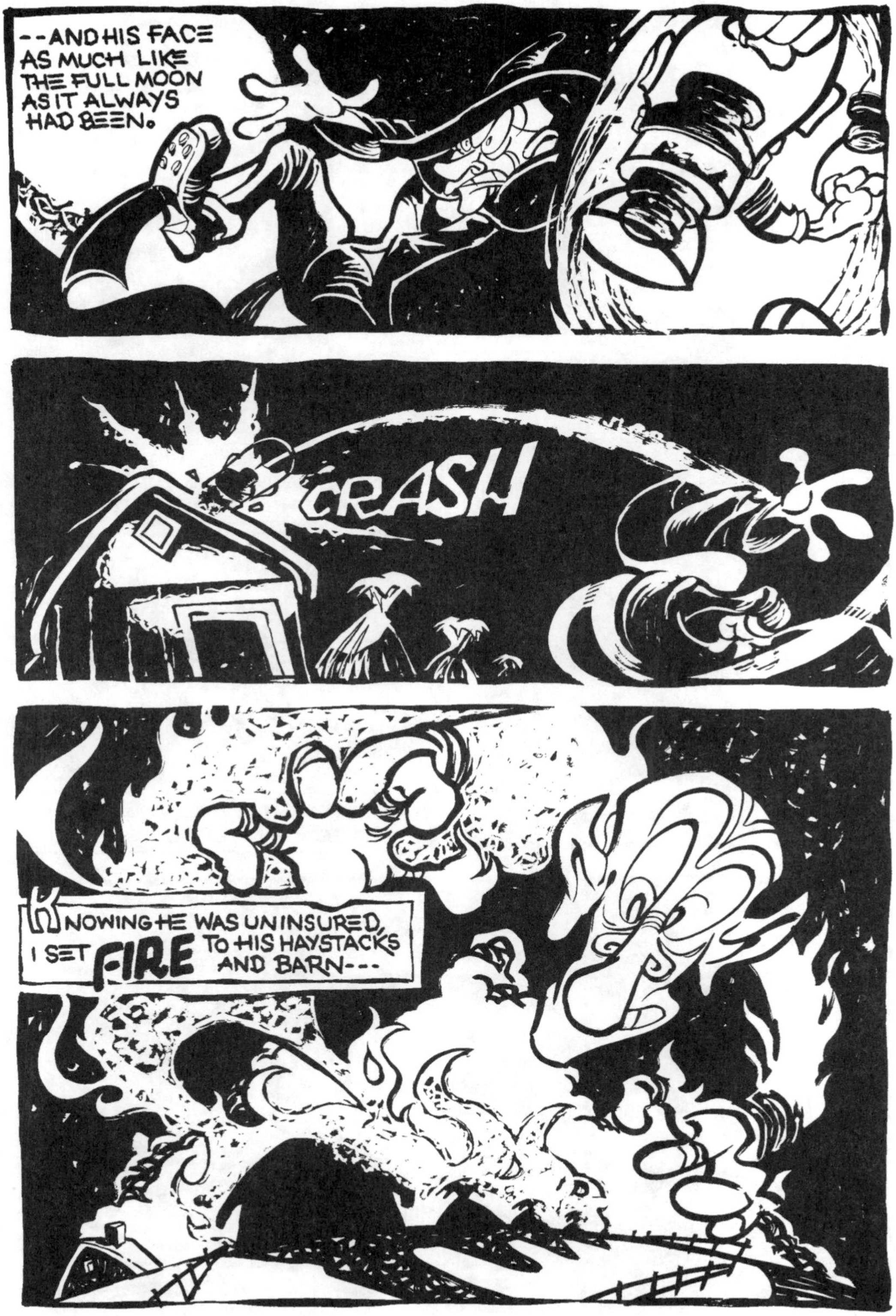
--AND HIS FACE AS MUCH LIKE THE FULL MOON AS IT ALWAYS HAD BEEN.
CRASH
KNOWING HE WAS UNINSURED, I SET FIRE TO HIS HAYSTACKS AND BARN---

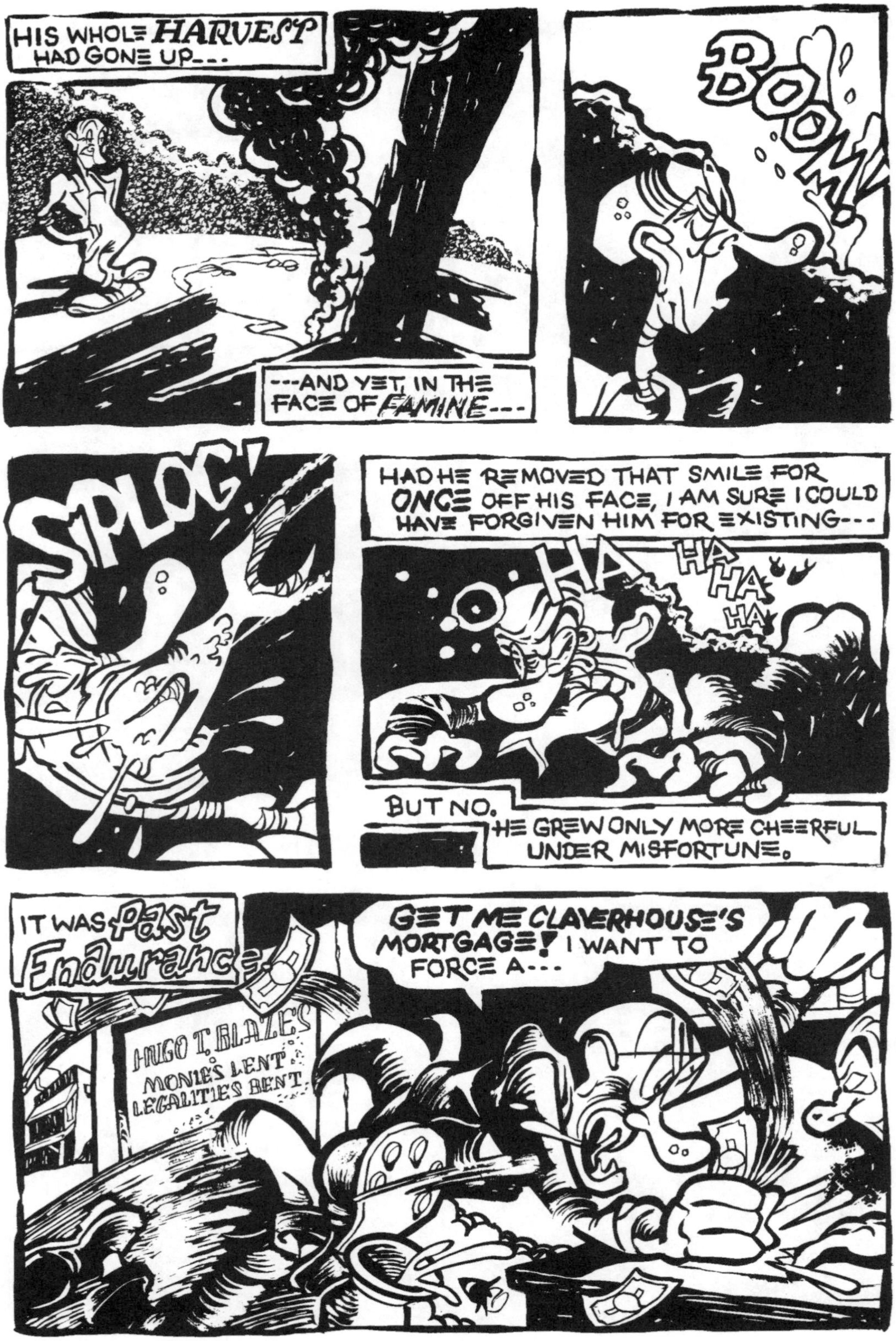
HIS WHOLE HARVEST HAD GONE UP---
---AND YET, IN THE FACE OF FAMINE---
BOOM!
SPLOG!
HAD HE REMOVED THAT SMILE FOR ONCE OFF HIS FACE, I AM SURE I COULD HAVE FORGIVEN HIM FOR EXISTING---
HA
HA HA HA
BUT NO.
HE GREW ONLY MORE CHEERFUL UNDER MISFORTUNE.
IT WAS Past Endurance.
GET ME CLAVERHOUSE'S MORTGAGE! I WANT TO FORCE A---
HUGO T. BLAZES
MONIES LENT
LEGALITIES BENT

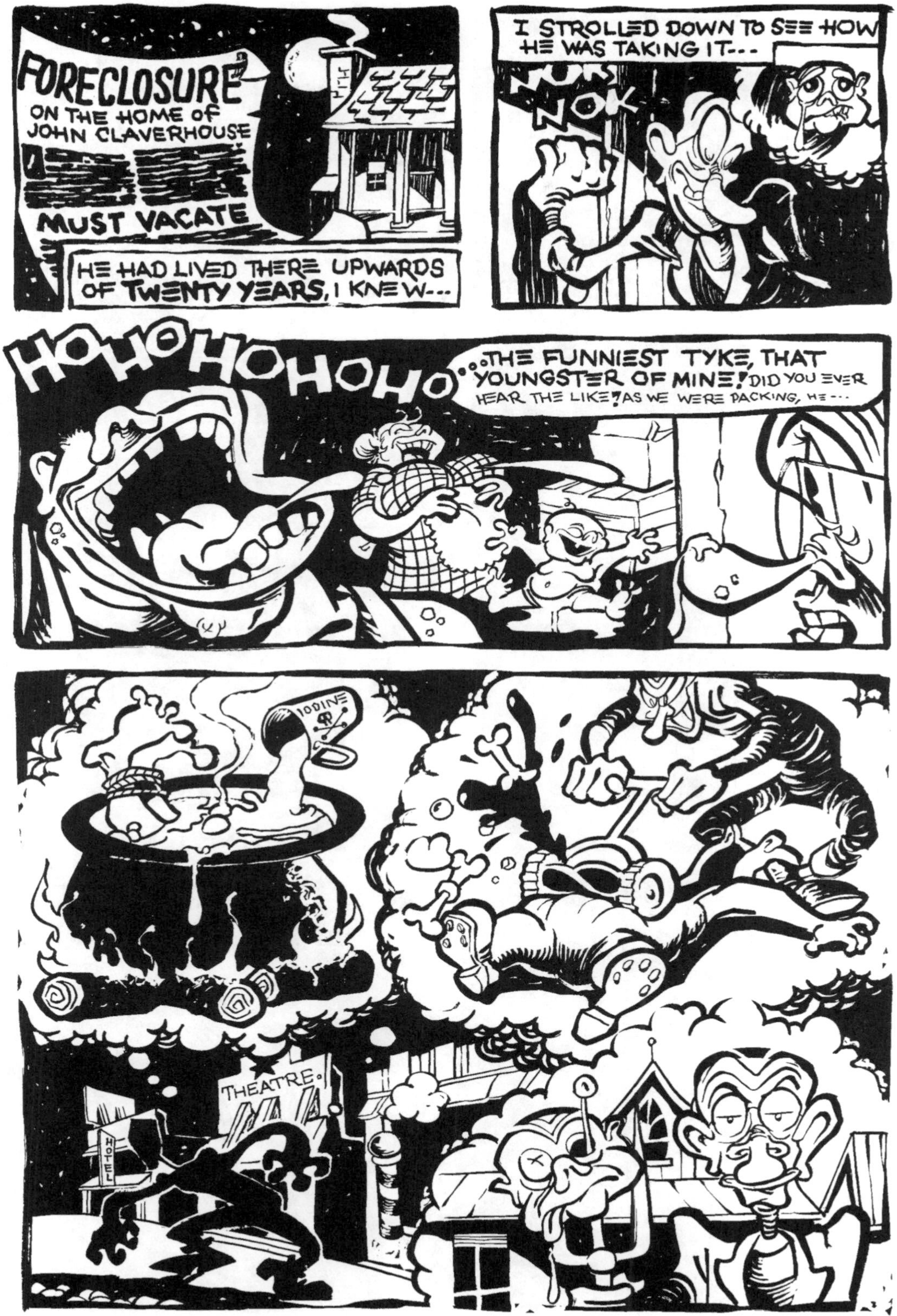
FORECLOSURE
ON THE HOME of
JOHN CLAVERHOUSE
MUST VACATE
HE HAD LIVED THERE UPWARDS OF TWENTY YEARS, I KNEW---
I STROLLED DOWN TO SEE HOW HE WAS TAKING IT---
NOK
HOHOHOHOHOHO
...THE FUNNIEST TYKE, THAT YOUNGSTER OF MINE! DID YOU EVER HEAR THE LIKE! AS WE WERE PACKING, HE---
IODINE
THEATRE
HOTEL

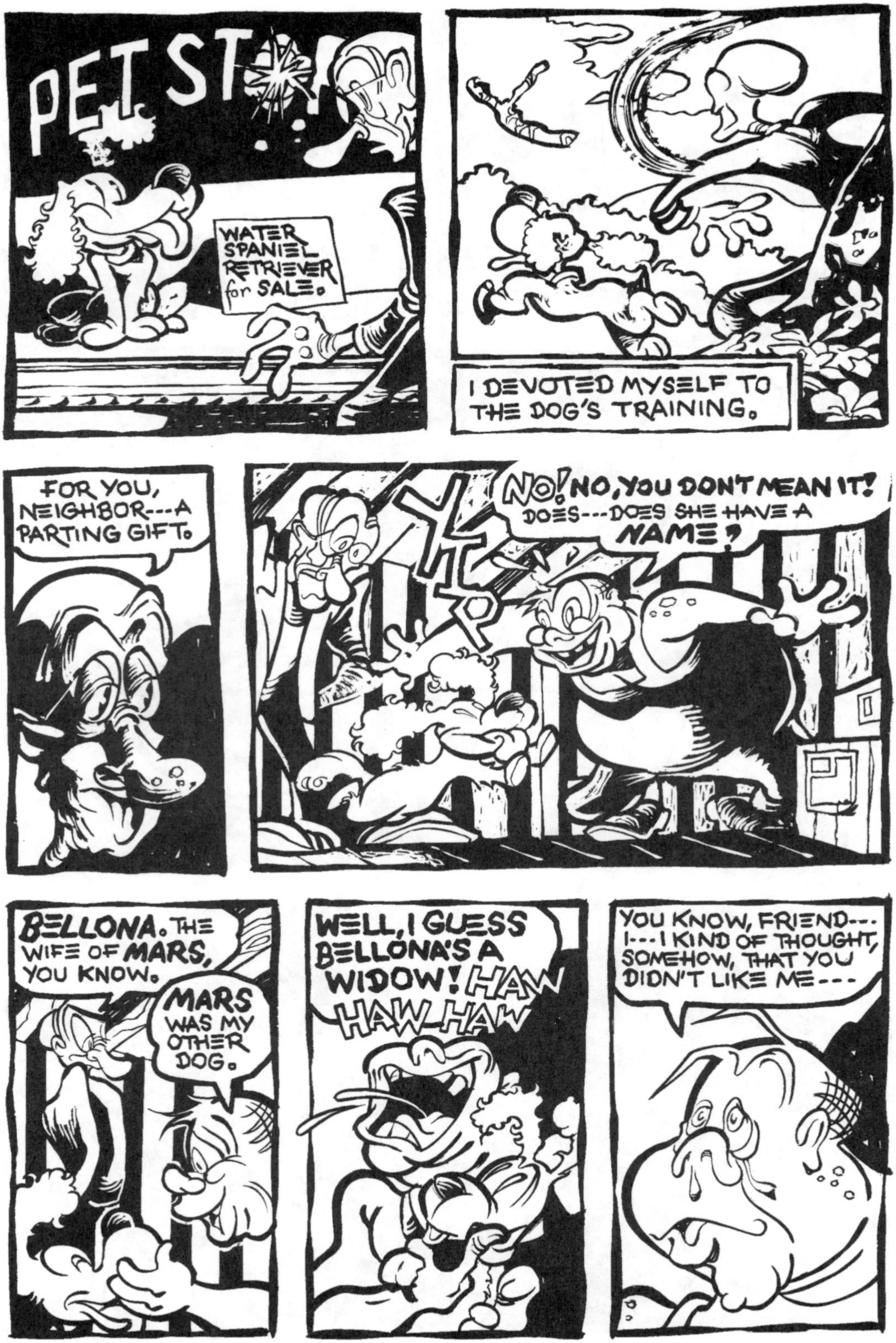
PET ST
WATER SPANIEL RETRIEVER for SALE.
I DEVOTED MYSELF TO THE DOG'S TRAINING.
FOR YOU, NEIGHBOR---A PARTING GIFT.
YIP
NO! NO, YOU DON'T MEAN IT! DOES---DOES SHE HAVE A NAME?
BELLONA. THE WIFE OF MARS, YOU KNOW.
MARS WAS MY OTHER DOG.
WELL, I GUESS BELLONA'S A WIDOW! HAW HAW HAW
YOU KNOW, FRIEND--- I---I KIND OF THOUGHT, SOMEHOW, THAT YOU DIDN'T LIKE ME---

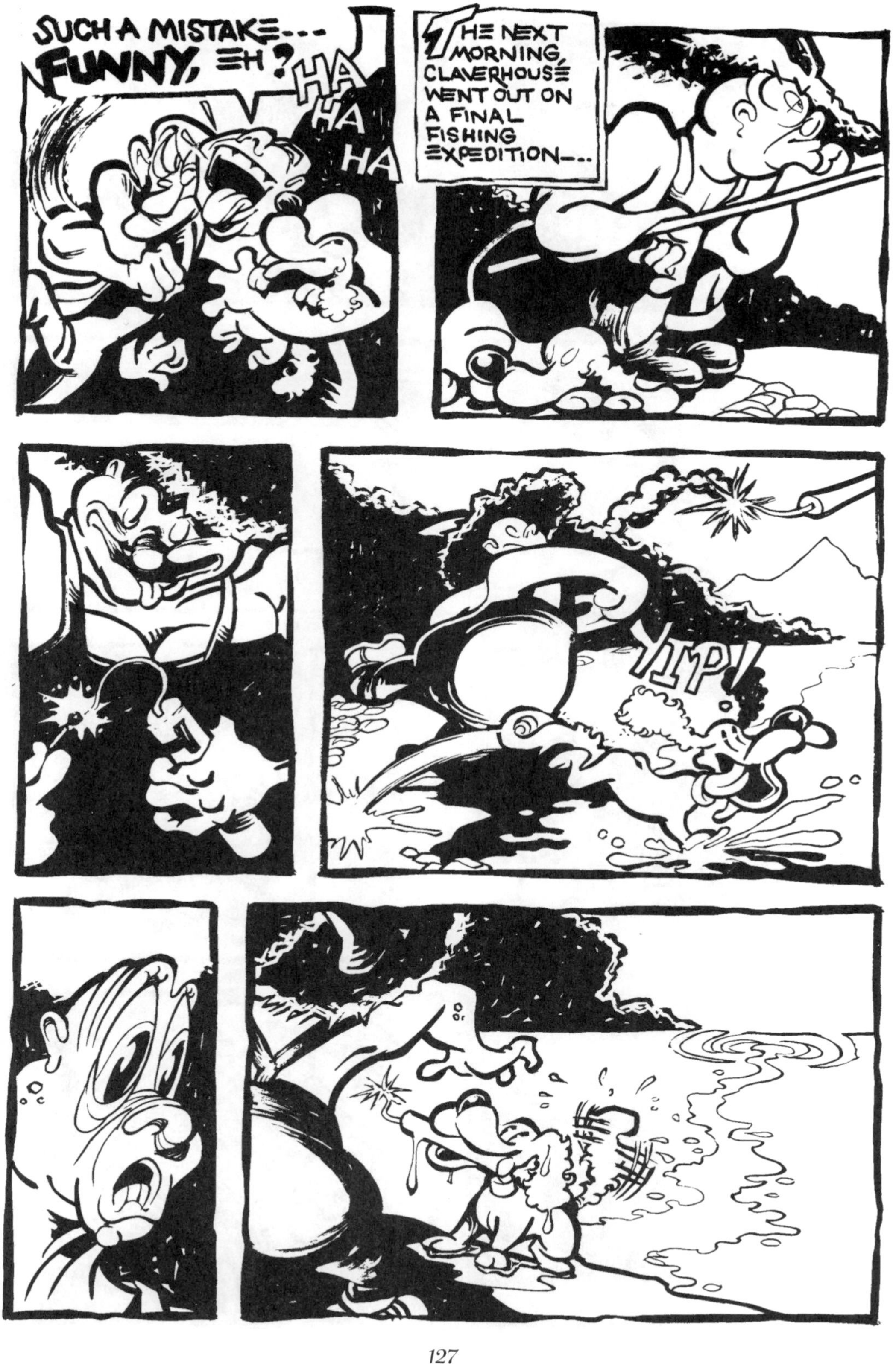
SUCH A MISTAKE... FUNNY, EH?
HA HA HA
THE NEXT MORNING, CLAVERHOUSE WENT OUT ON A FINAL FISHING EXPEDITION...
YIP!

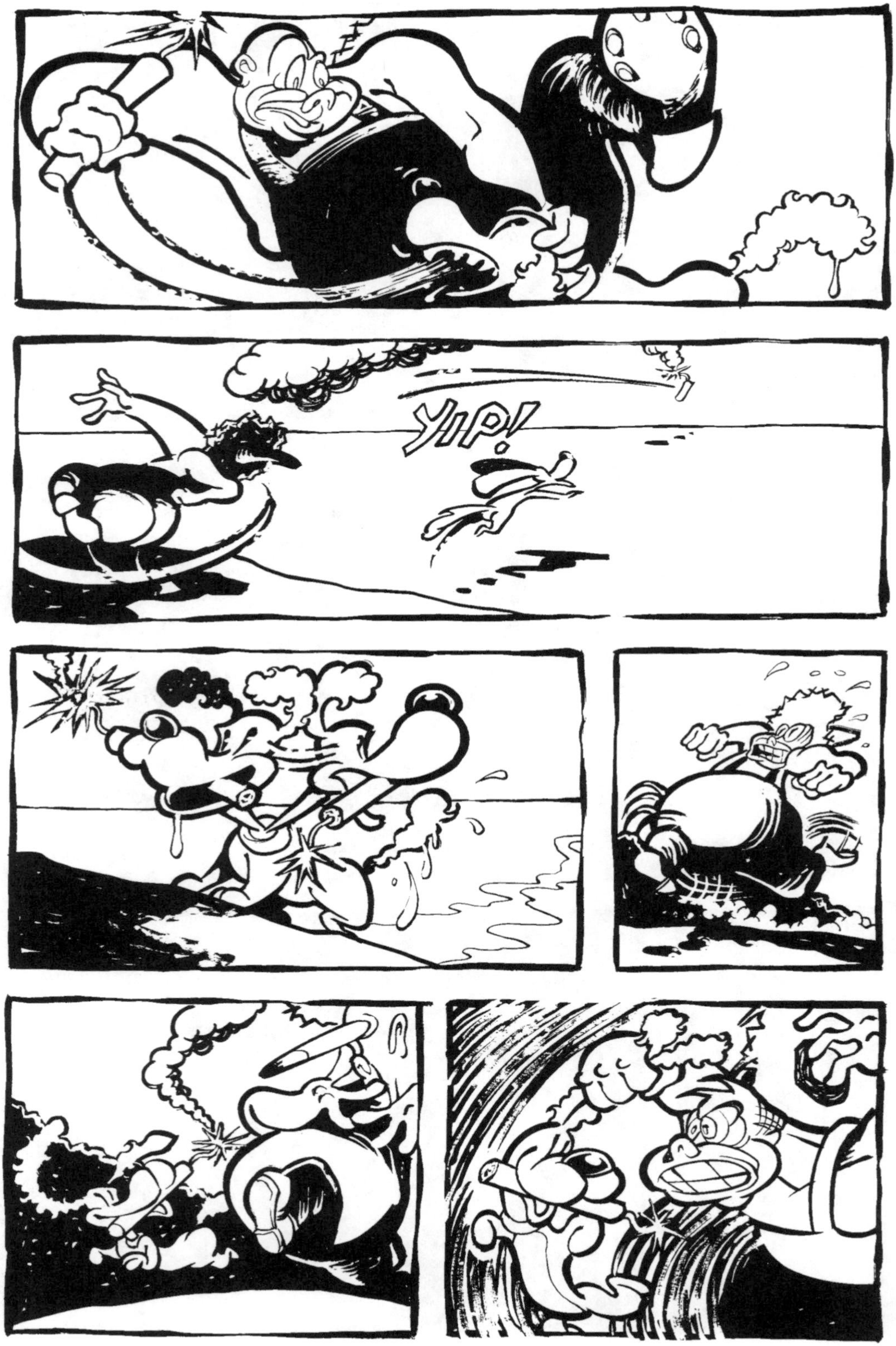
YIP!

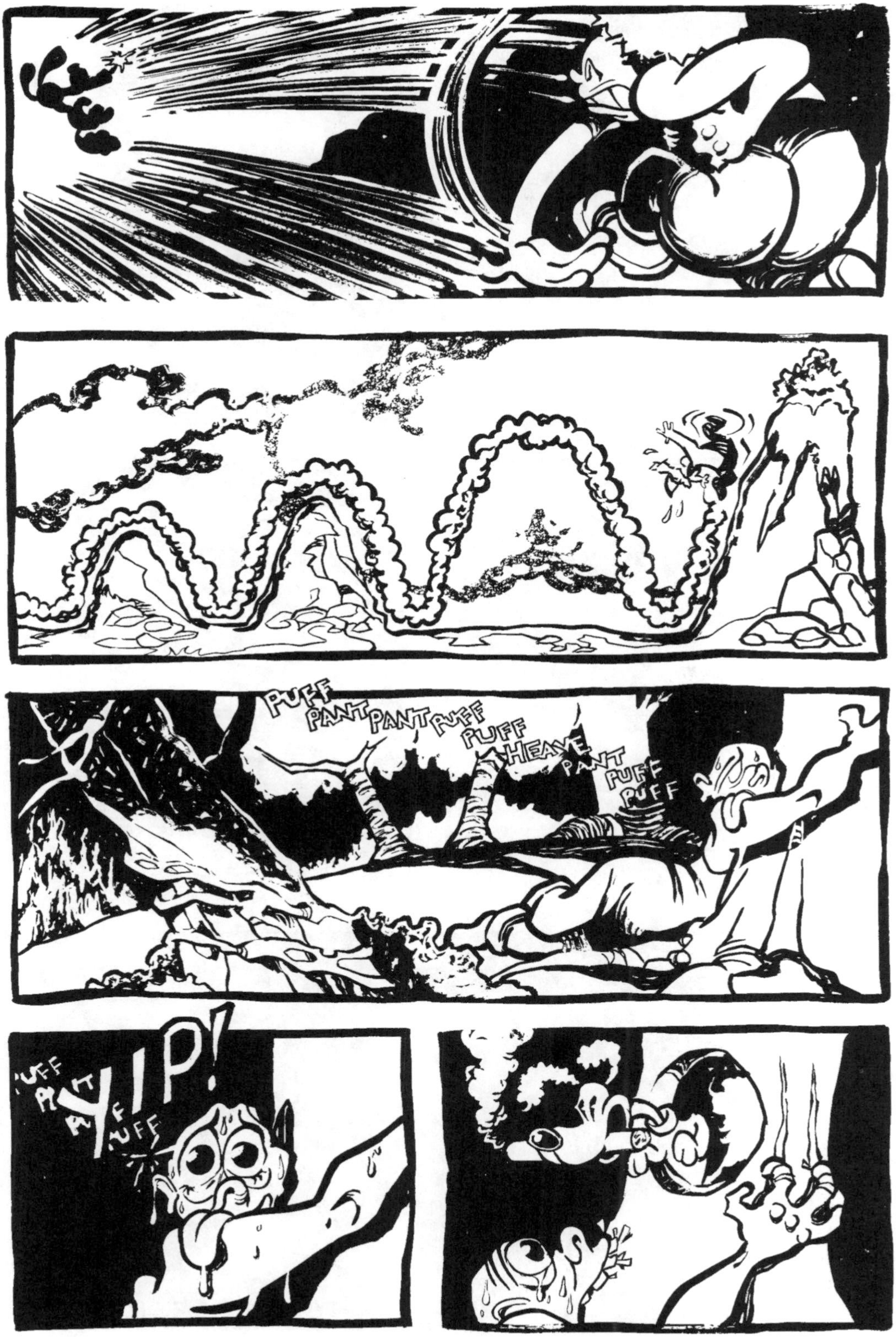
PUFF
PANT PANT PUFF
PUFF
HEAVE
PANT
PUFF
PUFF
YIP!

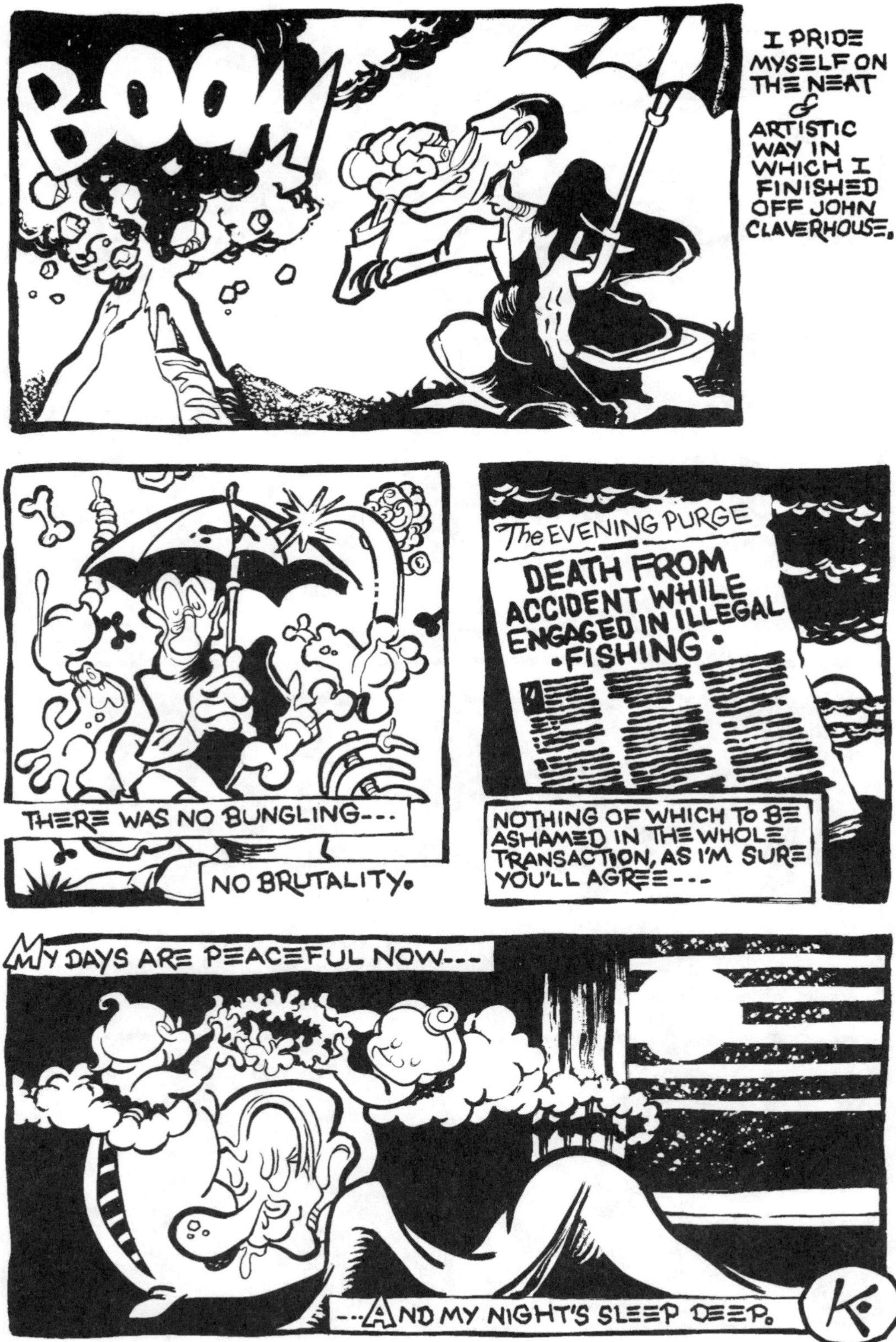
BOOM
I PRIDE MYSELF ON THE NEAT & ARTISTIC WAY IN WHICH I FINISHED OFF JOHN CLAVERHOUSE.
THERE WAS NO BUNGLING---
NO BRUTALITY.
The EVENING PURGE
DEATH FROM ACCIDENT WHILE ENGAGED IN ILLEGAL •FISHING•
NOTHING OF WHICH TO BE ASHAMED IN THE WHOLE TRANSACTION, AS I'M SURE YOU'LL AGREE---
MY DAYS ARE PEACEFUL NOW---
---AND MY NIGHT'S SLEEP DEEP.
K

HOW I BECAME A SOCIALIST

an essay by **JACK LONDON**

illustrated by **SPAIN RODRIGUEZ**

IT IS QUITE FAIR TO SAY that I became a Socialist in a fashion somewhat similar to the way in which the Teutonic pagans became Christians— it was hammered into me. Not only was I not looking for Socialism at the time of my conversion, but I was fighting it. I was very young and callow, did not know much of anything, and though I had never even heard of a school called "Individualism," I sang the paean of the strong with all my heart.

This was because I was strong myself. By strong I mean that I had good health and hard muscles, both of which possessions are easily accounted for. I had lived my childhood on California ranches, my boyhood hustling newspapers on the streets of a healthy Western city, and my youth on the ozone-laden waters of San Francisco Bay and the Pacific Ocean. I loved life in the open, and I toiled in the open, at the hardest kinds of work. Learning no trade, but drifting along from job to job, I looked on the world and called it good, every bit of it. Let me repeat, this optimism was because I was healthy and strong, bothered with neither aches nor weaknesses, never turned down by the boss because I did not look fit, able always to get a job at shovelling coal, sailorizing, or manual labor of some sort.

And because of all this, exulting in my young life, able to hold my own at work or fight, I was a rampant individualist. It was very natural. I was a winner. Wherefore I called the game, as I saw it played, or thought I saw it played, a very proper game for MEN. To be a MAN was to write man in large capitals on my heart. To adventure like a man, and fight like a man, and do a man's work (even for a boy's pay)—these were things that reached right in and gripped hold of me as no other thing could. And I looked ahead into long vistas of a hazy and interminable future, into which, playing what I conceived to be MAN'S game, I should continue to travel with unfailing

health, without accidents, and with muscles ever vigorous. As I say, this future was interminable. I could see myself only raging through life without end like one of Nietzsche's blond beasts, lustfully roving and conquering by sheer superiority and strength.

As for the unfortunates, the sick, and ailing, and old, and maimed, I must confess I hardly thought of them at all, save that I vaguely felt that they, barring accidents, could be as good as I if they wanted to work real hard, and could work just as well. Accidents? Well, they represented FATE, also spelled out in capitals, and there was no getting around FATE. Napoleon had had an accident at Waterloo, but that did not dampen my desire to be another and later Napoleon. Further, the optimism bred of a stomach which could digest scrap iron and a body which flourished on hardships did not permit me to consider accidents as even remotely related to my glorious personality.

I hope I have made it clear that I was proud to be one of Nature's strong-armed noblemen. The dignity of labor was to me the most impressive thing in the world. Without having read Carlyle, or Kipling, I formulated a gospel of work which put theirs in the shade. Work was everything. It was sanctification and salvation. The pride I took in a hard day's work well done would be inconceivable to you. It is almost inconceivable to me as I look back upon it. I was as faithful a wage slave as ever capitalist exploited. To shirk or malinger on the man who paid me my wages was a sin, first, against myself, and second, against him. I considered it a crime second only to treason and just about as bad.

In short, my joyous individualism was dominated by the orthodox bourgeois ethics. I read the bourgeois papers, listened to the bourgeois preachers, and shouted at the sonorous platitudes of the bourgeois politicians. And I doubt not, if other events had not changed my career,

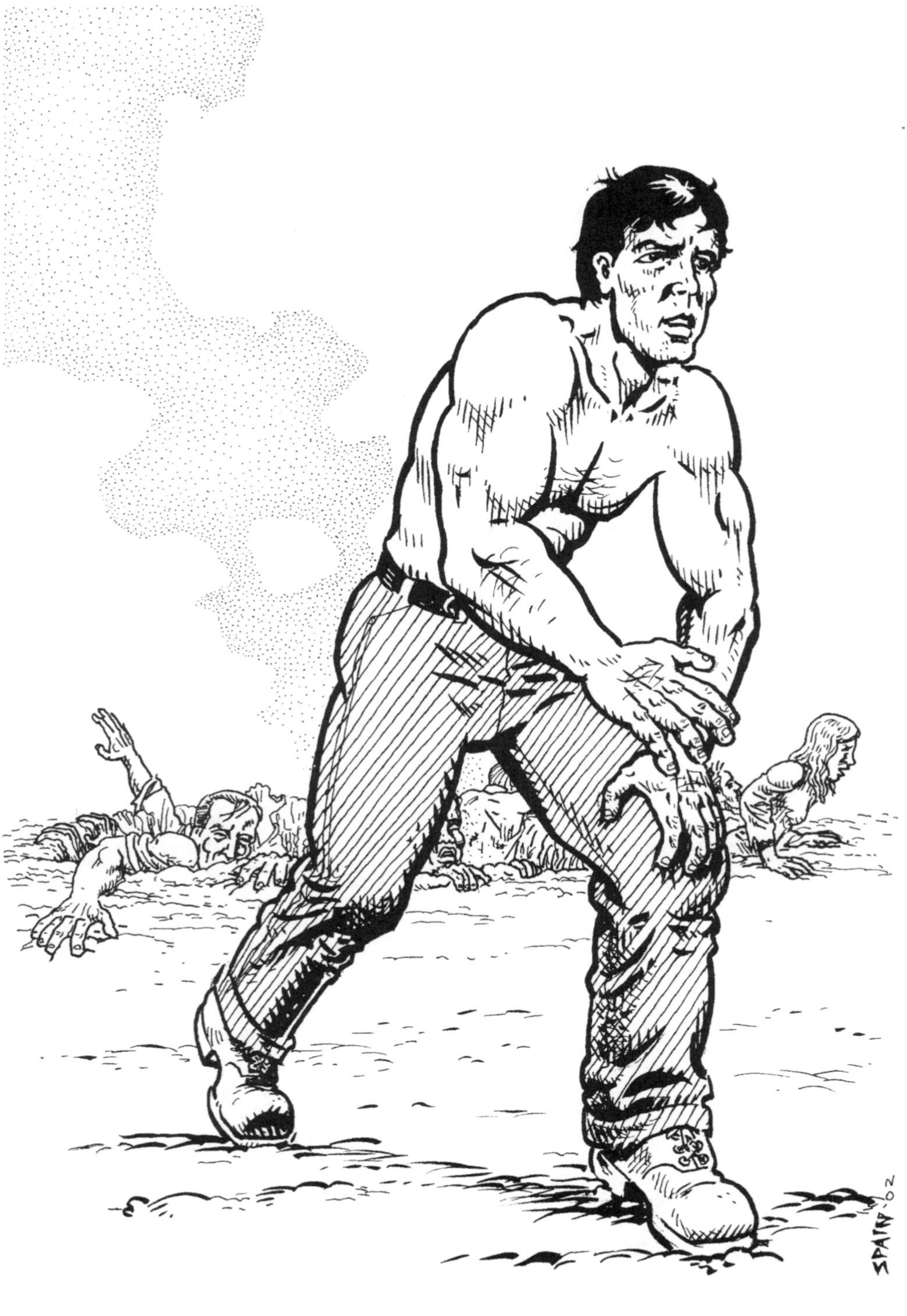
SPAIN '02

that I should have evolved into a professional strike-breaker, (one of [Harvard] President Eliot's American heroes), and had my head and my earning power irrevocably smashed by a club in the hands of some militant trades-unionist.

Just about this time, returning from a seven months' voyage before the mast, and just turned eighteen, I took it into my head to go tramping. On rods and blind baggages I fought my way from the open West, where men bucked big and the job hunted the man, to the congested labor centers of the East, where men were small potatoes and hunted the job for all they were worth. And on this new blond-beast adventure I found myself looking upon life from a new and totally different angle. I had dropped down from the proletariat into what sociologists love to call the "submerged tenth," and I was startled to discover the way in which that submerged tenth was recruited.

I found there all sorts of men, many of whom had once been as good as myself and just as blond-beastly; sailor-men, soldier-men, labor-men, all wrenched and distorted and twisted out of shape by toil and hardship and accident, and cast adrift by their masters like so many old horses. I battered on the drag and slammed back gates with them, or shivered with them in box cars and city parks, listening the while to life-histories which began under auspices as fair as mine, with digestions and bodies equal to and better than mine, and which ended there before my eyes in the shambles at the bottom of the Social Pit.

And as I listened my brain began to work. The woman of the streets and the man of the gutter drew very close to me. I saw the picture of the Social Pit as vividly as though it were a concrete thing, and at the bottom of the Pit I saw them, myself above them, not far, and hanging on to the slippery wall by main strength and sweat. And I confess a terror seized me. What when my strength failed? When I should be unable to work shoulder to shoulder with the strong men who were as yet babes unborn? And there and then I swore a great oath. It ran something like this: all my days I have worked hard with my body and according to the number of days I have worked, by just that much am I nearer the bottom of the Pit. I shall climb out of the Pit, but

not by the muscles of my body shall I climb out. I shall do no more hard work, and may God strike me dead if I do another day's hard work with my body more than I absolutely have to do. And I have been busy ever since running away from hard work.

Incidentally, while tramping some ten thousand miles through the United States and Canada, I strayed into Niagara Falls, was nabbed by a fee-hunting constable, denied the right to plead guilty or not guilty, sentenced out of hand to thirty days' imprisonment for having no fixed abode and no visible means of support, handcuffed and chained to a bunch of men similarly circumstanced, carted down-country to Buffalo, registered at the Erie County Penitentiary, had my head clipped and my budding mustache shaved, was dressed in convict stripes, compulsorily vaccinated by a medical student who practiced on such as we, made to march the lock-step, and put to work under the eyes of guards armed with Winchester rifles — all for adventuring in blond-beastly fashion. Concerning further details deponent sayeth not, though he may hint that some of his plethoric national patriotism simmered down and leaked out of the bottom of his soul somewhere — at least, since that experience he finds that he cares more for men and women and little children than for imaginary geographical lines.

To return to my conversion. I think it is apparent that my rampant individualism was pretty effectively hammered out of me, and something else as effectively hammered in. But, just as I had been an individualist without knowing it, I was now a Socialist without knowing it, withal, an unscientific one. I had been reborn, but not renamed, and I was running around to find out what manner of thing I was. I ran back to California and opened the books. I do not remember which ones I opened first. It is an unimportant detail anyway. I was already It, whatever It was, and by aid of the books I discovered that It was a Socialist. Since that day I have opened many books, but no economic argument, no lucid demonstration of the logic and inevitableness of Socialism affects me as profoundly and convincingly as I was affected on the day when I first saw the walls of the Social Pit rise around me and felt myself slipping down, down, into the shambles at the bottom.

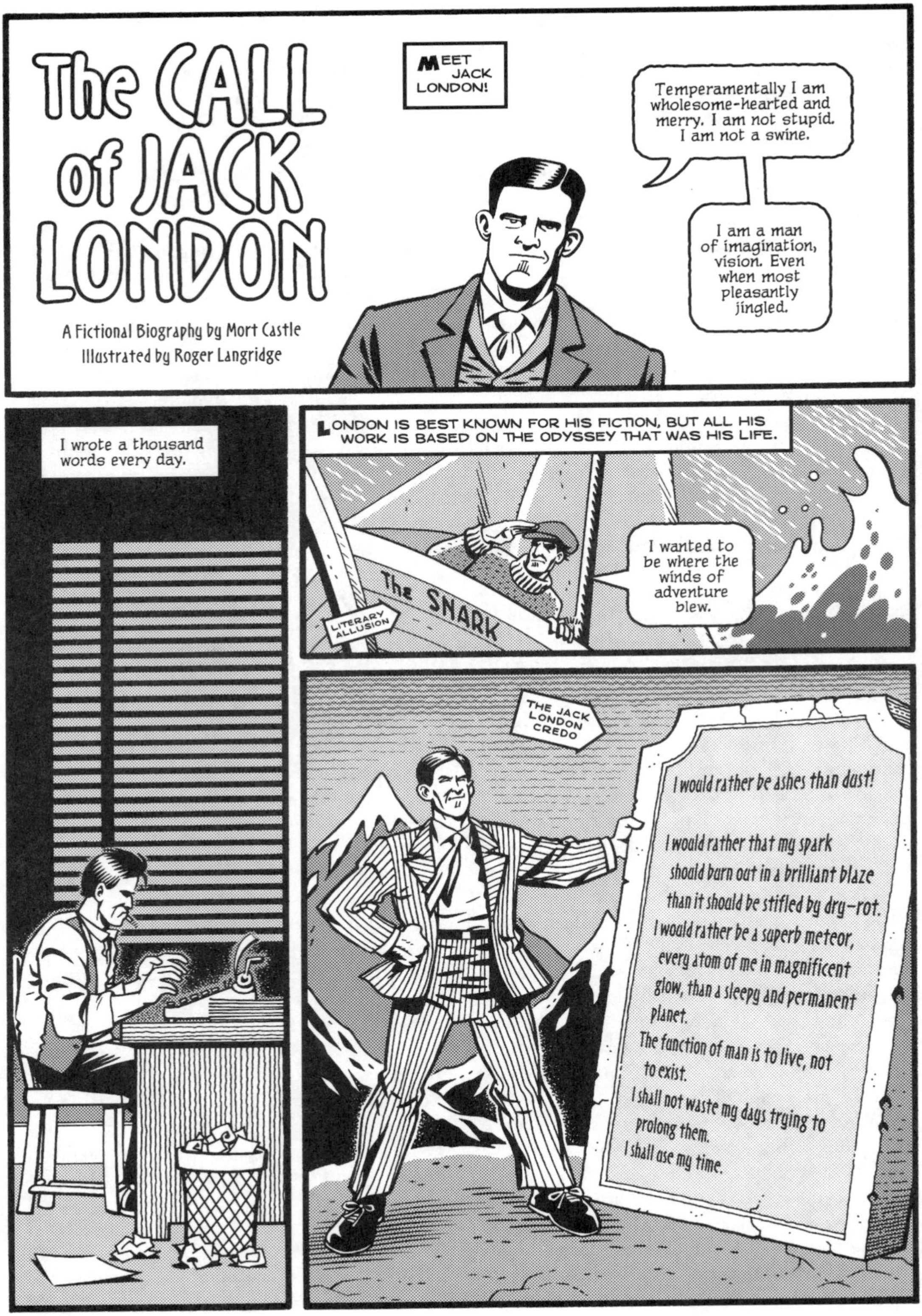
The CALL of JACK LONDON
A Fictional Biography by Mort Castle
Illustrated by Roger Langridge
MEET JACK LONDON!
Temperamentally I am wholesome-hearted and merry. I am not stupid. I am not a swine.
I am a man of imagination, vision. Even when most pleasantly jingled.
I wrote a thousand words every day.
LONDON IS BEST KNOWN FOR HIS FICTION, BUT ALL HIS WORK IS BASED ON THE ODYSSEY THAT WAS HIS LIFE.
The SNARK
LITERARY ALLUSION
I wanted to be where the winds of adventure blew.
THE JACK LONDON CREDO
I would rather be ashes than dust!
I would rather that my spark should burn out in a brilliant blaze than it should be stifled by dry-rot.
I would rather be a superb meteor, every atom of me in magnificent glow, than a sleepy and permanent planet.
The function of man is to live, not to exist.
I shall not waste my days trying to prolong them.
I shall use my time.

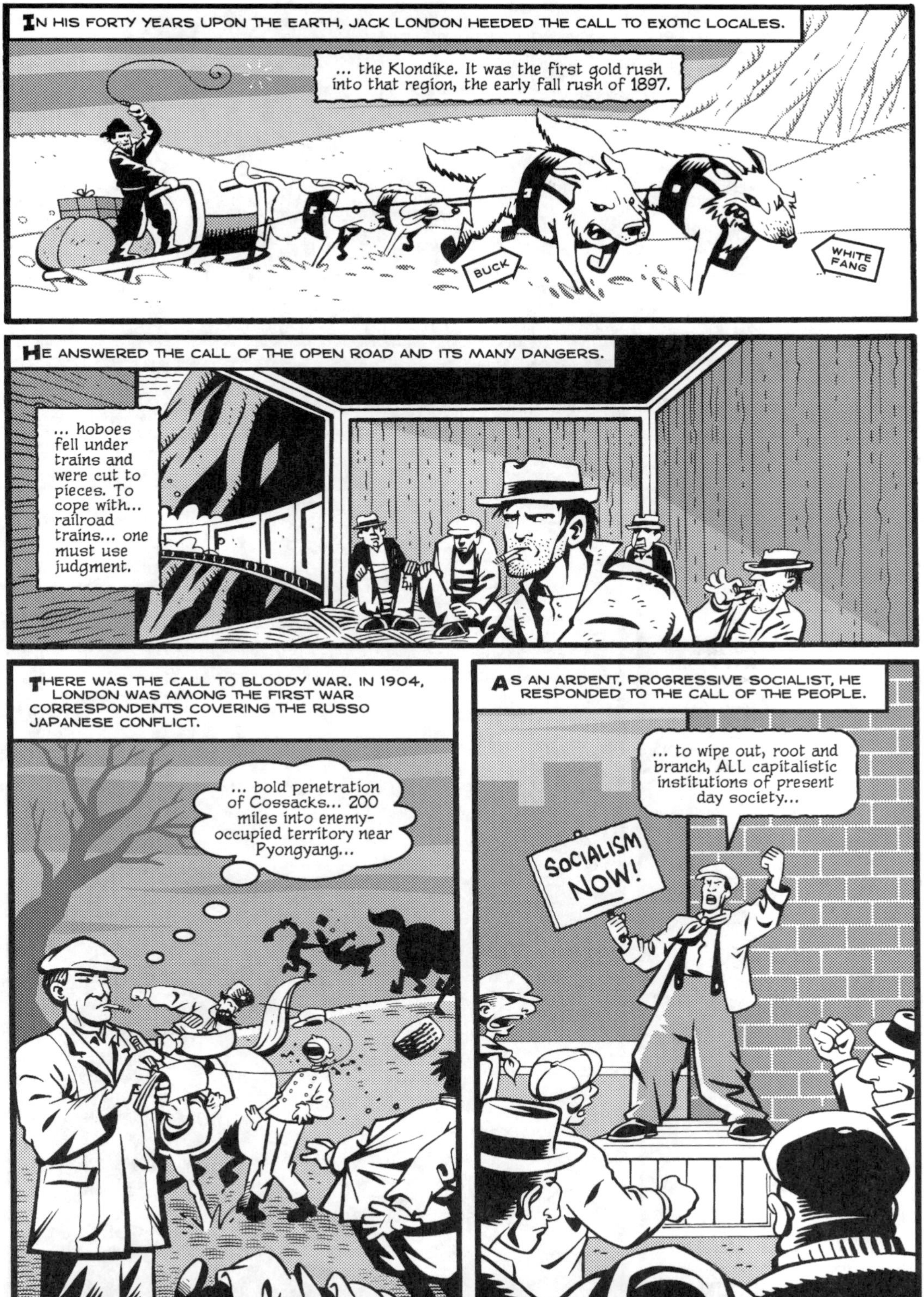
IN HIS FORTY YEARS UPON THE EARTH, JACK LONDON HEEDED THE CALL TO EXOTIC LOCALES.
... the Klondike. It was the first gold rush into that region, the early fall rush of 1897.
BUCK
WHITE FANG
HE ANSWERED THE CALL OF THE OPEN ROAD AND ITS MANY DANGERS.
... hoboes fell under trains and were cut to pieces. To cope with... railroad trains... one must use judgment.
THERE WAS THE CALL TO BLOODY WAR. IN 1904, LONDON WAS AMONG THE FIRST WAR CORRESPONDENTS COVERING THE RUSSO JAPANESE CONFLICT.
... bold penetration of Cossacks... 200 miles into enemy-occupied territory near Pyongyang...
AS AN ARDENT, PROGRESSIVE SOCIALIST, HE RESPONDED TO THE CALL OF THE PEOPLE.
... to wipe out, root and branch, ALL capitalistic institutions of present day society...
SOCIALISM NOW!

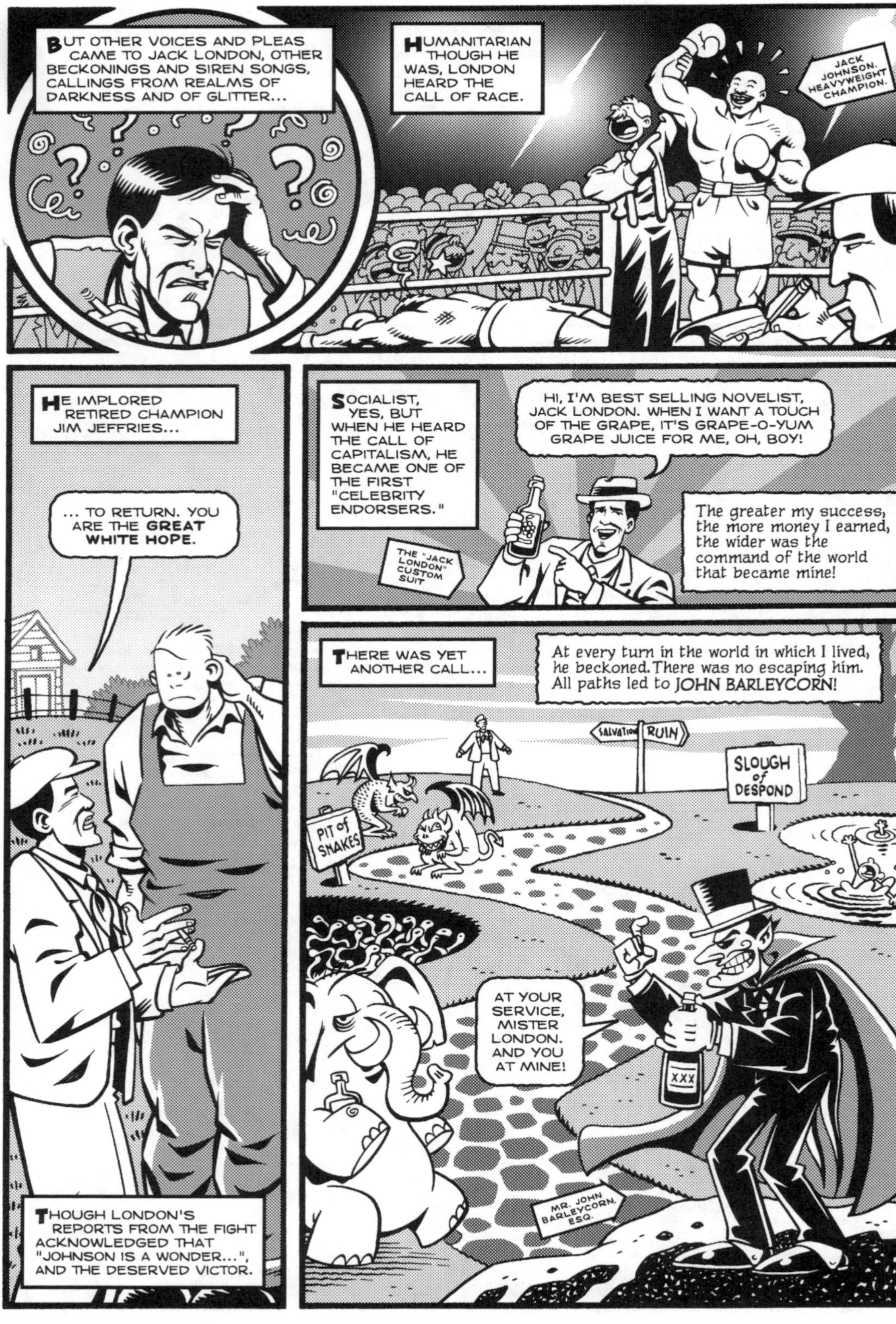
BUT OTHER VOICES AND PLEAS CAME TO JACK LONDON, OTHER BECKONINGS AND SIREN SONGS, CALLINGS FROM REALMS OF DARKNESS AND OF GLITTER...
HUMANITARIAN THOUGH HE WAS, LONDON HEARD THE CALL OF RACE.
JACK JOHNSON, HEAVYWEIGHT CHAMPION.
HE IMPLORED RETIRED CHAMPION JIM JEFFRIES...
... TO RETURN. YOU ARE THE GREAT WHITE HOPE.
THOUGH LONDON'S REPORTS FROM THE FIGHT ACKNOWLEDGED THAT "JOHNSON IS A WONDER...", AND THE DESERVED VICTOR.
SOCIALIST, YES, BUT WHEN HE HEARD THE CALL OF CAPITALISM, HE BECAME ONE OF THE FIRST "CELEBRITY ENDORSERS."
HI, I'M BEST SELLING NOVELIST, JACK LONDON. WHEN I WANT A TOUCH OF THE GRAPE, IT'S GRAPE-O-YUM GRAPE JUICE FOR ME, OH, BOY!
THE "JACK LONDON" CUSTOM SUIT
The greater my success, the more money I earned, the wider was the command of the world that became mine!
THERE WAS YET ANOTHER CALL...
At every turn in the world in which I lived, he beckoned. There was no escaping him. All paths led to JOHN BARLEYCORN!
SALVATION
RUIN
SLOUGH of DESPOND
PIT of SNAKES
AT YOUR SERVICE, MISTER LONDON. AND YOU AT MINE!
XXX
MR. JOHN BARLEYCORN, ESQ.

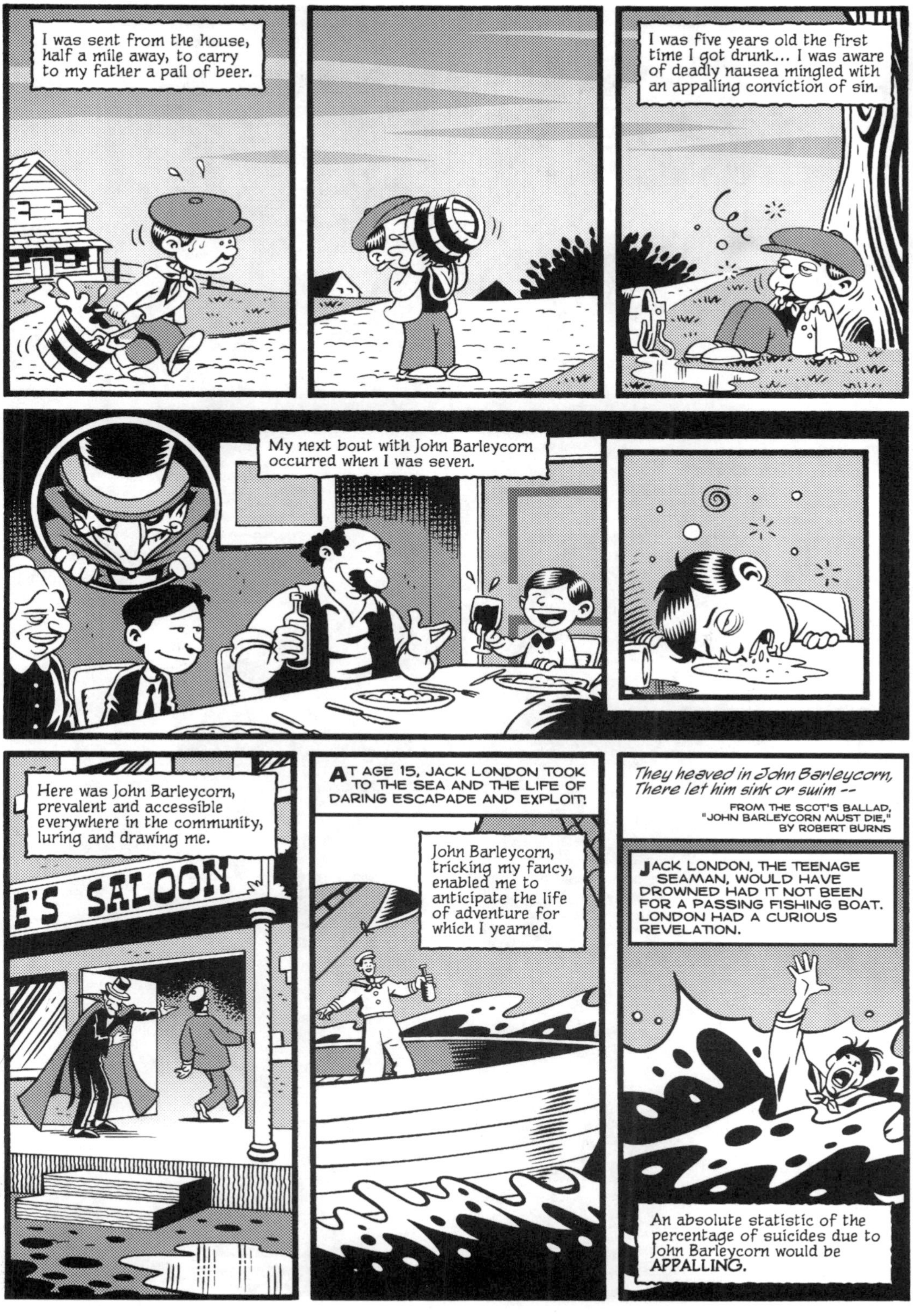
I was sent from the house, half a mile away, to carry to my father a pail of beer.
I was five years old the first time I got drunk... I was aware of deadly nausea mingled with an appalling conviction of sin.
My next bout with John Barleycorn occurred when I was seven.
Here was John Barleycorn, prevalent and accessible everywhere in the community, luring and drawing me.
E'S SALOON
AT AGE 15, JACK LONDON TOOK TO THE SEA AND THE LIFE OF DARING ESCAPADE AND EXPLOIT!
John Barleycorn, tricking my fancy, enabled me to anticipate the life of adventure for which I yearned.
They heaved in John Barleycorn, There let him sink or swim --
FROM THE SCOT'S BALLAD, "JOHN BARLEYCORN MUST DIE," BY ROBERT BURNS
JACK LONDON, THE TEENAGE SEAMAN, WOULD HAVE DROWNED HAD IT NOT BEEN FOR A PASSING FISHING BOAT. LONDON HAD A CURIOUS REVELATION.
An absolute statistic of the percentage of suicides due to John Barleycorn would be APPALLING.

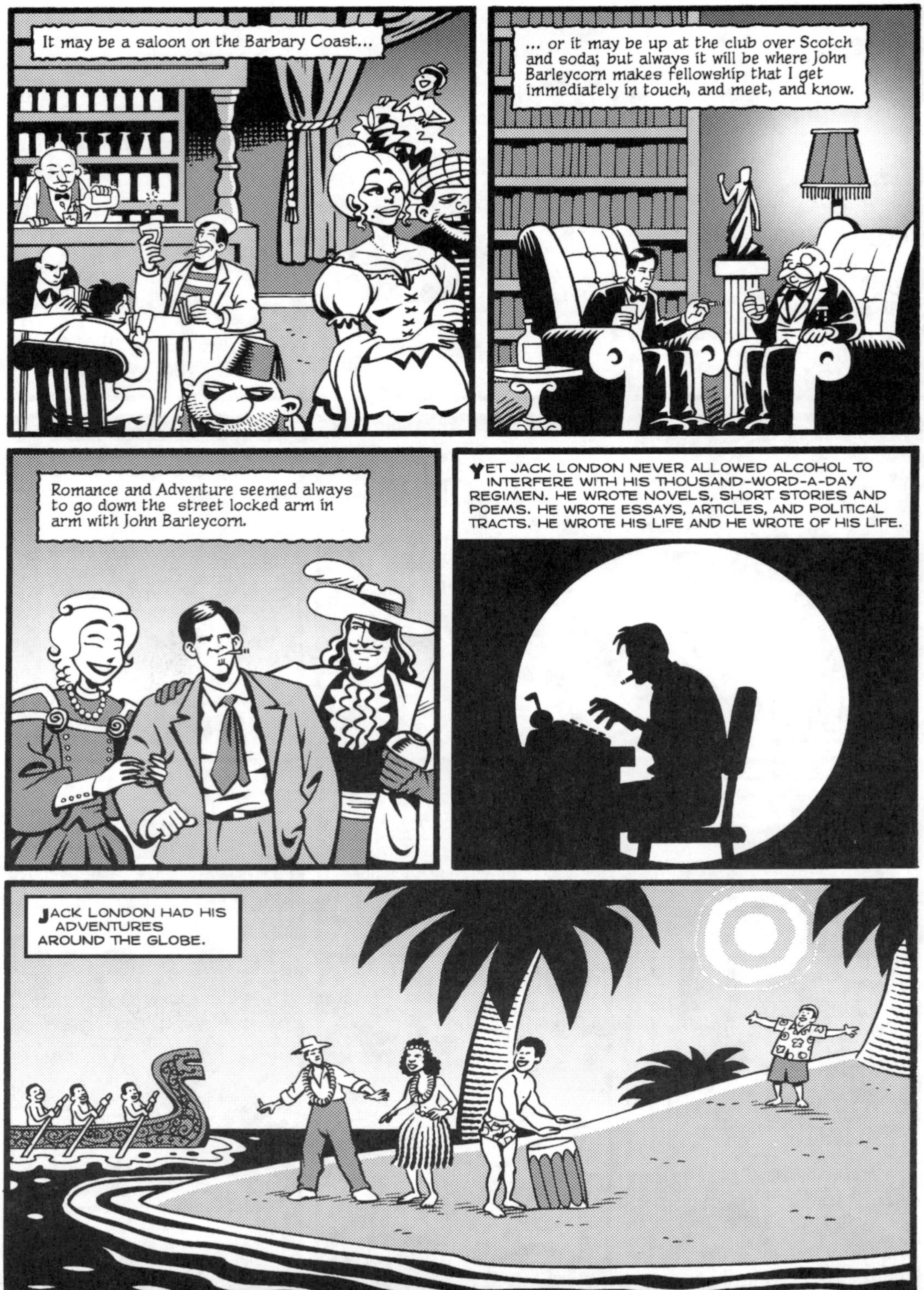
It may be a saloon on the Barbary Coast...
... or it may be up at the club over Scotch and soda; but always it will be where John Barleycorn makes fellowship that I get immediately in touch, and meet, and know.
Romance and Adventure seemed always to go down the street locked arm in arm with John Barleycorn.
YET JACK LONDON NEVER ALLOWED ALCOHOL TO INTERFERE WITH HIS THOUSAND-WORD-A-DAY REGIMEN. HE WROTE NOVELS, SHORT STORIES AND POEMS. HE WROTE ESSAYS, ARTICLES, AND POLITICAL TRACTS. HE WROTE HIS LIFE AND HE WROTE OF HIS LIFE.
JACK LONDON HAD HIS ADVENTURES AROUND THE GLOBE.

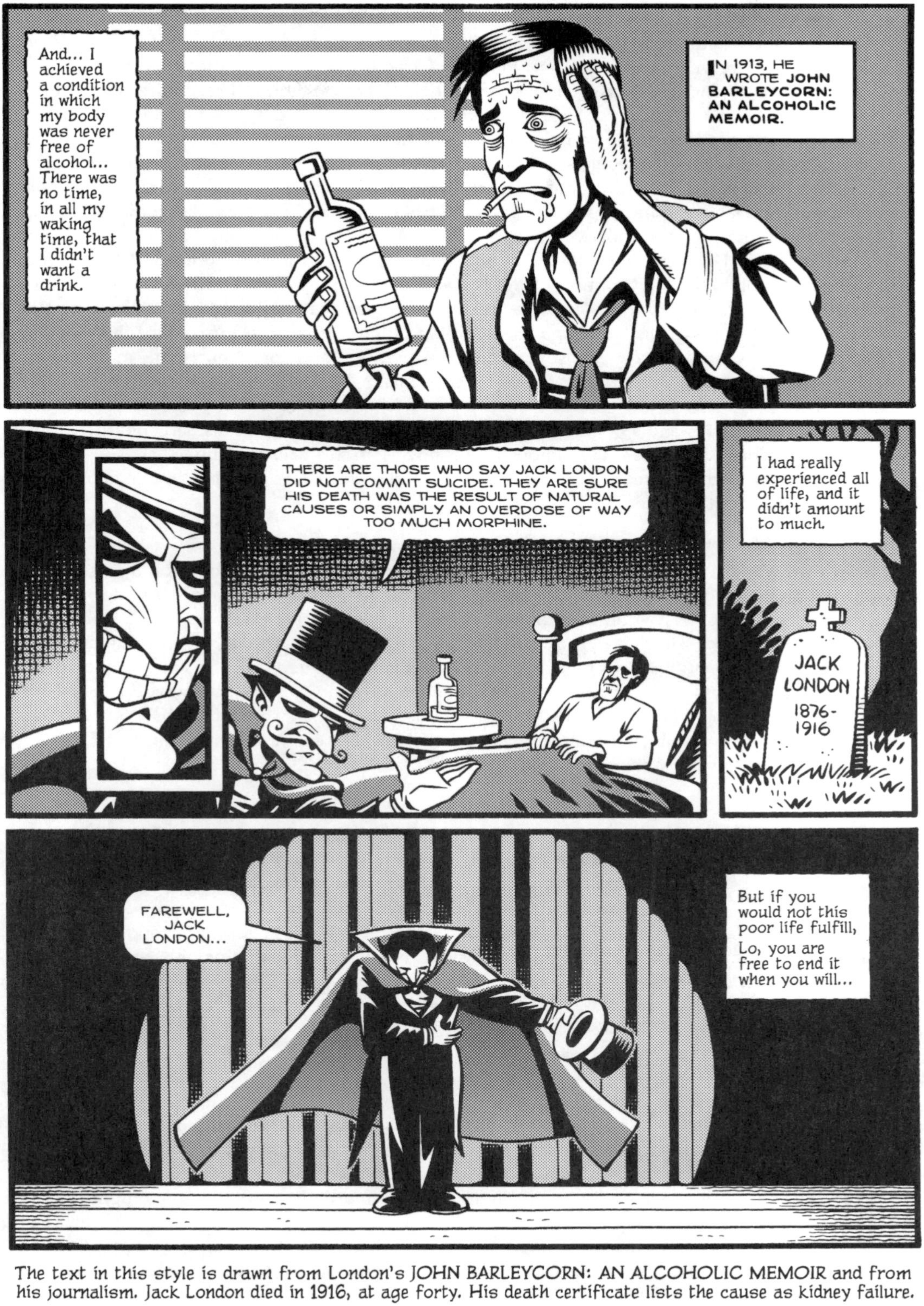
And... I achieved a condition in which my body was never free of alcohol... There was no time, in all my waking time, that I didn't want a drink.
IN 1913, HE WROTE JOHN BARLEYCORN: AN ALCOHOLIC MEMOIR.
THERE ARE THOSE WHO SAY JACK LONDON DID NOT COMMIT SUICIDE. THEY ARE SURE HIS DEATH WAS THE RESULT OF NATURAL CAUSES OR SIMPLY AN OVERDOSE OF WAY TOO MUCH MORPHINE.
I had really experienced all of life, and it didn't amount to much.
JACK LONDON 1876-1916
FAREWELL, JACK LONDON...
But if you would not this poor life fulfill,
Lo, you are free to end it when you will...

The text in this style is drawn from London's JOHN BARLEYCORN: AN ALCOHOLIC MEMOIR and from his journalism. Jack London died in 1916, at age forty. His death certificate lists the cause as kidney failure.

JACK LONDON

As a sailor, petty thief, hobo, prospector, rancher, war correspondent and socialist spokesman Jack London's life was as exciting, inspiring, and tragic as any of his many stories. London was born in San Francisco in 1876, an illegitimate child. His mother and stepfather were never far from poverty, and at the age of 13, Jack left school and began the life of a common laborer. But his appetite for reading allowed him to continue educating himself and his talent for writing of the experiences of his life would eventually make him, by the time of his death, the most popular author in America. When he was 17, Jack went to sea, where he found inspiration for his early stories and later, a great novel, *The Sea Wolf*. He then joined the Klondike gold rush, which formed the basis of his most famous stories and novels, including *Call of the Wild* and *White Fang*. Despite his professional and financial success London remained true to his working-class roots in his promotion of the socialist cause in America. He traveled to England and wrote *The People of the Abyss*, an examination of the deplorable conditions of the working poor. He served in Indochina as a correspondent during the Russo-Japanese war. In 1907 he and his wife departed on a seven-year ocean voyage and spent much time in the South Pacific, the inspiration for London's *South Sea Tales*. By 1913, while his career was at its peak, London's health was seriously deteriorating. The range and sheer volume of his work (51 books, 500 articles and 191 short stories) is astonishing, considering his early death in 1916 at age forty. While London is justly famous for his novels, in this volume we have chosen to concentrate on a wide selection of his shorter works, most of which have never been presented in illustrated form.

ARNOLD ARRE (cover)

Arnold Arre worked in several ad agencies in the Philippines before deciding on a career as a freelance artist, saying, "I guess I'm more of a storyteller than an advertiser." Arnold tells his stories through both illustration and comics, as can be seen by the examples on his website at www.arnold-arre.com. He has won awards for his graphic novels *The Mythology Class* (2000) and *Trip to Tagaytay* (2001). His most recent offering is *After Eden*, a 254-page graphic novel. In addition to comics work, Arnold still does commercial design and and has moved into gallery paintings. He had his first solo show, *Mythos*, in 2000, and was also part of the 2001 Filipino American Art Expo Exhibits in San Francisco and New Jersey. Arnold's art also appears in *Graphic Classics: Arthur Conan Doyle* and *Graphic Classics: H.P. Lovecraft*.

MARK A. NELSON (page 1)

Mark was a professor of art at Northern Illinois University for twenty years, teaching courses in illustration, printmaking, and drawing. He is currently working at Raven Software as a staff artist doing conceptual work, painting digital skins and creating textures for computer games. His comics credits include *Blood and Shadows* for DC; *Aliens* for Dark Horse Comics; and *Feud* for the Marvel Epic line. He has worked for numerous publishers, and his art is represented in *Spectrum #4, #5, #6* and *#8*. Mark's comics and illustrations have appeared in *Graphic Classics: Edgar Allan Poe, Graphic Classics: Arthur Conan Doyle* and *Graphic Classics: H.P. Lovecraft*. He is now working on an adaptation of *The Stranger* for *Graphic Classics: Ambrose Bierce*.

MARC ARSENAULT (page 2)

Marc is best known for his comics work as an art director and editor for Tundra, Fantagraphics Books (the Vaughn Bodé library and Robert Williams' *Malicious Resplendence*) and his own imprint, Wow Cool (www.wowcool.com). His illustrations have appeared in *Zero Zero, Hyena, Monster, Rare Bit Fiends, Maximum Rock N Roll* and on numerous record covers, T-shirts and concert posters. Currently, Marc is the art director for the martial arts equipment company Tiger Claw and spends his nights majoring in video art at the University of Tennessee. He says he enjoys bicycles, basketball, rollerblading, dive bars, haunted places, cotton clothing, cooking, and his son Luc Arsenault. Marc is also a musician, and has been a member of the "art group" Brown Cuts Neighbors since 1989.

ROGER LANGRIDGE (*pages 4, 134*)

New Zealand-born artist Roger Langridge is the creator of Fred the Clown, whose online comic strip appears every Monday at www.hotelfred.com. Fred also shows up in print three times a year in *Fred the Clown* comics. With his brother Andrew, Roger's first comics series was *Zoot!* published in 1988 and recently reissued as *Zoot Suite*. Other titles followed, including *Knuckles, The Malevolent Nun* and *Art d'Ecco*. Roger's work has also appeared in numerous magazines in Britain, the U.S., France and Japan, including *Deadline, Judge Dredd, Heavy Metal, Comic Afternoon, Gross Point* and *Batman: Legends of the Dark Knight*. His version of *Eldorado* was featured in *Graphic Classics: Edgar Allan Poe*, and he adapted *Master*, a rare Doyle poem in *Graphic Classics: Arthur Conan Doyle*. Called "insanely hardworking," Roger now lives in London, where he divides his time between comics, children's books and commercial illustration.

J.B. BONIVERT (*page 6*)

Jeffrey Bonivert is a Bay Area native with a varied background in independent comics as both artist and writer, contributing to such books as *Mister Monster, Turtle Soup* and *The Funboys*. His unique adaptation of Poe's *The Raven* appeared in *Graphic Classics: Edgar Allan Poe*, he contributed *The Los Amigos Fiasco* to *Graphic Classics: Arthur Conan Doyle*, and was part of the unique five-artist team on *Reanimator* in *Graphic Classics: H.P. Lovecraft*. Jeff's comic book bio of artist Murphy Anderson appears in *Spark Generators* (2002, SLG Publishing), and his Casey Jones / Teenage Mutant Ninja Turtles epic, *Muscle and Faith*, can be seen online at www.flyingcolorscomics.com.

ANTONELLA CAPUTO (*page 18*)

Antonella Caputo was born and educated in Rome, Italy, and is now living in England. She is something of a Renaissance woman, working as an architect, archaeologist, art restorer, photographer, calligrapher, interior designer, theater designer, actress and theater director. Her first published work was *Casa Montesi*, a weekly comic strip that appeared in *Il Journalino*. She has since written comedies for children and scripts for comics in Europe and the U.S., before joining Nick Miller as a partner in Sputnik Studios. Nick and Antonella have collaborated for several years, but *The War of the Worlds* for *Graphic Classics: H.G. Wells* was the first official Team Sputnik production. She is also collaborating with Italian artist Francesca Ghermandi on a story for *Graphic Classics: Ambrose Bierce*.

NICK MILLER (*page 18*)

The son of two artists, Nick Miller learned to draw at an early age. After leaving college, he worked as a graphic designer before a bout of chronic fatigue syndrome forced him to switch to cartooning full-time. Since then, his work has appeared in numerous adult and children's magazines as well as comics anthologies in Britain, Europe and the U.S. His weekly newspaper comics run in *The Planet on Sunday*. Nick's art will also be published in *Graphic Classics: Ambrose Bierce*. He shares his Lancaster, England house with two cats, a lodger and Antonella Caputo. You can see more of Nick and Antonella's work at http://www.cat-box.net/sputnik.

PETER KUPER (*page 28*)

Highly regarded by both fans and his peers, Peter Kuper has been active in the comics community since the early 1970s. In 1979 he co-founded the political comics magazine *World War 3 Illustrated* and remains on its editorial board. He has been an instructor at the School of Visual Arts since 1986 and is also an art director for the political illustration group INX (www.inxart.com). Peter's illustrations and comics appear regularly in *Time, The New York Times* and *MAD*. He has written and illustrated many books including *Comics Trips*, a journal of an eight-month trip through Africa and Southeast Asia. Other works include *Stripped – An Unauthorized Autobiography, Mind's Eye* and *The System*, a wordless graphic novel. His most recent book, *SPEECHLESS*, collects his career to date. Peter has recently completed an adaptation of Franz Kafka's *The Metamorphosis* which will be published by Crown in 2003. More of his work can be seen at www.peterkuper.com.

ONSMITH JEREMI (page 34)

Onsmith Jeremi has been in a number of collections including SPX 2002, Studygroup 12 #2, Proper Gander, and Graphic Classics: H.P. Lovecraft, as well as the anthology he helped start, Bomb Time for Bonzo. He also founded the (sometimes) experimental comics site, Comixwerks, with fellow cartoonists Henry Ng and Ben Chandler. Onsmith came from a small town in rural Oklahoma and now lives in Chicago, where he is currently working on his own publication and a new adaptation of The Squaw for Graphic Classics: Bram Stoker. To see more of his work, visit www.comixwerks.com.

KOSTAS ARONIS (page 42)

In addition to his illustration work, Kostas is an architect in Thessaloniki, Greece and also works as a scenographer for the theater, State TV and private channels. He teaches in a private school of arts in Thessaloniki and established the theater group "ACHTHOS," to create performances and installations with a comics aesthetic. In December 2002 Kostas organized the first Intervalkanian Comics Festival as part of Cultural Olympiade 2004 and he is now preparing the second one. His illustrations and comics have been published in books, on CDs, and in magazines and newspapers in Greece. His first book, Between the Legs – Unbelievable Stories, was published in 2001, and he is finishing his second, as well as preparing his next painting exhibition in Athens. To Kill a Man is the first work by Kostas to appear in the United States.

JOHN PIERARD (page 50)

John Pierard has had a varied career in illustration. After leaving the bosom of his beloved Syracuse University for New York City, he immediately found work in publications such as Screw and Velvet Touch Magazine, where he illustrated stories like Sex Junky (opening line: "She had a face like a madonna, and I came all over it..."). In a major departure, he then graduated to illustrating children's fiction including Mel Gilden's P.S. 13 series, and various projects by noted children's author Bruce Coville. He has worked for Marvel Comics, Asimov's Magazine and Greenwich Press. John's comics were published in Graphic Classics: H.G. Wells and he is now working on a story for Graphic Classics: Bram Stoker.

GERRY ALANGUILAN (page 62)

Gerry Alanguilan is a licensed architect who chooses to write and draw comic books. In his native Philippines he has created comics including Timawa, Crest Hut Butt Shop, Dead Heart and Wasted. In America, he has contributed inks on titles such as X-Men, Fantastic Four, Wolverine, X-Force, Darkness, Stone and Superman: Birthright, working with pencillers Leinil Francis Yu and Whilce Portacio. He is currently putting together Komikero, a portfolio of his sketches, illustrations and comics. Gerry has written the screenplay and is starring in an independent motion picture adaptation of his book Wasted, currently being shot in the Philippines. His adaptation of The Judge's House will be in Graphic Classics: Bram Stoker. More of his work can be seen at www.komikero.com.

HUNT EMERSON (page 66)

The dean of British comics artists, Hunt Emerson has drawn cartoons and comic strips since the early 1970s. His work appears in publications as diverse as Fiesta, Fortean Times, and The Wall Street Journal Europe, and he has also worked widely in advertising. Hunt has published over twenty comic books and albums, including Lady Chatterley's Lover, The Rime of the Ancient Mariner, and Casanova's Last Stand, and his comics have been translated into ten languages. He will be illustrating Professor Van Helsing's Vampire Hunter's Guide for Graphic Classics: Bram Stoker. You can see lots of cartoons, comics, fun and laffs on Hunt's website at www.largecow.demon.co.uk.

RAFAEL AVILA (page 74)

Rafael Avila was born in São Paulo, Brazil in 1975. He studied at the Pennsylvania School of Art and Design and the Maryland Institute, and he now teaches drawing at School 33 in Baltimore. His illustrations have appeared in Prairie Journal Trust, The Mystery Review and Potpourri Magazine. He has also done work for local rock bands, storyboard illustrations for

Eisner Communications and is currently engrossed in *Naked Soul*, a graphic novel of his own creation. Rafael cites comic books, melancholy song lyrics and German Expressionist art as his greatest influences. Samples of his work can be viewed at www.portfolio.com/rafaelavila, and in *Graphic Classics: H.P. Lovecraft*.

RICK GEARY *(page 83)*

Rick is best known for his thirteen years as a contributor to *The National Lampoon*. His work has also appeared in Marvel, DC, and Dark Horse comics, *Rolling Stone*, *MAD*, *Heavy Metal*, *Disney Adventures*, *The Los Angeles Times*, *The New York Times Book Review* and *Rosebud*. He has written and illustrated five children's books and published a collection of his comics, *Housebound with Rick Geary*. The fourth volume in his continuing book series *A Treasury of Victorian Murder* is *The Mystery of Mary Rogers* (NBM Publishing, 2001) and he is now finishing a fifth volume, *The Beast of Chicago*. Rick is the only artist to have appeared in all five volumes of *Graphic Classics* to date, and he will be represented by a new comics adaptation of *An Imperfect Conflagration* in *Graphic Classics: Ambrose Bierce*. You can view more of his art at www.rickgeary.com.

TRINA ROBBINS *(page 89)*

Trina has been writing and drawing comics for over thirty years, and since 1990 she has become a writer and feminist pop culture herstorian. Aside from her award-winning books on comics from a feminist perspective (her latest, *The Great Women Cartoonists*, was listed among *Time Magazine's* top ten comics of 2001), she has written about goddesses and murderesses, and her newest book is *Tender Murderers: Women Who Kill*. Currently, she scripts *GoGirl!* (Dark Horse), a teen superheroine comic with art by Anne Timmons. Early art by Trina was reprinted in *Graphic Classics: H.P. Lovecraft*, and she will be doing new illustrations for a fable in *Graphic Classics: Ambrose Bierce*. Check out her website at www.trinarobbins.com.

ANNE TIMMONS *(page 89)*

Anne was born in Portland, and has a BFA from Oregon State University. In addition to her collaboration on Lulu Award-winning *GoGirl!* with Trina Robbins, Anne's work includes the Eisner Award-nominated *Dignifying Science* and the comics version of *Star Trek: Deep Space Nine*. She has also drawn and painted children's books and covers and interior art for magazines including *Comic Book Artist* and *Wired*. Her art from the anthology *9-11 Artists Respond* is now included in the Library of Congress Collection. Samples of Anne's work can be seen at www.homepage.mac.com/tafrin.

LESLEY REPPETEAUX *(page 98)*

A Canadian born illustrator who currently resides in Los Angeles, Lesley claims she rarely sees the ocean due to the fact she's cramped up in her studio painting all day. She has participated in group and solo gallery exhibitions nationwide, and she has brought her intriguing left-of-mainstream imagery to publications including *Bitch Magazine*, *Cicada* and *The Progressive* as well as numerous alternative weeklies. Lesley's ghostly new comic book, *Outlook: Grim* will be released by Slave Labor Graphics in May 2003, and she is currently working on illustrations for *The Dualitists*, to appear in *Graphic Classics: Bram Stoker*. She invites you to take a peep at her portfolio at www.reppeteaux.com.

MATT HOWARTH *(page 105)*

Matt Howarth has spent his career mixing the genres of science fiction, comic books, and alternative music. Probably best known for his *Those Annoying Post Bros.* comic book series, lately he has been doing a variety of graphic adaptations of stories by Greg Bear, Vernor Vinge, and now Jack London. Other adaptations appeared in *Graphic Classics: Arthur Conan Doyle* and *Graphic Classics: H.P. Lovecraft*. Matt continues to explore the digital genre with a variety of on-line comics, plus his weekly music review column (at www.soniccuriosity.com). Currently, he is working on a new *Bugtown* comic book series for MU Press, and collaborating with New Zealander electronic musician Rudy Adrain on an upcoming album project. You are invited to visit www.matthowarth.com for more entertainment.

MILTON KNIGHT (page 105)

Milton Knight claims he started drawing, painting and creating his own attempts at comic books and animation at age two. "I've never formed a barrier between fine art and cartooning," says Milt. "Growing up, I treasured Chinese watercolors, Breughel, Charlie Brown and Terrytoons equally." His work has appeared in magazines including *Heavy Metal, High Times, National Lampoon* and *Nickelodeon Magazine*, and he has illustrated record covers, posters, candy packaging and T-shirts, and occasionally exhibited his paintings. Labor on *Ninja Turtles* comics allowed him to get up a grubstake to move to the West Coast in 1991, where he became an animator and director on *Felix the Cat* cartoons. Milt's comics titles include *Midnite the Rebel Skunk, Hinkley,* and *Slug and Ginger.* MU Press is currently publishing a revival of his most popular character, *Hugo.* Check for the latest news at www.miltonknight.net.

SPAIN RODRIGUEZ (page 132)

Manuel "Spain" Rodriguez, born 1940 in Buffalo, NY, first gained fame as one of the founders of the underground comix movement of the 1960s. After drawing comics in New York for the *East Village Other*, he moved to San Francisco where he joined Robert Crumb and other artists on *Zap Comix*. Spain's early years with the Road Vultures Motorcycle Club and his coverage of the 1968 Democratic Convention in Chicago as a reporter for *EVO* are chronicled in his collection, *My True Story* (1994, Fantagraphics Books). Along with autobiographical stories and politically-oriented fiction featuring his best-known character, Trashman, Spain has produced a number of historical comics. His story of Poe's astonishing choice for a posthumous literary agent, *The Inheritance of Rufus Griswold*, appeared in *Graphic Classics: Edgar Allan Poe*. Spain's work can be seen in the online comic *The Dark Hotel* at www.salon.com, and he is now working on an illustration of *Dracula* for *Graphic Classics: Bram Stoker*.

MORT CASTLE (page 134)

A writing teacher and author specializing in the horror genre, Mort Castle has written and edited fourteen books and around 500 short stories and articles. His novels and collections include *Cursed Be the Child, The Strangers, Moon on the Water* (2002, Leisure Books) and *Nations of the Living, Nations of the Dead* (2002, Prime Books). He has produced an audio CD of one of his stories, *Buckeye Jim in Egypt* (2002, Lone Wolf), and is the author of the essential reference work for aspiring horror writers, *Writing Horror* (1997, Writer's Digest). Mort has won or been nominated for the Bram Stoker Award, the Pushcart Prize, the International Horror Guild Award, the Emerson Fiction Award, the DeMarco Prize, and others. He has had several dozen stories cited in "year's best" compilations in the horror, suspense, fantasy, and literary fields. He has been a writer and editor for several comics publishers, and is a frequent keynote speaker at writing conferences. Mort is now working on a comics biography for *Graphic Classics: Ambrose Bierce* and on the introduction to *Graphic Classics: Bram Stoker*.

MICHAEL SLACK (back cover)

Michael works both as an illustrator and animator. His animations have screened on Noggin TV and Hot Wired's *Animation Express*, and his short film *Daryl* was recently shown internationally in the Short Attention Span Film and Video Festival. Print work has appeared in magazines and newspapers including *Time, Nickelodeon Magazine, PC Computing, Computer Gaming World* and the *NY Press*. His first comic book, *The Land of O*, received a 2002 Xeric Foundation grant and is distributed by Top Shelf Productions. Michael is now working on an adaptation of *The Hypnotist* for *Graphic Classics: Ambrose Bierce*.

TOM POMPLUN

Tom is a graphic artist with a background in both fine and commercial arts and a lifelong interest in comics. He designed and produced *Rosebud*, a journal of fiction, poetry and illustration from 1993 to 2003, and in 2001 founded *Graphic Classics*. Tom is currently working on *Graphic Classics: Ambrose Bierce*, scheduled for release in June 2003.